DEVON LIBRARIES
Please return/renew this item by the due date
Renew on tel. 0345 155 1001 or at
www.devonlibraries.org.uk

MO
5/24

The
Teacher

The Teacher

A **DS CROSS** THRILLER

TIM SULLIVAN

An Aries Book

First published in the UK in 2024 by Head of Zeus,
part of Bloomsbury Publishing Plc

Copyright © Tim Sullivan, 2024

The moral right of Tim Sullivan to be identified
as the author of this work has been asserted in accordance with
the Copyright, Designs and Patents Act of 1988.

9 7 5 3 2 4 6 8

A catalogue record for this book is available from the British Library.

ISBN (HB): 9781804545652
ISBN (E): 9781804545638

Cover design: Ben Prior

Printed and bound in Great Britain by
CPI Group (UK) Ltd, Croydon CR0 4YY

Head of Zeus
First Floor East
5–8 Hardwick Street
London EC1R 4RG

WWW.HEADOFZEUS.COM

For James Maw,
my erstwhile partner in crime. One of the funniest
and most talented people I know.

I

The victim's head was at a grotesque and unnatural angle to his body, which lay crumpled like a pile of laundry that had been thrown down the narrow staircase. The victim was a white male, probably in his eighties and quite tall. There was a long smear of blood where his head had made contact with the wall as his body slid down it. His neck was, in all likelihood, broken. One thing was beyond question, however. Alistair Moreton was very much dead. His dog, a large German shepherd, lay nearby, watching protectively as the police team did their work.

'Why call in the murder squad?' DCI Ben Carson asked the young PC who had been first on the scene. Carson sounded like he was in an episode of a US crime show from the fifties. He was attending the scene with DS George Cross as Cross's usual partner, DS Josie Ottey, was moving house. Carson's referencing the 'murder squad' – tantamount to talking about himself in the third person, thought Cross – was par for the course. He was often prone to these moments of self-aggrandisement. They irritated the hell out of Ottey when she was within earshot, but Cross rarely noticed, as he was generally too engrossed in whatever they were working on.

'He was alive when he fell,' explained PC Trevor Bain nervously.

'And how do you know that?' asked Carson, looking to Cross for approval of his demand for precision. None was forthcoming.

'You can tell from the amount of blood on the wall from the head wound. But I also noticed defence wounds on the deceased's hands,' replied Bain.

'From the fall, presumably.'

'I don't think so,' said Bain who was then immediately alarmed that he had just contradicted a DCI so brazenly. He took a deep breath and awaited the deserved reprimand.

'Why not?' asked Carson.

'Because they are puncture wounds, not consistent with a fall. More consistent with an attack.'

'Good work,' said Carson like the man manager and encourager he fancied himself to be. But in truth he was just trying to imply that he knew this full well himself and was testing the young officer. Training on the job, as it were.

'Consistent with the puncture to the chest, as well as what appear to be bites to his legs,' said Cross who was kneeling over the body.

'Do we need to call animal control?' asked Carson casting a nervous glance at the Alsatian who was still, seemingly, observing the scene.

'What makes you so sure they are dog bites?' asked Cross, standing up from examining the body. Something Carson hadn't done. As a rule he never did. The truth was he had something of an aversion to dead bodies. Bit of a problem when it came to being a senior member of the Avon and Somerset Major Crime Unit (MCU). He'd managed to solve this by claiming he was more use in the office coordinating the investigation than at the scene. He said it gave him an objective overview of the case they were working on.

'It would make more sense if it was a dog,' he said as assertively as he could manage. 'Was the stab the fatal wound? The cause of death?' Carson was, as always, in need of quick answers, whether accurate or not.

'I have no idea. The forensic pathologist will tell us,' Cross replied.

'Pretty obvious, I would've thought,' continued Carson.

'He has a massive injury to the back of his head. By the look of things a possible broken neck, either of which could have been fatal. Do you have any idea of the depth of the stab wound to the chest?' asked Cross.

'Of course not,' spluttered Carson.

'Yet you seem convinced it's the cause of death,' said Cross before leaving the room.

'Can someone get that dog out of here?' commanded Carson in an attempt to show everyone that he was really in charge.

But the animal had followed Cross out of the room. It was as if he was sure Cross was the one who'd have answers as to how his owner had died. Cross walked across the entrance hall into the living room.

It was a small cottage – probably eighteenth-century, Cross calculated. The ceilings were low with the occasional forehead-cracking beam, stretching wall to wall. The windows were leaded in a diamond formation which made the interior fairly dark, even when it was a bright day outside. There was a worn, plum-coloured velvet sofa opposite an open fire which was situated in an exposed brick wall. Also a leather armchair which wouldn't have looked out of place in a Pall Mall gentlemen's club. It had a brass reading lamp on a stand at its side. The previous day's copy of *The Times* was lying folded up on the floor, revealing a completed crossword in beautiful, meticulous, tiny handwriting. There were copies of *The Spectator* magazine, the *Times Literary Supplement*, the *London Review of Books*, the *New York Review of Books* and the *Times Educational Supplement* strewn on the floor surrounding the chair. A copy of Henry James's *Portrait of a Lady* was open on a small table next to it. On the book a pair of half-moon reading glasses, and next to them a glass of whisky, with about a finger of Scotch left in it. There was a pipe in an ashtray, together with a soft leather pouch filled with tobacco and a silver tamping tool. The end of the pipe had been bitten down. Cross was pretty sure if he examined Alistair Moreton's teeth, he would find them to be worn down and brown from holding the pipe in this mouth. There was a box of Swan Vesta safety matches. It spoke of a different era. The room itself had the sweet aroma of a thousand smoked pipes, also evidenced by the brown patina on the walls. The nicotine had given it a stain like a paint finish that many a fashionable interior designer might have been proud of.

The dog lay down in front of the armchair, presumably his habitual spot at the feet of its master. Cross looked at it for a moment and reflected how frustrating it was that this animal was probably a witness to what had befallen Moreton and yet wouldn't be able to tell them a thing. The dog noticed Cross's staring, got up, pushed its nose against the police officer's leg, mouth open, panting. Cross bent down to console it. This came perfectly naturally to him in a way that never happened with people in this kind of situation. He'd never had a dog, which had been a source of regret, but something he still thought about rectifying when he retired. As he stroked the dog, he looked around the walls of the room which were covered floor to ceiling with bookshelves. There were also piles of books, stacked on the floor. Moreton had obviously run out of room for his vast collection. But then Cross noticed something about the dog's mouth. Perhaps he had something he could tell them after all.

2

Cross saw Dr Michael Swift's SUV pull up and join the numerous other vehicles outside the cottage. He knew he'd be livid about the vehicles already parked outside, thus making any examination of the tracks leading up to the building pointless. He got out of the car, looked at them and shook his head, before making a point to Dr Clare Hawkins as she got out of the passenger side. They would now claim the scene and insist that everyone either left or donned white forensic suits. Cross would have normally been wearing one immediately upon his arrival, together with DS Ottey. But they were in the boot of her car and Carson, unsurprisingly, didn't have any in his. Cross thought the low-ceilinged location would pose a personally logistical challenge for the six-foot-eight Swift. He went out to greet them. It was a grey, wet day in the third week of September. An early morning downpour had filled the potholes in the lane. They reflected the clouds moving above like a hopscotch of animated mirrors.

'Hello, matey,' said Swift. Cross looked at him in horrified astonishment that he should address him in such a wholly unprofessional way, and at a crime scene no less. 'No need to look like that. I was talking to your friend,' Swift explained. Cross turned to see Moreton's dog standing behind him. Hawkins and Swift laughed.

'I see,' replied Cross, failing to see any humour in it.

Swift handed him a white forensic suit which he put on, as he and Hawkins both donned theirs. They performed this ritual in silence. This was because Swift and Hawkins knew Cross was averse to small talk, as well as being completely inept at it. Indeed, there were times when he was not entirely sure it was even taking place. They had also learned from experience that any attempts on their part to fill in the silence had two inevitable consequences. The first was that it made them appear stupid. The second that it annoyed the detective in a way that he found difficult to get back from. So the best tactic was silence. Carson, who hadn't learned this lesson despite having far more interaction with Cross than them, now appeared at the door.

'DCI Carson, this is an honour,' proclaimed Swift cheerfully.

'What do you mean?' Carson asked.

'Seeing you at a crime scene,' Swift replied.

Carson didn't know whether this was an implied slight, but the constant insecurity about his status meant he took it as such.

'I don't know what you mean by that. I frequently attend crime scenes. Otherwise, how would I be able to perform my job properly? Wouldn't you agree, DS Cross?' he asked.

'About the frequency of your presence at crime scenes or your ability to perform your job properly?' asked Cross.

Swift stepped in to save the situation from getting any worse. 'No disrespect was intended,' he said and offered Carson a paper suit as a peace offering.

'That won't be necessary,' came the reply. 'I'm returning to the office.' He looked at Cross who was now in his suit. 'Are you not coming, George?'

'I am not. I would've thought my attire would have suggested as much.'

'Very well, any questions before I leave?'

'You were my transport back to the unit—' Cross began.

'Constable, do you have a car?' Carson addressed PC Bain.

'Yes, sir,' he answered.

'Then please drive DS Cross back to the MCU when he's finished,' Carson instructed him.

'Yes, sir.'

'And another thing, call animal control and get them to pick up the dog,' Carson continued.

'No, don't do that,' countermanded Cross.

'Why not?' asked Carson.

'I believe the dog may be evidence,' continued Cross.

'What?'

'I believe the dog may be evidence,' Cross repeated.

'Of course,' replied Carson, as if he knew very well this to be the case. 'Call animal control anyway. It'll need picking up at some point.'

He got into his car and drove off.

The constable got his mobile phone out.

'Don't make the call, Constable,' said Cross.

'But the DCI—'

'Won't know anything about it. If you call animal control, there will only be one outcome. The dog will be destroyed,' said Cross.

'But if he bit the victim?' Bain protested.

'Don't make the same mistake as the DCI and jump to conclusions, Constable,' replied Cross. He turned to Swift. 'Dr Swift, we'll need a swab of the dog's teeth and mouth.'

'Really?' said Swift obviously apprehensive at the idea.

'Yes, there are traces of blood.'

This didn't make the prospect of swabbing the dog any more alluring. But Swift's fear was overtaken by his constant need to ingratiate himself with Cross. He was still, after a couple of years at the Avon and Somerset force, desperate to learn from someone he considered to be uniquely gifted when it came to solving crime. He put his large aluminium equipment case down and got out a swab kit. He walked over and knelt by the dog who immediately retreated.

'His name's Ricky,' said Cross.

'Ricky?'

'Short for Richard,' said Cross.

'Is that right?' answered Swift.

'As in Richard Wagner, according to Tom Holmes, the pub landlord who discovered the body. Ricky, sit.' The dog did so and Cross took hold of his collar gently.

'Perhaps I should speak to him in German,' Swift joked.

'I didn't know you spoke German,' replied Cross, impressed.

'I don't,' answered Swift, immediately regretting his lame joke.

'Then I'm not sure why you suggested it,' said Cross.

Swift decided the best policy was just to move on. 'Right, so now I'm just going to take a swab from your teeth, is that okay, Ricky?' he asked nervously as if explaining this to a small child. The dog was completely compliant.

'Could you also take a sample of his coat hairs?' asked Cross.

'Of course.'

Cross walked back into the house and saw Hawkins going about her work. Over the years of working with her he'd noticed how she was almost protective of the dead bodies she worked with, which he thought was generally indicative of her fastidious approach. It was as if she had a reverential respect for death. She worked away quietly, saying nothing to him as he came into view. She never felt the need to volunteer an immediate opinion at a scene, as many of her colleagues did, to prove to everyone that she knew what she was doing. She had also discovered that the quieter she was at a crime scene, the fewer questions she'd be asked. Questions she invariably wouldn't have the answers to as yet. She wouldn't have them until she'd got her client, as she referred to the bodies she worked with, back to the sanctuary of her mortuary table. There they would patiently reveal their secrets to her. Cross was unlike any other detectives she knew, as he generally never asked her a question at a crime scene. In the mortuary when her investigations were complete it was another matter. He was persistent, obdurate and detailed. As infuriating as he could be, he was still her favourite detective.

Cross stayed for a while because he liked to watch this team at work. He was intrigued by the way Dr Hawkins went about examining a body initially. Her process and routine were both considered and very systematic. He'd learnt a lot from just observing her. It had informed and reconfigured his initial approach to bodies at crime scenes. He was also fascinated by the way Swift walked into a room where a crime had been committed and just stood at the entrance for a good few minutes, taking it all in before he started processing it. He had noted how and where Swift started his search for the minuscule forensic clues that, so often unseen, ended up solving a case. He'd told Cross once that every location had its own language. You simply had to work out what that was before being able to interpret it.

3

Half an hour later Cross decided to leave Swift and Hawkins to get on with their work and pay Tom Holmes a visit. He'd gone back to the pub to oversee a delivery from the brewery. Cross walked down the lane and joined the main road. It smelled of damp vegetation. He looked up at the glowering sky. There would be more rain today and soon. He became aware of the patter of quick light steps behind him and turned to see Ricky following him. Cross stopped and looked at the dog. The creature was obviously going to follow him, so it seemed pointless to try and stop him.

As he approached the village of Crockerne, he saw a brewer's lorry parked outside the Hobbler's Arms. It was one of the first buildings you saw as you went into the village. Two men were dropping barrels off the back of the truck onto a fat bright blue crash mat on the ground. The barrels fell with a dull thud before being rolled with an echoing metallic clatter to an open trapdoor where they disappeared, followed by another distant, dull thud. Cross carried on into the village. He would come back when the delivery had been dealt with.

He walked down to the Avon with his canine companion. The tide was out, grey banks of mud slid their way down to the water. Boats in the tiny inlet sat on the riverbed at drunken angles as if exhausted after their maritime adventures. Cross knew something of the history of the village from his father, Raymond. From the eighteenth century onwards it had been the base for river pilots taking ships up the Avon to the port of Bristol. They would either be towed by the pilots or pulled from the towpath. The village was on a natural inlet and so became the focus for these men and their boats. But then the port opened at Avonmouth just a few miles away and there was no need for ships to go into Bristol any more. Everything could be moved from the new port by rail and so the pilots left.

There had also been a ferry that crossed the river from Crockerne to the other side and was in use till the nineteen seventies when the Avonmouth Bridge, which now overshadowed the village nearby, made it redundant. It must've been much like the Severn ferry, thought Cross, probably a lot smaller. He remembered crossing the Severn on the ferry with Raymond and his father's partner Ron, when he was a child. They would use it when visiting Ron's relations in Swansea, before driving through the Gower Peninsula. There was something adventurous about queuing for the ferry and making the crossing. It was the anticipation of it all. Then the Severn bridge had made the ferry redundant. The journey was much quicker, but much less interesting for the young Cross.

Apparently, the giant slopes of mud leading down to the water around the inlet covered up numerous old slipways. There was an air of the village's main life having resided in the past, Cross thought. It was so small, he wondered if everyone knew everything about everyone else. Whether this in turn might make things easier or more complicated for the police, he couldn't be sure. Small communities were often determinedly jealous of their secrets.

'Twenty-one pubs this village had at one time,' Tom Holmes began by telling Cross as they settled into two chairs in the pub. The bar had that morning-after sweet-and-sour smell of spilt beer and cooked food. Cross had been reluctant to go into the building. As he told Tom Holmes, he didn't like pubs. Tom pointed out they wouldn't be open for another hour, so Cross agreed to talk inside. Tom's wife, Mary, was busy with another young woman cleaning up. 'Poor old thing,' continued Holmes as he looked at Moreton's dog who had settled at the foot of another chair by the fireplace.

'Mr Moreton, do you mean?' asked Cross.

'No, Ricky, his dog. That's Alistair's chair,' replied Tom.

'I see, so Mr Moreton was a regular here, presumably?'

'Oh yes. Every night of the week.'

'Except for a Sunday,' said his wife who was obviously keeping a keen ear on the conversation.

'That's right. He didn't drink on a Sunday and was very strict about drinking at home. Only a single glass of Scotch before bed. But never on the Sabbath,' said Holmes.

Cross thought about the glass of unfinished whisky by Moreton's chair. He'd been killed on a Sunday night. So, either he wasn't as strict about drinking on the Sabbath as he made out. Or things had changed.

'So, he was religious?' asked Cross.

'I think so, I mean he went to church every Sunday. The vicar would be able to tell you more. Think she might have known Alistair as well as anyone in the village, if not better.'

'Did you know him well?' asked Cross.

'Yes and no. I mean, we saw a lot of him. But he kept himself to himself, mostly.'

'Did he have many friends in the village?'

Holmes paused as he considered how best to answer this.

'Alistair wasn't a popular figure in the village, to be honest.'

'Why was that?'

'People were suspicious of him.'

'Why?'

'I don't know really. Possibly because he was a bit of a loner. Never mixed with anyone. You'd see him in the shop, or the church, but he didn't talk much,' continued Holmes.

'Unless it was a parish meeting,' volunteered Mary.

'Oh, that's true,' chuckled Holmes. 'He always had a view on local issues and had a lot to say. He could be quite vocal, and his opinions weren't always popular.'

'He didn't care who he upset,' said Mary. 'Can I make you a cup of tea? I should've offered before.'

Cross hesitated. He really wanted a cup of tea, but wasn't sure it would be made in a way that he found acceptable. Ottey had told him that people were offended when he left cups untouched after one sip. So he generally refused.

'I have the feeling you're a leaf man. Am I correct?' she asked.

'I am.'

'And a china cup rather than a mug,' she went on.

'Yes. How very perceptive of you,' Cross replied.

'I'm a pub landlady. That's what I do. Read people. I'll just be a minute.'

'How long had Mr Moreton lived here in the village?' Cross continued.

'Ten, twelve years,' replied Holmes.

'Do you know where he came from?'

'Nope.'

'Do you know what he did for work, before he retired?'

'No. I thought maybe he'd been in the army, but he said he wasn't when I asked.'

'What made you think that?'

'Just the way he was. The way he spoke, walked, dressed. Always quite well turned out. Wore a tie even when he came to the pub, even when he was wearing a sweater. He had quite a military way about him, you know? Smoked a pipe. We put a stool outside the back door so he could smoke and drink his pint out there.'

A little later Mary arrived with a tray on which there was a teapot, jug of milk, cup and saucer and a plate of home-made biscuits. She put it on the table. Holmes reached over for a biscuit and she slapped his hand.

'They're not for you,' she reprimanded him. 'I'll let you decide when to pour, Sergeant.'

Cross said nothing. Then realised she had done something kind for him and he should acknowledge it.

'Thank you,' he said finally, just as Mary was beginning to think he was a little rude.

'When you say Mr Moreton wasn't popular in the village, was there anyone in particular he had an issue with?' asked Cross.

Cross noticed Holmes hesitate then look over at his wife to seek permission.

'Have you spoken to his neighbours? The Cotterells?' asked Holmes.

'I have not.'

'They won't be there, Tom,' said Mary. 'They're weekenders. Live in London during the week.'

'They shared a lane – well, technically it was Alistair's. They had an easement to use it. There was no trouble with the previous people and Alistair. But as soon as the Cotterells arrived it all kicked off. Went to court in the end.'

'What was the problem?'

'They complained that his hedge needed cutting. It was scratching their Range Rover, apparently.'

'How did Alistair respond?'

'He told them to get driving lessons,' replied Tom laughing.

'Then they tried to have it cut themselves. No one in the village would touch it so they found a company out of town. When they pitched up Alistair wouldn't let them go anywhere near it. Called the police,' said Mary.

'They complained his bins were blocking their access on collection days when they weren't even here. They were in London,' said Holmes. 'They'd installed security cameras and saw it on there. One time he had a delivery at a weekend and she took a photo of the van and claimed it was parked there all day.'

'The final straw was when they put up a gate on his land,' said Mary.

Cross was now drinking his tea, which met with his full approval.

'How did they manage that if they couldn't even cut the hedge without him intervening?' he asked.

'Alistair had a hip replacement last year. They waited till he was in hospital. As soon as he was fit again, he took the gate down. They called the police. It went to court,' said Holmes.

'They lost,' said Mary. 'Ordered to pay Alistair twenty thousand and costs.'

'Did they pay?' asked Cross.

'Only after he took them to court again to get the money,' she said.

'That was a joke. They claimed he'd slashed the tyres on the Range Rover.'

'Did they call the police?'

'Oh yeah. Alistair was charged. They had taken photographs and showed them in court. What they didn't know was that Alistair had installed a couple of cameras of his own. One of them covered the front of the house. He went through the footage and found Cotterell slashing his own tyres. The judge threatened them with jail time if they didn't pay the original fine within seven days, and added another five grand for wasting the court's time.'

This interested Cross.

'Did Moreton have any family? Visitors?' he asked.

'His son. The MP. He came pretty much every month on a Sunday. Went to church with him. Good for the public profile, no doubt,' said Tom.

'That's unfair. He was a very dutiful son. They came in here for Sunday lunch when he was over. He seemed very fond of his dad,' said Mary.

'As for other visitors, well, the cottage isn't that visible from the main road. So, it's possible,' Holmes answered.

'But he never mentioned it?' Cross asked.

'Of course not.'

'Why do you say that?'

'Because that would have required a conversation, Sergeant.

Something you never really had with Alistair. He'd just ask for his pint and sit down. That was it. Just grunted if you asked him how he was, commented on the weather.'

'And yet you seem to know a lot about the court case. How is that?' Cross asked.

'Because I went along to support him. And when I couldn't go Mary went,' Holmes replied.

'Why?'

'Because we considered him to be a friend, Sergeant,' replied Mary with a tone that implied this much should have been obvious.

'How had Alistair seemed recently?' Cross asked.

Mary and Tom exchanged an awkward look which didn't go unnoticed by Cross.

'Difficult to say,' Tom replied.

'Why?'

'We hadn't seen him for a couple of weeks,' Mary explained.

Cross looked at his notes. 'But you said he came in every night without fail, except for Sundays,' he said.

'Not for the last couple of weeks,' Tom said hesitantly.

'I went up to the house after a couple of days. You know, to make sure he was all right,' said Mary.

'Did you speak to him?' asked Cross.

'I did.'

'And how did he seem?'

'Well, you know. Much like normal really. Not very talkative,' Mary replied.

'Tell him, Mare,' her husband urged her.

'No, it's probably nothing,' she replied.

'Let him be the judge of that.'

She looked at Cross, possibly apologetically, he thought, though he couldn't be sure.

'Well, it's just that I got the feeling he didn't want me to go in,' she said.

'Did he normally let you in?' Cross asked.

'Yes. I'd often pop in on the pretext of passing and do a bit of cleaning for him,' she said.

'The woman has OCD,' Tom laughed.

'Really?' asked Cross.

'No, I don't. He just thinks he's being funny,' she said.

PC Trevor Bain now walked through the front door. 'I have to go back to my station. So can I drive you back to Bristol?' he asked.

'Why?' asked Cross.

'Because it's about to chuck it down,' he replied.

Cross looked at him, trying to work out what that had to do with anything.

'I'd like to leave before the rain,' Bain began to explain. 'And you won't want to be getting wet making enquiries.'

'I have an umbrella and a mackintosh for such situations,' Cross pointed out.

'I see. Well, it's just that the heater in the squad car doesn't work and with the two of us it'll steam up before we've left the village.'

This made complete sense to Cross.

'The tea was most proficiently made,' said Cross, thinking that Ottey would be pleased with his manners. 'I'll be in touch again soon,' he said to the landlord and his wife.

'What about the dog?' the young constable asked.

Cross looked at Ricky who was by now asleep.

'My boss wants animal control to pick up the dog,' he told the publican.

'We'll have him,' replied Holmes immediately.

'What?' asked Mary.

'We'll have him. Look at him. He's completely at home,' he pointed out.

'And who's going to walk him and pick up the dog shit?' she asked.

'You. Obviously,' he said. Her jaw dropped open in outrage at such a suggestion. 'Me, of course,' Tom laughed. 'Look, if it doesn't work out then we'll take him to a refuge, but for now let's at least give the poor bugger a chance.'

As if on cue Ricky woke up, cocked his head and gave Mary an imploring look.

'All right, all right. But you're on probation,' she announced.

'Who, me or the dog?' asked Holmes.

'The both of you.'

4

Cross's partner DS Josie Ottey had taken a week off to move house. She had, rather fancifully as it turned out, imagined that moving home would provide a welcome break from the emotional strains and stresses of solving gruesome murder cases. She had neglected to factor in her mother Cherish, who was also moving into the self-contained flat at the bottom of the new house. There had already been more personal politics flying around the kitchen the first morning than at a staff meeting in the MCU discussing involuntary redundancy.

Packing up her flat had taken more time than Josie had allowed. She had decided, eminently sensibly in her opinion, to discard things as she went along. Stuff that had accumulated in the flat and hadn't been looked at once in the years since they had been carefully put away for safekeeping. The problem was that she kept stopping and studying things out of a nostalgic and affectionate curiosity. There were many little surprises along the way that alleviated the tediousness of the task at hand. She went on to chuck a lot of it, but it became a long-drawn-out, staying-up-until-three-in-the-morning process. Terrible paintings by the children from their toddler years were, however, sacrosanct. This despite teenage howls of embarrassed protest.

The problem with her mother hadn't really surfaced till Josie and the girls moved into the house themselves. Cherish had moved into her flat a few days earlier, on the day of completion – when they were supposed to, as she continually reminded her daughter. But Josie was wrapping up a case at work and had to postpone, a bone of contention with her mother which set the tone for the day. Cherish announced that she was completely free to help her daughter. It started well but things reached fever pitch when they got into the kitchen. The main problem was that Cherish started putting things in the cupboards she thought most sensible and practical. Unfortunately, this often didn't align with Josie's opinion and they clashed in a way that was oddly reminiscent of Carla and Debbie's, her daughters, daily sibling warfare. It wasn't so much that Josie disagreed with these choices. It was her mother's usual presumption that she knew best that really annoyed her.

'Why have you moved the cutlery?' she asked her mother as she was about to put a handful of forks into a drawer that now contained neat piles of dishcloths and hand towels.

'I haven't. I moved the kitchen tools.'

'That's what I meant,' Josie lied in reply.

'Because that drawer is under the part of the work surface where I'll prepare the vegetables when I'm cooking,' replied Cherish.

'Why wouldn't you prepare the vegetables over there?' Josie asked. 'I mean, that's where I would naturally do them.'

'Because here is above the food waste bin and next to the sink. It makes sense.'

'What if I don't want to do my food prep there?' asked Josie. 'It is my kitchen, after all.'

Cherish gave her that familiar maternal look which said, wordlessly, don't talk rubbish.

'Stop just making a point and fussing about stuff you're not really bothered about. We both know you'll be happy just so long as you know where the corkscrew is,' Cherish finally said.

'Mum!' said Josie, genuinely outraged at this portrayal of her, at the same time as being irked at the truth of the statement.

'Speaking of which, why don't you put that knowledge to good use right now and get us a drink.'

'You know what would be more helpful?' Josie replied.

'I thought I was being helpful,' Cherish replied.

'And you are. It's just that it's suspiciously quiet upstairs and I'm worried what the girls are up to. Could you possibly go and check?' she asked with heightened politeness, immediately giving away the fact that she had a hidden agenda.

'Sure,' Cherish muttered, just this side of audibly.

'What?' asked Josie, despite her instincts warning her not to rise.

'Well, it's just that it might be easier if I continued to organise the kitchen the way I like it, as I tend to use it a lot more than you when I'm looking after the girls,' she replied. With that grenade of hardcore guilt lobbed with practised precision in her daughter's direction, she left the room.

Half an hour later they sat in the living room surrounded by packing boxes. There was so much more to do. Josie was beginning to think the week she'd taken off might not be enough. She also knew herself well enough to know that she wouldn't make time to get properly organised at home once she'd returned to work. She looked around the room and felt uneasy. She didn't know why, initially. Then it dawned on her. It felt like she was sitting in someone else's room. It didn't feel like home.

'I think we should repaint this room before we unpack,' she said finally.

'Really? I quite like it.'

It was an off-white with deeper shades of off-white on the woodwork. It looked like a room hiding in plain sight.

'You'll need to take more time off if you want to do that,' Cherish observed.

'I can't do that. We're short staffed enough as it is.'

But the truth of the matter was that her boss, DCI Ben Carson, had been uncharacteristically accommodating about her taking time off. In fact, he'd insisted she took as much time as she needed. Normally, such requests were greeted with a look of betrayed reproach. Treated like a personal affront of friendship-ending proportions. But this time he'd even given her a lecture about the importance of family in life, as if it were a new concept to her. This was undoubtedly everything to do with the fact that Carson had recently become a father for the first time. He behaved as if it was the first time it had happened to anyone in the history of mankind, which was both irritating and endearing. His smartphone screen was in danger of being worn out with the amount of swiping through photographs he was doing when showing pictures of his baby daughter, Flora, to anyone in his vicinity.

'But you're owed so much time off,' Cherish pointed out.

'I know but I'm not sure my boss sees that as a problem.'

'How is he?'

'All right, as far as I know. But his world's about to be turned upside down. He and his wife have had their first baby.'

'Really? I didn't even know he was married. You never mentioned it.'

'Why would I?' Josie asked.

'I think that's amazing considering all his... you know, difficulties.'

Josie frowned for a moment then realised what her mother was talking about.

'Oh, for God's sake, I'm not talking about George, and how many times do I have to tell you, he's not my boss,' Josie protested.

'Well, you say that. But the way he has you running around all the time, I can be forgiven for forgetting. I wonder how he's getting on without you?'

'Good question. I do worry about him, to be honest.'

'Well, you shouldn't. They'll have found someone else to work with him,' Cherish consoled her.

'That's exactly what worries me.'

'Any chance of some more wine?'

Josie reached for the bottle and topped her mother's glass up. She smiled at her with a sudden rush of love that warmed her stomach like a shot of single malt.

'I know I don't say it enough. But I am grateful for everything you do for us,' she said.

'Oh, don't be ridiculous,' Cherish replied. Josie smiled gratefully. 'You never say it at all.'

5

'It's got to be someone in the village,' was the characteristic sweeping judgement Carson began the meeting with at the Major Crime Unit the next morning. A couple of other detectives nodded in agreement. One, who was new to the department, sitting next to Carson, spoke up.

'It makes complete sense. We should concentrate our efforts there and move quickly. I'm confident we should have this wrapped up by the end of the week.'

Carson smiled.

'I'd like to introduce DI Bobby Warner. He'll be joining us for this investigation as Ottey deals with her house move.'

'Morning,' smiled Warner.

This was a surprise to Cross as Carson had told him only yesterday morning that he himself would be filling in for Ottey. It was good for him to keep his hand in, on the ground, he'd told them all. Now this. Cross wondered what had happened in the intervening twenty-four hours.

'DI Warner is from Kent Police and has an enviable reputation for his speed at closing cases. We're lucky to have him for this interim period. He'll work alongside DS Cross but obviously as a DI will take the lead on any decisions and lines of investigation,' Carson went on, his face turned to Cross to see if there was any reaction from him. There wasn't.

'Right, let's get to it!' Carson announced.

Cross was out of his seat, across the room and into his office like a bullet.

Carson turned to Warner. 'Remember what I said,' he cautioned him.

'Of course. I shall tread lightly with Cross,' Warner replied reassuringly.

What he understood to be the meaning of that expression, or indeed his understanding of what Carson had told him about Cross earlier, was brought into question half an hour later, when he marched across the open area towards Cross's office carrying a chair. Behind him were two uniforms carrying a desk he seemed to have requisitioned from somewhere. He opened the door without knocking and placed the chair against the wall opposite the shocked Cross's desk.

'What do you think you're doing?' asked Cross.

'I would've thought that was obvious,' replied Warner.

'I can see you're moving a desk into my office. The question actually was what you *thought* you were doing,' Cross pointed out.

'We're a team, George.'

'DS Cross,' Cross corrected him.

'DS Cross, and as such it makes much more sense for us to share an office,' Warner explained.

'Not to me. I don't want to share an office,' said Cross.

'Well, as the junior member of the team if you're going to reject my offer of a shared office, I suggest you move your desk elsewhere,' Warner replied defiantly.

'I have a special arrangement.'

'You *had* a special arrangement,' said Warner.

'Have you discussed this with DCI Carson?' asked Cross as the two uniforms deposited the desk opposite his.

'I have not and nor do I intend to.'

Cross looked outraged. Police staffer Alice Mackenzie, observing this encounter from the open area, was concerned. There was something about the way Warner was going about this which made her think it was deliberately provocative. Like he was trying to make a point. He also looked like he was enjoying it.

Cross got up from his desk, walked out, and went straight to Carson's office. The DCI was in the middle of a meeting, but Cross knocked on the door and started speaking immediately. It was odd that he should knock as his sense of decorum dictated, then immediately interrupt in such a rude manner.

'He is moving a desk into my office,' said Cross. '*My* office,' he repeated as if to make his point.

Carson thought about this for a moment, nodded apologetically to the other detective, who took the hint and left, and tried to figure out how to deal with this.

'Well maybe it's time for a change, George. In the office accommodation arrangements, that is,' he began, knowing this was going to be a difficult conversation.

'We had an agreement. You cannot simply renege on it,' replied Cross whose indignation had now rendered his cheeks a delicate shade of pink.

'I know, but why don't you just give it a go?'

'I cannot and I will not,' spat Cross like a displeased child.

Carson realised that he was now in an extremely awkward position. He didn't know who he was more annoyed with. Cross for his obdurate refusal to comply or Warner for completely disregarding what he'd told him not an hour before. He'd made it quite clear how Cross worked and how his value to any investigation outweighed people's accusations of his getting special treatment. Carson never denied this was a fact, partly because he knew he had the support of the chief. But Warner had now created an impossible situation. Carson couldn't countermand him as he outranked Cross and his request wasn't exactly outlandish. Unless, of course, you were unfamiliar with Cross.

'Is there a problem?' Warner asked innocently, having appeared at the door.

'You know very well there is,' replied Cross.

'If I knew I wouldn't have asked.'

There was a silence during which both Warner and Cross looked to Carson for an answer. He hated these situations at the best of times, despite the fact that he prided himself on his man-management skills. He hated them even more when they involved Cross because invariably the situation could only be solved by his taking Cross's side. But that wasn't an option here.

'George, I'd like you just to see how this new arrangement goes,' he began. 'I know it's not what you're used to, but let's just see what happens.'

Cross was about to reply when Mackenzie appeared with a note which she gave to Cross. He read it then looked up at Carson.

'The Cotterells have come back from London and are happy to be interviewed,' he said.

'The neighbours?' asked Warner.

'Correct,' said Cross.

'Well come on. Let's go,' said Warner already on his way to Cross's office to get his car keys. Cross didn't move. Warner reappeared, keys jangling purposefully in his hand. 'Are you not coming, DS Cross?'

Cross neither moved nor answered.

'Fine. Suit yourself. I'll go on my own.' He then strode out of the office like the man on a mission he was.

'Are you really not going with him, George?' asked Carson.

'I am not,' he replied.

'Then how are you going to get there? It's a bit far for a bike, isn't it?' asked Carson.

'Definitely. But then I have no intention of going to the village,' he said.

'Why not? Please don't make things difficult from the get-go.'

'Because the Cotterells are waiting in the Voluntary Assistance suite downstairs,' said Cross looking at the note. As he then left the office Carson couldn't help but smile at the wily old detective. He spotted Mackenzie also smiling.

'That will be all, thank you, Alice,' he said.

'Yes, sir,' she replied knowingly.

6

Cross read the couple's body language as entitled and inconvenienced, as soon he came into the VA suite. Tamsin Cotterell looked around her immediate vicinity as if searching for hidden germs. She was in her early thirties and clearly pregnant. Barnaby Cotterell was a little older, late forties possibly. He was well built and sat with an attitude that said he considered his physique to be a useful attribute in any given situation, but particularly ones with an element of confrontation. As if his mere presence was a negotiating tool in itself. The main thing that struck Cross's ultrasensitive olfactory system was the invisible cloud of scent that hung in the room. What made it almost unbearable for the detective was the fact that it was a clear case of two conflicting perfumes that had absolutely nothing in common and were fighting for superiority. This made him wonder whether couples should consult with each other first thing in the morning about their respective scents for that day, in the same way they might discuss clashing outfits. He walked over to the window and opened it.

'Good idea, it is rather stuffy in here, don't you think?' Tamsin asked Cross.

'Not particularly,' answered Cross. 'I've opened the window because I find yours and your husband's liberal application of perfume nauseating.'

Her mouth dropped open in shock.

'Why are you here?' Cross asked as he sat.

'Our neighbour has been murdered,' said her husband as if explaining the obvious to an unintelligent underling.

'Correct. Did you do it?' Cross asked.

'No,' he replied.

'So, again. Why are you here?'

'Because we wanted to get ahead of it,' replied the wife.

'Get ahead of what?' asked Cross.

'The situation,' she explained, looking at her husband as if to ask what they were dealing with here.

'What situation?' asked Cross.

'Are you being deliberately obtuse?' asked Barnaby Cotterell.

Cross made no reply. Not because he was offended in any way and wanted to indicate this. He was simply trying to ascertain whether this had been said out of innate arrogance or incipient fear. This couple had driven back down from London having made the journey home less than thirty-six hours earlier. What time had they got up that morning? He also wondered whether, as they lived in London, they had that oft-held metropolitan prejudice about policemen outside of the big city – that they were either stupid, bad at their job or probably both.

'I am not, deliberately nor otherwise. Why are you here?' he asked again, as if it were the first time.

'Our neighbour has been murdered,' Barnaby Cotterell repeated. He was beginning to sound exasperated.

'Did you do it?' Cross asked again.

'No!' said Tamsin.

'I'd like to speak to your superior,' added her husband.

'Where were you the night before last?' asked Cross, ignoring him.

'On our way back to London,' said Tamsin, relieved that the conversation was finally moving on.

'From where?' asked Cross.

'Crockerne, obviously,' replied Barnaby.

'Why is that obvious?' asked Cross.

'Because that is where our house is,' said Barnaby.

'What time did you leave?' asked Cross.

'Around eight.'

'And now you've driven all the way back down from London. Have you taken time off work?' Cross went on.

'I have. Tammy is on maternity leave.'

'Why?'

'Why what? She's pregnant, that's why,' replied Barnaby testily.

'Why did you feel the need to come back so quickly? Come back to see the police, more specifically?' asked Cross.

'Are you serious?'

This was a question Cross was asked a lot in the course of his work. It puzzled him as it seemed perfectly obvious that he was being serious. He had taken to not answering it.

'Our neighbour has been murdered,' Barnaby reiterated.

As this was simply a statement and didn't answer Cross's question, he again said nothing. Just looked at them. He was still waiting for an answer.

'We and Moreton didn't get along,' Barnaby said finally. 'Our relationship wasn't what you might call neighbourly or cordial.'

'What would you call it?'

'He was an antagonistic old bastard, short and long of it.'

'Barnaby,' his wife cautioned.

'How exactly was he antagonistic?' asked Cross.

'Right from the get-go he was a problem,' said Tamsin.

Cross now opened his file.

'Would this have something to do with the lane next to his property?' he asked.

'Yes. The lane we shared,' Tamsin said.

'His lane which you had use of through an easement,' Cross pointed out.

'That's what I said,' she insisted.

Cross looked at her but decided not to pursue this.

'You went to court. Twice,' Cross noted.

'Yes,' Barnaby replied with a sigh. He knew where this was going.

'And lost on both occasions. The second actually concerning

the non-compliance of the first judgement,' Cross pointed out. 'Non-compliance in the form of non-payment.'

Neither of them replied. Cross continued to read, turning the pages over in his file with concentrated deliberation.

'You accused Mr Moreton of slashing the tyres on your Range Rover,' Cross continued.

Again, no reply.

'You must have known he had a security camera on the back of his property but were obviously unaware this camera covered the front part of the property where you park your car. Which revealed you late at night, slashing the tyres of your own vehicle, Mr Cotterell. That can't have reflected well on you in court.'

Cross then went back to the folder and continued to read. He came across something which obviously surprised him.

'You also accused him of constantly blocking the drive with vehicles. You provided a photograph showing a van blocking Mrs Cotterell's car. But it transpired this was a delivery van who had wrongly attempted to make a delivery addressed to you, at Mr Moreton's house. The driver left the van where it was, then walked up to your house to make a delivery. But he was unable to because Mrs Cotterell had driven past him, then photographed her car being blocked by the van as an attempt to provide evidence against Mr Moreton. To prove your point, as it were.'

Cross now looked up and attempted to seem puzzled.

'And yet you claim he was the problem. An interesting way of looking at it. In the light of all this I'm beginning to understand your speedy return today,' he said.

'Well, yes. That is why we're here,' said Tamsin, nervously.

'It was obvious you might point the finger at us,' said Barnaby.

'Except, of course, that we haven't. However obvious it might have seemed to you, Mr Cotterell. Did you need to buy petrol for the journey to London when you left Crockerne?' Cross asked.

'Yes,' Barnaby replied.

'Do you have a receipt?'

'I do.' He got his wallet out of his jacket and produced a receipt which he handed over.

Cross examined it. 'Well, that certainly accounts for your whereabouts at eight seventeen that night. But not your wife's.'

'She was with me, obviously,' he replied.

'Again, our understanding of what is obvious or not plainly differs.' He closed the file. 'I need to amass more information before questioning you further. Would you object if we had a look around your property, the house and gardens?'

They looked at each other, which Cross noted.

'Not at all,' replied Barnaby.

Cross got up and walked to the door. He turned.

'Oh, one last question. Do you own a dog?'

'We do. Two, actually.'

'What breed?'

'Rhodesian Ridgebacks.'

'Do you bring them to the country with you at weekends?'

'Obviously,' replied Barnaby Cotterell.

'Obviously,' repeated Cross. 'There you go again.' Then he left.

The couple looked at each other, not sure what to do next. They were saved by a PC opening the door and offering to show them out.

7

'I suppose you thought that was funny,' Warner said as he barged into the office.

'What?' asked Cross innocently.

'Sending me off to Crockerne when you knew very well the neighbours were in the VA suite.'

'Firstly, I didn't send you anywhere, DI Warner. You rushed off without bothering to ascertain the exact whereabouts of the Cotterells. Secondly, you should probably be aware that I am not known for my sense of humour. Quite the opposite, in point of fact,' Cross replied.

'Carson's office, now!' Warner announced before striding off through the open area. Cross remained where he was as he wasn't entirely sure what the DI's statement meant. Warner's face, now a virulent red, reappeared at the door.

'Are you coming?' he barked.

'Of course. You should have asked,' said Cross, getting up.

This stopped Warner in his tracks for a moment before he turned and marched off again. Cross followed obediently and wondered, as he walked by her desk, why Mackenzie was grinning from ear to ear.

Carson was sitting in his office as Warner leant on his desk and held forth. Cross stood at the door. Carson didn't like Warner's posture in the least, but decided the DI was wound up enough without him adding more fuel to his ire.

'He let me go there in full knowledge that the suspects were here, downstairs,' proclaimed Warner.

'Suspects?' asked Carson.

'The neighbours,' replied Warner.

'It might be more useful, if not accurate, if we were to refer to them as persons of interest at this juncture,' Cross pointed out.

'Shut it,' spat Warner, turning towards Cross.

Cross looked behind him and saw that the door was indeed open. He pushed it shut.

'Are you trying to be funny?' asked Warner.

'I'd remind you of my recent comment about my relationship with humour,' said Cross.

Warner turned back to Carson who was struggling to suppress a smile.

'He wasted a good two hours of my time,' he said.

'The village is actually only a twenty-five minute drive, sir,' Cross pointed out to Warner. 'So, fifty minutes' driving in addition to a generous ten minutes to ascertain the Cotterells weren't there. It was probably no more than one hour.'

'I took the opportunity to look around and familiarise myself with the crime scene; I wasn't going to let it be a totally wasted trip,' replied Warner who didn't know Cross well enough to realise he was just digging a hole for himself.

'So, to be clear, we are in fact talking about you wasting just the one hour of your time as you managed to put the other to good use. But having said that it occurs to me that as you did put the time to good use, we cannot really consider the one hour's driving to get you there and provide you with the opportunity you describe, as a waste of time as without it you wouldn't have been able to examine the crime scene and familiarise yourself with the village. Which means, in essence, neither I nor you have wasted two hours of your time,' Cross said, perfectly seriously.

'Do you want a slap, mate?' Warner said before he could stop himself.

'DI Warner, I will not tolerate that kind of language or threat in my office nor anywhere else in the MCU,' said Carson with surprising authority.

'Apologies, sir,' muttered Warner.

'It seems to me there has been a lack of communication here. Plain and simple. You two don't know much about each other. There will need to be a period of acclimatisation and getting familiar with each other. Bobby, George here is one of my best detectives and I'm sure he won't mind me telling you this, but he has Asperger's Syndrome—'

'Autism Spectrum Condition,' interrupted Cross.

'Oh, I'm sorry, George. I thought you told everyone you preferred—'

'I did further research and have changed my position on the matter.'

'Of course. Good to know. George has Autism Spectrum Condition—'

'Also known as Autism Spectrum Disorder. But I don't see it as a disorder. Just to be completely clear,' Cross interrupted again.

Carson eyed him but decided this was not the time for a discussion, though this clarification was useful.

'Which means he works differently to most of us and we need to understand that,' Carson finished.

'That seems a little indulgent if you don't mind my saying so, sir,' replied Warner.

'As it happens, Bobby, I do. This has nothing to do with favouritism, just pragmatism. You may be unaware of this, but George has the highest conviction rate in the force,' Carson informed him.

'By far,' Cross elaborated.

'Which begs the question why he's still a detective sergeant,' said Warner as if this had to prove something was amiss somewhere.

'I have no desire to run a team nor fulfil any other tasks required by such a rank,' Cross replied.

'That's a good excuse,' scoffed Warner.

'You're a good detective, Bobby. So I'm told. But we have yet to work together. You'll have to find a way to work with George and he with you, if you're to get on here. But we've discovered compromise is not his strong suit. So you as senior officer will need to take the lead,' Carson finished by saying.

'Yes, sir.'

'That'll be all. George, stay behind for a minute,' said Carson.

Warner walked to the door, annoyed at being dismissed in the presence of a junior officer. Cross remained where he was.

'Are you not going to open the door?' Warner asked.

'No. I'm not leaving,' Cross pointed out.

Warner turned to look at Carson.

'Choose your battles, DI Warner,' he said.

Warner left.

'Would you like me to get Josie back early from her leave?' Carson asked.

'No,' replied Cross horrified, not by the idea of her being summoned back, but by the assumption he couldn't cope without her.

'I want you to know that I understand how difficult this might be for you. So, if you need anything, just ask.'

'Yes, sir.'

Cross didn't move even though it was clear the meeting was over.

'You can go.'

Cross opened the door then turned back into the room.

'There is one thing I do need,' he said.

'I'm not going to ask Warner to move his desk out of your office, George,' said Carson.

Cross paused for a second as he processed this, nodded then left.

8

'**R**ight, George,' said Warner as Cross walked back into the occupied territory of his office. 'What would be your preferred course of action?' Anyone else would have been well aware of the sarcasm dripping off this enquiry. But not Cross.

'I'd like Mackenzie assigned to the case for a start,' began Cross.

'Is she the young blonde?' asked Warner, looking at her in the open area.

'I'll text her.'

'You're kidding, right?' said Warner opening the door. 'Miss Mackenzie, could we have a moment of your time?' he asked politely.

Alice got up and walked over.

'The name's Alice,' she said walking past him as he held open the door.

'Bobby,' he replied. 'So, George, what do you want Alice to do for us?'

'Alice. I'm not sure a man of Moreton's age will have much of a digital presence, but let's not make any assumptions. Here is what I know about him thus far,' he said handing over a sheet he'd typed up.

'Thank you,' she said taking it and making for the door. Warner turned to Cross.

'She attached to anyone?' he asked as he watched Alice leave.

'No one in particular, she'll work with whomever she's told to,' replied Cross.

Warner looked at him like he was from another planet but decided against making a comment.

'Right, well, I think I'll go and see the pathologist,' he said instead.

'She won't have anything useful for you as yet,' Cross cautioned him as he busied himself on his computer.

'Okay then, back to the village it is.'

Cross said nothing as Warner made for the door. He then turned.

'Are you not coming?'

'I am not.'

'Well, I'd like you to,' replied Warner.

'Is that an order?' Cross asked.

'Sure. If that makes it any easier.'

Cross got up and gathered his things.

'Do you mind if I smoke?' Warner asked getting a packet of cigarettes out of his pocket as he drove them to Crockerne.

'I do and my preference would be for you also to keep both hands on the wheel while the vehicle is in motion,' Cross replied.

'You know you speak like an instruction manual, don't you? I'll open the window,' said Warner, ignoring Cross's objection.

'It makes no difference to me—' said Cross.

'Thanks. You'd be amazed at how tight arsed people are about smoking these days,' he said, putting a cigarette in his mouth.

'—whether the window is open or not. The force's policy on smoking is quite clear on the matter of smoking or vaping within a departmental car. It is expressly forbidden,' replied Cross.

Warner looked at Cross.

'Please keep your eyes on the road.'

'Wow, this is going to be fun,' Warner observed.

'Interesting you should have any expectation of a murder investigation being fun. You should talk to my colleague DS

Ottey. She manages to find humour in the most unlikely of places.'

'Is that right? Something tells me that doesn't apply to you.'

'Oh, absolutely not. As I've already mentioned, I believe I'm quite notorious for not having much of a sense of humour,' replied Cross.

Warner looked at him again. 'Now I don't know if you're taking the piss or not.'

'Again, perhaps you could concentrate on the road ahead while you decide,' replied Cross.

Warner decided the best policy here was to change the subject. Maybe talking about the investigation and a strategy would be easier.

'Where shall we start in Crockerne?' he began by asking.

'As it wasn't my idea to come back to the village and I haven't had time to form a coherent strategy, I'll follow your lead. You are the SIO,' Cross replied.

'Well, obviously we need to take a close look at the neighbours. They have to be prime suspects. You must've been thinking the same thing. I like them for this. What are you doing?' he asked Cross who was busy writing in his notebook.

'I'm writing a plan of action,' replied Cross.

'Okay, well let's go and interview the Cotterells.'

'I've already interviewed them,' Cross pointed out.

'Not properly.'

'That is an opinion based on absolutely nothing, sir. If you have such a strong feeling you must follow it up and interview them. I have nothing to add to the conversation I had with them this morning.'

'So how do you intend using your time?' asked Warner, straining to keep his temper.

'I would like to visit the shopkeeper, then Mr Toby Bath and the Reverend Alison Smith. Mr Bath is head of the local parish council. The Reverend, well, that should be obvious,' said Cross.

'Fine, go. I don't have time for this.'

'Time for doing a proper investigation?' asked Cross.

'Just go before I say something you'll regret,' said Warner.

'I'm fairly sure the correct expression is—'

'Go!' ordered Warner, glad to see the back of him. He was pretty sure he'd get to the bottom of the case quicker on his own and without the help of the esteemed George Cross.

9

Cross walked up the main street of the village to the local shop. It had become an outpost of a nationwide chain of supermarkets recently, but according to Tom was still run by the man who'd owned the shop previously. He'd been there for forty years. Quite astute business of the supermarket to keep him on, thought Cross. It would alienate the village less and he would already be aware of their individual needs. His name was Patrick Withey.

'How often did Mr Moreton shop here?' Cross began by asking.

'A couple of times a week. He did his main shop on a Thursday,' answered Withey.

'Did you know him well?'

'As well as anyone could say they knew Alistair. He actually worked for me for a while.'

'In the shop?' asked Cross.

'No.' Withey laughed at the absurdity of this notion. 'He would've frightened the customers away. He did my paper round. Oldest paper boy in the UK, I used to joke.' Cross wasn't exactly sure why this was a joke, as in reality it was quite probably true. 'He wouldn't take any money either. Told me to put his wages in the collection box at the church.'

'And did you?' asked Cross.

'Of course,' answered Withey slightly affronted. 'He said it was a good way of getting him out of the house and taking some exercise. Always on time, early in fact, as he often helped me sort out the orders.'

'Why did he stop?'

The shopkeeper paused for a moment, as if maybe aware his answer didn't reflect well on him or the village.

'People complained,' he said finally.

'Why? About what?' Cross asked.

'They didn't like him delivering their papers,' he said awkwardly.

'What time did he do his round?' Cross went on.

'Six thirty in the morning.'

'Then presumably no one saw him.'

'Not initially, no, then someone did. They were leaving early one morning to go on holiday. When it got around, people complained. They said they'd cancel their order if he continued. I know it was wrong, but that was before I sold the business and things were tough,' Withey explained.

'I see.'

'And now look what's happened; I couldn't believe it when Tom told me yesterday. It's definitely murder, is it?'

'I would say so, yes,' replied Cross. 'How often did you see Mr Moreton?'

'Every day. He'd come in to get his paper. *The Telegraph.*'

'Every day,' repeated Cross, writing it in his notebook.

'Well, when I say that. Except for the last couple of weeks,' Withey said. 'He stopped coming.'

'When was this?' asked Cross.

'Like I said. The last couple of weeks. I went up to see if he was all right. He said he'd been under the weather. So, I asked him if he'd like the papers delivered till he was back on his feet.'

'And what was his reply?'

'He said yes. He'd like that.'

'So, you saw him.'

'Yes, just that once.'

Withey thought for a moment then suddenly looked up. 'Oh God, you don't think it could be someone from the village, do you?' he asked.

'I don't think anything as yet but more to the point – do you? After all, you must know everyone here,' asked Cross.

'Look, he wasn't popular in the village, but that was mostly because people thought he was a little odd. The way he kept himself to himself and didn't really want anything to do with the village or the people,' Withey replied.

'Unless it was a parish meeting,' Cross pointed out.

Withey smiled at this. 'Oh, you've heard about that, have you? Yes, he was a great one for causes or, more accurately, points of principle as he constantly told us. A great one for a point of principle, Alistair.'

'Which wouldn't have added to his popularity I should think.'

'Village gossip is exactly that. It's not something that is particularly interested in the truth. Far from it. Take the Turnbull girl nonsense, for example.'

'Go on,' said Cross making a note of the name.

'She was a young girl who went missing from the village about six or seven years back,' Withey told him. 'She was eleven – Kylie. Everyone was out looking for her, everyone except for Alistair, but that was completely understandable in the circumstances.'

'Why?' asked Cross.

'People had started pointing the finger. Said if anyone local had taken Kylie, it had to be him. He was the last person seen talking to her. They arrested him in the end.'

'I thought no one in the village talked to Moreton,' Cross said.

'On the whole, yes. But people had noticed her talking to him quite a lot before she went missing. The police then got a warrant for his house and searched it. They found some of her hair on a chair,' Withey went on. 'He claimed he had helped her with her reading.'

Cross continued to write in his notebook.

'Kylie was dyslexic. But for everyone the hair made it a foregone conclusion. You lot charged him. It was all over the papers. "Retired teacher took girl". It was disgraceful. Then Kylie turned up. She was in London. Run away. Having trouble at school, but mostly trouble at home with her stepdad. She accused him of abusing her. As soon as she saw Alistair had been arrested, she went to the nearest police station. Backed up everything Alistair had told them. He was teaching the poor girl to read. She was very grateful. She liked him for taking the time.'

'I do remember that now,' said Cross.

'But even now people still think he did it. When nothing actually happened. Can you believe how stupid that is?' said Withey. 'Kylie and her family moved away a year later. Without the stepdad.'

'Is he still here?' asked Cross.

'Malcolm? Yes,' replied Withey. 'You don't think... Come to think of it he was one of the first to point the finger at Alistair. Straight-out accusing him of being a pervert and taking her. They had a massive row after she pitched up. Alistair attacked him.'

'Did anyone witness that?' asked Cross.

'Dozens of people. Went after him with a stick in the pub. A bamboo cane, like from a garden.'

'What's this individual's surname?' asked Cross.

'Fisk. Malcolm Fisk. Tom barred him. He'd always have a go at Alistair after he'd had a few drinks, apparently,' Withey went on, as if he was convincing himself out loud that Fisk had to be a prime suspect.

'Where does Mr Fisk live?' asked Cross.

'Number twenty-seven on the lane. But he's a long-distance lorry driver, so chances are he won't be at home.'

Cross put a card on the counter.

'If anything else occurs to you, call me on this number,' Cross instructed him.

'I assume you've heard about the neighbours,' Withey went on as if he wanted to prevent Cross from leaving.

'The couple from London?'

'Yes. He had a lot of trouble with them,' Withey continued.

'What are they like?' Cross asked.

'Couldn't tell you really. The only time she's been in the shop, she made a point of saying they did all their shopping in London where the produce was so much better and brought it down with them. When I asked if they wanted the weekend papers, she replied they came into the sticks – her expression, not mine – to get away from all that.'

As predicted, Malcolm Fisk wasn't in. Or if he was, he wasn't answering the door.

IO

Cross walked through the village towards a small house which had a very ordered, traditional cottage garden at the front. Roses abounded in various pale shades of yellow and pink, together with pots of nasturtiums, lobelias and a large collection of different types of fuchsias. As he walked up the path the air was filled with the scent of thyme. He looked down and saw that in the cracks between the paving stones small clumps had been planted. So as the visitor came towards the house their feet crushed the herb and they were greeted with a fragrant welcome. He pulled an old cast iron bell pull. A bell rang inside the house. Not an electric one, but an actual bell sounded by a clapper.

After a few moments the door was opened by a woman in her seventies wearing a floral housecoat and a pair of Marigold gloves. An Hermès scarf was tied around her head of white hair. But it was all carried off with a supremely confident elegance.

'Hello,' she said brightly. 'Can I help you?'

Cross held up his warrant card.

'DS George Cross,' he informed her.

'Oh, you must be here about poor Mr Moreton. What a terrible thing.'

'Are you Mrs Toby Bath?'

'I am Mrs Deborah Bath, yes,' she corrected him with a twinkle in her eye. 'Would you like to speak with my husband about the parish council?'

'I would.'

'You'll find him in his greenhouse. He really should put a bed

in it the amount of time he spends in there. Come in.' She waved
him on.

Cross walked through the low-ceilinged house into a narrow
garden at the back. It was a well-stocked garden. Barely an inch
of soil was visible anywhere. A varied floral scent filled the air. A
gap in a well-trimmed tall hedge led into a wilder section of the
garden with long grass and a small orchard. But before then was
a vegetable garden filled with lettuces, onions, herbs and a tall,
long pyramid of runner beans. There was a greenhouse to the
side in which a man could be seen working. Cross approached
the entrance. The glasshouse was filled with tomatoes, peppers
and cucumbers. The man was working at a bench to one side
potting on seedlings. He was wearing a baggy pair of reddish-
brown corduroy trousers, held up by a pair of wide braces, a
thick checked Viyella shirt and knitted tie. Over this he wore
a green apron which had a leather tool belt around it. Cross
thought he had to be impossibly hot on a day like this, let alone
in a sweltering greenhouse.

'Mr Bath?' Cross enquired.

'Yes,' replied the man without turning round.

Cross held up his warrant card despite the man still not
looking at him.

'My name is George Cross. I'm investigating the murder of
Alistair Moreton.'

This got Bath's attention. He turned immediately.

'Oh, yes. I've been expecting you. Let me just get cleaned up.'

A few minutes later they were sitting at a table outside the
back door of the house.

'An absolute pain in the backside. My backside in particular,'
Bath answered in reply to Cross's first question about Moreton.

'In what way?'

'Well, as I'm sure you're aware, I'm the chair of the Crockerne
parish council,' Bath went on with the habitual air of self-
importance that seemed to come with holding such positions in
small communities. 'For someone who had so little to do with the

48

village or the people within it, he had an awful lot of opinions about the affairs of Crockerne.'

'Were there any issues that were particularly troublesome?' asked Cross.

'Any? There were dozens. That man had an opinion on everything. Whether he had the knowledge to back it up or not was often a matter for debate.'

'Was he on the council?'

Bath scoffed at the very idea. 'Good Lord no. No one would have voted him on. But he came to all the public meetings. Every single one during his time here. Before his arrival they lasted an hour to maybe an hour and a half. With him, they regularly became two to three hours long. He loved the sound of his own voice.'

'What were his particular concerns?'

'Anything! Literally anything. I'll give you an example. A few years ago, we had to design a one-way traffic system for the village. As you've probably noticed the lanes here are very narrow and it was virtually impossible to have two-way traffic. Constant bottlenecks and arguments about whose right of way it was. Naturally, the county council held a consultation. Moreton tabled over a hundred questions and concerns. He held the bloody thing up for over a year. The council almost put its hands up in surrender. We nearly lost the scheme because of one man, when the entire village was in favour of it. Moreton objected to the introduction of parking restrictions and residents' bays and he didn't even own a car! He had things to say about the shop changing its opening hours which wasn't even a parish council matter. That didn't stop him bringing it up and talking about a loss of amenities. The dates of the annual fair, which he never came to, not once. He made everything impossibly difficult. It was as if that was his sole purpose in life. To make my life a bloody misery.'

'That must have been very frustrating for you,' Cross commented.

'Now, I'm going to say this because others will say they heard me say it and it's true. I often wanted to kill the bloody man.'

'And did you?' asked Cross.

'I did not,' he replied, genuinely shocked by the question. 'And despite my dislike for him, I feel terrible about what has happened. We all do. Well, except for the Cotterells, of course. But then again, they're not villagers really. We had a responsibility of care for him, as with everyone else in the village. But we did our best to neglect and as chair of the parish council I must bear the brunt of,' he said tragically.

'Why are you responsible?' asked Cross.

'Because if we'd paid a little more attention to him... What am I talking about? *Any* attention to him, this might not have happened. We shouldn't have been put off by his outward demeanour. People can often be awkward and difficult when they don't mean to be. Don't you find?'

Had anyone else been with Cross they would have felt the question was, perhaps comically, a little close to home. It didn't strike him as such.

'Were there people in the village who were particularly antagonised or inconvenienced by Mr Moreton's interference in village affairs?' Cross asked.

'Everyone was antagonised, but only because no one likes a busybody, especially when they take up so much of everyone's valuable time. Nothing more serious than that. His murder is baffling. I can't believe it was anything to do with someone in the village, but then again, I suppose you must hear that all the time.'

'What about the neighbours?'

'That did get a bit bloody. Naturally everyone sided with them at the outset.'

'Why?'

'Well, it didn't take a huge stretch of the imagination to picture what life must've been like to be his neighbour. I mean, if his behaviour at parish meetings was anything to go on. Everyone thought he might have been making their life hell. But when the details emerged at the first court hearing, people took his side. In a weird way it changed people's attitudes to him altogether. They started to ask him how it was going and if the Cotterells had paid up. At the second hearing some people spoke for him, others even just turned up to show their support.'

'Was he grateful?' Cross asked.

Bath laughed. 'You didn't know the man, Sergeant. Put it this way, if he was grateful he never showed it.'

'What do you make of the Cotterells?' asked Cross.

'Truth? Not good people. I don't like them. In part because they don't seem to like us. They're outsiders, second-homeowners what's more. They make no effort to be a part of the village, even for three days a week. They think that just because they come from London they're in some way better than us. The only time they came to the council – and not to a meeting mind you, but quietly to each member – was when they tried to drum up support against Moreton. They tried all sorts of ways to persuade us. You wouldn't believe,' said Bath.

'I'm a policeman. You wouldn't believe what I'd believe,' Cross remarked which, to his surprise, caused Bath to laugh. 'Bribes?'

'Correct, and when that didn't work they offered to contribute to the village financially. A sort of community bribe, if you like. They must've thought that would be cheaper than a court fine.'

Cross didn't make it as far as the vicarage as he encountered Alison Smith in the village street. She suggested they go to the local tearoom. She was in her thirties, Cross estimated, and had an eager, enthusiastic quality about her in the way she moved, spoke and gestured. Her hands and arms were in a state of perpetual motion. Her facial expressions were over-articulated to the point of exaggeration. As if to make them more easily read. For Cross though, the artifice in this actually made her more difficult to read. She went from laughter to concern in the blink of an eye when asking about the tearoom owner's elderly parents as she took their order.

'So, poor old Alistair. I'm not really sure how I can help, Sergeant,' she began, with a handwringing expression of apologetic sympathy. 'I can't think of anyone who would want to cause him harm. Isn't that the first thing you usually ask in these situations?'

'It is not,' replied Cross.

'Oh, right,' she said scooping her blonde hair into a ponytail and securing it with a hair tie, as if she now understood this was serious business. Either that, or to ensure her dog collar was definitely visible.

The tea arrived in a china pot with cups and saucers which Cross thought was a positive start. Then he saw the tea strainer and realised that there was every chance it might prove to be his second acceptable cup of tea in the village. Crockerne was performing admirably in the proper-cup-of-tea stakes.

'So how can I help?' the vicar asked, face-width smile accompanied with a furrowed, concerned brow.

'Alistair Moreton was a regular churchgoer. As his vicar, did you have much contact with him?'

'Of course. Although he was Catholic, he came to our services. For the convenience only, as he would constantly tell me,' she laughed.

'Did you know him well?'

'As much as anyone, I suppose. Actually, that's not true. I think I knew him much better than most in the village, certainly after our tricky start.'

'"Tricky" in what way?'

'I've only been in the parish for four years. Before that there was a male vicar. Whether it was Alistair's Catholicism or just downright misogyny I don't know, but he was vehemently opposed to my appointment.'

'Because you're a woman?' Cross asked.

'Correct. He had no truck with female vicars. He objected

strongly, wrote letters to the parish, emails, you name it. This from a man who didn't even come to the village church at the time. He probably would have started a petition but realised no one in the village would have signed it. He frequented a Catholic church about five miles away.'

'But he ended up in your congregation? Why the change of heart?' asked Cross.

'A broken hip. Last year. He was in hospital for a while. I visited him when he came home. Encouraged him to take short walks with me. We got to know each other slowly. Then he decided to worship at the village church until he was able to go back to a "proper" one, as he put it. But he never did.'

'What did you think of him? Once you got to know him?'

'A complex character. Very private, almost to the point of being a recluse. Very set in his ways, but overall very misunderstood. People were suspicious because he kept himself to himself. They never really got over the missing girl.'

'Kylie Turnbull?' Cross volunteered after consulting his notes.

'That's right. Even though it had nothing to do with him, they never got past it. Mud sticks, even when you're completely innocent it would seem,' she said sadly.

'Do you know Malcolm Fisk?'

'Only on nodding terms. He's not a churchgoer. Saw him this morning actually.'

'Do you know who he works for?'

'Hammonds, in Avonmouth. He brought one of the artics into the village for a fete day. It was huge. I have no idea how he managed to get through the lanes. The kids loved it. He let them climb all over the thing. You don't think... I mean, they were always at each other's throats.'

'I haven't spoken with him yet. Did you learn anything about Moreton's life? His past?' Cross asked.

'Yes. He'd been married. His wife died about thirty years ago. I don't think he ever got over it. They had a son.'

'Did he see him much?'

'Quite regularly, which speaks volumes.'

'In what way?' asked Cross.

'Well, I can't imagine Al was the easiest of fathers. He had high, somewhat unrealistic expectations of people and the way they behaved. Had a lot to say about the world, politics, mostly critical. He thought unemployment was self-inflicted and that there was a malaise of laziness in the country encouraged by a ludicrously generous benefit system. The only time he seemed content, at peace, even, was when he talked about literature. It was his safe place. He found sanctuary in the written word. But his son was devoted,' she replied.

'Did he have a military background at all?'

'I thought he might initially. But no. He did his national service but that was it. He ran the cadet force at a couple of schools. He was a teacher, you see. Ended up being headmaster at a small Catholic prep school somewhere. Don't know where. He seemed quite reluctant to discuss that part of his life.' She then laughed. 'What am I talking about? He was reluctant to talk about any part of his life.'

'Did you meet the son?'

'Yes, he popped in to see me occasionally. To ask after his dad. Get the truth of what was really going on, he said.'

'Do you have contact details for him?'

'I do,' she said, looking for her phone. 'He was here yesterday afternoon, obviously. As soon as he heard. He's an MP in Dorset. Sandy Moreton's his name.'

'Oh, I know of him. Famous for his right-wing views on immigration, gay marriage and abortion. Recently lost the Tory party whip,' remarked Cross.

'Not only that, his constituency has just successfully petitioned for his recall. There's going to be a by-election. It was announced on the day of Alistair's murder.'

'Really?' Cross made a note of this. 'Had anything happened in Alistair's life recently, changed perhaps? Did you notice any difference in his mood, behaviour?'

She thought about this for a moment, hand to chin, lined brow to communicate how seriously she was considering it.

'If I'm honest, which let's face it should be a given with a vicar' – she laughed heartily at this but elicited no response from Cross – 'he didn't seem himself recently. He did have this ongoing dispute with his neighbours but that had never affected him before. And he'd won, after all. But he missed church for a couple of Sundays. I thought he might have gone away until I remembered he never went away. Anyway, I asked Tom, he runs the pub. But you'd know that, wouldn't you? He discovered the body, didn't he? I should pop in and see them,' she said, making a note in a vast, well-annotated diary. 'I asked him if he'd seen Al but he hadn't. So, I popped up there to make sure everything was okay.'

'Was he there?'

'He was. Yes. But he didn't invite me in which was odd. Though, *wouldn't* let me in might be more accurate.'

'When was this?' Cross asked.

'Just a couple of weeks ago. He didn't come to church after that. I was going to go up there this week. But obviously...' She tailed off.

Cross made a note of this.

'The thing is, Sergeant, and I know you'll probably think this is silly, but when I went up to Alistair's house, I was convinced there was someone else there. In the house.'

Cross thought about this for a moment. It occurred to him that for someone who didn't involve himself in the life of the village and was something of an outsider, Alistair Moreton had at least two people in the village looking out for him. Maybe this was a benefit of living in such a small tight-knit community. He then got up and left the shop unceremoniously. She was quite startled by his sudden departure and equally taken aback by his reappearance a few seconds later when he walked up to the counter and paid before leaving again without even glancing in the vicar's direction.

Malcolm Fisk did, in fact, have a criminal record. Mostly from his early twenties, it had to be said. It had involved burglary, assault and, possibly more interestingly, some minor drug offences. He was obviously back from his latest driving job, if the vicar had seen him. Cross called in on him at his cottage. Fisk wouldn't let him in and so they were sitting on a bench by the river inlet in the village.

'Interesting name, Fisk. Particularly appropriate when you consider where you live,' Cross began their conversation with him. Fisk worked for a national haulage company, recently rebranded as a logistics firm. It was based in the south-west. It did a lot of business out of Avonmouth Docks. Moreton had unsuccessfully applied for injunctions against Fisk.

'Is it?' Fisk replied with distinct disinterest.

'Is your family from around here originally?' Cross went on, not in the least discouraged.

'Yeah. I live in my gran's house. Well, it's mine now.'

'Fisk unsurprisingly derives from the word fish. First used in the UK in the Middle Ages, I believe. Were your family fishermen at some point?'

'No idea, but we've always been working the water in one way or another. My grandparents were pilots here. My dad then worked in the docks at Avonmouth,' said Fisk.

'But you chose a different path,' Cross commented.

'I did a bit, yeah. Started driving at the docks before they had a load of redundancies. Look, what is this all about? I'm knackered. I need a kip.'

'Where do you drink?' Cross asked.

'Drink?'

'Well, you've been barred from the only pub in the village. Where do you go?'

'Oh, I see. Well, maybe that'll change now the old bastard's dead,' said Fisk.

'Interesting way of describing a murder victim to a police officer investigating his death,' Cross pointed out.

'It wasn't nothing to do with me,' spat Fisk.

'His murder?' asked Cross.

'Well, what else are we talking about?'

'Where were you on the night of Mr Moreton's murder? Sunday night?'

'I was working.'

Cross nodded slowly at this information.

'That's good. If I were someone who was in a widely known antagonistic relationship with a person who later ended up murdered in the village where that antagonism was on view on a daily basis, I would make sure I knew where I was at the time he was murdered. You didn't get on with him, did you?'

'That's an understatement. The man was a bloody pervert. Everyone knew it. I was the only one to call him out on it and it got me barred from the pub. If anyone should've been barred it should've been him. Bloody paedophile. I've got every right to protect my own.'

'Except that by the time it happened your "own" were no longer any such thing. They'd been long gone. You were still trying to point the finger at him despite the fact that Kylie and her mother had moved away years ago. Moved to get away from you.'

'Not true.'

'Many people thought you'd killed her, didn't they? Classic case of a stepfather abusing his stepdaughter then killing her. They'd seen men like you on the television pleading tearfully for the return of their beloved stepdaughter knowing full well she was dead in the loft where they'd wrapped her up in a carpet and bin bags a few days before,' Cross pushed.

'No one in this village thought that,' Fisk protested.

'Because you had them all looking in Moreton's direction.'

'Because I thought he'd done something to her. She was spending way too much time with him. It wasn't right.'

'But it wasn't wrong either. He was teaching her to read. Helping her with her dyslexia.'

'So he said.'

'So she said,' Cross pointed out.

'That girl's a liar.'

'Is her mother a liar as well? Her mother who called the police on three separate occasions claiming you'd assaulted her?'

'Nothing happened.'

'No, she changed her story on all three occasions until Kylie went missing and then it all came out.'

'All lies,' said Fisk.

'I'm surprised you still live here,' commented Cross.

'Why should I move? I've done nothing wrong.'

'Where were you on Sunday night?' Cross asked.

'Like I said. On a job. Europe.'

'I'll need proof.'

'Then call the company.'

'I already have.'

Fisk took this in and said nothing. Nothing was said as they just looked at each other.

'I'm sure like many people you have little or no respect for the police. But surely you knew we'd check. Where were you?'

'At home.'

'Alone?'

'Yep.'

'Pity you'd got yourself barred from the Hobbler's Arms. Could've been a useful alibi, plenty of witnesses. You used to go down there regularly before the bar. And all because of Alistair Moreton,' Cross went on.

'I didn't kill him. End of.'

'Would you allow us to take a saliva sample from you, Mr Fisk? To get a DNA sample?'

Fisk scoffed at the very idea.

'You've got to be kidding. Why would I do that?' he asked.

'To enable us to eliminate you from our enquiries,' Cross reasoned.

'Absolutely not.'

'Why not?'

'I know what you lot are like. I probably look like I'm good for this with my history with Moreton. You'll make your minds up I did it. People in the village will tell you I probably did. No witnesses though. No alibi, but no proof neither. But that won't matter. You'll push for a confession and when you don't get it, hey presto, my DNA turns up magically at the crime scene,' he said.

'I can assure you—' Cross began.

'You're police. Your assurances don't mean a thing.'

He then got up and shuffled away.

12

Cross returned to Moreton's house. Breaks in people's behaviours, particularly their routines, always got his attention. This was partly because he was a slave to routine himself. He liked regularity in his life. It removed unpredictability. He hated surprises in his personal life but thrived on them at work in an investigation. They so often led to a rewarding line of enquiry. Why had Alistair Moreton stopped going to church and the pub in the last couple of weeks of his life? Was it his health? Cross made a note to visit the local GP. Was there anything in the vicar's sense that there was someone else in Moreton's house when she visited? Cross himself never had a sense or feeling about things, particularly when it came to investigations. When colleagues had a feeling or instinct, he would listen in case it related or dovetailed with a fact, but in general he gave them short shrift. But with witnesses it was different. Depending on the circumstances, though. With them if they had no vested interest in a case sometimes their feelings about what they'd seen or observed were indicators of something which couldn't just be ignored. Both the vicar and the landlady had felt Moreton didn't want them in his house. Why?

Swift and his team were still at the cottage, processing it. Cross donned a white forensic suit and shoe covers as he wanted to have another look around before he went over to see Warner at the Cotterells' house. He started in the kitchen. He was looking for any signs of someone else's presence. But there were no plates or cups left out unwashed. Everything was clean and in its place. Moreton was obviously a very organised and clean housekeeper.

Cross went up to the first floor and looked in the spare bedroom. It was a dark room imbued with the abandoned air a room will cultivate when it hasn't been used in some time. The bed was covered with an old pink candlewick bedspread. A memento mori from a previous age of Moreton's life with his wife, perhaps. The bedspread was rumpled, which attracted Cross's attention. He walked across to the master bedroom door where Swift was bent over at work. The ceilings were low and with his height he couldn't stand up comfortably in the eaves of the room. Cross thought it probable that Swift might have a stiff back over the ensuing days.

'Dr Swift?'

'DS Cross,' he replied.

'Have you processed the spare bedroom?' Cross asked.

'Not yet.'

'Could you examine the bedspread and also the pillow closely?'

'Of course. What am I looking for?'

But Cross had gone.

He went into the small kitchen. There was a wooden table with two chairs. Shelves contained herbs and condiments. Saucepans hung from the ceiling. There was an old cream-coloured Aga which was still in use. Another CSI was processing the room.

'Have you gone through the contents of the bin and those outside?' Cross asked him.

'Not yet.'

'I'd like to go through them with you then,' said Cross in such a way that implied it should happen immediately.

They removed the plastic bag from the small round steel pedal bin. The lid flapped shut with a noisy rattle. They then emptied the bag of rubbish onto a plastic sheet. There was nothing exceptional in it. Nothing Cross wouldn't have expected. But it was different when it came to the recycling outside. Moreton was obviously a conscientious recycler with plastic, glass, tin and paper all carefully sorted into different bags. Cross was impressed. But what really caught his eye were several empty cans of strong lager and energy drinks, together with large empty plastic bottles of cheap strong cider. Neither seemed the natural drink of choice for an eighty-something-year-old man. Cross also knew from Tom that Moreton was very strict about drinking at home. Just the single nightcap of good barrel-aged Scotch was his limit, though Cross suspected it might well be a case of a four-finger-filled tumbler rather than one. The strong lager and cider, both with a high alcohol content, seemed out of place, but not as much as the garishly coloured energy drink.

Cross began to help the forensic investigator put all the rubbish back into the bags. This impressed the man who was more used to CID looking at what they wanted to, generally making a mess and then leaving it for someone else to clear up. As if their time was so much more valuable than other people's and in a way they would never understand.

'It's all right, I can do this,' the young man offered.

'It'll be quicker if we do it together,' Cross reasoned.

He was taking off the forensic suit at the front door of the cottage a few minutes later when another forensic investigator approached him from the garden holding up a transparent plastic evidence bag.

'DS Cross?' he asked.

'Yes.'

'I found this over there,' he said, pointing at a numbered yellow marker in the grass.

Cross took the bag and looked at it closely. Inside it was an old chisel with a narrow blade covered in blood.

'I'm fairly sure that's blood,' said the CSI. 'Murder weapon perhaps?'

'We don't actually have a cause of death as yet,' Cross replied pedantically. 'But it could certainly be the weapon that was used to stab him in the chest. Could you hold it up?' He then took several photographs of the chisel and walked away.

He heard the bemused CSI mutter under his breath, 'You're welcome.' He wondered why so many people did this as he walked away having spoken with them. He added it to his mental list of questions to ask Ottey.

13

Cross walked down the lane which was at the centre of the dispute between Moreton and his neighbours. It passed close to the old man's kitchen window before curving off to the right. The crops in the fields opposite the cottage had been harvested. Big black bales of plastic covered silage littered the countryside like giant liquorice sweets. It was good to see crops being grown. Cross was dismayed at the current trend for farmers to lease out their land to energy companies who then filled them with rows of solar panels like some sort of technological terracotta army. It seemed a strange choice of priorities when food was still at a premium in the world. But then again, farmers had to make a living.

The Cotterells lived in a converted barn at the end of the lane. The border of their property was clearly marked by new light-coloured gravel that had been laid up to the house. It was a mostly wooden structure, stained fashionably black, with a large glass panel in the middle of its façade. The door was to one side of this and so carefully concealed as to be almost invisible. There was a matt black intercom box to one side. Cross pressed the button.

'Hello?' said a female voice.

'DS Cross, Avon and—'

'Push the right side of the door,' he was instructed.

There was a delicate click of a lock being released. Cross pressed on the right-hand side. The door was huge, at least six feet wide and ten feet tall. It was cantilevered and opened on a central axis. Its movement was fluid and involved almost no effort on Cross's part. He then walked across the polished cement floor of the small hall, into a large open-plan living space. This was no comforting country chic interior. It was mostly exposed concrete and mid-century furniture. Nothing was out of place. It took the notion of minimalism to an extreme. Warner was sitting on a sofa that looked like it had come out of a nineteen-sixties edition of *House and Garden* devoted to the Scandinavian design that was so in vogue at the time. The Cotterells sat on an identical one facing him. Coffee mugs and a cafetière were on a low table made out of the same concrete as the floor, giving the impression they had both been fashioned out of the same pour.

'You've met my colleague – DS Cross,' said Warner.

'We have,' responded Barnaby Cotterell without enthusiasm.

'Well,' said Warner placing his hands on his knees with some intent. 'This is probably a good time to stop.'

'Are we free to go back to London?' asked Barnaby.

'Is that everything?' asked Tamsin.

'You are and no it's not. Far from it. I'd appreciate you keeping in contact. You don't have any plans to go abroad currently, do you?' Warner asked.

'We do not,' replied Barnaby.

'Okay. Thank you,' said Warner getting up and walking towards the front door. But Cross stayed where he was.

'When did your problems with Alistair Moreton start?' Cross began.

Warner turned, surprised that Cross hadn't taken his cue to leave and had started questioning the couple.

'From the moment we moved in,' answered Tamsin.

'That's not entirely accurate, is it?' said Cross.

'When else could it have started? We didn't meet him until after we'd moved in,' Tamsin remonstrated.

'Had you attempted to meet him before then?' asked Cross.

There was a slight hesitation from the two of them, he noted.

'Yes. We'd knocked on his door a number of times and left notes. He answered neither,' she explained.

'Why were you so keen to meet him?'

'We were just being neighbourly. Didn't you introduce yourself to your neighbours when you first moved into wherever you live?' she went on.

'I did not. But that is immaterial. Your answer isn't entirely true, is it?' replied Cross.

'I beg your pardon?'

Warner was irritated but decided to let Cross continue. It was important for them to present a united front.

'Was your initial approach to Mr Moreton before or after your first planning application was turned down?'

'I don't remember.'

'How many times was your application turned down?'

She didn't answer. Her husband finally said, 'Four.'

'Which meant what, in terms of delaying the commencement of building works?' Cross continued.

'Well over a year.'

'That must've been very frustrating.'

'Of course,' said Tamsin as if he'd stated the obvious.

'And expensive,' Cross pointed out.

'To an extent,' replied Barnaby.

'Planning is a difficult field to navigate,' Cross commented.

'It can be, yes,' agreed Barnaby.

'Why was your application so problematic? Why all the refusals and delays?' asked Cross.

'There were objections,' replied Tamsin.

'From whom?' asked Cross. There was a pause.

'Alistair Moreton,' replied Barnaby.

'That's right. He successfully had all four applications turned down. Now, I'm no expert in planning, but it seems as though he managed this almost entirely single-handed.'

'He did.'

'At one point you even attempted to start groundworks, before a final decision had been made. Under the mistaken impression that they came under a part of the application which wasn't being contested.'

'Correct,' replied Barnaby.

'We thought we were allowed to,' Tamsin pointed out.

'But Moreton objected and you had to stop. Stand down your builders.'

'Again, correct.'

'Again, expensive and frustrating,' said Cross.

'It was.'

'You were still trying to get planning permission in the winter of that year. You'd probably imagined spending Christmas in your beautiful new home,' Cross observed.

'What's your point?' asked Barnaby irritably.

'My point is that you were not entirely well disposed to Mr Moreton by the time you moved into your house.'

'I wouldn't deny that.'

'You took every opportunity to confront him,' Cross went on.

'If you say so,' replied Tamsin.

'Oh, it's not me,' said Cross. 'You must be aware that he kept a log. It was produced in court. Timings, contemporaneous notes, even photographs.'

'Him and his bloody Polaroid,' muttered Barnaby.

'The court case you lost.'

This was followed by silence until Warner decided to speak.

'Neighbours have killed neighbours for a lot less,' he pointed out.

'We didn't kill him,' replied Barnaby.

'Interesting you say "we",' observed Cross.

'Why?' asked Tamsin.

Cross ignored her and turned to look through the window at the garden stretching away from the building. At the bottom of it was a small old agricultural building, a bothy, which had been renovated in much the same style as the barn they were in.

'You've converted your bothy into a workshop,' said Cross.

'How do you know that?' asked Barnaby defensively.

'Because I've read all of your planning applications, Mr Cotterell. It's purely for recreational purposes, apparently.'

'It is.'

'Which one of you uses it? Or is it for both of you?'

'It's his. His rural bat cave,' Tamsin said with good humour.

'What is it you use it for?' Cross asked Barnaby.

'Woodwork.'

'You're a joiner?' asked Cross in an effort to sound impressed.

'An amateur one, yes.'

'Although you'd never know it the way he holds forth about his expertise to whoever will listen,' said Tamsin, laughing. Cross resisted his immediate urge to correct her grammar.

'That's just not true,' commented Barnaby.

'He bought himself a bloody lathe, for God's sake. It's massive,' said Tamsin.

'Really?' asked Cross now genuinely interested.

'It's old. Second-hand. And massive,' agreed Barnaby. 'But a fabulous piece of kit.'

'That's why you'll see so many bloody wooden finials on all the fencing and trellis. That's all he can make. Balls,' said Tamsin laughing again.

'Got to start somewhere,' Barnaby protested.

'I'd like to take a look.'

'Why?' asked Barnaby.

'Two reasons. Firstly, I'm carrying out an investigation into your neighbour's murder. Secondly, I'm interested on a personal level. My father was an engineer. It will interest him and give me something to tell him about when I meet him tomorrow for our weekly supper. Normally I'm unable to discuss my work with him, but this will be a welcome exception,' replied Cross.

'Then of course,' replied Tamsin.

'DS Cross, we do actually have a lot to be getting on with,' Warner pointed out.

'What, exactly?' asked Cross.

This flummoxed Warner who immediately wished he hadn't said a thing.

'All right, just make it quick please.'

'You should join us. Have a look at his massive lathe,' said Cross.

'I have no interest...' Warner began but then wondered why Cross would say this. He didn't know him well enough yet but knew enough to realise that social niceties were not Cross's forte. Maybe it was relevant to the investigation.

'Okay. Very well,' he said.

The garden was quite formally laid out and looked as though no expense had been spared. The couple from London obviously had a lot of money. It was elegant and symmetrical but Cross thought it still had a few years to go before it revealed exactly what the designer had in mind. They walked through a series of wooden arches that had climbers straining to meet each other in the middle.

'Have they flowered at all yet?' asked Cross looking at them.

'The wisteria? No. It can take eight years, so we still have a few to go,' replied Tamsin. Cross thought the garden must be her domain in the divvying up of marital responsibilities.

They all had to lower their heads slightly as they entered the bothy, the door frame was that low. Along one wall was a large industrial lathe and a lethal-looking table saw.

'How on earth did you manage to get them in?' asked Cross looking back at the door.

Barnaby Cotterell laughed with a sense of pride. 'Had to lower them through the roof with a crane before we restored it. No idea how we'll get it out if we ever move.'

'You bought old machinery, I see,' said Cross. 'Raymond, my father, would approve.'

'I think old machinery is often as good if not better than modern versions.'

'Can I see it work?' Cross asked.

'Of course.'

This was too much for Warner.

'I'll see you in the car, Sergeant. I'm going to call the pathologist,' he said pointedly, as if to remind Cross that they were actually investigating a murder.

'Would you like to turn a piece of wood?' Cotterell asked Cross.

'Really?' replied Cross.

'I'll walk back with you,' sighed Tamsin. She and Warner left.

Five minutes later, Cross was wearing an apron and under the guidance of Cotterell was turning a piece of wood. Shavings fell to the floor. Cross's face was a picture of almost childlike concentration. He stood back to admire his work. All he'd made was a small cylinder, but his pride was obvious.

'You're a natural,' proclaimed Cotterell.

'I am,' Cross agreed.

The workshop had been designed to be neat, tidy and organised with hooks on the walls for a regimented collection of tools. But there were several gaps in their ranks. Tools lay around the place, left where they'd been used. The floor was covered with a carpet of wood shavings and sawdust. Cotterell didn't seem to clear up behind him as he worked. Most of the missing tools lay on a large old wooden worktable. It had the scars of decades of use. Chips, chunks, saw marks, drill holes and a surface burnished into a patina of hard graft. Cross ran his hand over it as he took off the apron.

'It was my grandfather's,' Cotterell informed him. 'He was a carpenter. A proper one, unlike me. But it's probably where I got the interest from. It was in my father's garage for years. He never used it, so gave it to me.'

'It's been well worked,' commented Cross.

'Hasn't it? I actually get quite emotional at times, thinking of all the hours he spent at it. All the things he created.'

Cross looked at the tools on the table and picked up a chisel.

Cotterell quickly took it from him and hung it in its rightful place. He began picking up all the other tools and putting them back.

'Not the tidiest of workers,' he said as he did this. Cross noticed that there were several chisels on the wall. All quite old, by the looks of it. But what interested him more was that when Cotterell had finished putting all the tools back there was a space left for another chisel. Just as he was about to comment Cotterell picked another up off the floor and put it in the gap. Unlike the others, this one was new and had a different handle.

'Are those chisels your grandfather's?' Cross asked.

'They are. Well, all except for this one. This one's new, obviously.'

'A replacement?' asked Cross.

'Yep. Broke the old one. Really annoying. My grandfather would be furious.'

Cross said nothing. Didn't reveal an old, bloodstained chisel, identical to his grandfather's set, had been found in Moreton's garden. He wanted to piece a few more things together. Wait for the forensic results on the chisel before doing anything further. He suspected that were he to reveal its existence to Warner now he would rush to an arrest. Cross was in no such rush. Warner wouldn't become aware of it till the next morning. Whether he would then wait for the results, to discover whether it was evidence against the Cotterells, was another matter.

14

'Hey! How are you, mate? ... Great, I'm in Bristol. Wondered if you might like to hook up?' Warner shouted into his mobile at his desk opposite Cross. Mackenzie was sitting opposite Cross.

'I wasn't able to find out much online about Moreton, as I suspected would be the case,' she said.

'Probably not long. Few days max. Should have this wrapped up at the end of the week,' continued Warner.

'He was a teacher for a while,' Cross told Mackenzie.

'Right,' she replied.

'That'd be great. Why don't we grab a bite to eat while we catch up?' continued Warner.

'He was a headmaster at a small Catholic school somewhere,' Cross informed Mackenzie.

'That's interesting,' said Mackenzie making a note.

'His son is Sandy Moreton,' said Cross.

'That rings a bell,' said Mackenzie.

'Seven thirty. See you there. Look forward to it,' said Warner.

'MP in Dorset. Was a minister but lost his job after an inquiry found him guilty of bullying his staff. He then lost the Conservative party whip, and now he's been recalled and there's going to be a by-election,' Cross told her.

'Oh, I know who you mean. Tory, well, ex, I guess. Vocal Brexiteer, pro-life, Catholic fundamentalist. Didn't he say something about reinstating the death penalty?' Mackenzie said. 'Do you want me to follow up with him? Shouldn't be too hard. He's a right political rentagob.'

Cross noticed that Warner was now fiddling with his phone. He seemed to have two. One for work. One for personal use, presumably. It was the latter he was typing in. It was easily identifiable as it had a West Ham FC case.

'No need. He already has a family liaison officer. But I think we'll hear from him very soon. He's very vocal on policing issues and his father's murder will doubtless provide him with a unique opportunity to do some more self-promotion. It'll be another topical way of getting himself into the public eye,' replied Cross.

'Blimey, I didn't realise you were such a cynic, DS Cross,' said Warner checking his watch and getting up. 'I'm going out for a fag. Anything I should know about?'

'That would depend,' replied Cross.

'On what?'

'What the parameters are of what you believe you should know, as SIO on a murder case, of which you should be appraised,' replied Cross.

Warner looked at Cross and then at Mackenzie.

'Friday can't come soon enough,' he said.

'What happens on Friday?' she asked.

'I'll have this case wrapped up and will be able to bugger off,' he said, leaving the office. Mackenzie turned to Cross.

'Are you okay?' she asked.

'In what sense?'

'Having him in your office. With a bloody desk. Making personal calls on his phone.'

'In that case no. But I haven't concluded yet how best to resolve the situation,' he replied.

'Well, if there's anything I can do, let me know.'

He didn't reply and so she left.

Cross continued quietly going about his research. He began with the Cotterells. He discovered that she came from quite a wealthy background and worked in the PR department of the family firm. Barnaby Cotterell was an orthopaedic surgeon in a London hospital and had spent time in the Territorial Army.

Cross found himself wondering whether his carpentry skills came in useful in the operating theatre. This thought made him shudder so he moved on quickly. They were expecting their first child. He had just been made a consultant. Things were looking pretty positive in the lives of the young couple.

Cross's methodical research was interrupted half an hour later when he heard his name being bellowed across the department. He looked up to see Warner bearing down on him, yelling as he held up a plastic evidence bag for everyone to see.

'Cross! Cross!'

Cross went back to his computer screen. The door then burst open with such force that it slammed violently against the office wall. He jumped. Even though he was aware of the impending interruption, he wasn't prepared for the violence of it.

'What the fuck is this?' Warner demanded, brandishing the evidence bag in front of him. Cross could see it contained the bloodied chisel which had been found the previous day.

'It's an evidence bag,' replied the startled Cross.

'Don't be a smart arse.'

'I'm not.'

'You were told about this at the crime scene.'

Cross didn't say anything as a question hadn't been asked.

'Why didn't you say anything to me, the SIO?'

'I didn't think it necessary at the time and knew you'd find out about it in due course,' replied Cross.

'Are you trying to be funny?'

'I am not.'

'You obviously thought it relevant or else you wouldn't have asked to see Cotterell's workshop,' Warner went on.

'Correct. I then discovered Cotterell had a set of chisels identical to that one. One was missing. He claimed to have broken it.'

'And you're only telling me this now because?' asked Warner.

'Because you hadn't asked till now and I also didn't see the need,' Cross replied.

'What? How does that make any sense?'

'Whether it makes any sense to you or not is neither here nor there. I didn't see the need.'

'We should've arrested him.'

'Why him in particular and not her?'

'It's his chisel.'

'If it is, which we don't actually know, she could also have had access to it,' Cross pointed out.

'The chances are it is and yes, you're right. So we should've arrested them both,' replied Warner.

'Arresting them would have been precipitate,' said Cross.

'Are you joking?' shouted Warner getting more exasperated.

'I am not,' said Cross who just stared at him. Warner was at a loss. He'd never encountered anything like this before.

Carson appeared, having heard Warner yelling from his office. He looked at the audience of detectives hanging on every exchange between Warner and Cross, curious to see how it would pan out. He tried to get them back to work with an authoritative look. He didn't succeed. He got to Cross's door and said, 'My office.'

He then walked away before returning.

'George, I'd like you to come to my office now,' he said.

Cross got up and walked past Warner, who then followed.

Carson examined the chisel in the bag. Warner leant against the side wall of the office, arms folded. His attitude said that the evidence spoke for itself, and he was confident Carson would quickly take his side.

'So, you were aware of this piece of evidence?' Carson asked Cross.

'I was,' he answered.

'Do you think it likely to be the murder weapon?'

'We have no COD as yet,' Cross replied.

'Is he serious? No cause of death? A man is stabbed in the

chest, a bloody chisel is found in his garden with a blade which, to my untrained eye, looks about the same width as the puncture wound in the victim's chest, and he's not sure it's the murder weapon?' asked Warner.

'George, would you care to answer that?'

'The likelihood is that the chisel was indeed used in the assault. Whether it killed the victim and is therefore the murder weapon has yet to be ascertained,' Cross replied.

'He was stabbed in the chest with it, mate,' spat Warner.

'Do you know the depth of the chest wound, Bobby?' asked Carson, echoing Cross's exact same question to him at the scene, as if it had just occurred to him.

'I do not,' admitted Warner reluctantly.

'George, why didn't you tell DI Warner about the chisel at the crime scene yesterday? It was clearly of interest. You obviously thought so because you asked to see the workshop. So why not tell him?' asked Carson.

'Because I knew he would rush to make an arrest.'

'Too bloody right, mate,' said Warner looking at Carson as if to show him what he was up against.

'You told me he had a reputation for closing cases quickly,' Cross went on.

'Which I do.'

'Sometimes at such speed, it would seem, that cases don't hold up in court,' added Cross.

'Says who?'

'Says your record, sir,' replied Cross.

'Are you listening to this?' Warner asked Carson in disbelief. 'My DS, my subordinate officer, is checking up on me!' He laughed at the absurdity of it.

'I like to know who I'm working with—' began Cross.

'Working *for*, Sergeant,' Warner reminded him.

'Correct. Who I'm working for,' replied Cross. 'As I was saying, DCI Carson, I thought such an arrest prior to obtaining results from forensic testing of the weapon would only result in an early result and wasting time in our custody window with our suspects until such results surfaced.'

'That does make sense, Bobby,' Carson pointed out.

'Bollocks,' was the response he got.

'Anything else, George?' asked Carson, ignoring Warner.

'Seriously, are you going to side with him every time something like this happens?' asked Warner. Again, Carson ignored him.

'George, was there anything else?' Carson asked again.

'Alistair Moreton hadn't been to church for two weeks, neither had he been to the pub which he frequented without fail six nights a week. This was completely out of character,' Cross informed him.

'What has that got to do with anything? A bloodstained chisel most likely belonging to his neighbour was found in his garden and will most likely prove to be the murder weapon,' said Warner, emphasising 'most likely' sarcastically for their benefit.

'George, you may go,' said Carson. Cross left the office immediately.

'Bobby, sit.'

'That man is going to drive me nuts,' Warner said as he sat.

'Sure. I get it. We all get it. But listen. You're annoyed because you're used to people playing games. People dicking around. George doesn't do that. He's incapable of it. He's never trying to score points. He likes the odd bit of praise, but he'll never jump the queue to get it and never take credit for someone else's work. Nothing is personal with him even when it can come across that way. It just isn't. And yes, he drives us mad at times. But everything he does is in the best interests of the case,' Carson explained.

'He should've told me about the chisel,' Warner replied.

'Sure, and most people would have. Even though it's fairly obvious to you and me that the chisel is going to be material to the case. That it's probable it belongs to Barnaby Cotterell and he used it in the assault. But none of that is enough for Cross. He needs evidence,' said Carson.

'It is evidence,' maintained Warner.

'In all probability, yes. You and I both think that, but he doesn't. He didn't tell you because he felt the timing wasn't right for an arrest. An arrest he correctly thought you'd make. In effect he was trying to stop you from wasting any time before we got forensic confirmation.'

'That's not his call to make. I might have got a confession.'

'You know what? You might have. What is more, George believes in protocol and the chain of command—'

'You wouldn't know it.'

'And if you pointed out that he was in breach of that he probably wouldn't do it again.'

'Good point. So, I should tell him.'

'Sure. If you want,' said Carson.

'I sense a "but" there, sir.'

'If you do that, which you're perfectly entitled to do, well, it's just that putting him on a leash like that, you run the danger of not getting the best out of him, that's all. But it's your call. And I'll support you as the SIO. But I wouldn't do it.'

Warner thought about this for a moment, then slowly shook his head, as if it was a lot to process.

'His way is unorthodox, but the key is, if he infuriates you, to remember it's not his intention. Far from it.'

'Okay, boss. I'll try.'

'Good man. I would say you might even be surprised, that you might even learn something. But I have a feeling that just might make things worse. Don't take the things he does or says personally and you'll be okay.'

'Right,' said Warner unenthusiastically. He got up to leave.

'One other thing, Bobby. When something occurs to George that things aren't right, nine out of ten times he's right.'

Warner nodded then went to the door and turned back into the room.

'You know what, sir. He may have his ways and that's fine. But so do I. I have something that man will never have. A good nose for a suspect. A gut, and I'm telling you now that Cotterell is our man. It couldn't be more straightforward,' he said.

'And you know what? If you're right no one will be more pleased than George Cross. As long as everything is lined up correctly behind it.'

For Carson the evidence did seem to be stacking up against Cotterell quite convincingly. This was pleasing, not just because a quick resolution would reflect well on him but also because the Warner–Cross situation seemed to be boiling up. His anxiety about this had been further exacerbated by a call from Ottey earlier that morning. She'd asked for more time to sort out her move which Carson had granted her willingly. The quicker the case was wrapped up, the quicker he could get Warner out of Cross's office and peace would be restored.

15

Josie had been uncharacteristically decisive in choosing a bold new colour for the front room. The first coat had gone on and she was pleased with the look. It was a kind of Victorian dull red. She thought it made the room cosier and, more importantly, hers. Of an evening when the girls and her mother had all gone to bed, she found decorating late into the night, on her own, very therapeutic. Especially with a glass of Chardonnay in her non-brush hand. It had also broken her out of the fog of navel-gazing misery which had descended on her recently, like a heavy winter mist hanging underneath Clifton Suspension Bridge. She was convinced how tragic her life had become. She'd ended up living with her mother in her forties. This was, of course, a completely untrue and simplistic description of the situation. Her mother had basically 'bought' the basement flat so that Josie could afford the house. It was also hugely convenient for her mother's readily available childcare services. But depression and self-pity had no time for the niceties of actual truth. At times like that her bleak mood required a different, self-indulgent, interpretation. There was some truth in the fact that being around her mother all the time, or her mother being around her all the time which seemed like a more accurate description of the situation, made her feel and, at times, behave, like a fifteen-year-old. In her defence this was partly because her mother often spoke to her in the same despairing almost defeated tone that she always had done as the parent of an incomprehensible, uncomprehending alien of a teenager. Cherish's facial expressions hadn't changed in the intervening years, either. Why would they? But the fact that Josie associated them all with her teenage years put her right back there. So, her forty-three-year-old self often reacted like a turbulent teenager. It was a self-perpetuating cycle she couldn't break.

She also harboured the fear that living like this meant she would never meet another partner. The children would inevitably leave home and then she'd be left alone with her mother. Two old women living together. As they got older people would inevitably ask if they were sisters. The thought of this sent shudders through her already over-shuddered frame.

This had all been brought to the forefront of her mind when she came across two large storage boxes which had been kept in the back of the flat attic. They were labelled simply 'M'. A chill came over her as soon as she saw them. As if she'd suddenly remembered something important that she'd forgotten to do. They contained a few things she'd held onto from her life with Mark, her husband and the father of the girls. She kept them for herself, but more for the children.

Cherish had never been entirely sure about Mark. Never really trusted him. But then again, she never really trusted anyone when it came to her daughter. Mark was a social worker. A breed she had come to have a deeply entrenched suspicion of over the years. She had come to love him, though, as she began to understand his outlook on life. She admired his fervent, non-negotiable, belief that equal opportunity was a basic human right. When she witnessed how much time and emotional energy he put into his 'clients', as he called them, she couldn't help but be impressed and wish the world had more young men like him. At times she even felt he overindulged them. He had an unerringly developed ability to see the best in everyone.

These were all the qualities which initially attracted Josie. She felt this charismatic and confident young man made up for her inadequacies in the compassion and humanitarian stakes. In many ways her being able to cope with Cross was a legacy of her time with Mark. Initially things had been wonderful in the relationship. They tolerated and admired each other's total commitment to their jobs. But this was to have a deleterious effect on the marriage. They were always so busy with work. Worked so many nights. The confidence that their relationship was strong enough to ride this out actually just led to its being neglected. Before they knew it, the bedrock had crumbled and they were left looking at the dust of their former love just scattered around their feet. Unfixable. Tensions that had either not existed earlier or had been happily tolerated suddenly became the focus of each other's frustration. She accused him of having an ingrained suspicion and dislike of her 'being police'. She herself had had her fair share of frustration at the hands of various social service departments in the south-west during the course of her work. So, there was a reciprocal mistrust, albeit latent and mostly unspoken. More and more often they found themselves on opposing, intransigent, sides of an argument about something that had happened in their respective work lives.

They'd always wanted another child after Carla, but Josie had a couple of miscarriages. She felt Mark blamed her work for the loss of the pregnancies and eventually called him out on it. They went on to have a frank and upsettingly mature discussion of ending the marriage in an amicable way. They would co-parent in an unselfish manner. It seemed heartachingly sensible. The comfort sex which had inevitably followed such a painful conclusion resulted in Josie's pregnancy with Debbie. This seemed to change everything. They made the decision to make the marriage work and drew up a list of compromises and allowances each would commit to. It was one occasion on which his conflict resolution skills as a social worker were put to good use. They would make their family the priority, and their work, work for them. Not the other way round.

That summer, when Debbie was four months old, they had her christened at the church Josie had grown up in. It was a beautiful day. Everyone was dressed brightly, ready to celebrate this new life and party. It was joyous in the true sense of the word. Then, without any warning, as they left the church to go back to the flat for a christening tea with their friends, Mark collapsed and died. He'd had a massive catastrophic heart attack. A myocardial infarction, the death certificate informed her coldly. There had been no warning signs. He was only thirty-eight. At the moment it happened Josie had thrust her baby into her horrified mother's arms and given her husband CPR. She remembered later thinking, 'Don't do this. Please don't do this. Not today. Not ever.' There were dozens of small children crowded round, watching in confusion, wondering what was happening as Josie thumped her husband's chest and vainly tried to get oxygen to his brain. It was the last time she would ever kiss him.

She opened one of the boxes. She immediately smelled him and smiled. A bottle of his cologne had leaked all over the contents. There were some photographs. Most of the good ones were in other boxes and would adorn the sitting room with his memory. There was a particularly hideous tie of his which she had always hated, and he pretended to love, just to annoy her. It was the only one she'd kept. His favourite cardigan which she had always joked he was too young for and added ten years to his age. What she would have given to have had those years now.

In many ways the manner and sudden nature of his death had shaped who she now was. In the initial stages of bereavement, she'd found people's constant expressions and outpourings of condolence not just exhausting but also guilt-inducing. The truth was they'd pretty much decided to part before the pregnancy. Because of this she almost felt like a fraud as a grieving widow. It had also made her compulsively honest about things. She'd even told the children that everything hadn't been rosy with the marriage. She didn't want to make it out to be some idyllic thing they'd all lost. It was coming up to a decade since his death. She sometimes resented the fact that she still thought about it every day. She even congratulated herself when he ceased to be her first thought as she woke up and opened her eyes. She was absurdly pleased one morning when she realised the first time she'd thought about him was twenty-five past ten. Some sort of record. She was still angry with him for dying. Then angry with herself for being angry.

Her work had definitely suffered because of his death. It was hard being a single mother of two and a detective, despite help from her mother. Before Mark had died she'd been openly ambitious. But that ambition had faded quickly. Receded into the memory of a previous existence. Now she was in her forties and still a detective sergeant. She'd recently decided to put this right and work towards promotion. She felt guilty that this would mean leaving Cross's side. But she couldn't add him to her list of responsibilities, however fond she was of him. She'd decided, perhaps wrongly, that being a detective inspector might give her more control of her working life and hours.

Asking Carson for more time off was against all her sensibilities and natural instincts. She was hypersensitive as to how she was perceived at work as a single mother. How much she was seen giving to the job compared to others. This then progressed to her overcompensating and often working longer hours and much harder than her contemporaries. She'd expected pushback from Carson when she asked. But in his new post-natal incarnation, he was incredibly gracious and accommodating. Even telling her that family was more important than anything else. Was a privilege and should be treated as such. How long this would last was, of course, open to question.

16

Warner was no fool when it came to managing the internal politics of the police force. He felt that George Cross was overindulged in a way he'd never encountered before. He was treated like an out-and-out favourite by Carson. But he wouldn't fight that battle. He was way too smart for that. However, he didn't have the time, literally or figuratively, to just sit back and let Cross work through his laboured, tortuous, process. It was too slow, reactive and regressive for him. The solution was to leave Cross to his own devices while working the case his own way, which he was pretty sure was the only and best way to get a result. With this in mind he drove back into Crockerne with another detective and two uniformed officers to arrest Barnaby Cotterell. He didn't bother to let anyone know, as he was the SIO on the case and so didn't have to. He attempted to convince himself that he wasn't trying to prove a point. But he knew he was. It didn't matter. He'd have a confession from Cotterell within the next twenty-four hours.

Michael Swift was still at Moreton's house processing the scene. He saw Warner and the squad car driving down the lane to the Cotterells' converted barn. He walked through to the back bedroom where he had a view of it parking up. He was surprised not to see Cross getting out of the car as well. It was annoying, as he had a question for him. He watched as Barnaby Cotterell opened the door and listened as Warner spoke to him, then cuffed him. His wife appeared and took in what was happening. She grabbed a coat, but something her husband said to her stopped her. She then stood and watched as uniform put him into their car. Swift got out his phone and speed dialled a number.

'Alice, can you call me when you get this message?' he said.

Cross seemed remarkably unfazed when Mackenzie told him what had happened and that Cotterell was now in the custody suite.

'Aren't you bothered Warner didn't tell you?' she asked him.

'Bothered?'

'Well, he's making decisions without you.'

'He's the SIO,' he pointed out.

'Are you going down?'

'I am not.'

'May I ask why not?'

'You may,' he said and duly waited for her to do so.

'Why not?' she asked finally.

'Because I have no interest in talking to Mr Cotterell at present.'

'Okay.'

Warner settled into the interview room seat alongside a DC Matt Murray. He'd chosen Murray specifically because he'd noticed in the last few days a few expressions of disdain and eye-rolling from the young man, on the rare occasions Cross had spoken in meetings. He didn't know for certain but was fairly confident Murray would turn out to be an ally.

Cotterell had surprised them by not insisting on getting a lawyer down from London, thus keeping them waiting. Instead he made do with the duty solicitor available. He explained, when asked why he'd done this by Warner, that he was innocent and had no need of an expensive London lawyer. Added to the fact that he wanted to get it over and done with as soon as possible.

'Mr Cotterell, how would you describe your relationship with Mr Moreton?' Warner began by asking.

'Non-existent.'

'George,' said Carson as he came into Cross's office gingerly. 'Were you aware that Bobby has made an arrest? He's brought Barnaby Cotterell in.'

'I was, sir.'

'Okay. Did you not want to make the arrest with him?'

'I wasn't asked. He was accompanied by DC Murray.'

'I see... and you're all right with that?' asked Carson tentatively.

'I am.'

'You are... Is that because you are happy with Bobby's course of action?'

'I am more than happy with anything he does which keeps him out of my office, thereby affording me some peace and quiet.'

'Right, okay,' said Carson, leaving. In truth he was as unsure about how to proceed as he had been when he arrived. So he did what he always had recourse to in these situations. Absolutely nothing.

An hour later Mackenzie knocked on Cross's door again.

'Sandy Moreton's in reception. DI Warner is still interviewing Barnaby Cotterell,' she said.

'Okay,' said Cross getting up. He picked up a notepad and left the office. 'Is the VA suite available?' he asked.

'It is. I checked.'

Cross liked this efficient foresight.

'Would you like me to come with you, sir?' she asked.

Cross was about to answer no, as he saw no need. But he took a moment to think about this. He was about to deal with a presumably grieving son. Normally he had Ottey with him on these occasions but not today. Mackenzie would definitely be more alert to the sensitivities of the situation and without Ottey it made a lot of sense.

'Yes,' he replied.

Warner slowly built up a picture of conflict between Cotterell and Moreton. None of it was contended by Cotterell. He agreed with it all, no matter how unflattering and at times petty a portrait it painted of him. He was perfectly cooperative and hadn't resorted to the 'no comment' mantra once. Warner felt this was just an act of bravura which he'd seen in interview rooms many times before. The psychology of it was that if you were willing to accede to questions that didn't seem to help your case, your denials would be more readily accepted. As the interview progressed Warner became more and more confident that Cotterell was his man. When he thought the time was right, he produced his smoking gun. The chisel. He slowly brought it up from under the interview table with all the deft showmanship of a sleight-of-hand magician.

'Do you recognise this?' he asked Cotterell.

'It's a chisel,' Cotterell replied.

'Your chisel, in fact.'

'Difficult to say. They all look the same.'

'This one looks very much like the others in your workshop. Your grandfather's, if I remember clearly.'

Cotterell said nothing.

'It's been confirmed with the forensic pathologist that this was the murder weapon. It punctured the aorta causing a catastrophic bleed. At least it would have been quick. Was it quick, Barnaby?'

'How awful,' replied Cotterell looking at the chisel, horrified.

'Is it your chisel, Barnaby?' asked Warner.

'I didn't kill him.'

'Interesting response. Does that mean you recognise it as your chisel?'

'I'm assuming it has the initials TC burnt into the top of the handle?'

Warner made a play at having a close look although he already knew the answer.

'Slightly faded, but yes it does. Along with your DNA.'

'I'd like to speak with my client,' said Cotterell's solicitor.

Sandy Moreton was a red-haired man in his early fifties. He had a lined neck and face which betrayed a vulnerability to the sun. But it also added to a look of disdain which seemed to be the default expression of a man used to getting his own way and intolerant when he didn't. He wore a blue suit with a bold pinstripe which was meant to be a statement. But it looked a little anachronistic, as if from another era. A time when such a pinstripe might cause alarm or fear. Either Moreton was out of touch sartorially or he'd inherited the suit from his grandfather.

'Mr Moreton, how can we help?' began Cross.

'Oh, now let me see,' Moreton replied, enhancing his sarcasm with a ponderous stroking of his chin. 'My father has been brutally murdered. Why don't we start there?'

'We're so sorry for your loss,' said Mackenzie.

'If you really are why didn't you begin with that?' asked Moreton.

'We're sorry for your loss,' repeated Cross, taking his cue from Mackenzie.

'I'm not sure if you're aware I'm a Member of Parliament and have several friends in the justice department,' Moreton proclaimed.

'I am aware you're an MP, who has just been recalled, but unsure how your having any friends in the justice department can be of any help to anyone,' said Cross.

'What progress have you made?' asked Moreton, ignoring this.

'Our investigation is at an early stage. We are still making preliminary enquiries,' replied Cross.

'Would you care to elaborate?' This asked in such a way that it was meant as an instruction.

'I would not.'

'Oh, really?' replied Moreton, surprised but at the same time relishing the opportunity to put Cross in his place. He was the type of man who always took the opportunity for a confrontation regardless of whether it actually existed or not. 'In that case perhaps you would like me to call my friend the chief constable and see if he could join us.'

'I would not,' replied Cross.

'I thought as much.'

'He's immensely busy and would have nothing to add to this situation, other than platitudinous assurances. That might be what you're after. But it would serve no practical purpose,' replied Cross. Mackenzie was starting to enjoy this, as she'd developed an instinctive dislike for Moreton in the short time she'd been in his company. This was not just because of his arrogance but also the presence of what she was fairly sure was a love bite protruding just above his collar. There was something distasteful about this on a man of his age, she thought.

'Do you have any idea who you're talking to?' asked Moreton with growing disbelief.

'I do. You gave your name to reception and you've already reminded me that you're an MP with friends in the justice department,' said Cross.

'I'd like to talk to your superior,' replied Moreton.

'Mackenzie, would you go and see if DCI Carson is available?' said Cross.

'Of course,' she replied and left.

Cross sat where he was and offered nothing new to Moreton. He didn't attempt to make conversation or see if Moreton had any further questions. Moreton quickly busied himself with his smartphone.

★

Warner sat down opposite Cotterell and his brief in the interview room again.

'So, Mr Cotterell, is this your chisel?' Warner repeated.

'It is, yes, which would account for my DNA being on it, obviously,' began Cotterell.

'The chisel you said you'd broken, thrown away and replaced?'

'Correct.'

'So how do you explain this? What happened to it?' he asked, looking at the chisel in the evidence bag.

'I lost it,' said Cotterell, shifting in his seat at the obvious awkwardness of this reply.

'You lost it?' Warner replied with sympathetic understanding that reeked of scepticism.

'Yes.'

'Do a lot of woodwork outside of your workshop, do you?' Warner probed.

'I was making a sign for the house on a post at the bottom of our drive,' sighed Cotterell.

'Is that the sign opposite Moreton's kitchen?' asked Warner.

'It is. On our property, just to be clear.'

'Of course. So how did you come to lose it?'

'I don't know. I took several tools with me. It must've fallen out of my bag. I didn't realise till the following weekend – I'm not the tidiest of workers – when I was clearing up the workshop and saw there was a gap in the chisel rack.'

'Did you look for it?'

'I did. I knew exactly where I'd last used it. I went back to where I'd been working. Traced my steps to and from the house. But it wasn't there,' Cotterell explained.

'Did you ask Mr Moreton about it?'

'I did not. We weren't exactly on speaking terms at the time.'

'When was this?'

'I don't know, six or seven months ago. Something like that.'

'So, what did you think had happened?'

'Well, someone had obviously picked it up. In all likelihood I thought it was Moreton and turns out I was right.'

'Why did you lie to us about breaking it?' asked Murray.

'Why do you think?' came the answer.

'I have no idea. That's why I'm asking,' Murray went on.

'I don't know. It was instinctive. Because I knew what it would look like, I suppose,' Cotterell replied.

'What? What are we talking about here?' asked Murray.

'If it was my chisel that killed him.'

Murray made no reply. Warner considered this answer for a moment.

'I can see that. But at the time we asked you about it, we hadn't told you that a chisel was the murder weapon,' he pointed out.

'It didn't take a criminologist to work out why your colleague asked to see my workshop, and then asked about the chisel.'

'I'm sorry but I'm not buying that. It's quite the leap. Big assumption. No, the answer is you'd used it to kill your neighbour,' said Warner.

'That's just not true.'

'Mr Cotterell, your missing chisel, which you had lied about, was found covered in your neighbour's blood. How can you explain that?'

Cotterell made no answer. Warner just let it hang there for a while. 'In between his house and yours. Where you dropped it on your way back to your car before leaving for London.'

'Two things, Inspector. Firstly, why would I leave it there in the garden, and secondly, how could I have done it when I was already well down the M4 on my way to London?' Cotterell pointed out.

'People do a lot of careless things in the aftermath of killing someone. Adrenalin is coursing through the body. Disbelief at what they've just done. Often because they hadn't meant to do it. People do a lot stranger things than just leaving a murder weapon in close proximity to the scene of the crime,' Warner answered.

Cotterell had made a good point but Warner was perfectly calm. He'd been in this game a long time and Barnaby Cotterell was his man. Something would turn up soon to prove it. Warner could just feel it.

He called for a break.

17

Neither Sandy Moreton nor Cross had blinked in their war of silence. Carson then appeared.

'Mr Moreton, I'm so sorry for your loss,' he began with.

'Thank you.'

'Rest assured we are doing everything in our power to get to the bottom of this awful tragedy and bring the culprit to justice.'

'Well, I'm not,' replied Moreton.

'I'm sorry?' replied Carson.

'Assured. Far from it. Having spoken to this imbecile who is, I believe, a detective on this case, I think I have more chance of becoming prime minister than you solving this case.'

'I see... Well, of course DS Cross is not the only detective working on this case. We have an entire team of detectives investigating. Though I think it only fair to tell you George here is one of our very best,' replied Carson.

'Is that so? Then you've either set the bar really low when it comes to recruitment, or the police force is in a more parlous state than everyone currently believes.'

Mackenzie risked a quick glance at Cross. If he had reacted at all she couldn't see it. He was his usual inscrutable self, not moving a muscle. Not a cheek tremor in sight.

'Well...' was all Carson had to offer to occupy the pregnant pause which had enveloped the room.

'You should know I've just emailed the chief constable to express my dissatisfaction. You're aware, I take it, that because of my public profile this story has already become front page news,' Moreton continued.

'I see...' said Carson, sending an annoyed look in Cross's direction.

'We are aware,' said Cross. 'Just puzzled as we hadn't notified the press when the articles appeared. Too good an opportunity to miss, I suppose. I imagine you don't get that much opportunity to appear on the front pages of the press and with a by-election looming you must need all the publicity you can get.'

Carson couldn't believe what he was hearing and was about to remonstrate with him when the door opened and Warner walked in.

'Gosh, quite the party,' he said, glaring at Cross and Mackenzie. 'My invitation must have got lost in the post.' He offered his hand to Moreton. 'Detective Inspector Bobby Warner. I'm the senior investigating officer on the case. I'm so sorry for your loss.'

'As it appears are all of you, however—' began Moreton.

'I'm sure you want to know what progress we're making. I have a suspect in custody who I am in the process of interviewing. He will be charged by the end of the afternoon,' interrupted Warner.

'Excellent. I'm surprised your colleagues weren't aware of this development,' said Moreton clearly taken aback.

'I was of course aware, but I like to give my team their head which is why this department has such a rapid success rate,' explained Carson. But Moreton wasn't listening. Instead, he was fishing around in his wallet and producing a business card on which he proceeded to scribble something on the back of. He then held it out to Warner.

'My card. That's my personal number on the back. Please keep in touch with me directly. I daresay when this case has been solved having the personal number of a prominent MP might come in quite useful,' he said with unbridled arrogance. 'Who is the man in question?'

'His neighbour,' replied Warner.

'Well, no surprises there. The old man gave him a sound beating in court. Isn't he some kind of surgeon?' asked Moreton.

'Orthopaedic,' replied Warner.

'No stranger to breaking bones then,' replied Moreton, laughing at his own joke. He was joined in this by both Warner and Carson. Mackenzie was thinking how she couldn't dislike him any more than she already did. Cross appeared to be unmoved.

18

When Cross got back to his office Warner was already studying something on his desktop computer.

'Jesus,' he said as Cross sat at his desk. He then began to type furiously on his keyboard. He leant forward and looked at the screen even closer.

Cross found a report from Swift about the chisel waiting for him on his desk. He'd noticed that when Swift came across something important to a case, he printed the report up and left it for him, rather than just emailing a copy across. Cross understood the logic. If it was in a folder on his desk it was natural to look at it immediately, as soon as you saw it. Whereas an email could just sit in your digital inbox, ignored for a while. He read the report carefully. The blood on the blade was a match for Alistair Moreton. Cotterell's DNA was also present on the handle which was unsurprising as it was his chisel. It didn't, per se, prove anything. But what drew Cross's attention was the fact that there was an unidentified partial fingerprint. It wasn't in the system.

'Were you aware before you spoke to Sandy Moreton that there was an unidentified fingerprint on the chisel?' Cross asked Warner.

'Of course,' he said, still concentrating on his computer screen.

'Doesn't that concern you?'

'It's probably the wife's. It's irrelevant. His DNA is on the weapon because he killed him. And with this,' he said, nodding at his screen, 'it's irrefutable. The print's neither here nor there. Check your email.' He looked at his watch then got up and left.

Cross checked his email. There was a new flagged one from Catherine who did all their CCTV and traffic camera investigation. 'Please view the video ASAP' was all the email said. Cross clicked on the attached video file. It was footage from one of Moreton's security cameras on the back of his house. It was motion-activated and showed the front of the Cotterells' barn and the entrance to their drive. At 20.02 on the night of the murder the Cotterells' car with the couple in the front seats left the property. The next piece of footage was time stamped 20.52 and it showed the same car coming back into the drive. The automatic security lights caused a whiteout flare of the image then Barnaby Cotterell got out of the car and went into the house. At 20.57 he reappeared with a small holdall in his hand. He put it in the boot of the car then walked round to the driver's window. As he was about to get in the car he looked up in the direction of the camera, at Moreton's house. He leant into the car to talk to his wife. Then looked over at the house again. After a couple of seconds he walked towards the camera and out of sight. The footage stopped then started again as Cotterell ran over to the car, got in and drove away at speed.

Cross replayed the footage carefully before getting up and leaving the room. He went to a room adjacent to the interview room, where Warner's interview with Cotterell was being relayed onto a monitor. Carson was already there.

'George, has Bobby told you what's going on?' he asked.

'He has not.'

'But do you know? He seems pretty excited.'

'I do,' said Cross turning his intention to the monitor and watching as Warner began. Carson decided not to pursue it as he was about to find out anyway. Murray entered the interview room and sat at Warner's side. Carson hadn't made any comment about what he saw as Cross's being sidelined in the case. It was up to Warner how he ran his team. At the very least this meant that he'd have fewer personality clashes between them to deal with. If Warner was as quick as he claimed to be, he'd leave them soon enough, go back to his own unit and Ottey would return.

Cross looked at Warner. He had begun to understand his colleague's facial expressions and body language, having studied him in the past few days. Warner looked confident and almost pleased with himself. Like a schoolboy at the end of year prize-giving who, having been given insider knowledge that he was definitely getting the top prize, then attempted to look innocently and genuinely interested in 'discovering' the outcome, while giving nothing away. It resulted in an air of smug complacency.

'Barnaby,' Warner began, 'you told us you left your house at around eight o'clock on the night of Alistair Moreton's death.'

'Correct.'

'And you filled your car at a local petrol station shortly after,' Warner said slowly, consulting his notes as if to make sure this was accurate and that he wasn't getting anything wrong.

'You have the receipt,' Cotterell pointed out.

'We do,' Warner confirmed. 'So, what happened then?'

'I've already told you this,' replied Cotterell with the first signs of irritation. 'We drove to London.'

'You have. But the trouble is that's not true, is it? It's a lie,' said Warner, the threat unmistakable despite the overtly friendly tone. Cross detected a triumphal eagerness in Warner. As if he couldn't wait to deliver the damning evidence he had. Cotterell made no reply. He could obviously sense that Warner had something up his sleeve.

'What actually happened is that you went back to your house in Crockerne almost an hour later,' he said.

'Tamsin had forgotten her hospital overnight bag. She insisted on going back for it,' said Cotterell.

'And did you forget to mention it?' asked Warner.

'Obviously not.'

'So why not tell us?'

'Why do you think?'

'Because you killed Alistair Moreton and it might be a bit of a giveaway?'

'I did not. But I knew it would cause suspicion,' replied Cotterell.

'At last, a little bit of honesty. But not quite enough. You know it would play out a lot better in court if you just told us now, what happened. How you came to kill him,' said Warner.

'I didn't bloody kill him,' Cotterell refuted.

Warner opened his laptop, taking his time to find whatever it was he was looking for. He turned it to face Cotterell.

'Perhaps you could explain this then,' said Warner. 'For the tape I'm now showing Mr Cotterell video taken from the victim's security camera at the back of his house. The tape appears to show that after arriving back at the house and retrieving a bag he stops to talk to his wife as he's about to get into the driver's seat. He looks in the direction of the camera, therefore Mr Moreton's house, twice, before walking towards it and disappearing from frame. Which would indicate he went to the house. The motion-controlled camera then records him shortly after, running from the house, and getting into his car which then drives away at speed.'

'We've got him,' said Carson, together with an involuntary handclap.

Cross said nothing.

'What happened, Barnaby? Why did you look at Moreton's house? Did he shout at you? You complained in court that he would often shout abuse at you from his kitchen window when you were in your drive or garden. Is that what happened? Was it one insult or threat too many?' Warner pushed on.

'I'd like a word with my client,' said the lawyer.

Cross followed Carson out of the room. They met Warner in the corridor outside.

'Congratulations,' said Carson, extending his hand.

'Thanks. Told you he was our man,' Warner replied, looking directly at Cross. 'Instincts may not be to everyone's taste, but I have a lot of faith in mine, sir. They can sometimes lead to the heart and soul of a case. Wouldn't you agree, George?'

'On the contrary,' Cross replied, noting Warner's use of his Christian name. He thought this was probably an attempt to make his remark all the more patronising as Cross had made it perfectly clear he preferred Warner to use his rank and surname when being addressed.

'Nothing good about a sore loser, George,' replied Warner.

'I had no idea this was all a game to you, DI Warner,' said Cross.

'All right, all right,' said Carson attempting to head off any potential conflict. 'Very impressive, Bobby. I'll get straight on to the CPS.'

Cotterell was kept in police custody overnight.

The evidence was compelling, even for Cross. Cotterell had lied to them about the chisel. His DNA was on the handle. Now it appeared he'd lied about his movements on the night. Most damning of all it did appear he went in the direction of Moreton's house at the time of the murder. In his office the next day Cross studied the footage a few more times. He then saw Dr Michael Swift come into the open area of the office with a cup of coffee for Mackenzie. He attempted to give it to her in front of everyone, in a relaxed 'So I'm just bringing a colleague a coffee, nothing to be read into it. We are definitely not in a relationship' kind of way. So nonchalantly did he place it on the very edge of her desk, that he almost missed it entirely. This of course screamed out to the assembled collective of gossip-starved detectives in the office, THEY'RE SO SHAGGING! Their repeated dismissals when the subject was brought up did nothing to allay the rumours. But he still persisted in bringing her coffee whenever he came over, despite her pleas for him to stop. He saw no harm in it. She told him this was because he worked in an entirely different building and didn't have to deal with the smirks and knowing, sometimes pitiful, looks which followed his every visit.

'How would you feel if the boot was on the other foot and I did it to you?' she asked.

'What?'

'Brought you coffee in your office?'

He thought about this for a moment.

'Um, grateful?' he tried to suggest.

19

Warner decided to have 'one more go' at Cotterell that morning and see if he could get a confession out of him before he was charged. It would make everything much neater. Cross watched the interview on the monitor in the next room. Barnaby Cotterell already seemed a different man to the one who'd been brought in the day before. He was now dressed in a baggy tracksuit top and bottoms provided for him by the custody sergeant, as his own clothing had been taken away for testing. He looked shrunken. People often did after a night in the cells. But whether this was because he'd been caught and it was all over or because he couldn't believe the nightmare he found himself in when he'd done nothing wrong, Cross couldn't be sure. It wasn't just the fact that it was all too easy that meant Cross wasn't sure about his guilt. The evidence definitely pointed in his direction and he certainly hadn't helped with all the inconsistencies in his statement. But, for Cross, there were still some questions to be answered.

'Barnaby, why don't we just get this over and done with. Man to man. Have done with it,' Warner began. 'Look, I completely understand that Alistair Moreton was a tricky old bugger. It must have been so difficult. I know how these things can get out of hand in a second. I see it all the time. You're a busy man in a high pressure, stressful job. Quite physical, orthopaedics, I'm reliably informed. The house in Crockerne, the weekends there were supposed to be peaceful. Your little pool of calm, if you like. But then you find yourself with the neighbour from hell. Determined to stand in your way at every turn and make your life difficult. Before you'd even moved in, for heaven's sake. Before you'd even met him, he'd become a pain in your arse. Your wife is pregnant. What did he say that night that finally made you snap?'

'No comment,' replied Cotterell.

'What was it that finally made you lose it after all that time?'

'I didn't lose anything. I thought I heard something.'

'Okay, and what was that?'

'Something that didn't sound right.'

'What?'

'A scream, or a yell. Shouting. Dogs barking. I thought Moreton might be in trouble, so I went to investigate.'

'You went to help the man who was the bane of your life? I don't think so. Just tell us what he said, Barnaby.'

'I went in and he was at the bottom of the stairs,' continued Cotterell, ignoring Warner.

'Now that's just not true, is it?' said Warner quietly.

'I checked his pulse. He was dead.'

'Because you stabbed him with your chisel,' said Murray holding up the evidence bag with the tool inside it. Cotterell couldn't look at it.

'He was still warm,' said Cotterell, now almost speaking to himself.

'Because you'd just killed him. You checked his pulse instinctively to find out what you'd done. How far this had gone,' offered Warner.

'It could only have just happened,' said Cotterell, thinking out loud. Something dawned on him. He looked up at the SIO across the table from him for the first time in the interview. 'He was still there. Must've been. The killer must've still been there when I went in.'

Warner paused. But he wasn't considering this possibility.

'I'm going to give you one last chance to tell me the truth, Mr Cotterell. Let me jog your memory. This is how I see it. You went in. He was upstairs. You challenged him for whatever he'd shouted at you. Maybe it was something about your wife that really hit a nerve. But it was enough to make you go in and attack the old man. I'm not sure you actually meant to kill him. But you did. That's it, isn't it? It was an accident. It was over before you knew what had happened and then you were taking his pulse,' said Warner.

'I didn't kill him; accidentally or otherwise. I did not stab that man.'

'With your chisel. You did not stab that man with your chisel?' asked Warner as if pointing out the absurdity of this claim. Something occurred to Cross as he watched this exchange. He made a note in his book.

Warner was suddenly gimlet-eyed as if he'd now made a decision he didn't really want to make. Had done it with great regret. Forced into it by the man sitting opposite him.

'We're done here. Barnaby Cotterell, you're going to be charged with the murder of Alistair Moreton on 17th September 2023.'

He then got up with a look of completely insincere regret, that he'd done all he could to help, that it was now out of his hands, and left.

20

Cross was in his office studying the CCTV footage of Cotterell taken from Moreton's security camera when Warner returned with a triumphant swagger through the open area where some of the junior detectives even clapped.

'He's being charged,' he said as he slumped into his chair with an air of great satisfaction, leaving the door wide open in the certain knowledge it annoyed Cross.

'So I understand,' replied Cross.

'Is that all you have to say?'

Cross thought about this for a moment.

'No, it isn't. But I don't see any purpose in saying any more, as it will only result in conflict which, on the whole, I try to avoid.'

Warner was about to reply when Carson appeared at the door.

'Congratulations, Bobby. Quite the result.'

'Thank you.'

Carson turned to Cross.

'Quite something, eh, George?' he said.

'That would depend on your definition of "something",' replied Cross.

Carson realised immediately all was not well with Cross, but judged it best left alone in the moment of victory.

'Spit it out, DS Cross,' Warner said, unable to resist the lure of a good fight, and one he was bound to win.

'Spit out what? I have nothing in my mouth,' Cross replied. He then opened his mouth wide and stuck out his tongue like a child trying to prove they'd eaten their broccoli. Warner stepped back in disgust.

'George is never celebratory when it comes to charging a suspect and concluding a case. Are you, George?' said Carson quickly stepping in to defuse the situation.

'I don't find it a cause for celebration.'

'Nah, it's more than that. You think I've got it wrong, don't you? Care to elaborate?' Warner tried to goad Cross.

'I do not. Care to,' he replied.

'Well, as your superior officer I'm ordering you to,' said Warner.

Cross thought about this for a moment. He obviously had no choice.

'Alistair Moreton's behaviour changed significantly in the two weeks leading up to his death,' he began.

'Oh, not this again,' Warner protested.

'Very well, let's discuss the chisel,' Cross continued.

'What about it?'

'I can't see it in Cotterell's hands on this CCTV,' said Cross indicating his laptop.

'He said he'd lost it,' interjected Carson.

'So you've decided to go along with a selective part of his narrative. That he'd lost the chisel. Then sees it upstairs and uses it to kill Moreton,' Cross said.

'Possibly,' replied Carson.

'You're picking and choosing parts of his story you want to believe. But if he killed Moreton with the chisel, is it not more likely that he would have had it with him going into the house?' Cross pointed out.

'Look, the chisel is the murder weapon. That's been established. His DNA is on it. It's more than possible he lost it like he said, then picked it up in the house, accused Moreton of stealing it, they fight and he kills him with it,' Warner said, getting increasingly irritated.

'So, we are to… assume,' Cross said the 'a' word with as much distaste as he was able to muster, 'he went into the house, happened to see the chisel left out in plain sight, took it and used it to kill Moreton.'

'Possibly,' said Warner.

'I've never considered "possibly" a sufficient criterion either to charge someone with murder or argue the case successfully in front of a judge,' Cross went on.

'George always does this. He has a habit of challenging us when we've charged someone,' said Carson apologetically.

'Your case is full of possibilities, theories and maybes. Sufficient for a defence barrister of even the meagrest of talents to cast enough doubt in court,' said Cross.

'Not my problem. If they can't prove it, that's their problem,' said Warner.

'An interesting point of view, sir. Not entirely satisfactory I would've thought,' reflected Cross.

'Enough of this. I'm taking the team to the pub,' said Warner.

'You should. Go and celebrate,' Carson encouraged him.

'I trust you won't be joining us?' Warner said to Cross.

'Oh, George never goes to the pub,' Carson answered for him, trying to head off another argument.

Warner left. Carson turned to Cross.

'I think you might be wrong about this, George. Everything would seem to point in Cotterell's direction.'

'I agree,' replied Cross.

'You do?' said Carson, surprised and unable to contain his relief.

'It would "seem to", yes,' replied Cross.

Carson shook his head.

'Please don't cause any trouble.'

'I'd like to speak to Cotterell,' Cross told him. Carson's face fell.

'What? Why, George? Why must you always do this?'

'Do what? My job?' Cross replied.

'But Cotterell has been charged.'

'I'm aware of that. But I still have some questions I'd like to ask.'

Carson was about to object more strongly when it occurred to him that in situations like this Cross was often right.

'All right. You have my permission,' he sighed.

'I have no intention of speaking to you until my lawyer has arrived from London,' Cotterell said immediately.

'I'd like to talk to you about Mr Moreton's behaviour in the weeks before his death,' Cross persisted.

'No comment.'

This was as far as Cross got. Cotterell's being charged had understandably changed the situation completely. The evidence pointed very firmly at him, and he hadn't helped his case by lying to the police on two occasions. But for Cross something about it didn't make sense. Not that murders always made sense. He wanted to know what had made Moreton change his routine over the last couple of weeks. Something had happened and whatever that was, Cross thought it might well have been relevant to his death.

He'd visit Tamsin Cotterell in the morning.

21

George was pleased that Stephen, the priest of the church where he practiced the organ, had spent most of that day, as he did every Thursday, baking with the ladies of the parish. The presbytery was suffused with the welcoming and comforting smell of freshly baked cakes. Tonight's offering was a delightfully light Victoria sponge with a generous centre of thick cream and home-made strawberry jam. As it was the first Thursday of the month his mother, Christine, had sat in on his organ practice as per their agreement.

'You really should give baking lessons,' Christine said approvingly. 'I'm sure you'd be oversubscribed.'

'You're not the first to suggest that. But unfortunately this kitchen is too small and I only have the one oven,' Stephen replied.

'Couldn't you use the church hall?' she went on.

'No access to ovens and with more people baking, we'd need more than the one,' Stephen reasoned.

'What about internet classes?' She clearly wasn't going to let this go. 'I can see you becoming an overnight TikTok sensation.'

'I think not.'

'I fail to see the point of doing it on TikTok,' George said, entering the conversation for the first time.

'I'm surprised you've even heard of TikTok,' replied his mother.

'You would be surprised at what I come across in my work,' he pointed out.

This was fair enough. There was then a pause in the

conversation. If George had been generally more aware of such things, he would have seen the subtle look between his mother and the priest. It was an unspoken enquiry on her part and a nod of approval on his. Whatever it was she wanted to say, which Stephen was aware of, now was the appropriate moment to say it, apparently.

'George, I have a timeshare flat in Calpe, Spain, George. My husband, Duncan, and I have had it for over forty years. Obviously with his situation, his Alzheimer's, we haven't been able to visit and I haven't felt able to go on my own. But certain things, administrative things, need attending to. So I thought I might go in a couple of weeks,' she informed Cross innocently. He wondered why she was telling him this. It wasn't any of his business.

'As you know, Duncan can't come with me but the home he's in is quite happy for me to go. The truth is, he won't even know I've gone, sadly. But I don't want to go on my own. So I've asked Raymond if he would like to accompany me.'

'I see,' said Cross, realising in the moment that he was actually shocked at the very suggestion. The usual, uncomplicated eating of cake and drinking tea after practice had been hijacked by the kind of personal conversation with his mother he had hoped to avoid.

'I'm afraid you don't. Raymond has said no. That he can't. You and I know full well what the reason is,' she went on.

'He doesn't like hot climates and is quite particular when it comes to his food.'

'Don't be naive, George,' said Stephen.

'I fail to see how that response qualifies in any way as being naive,' refuted George while at the same time failing to see how this had anything to do with the priest. George hadn't noticed how integral a part of his inner circle Stephen had become over the years. In fact, in all of theirs – Raymond, Christine and George. Although it could be said that George had failed to notice the existence of the inner circle itself.

'He won't come because of you, George. He doesn't feel he can leave you on your own. We all know that to be the case,' said his mother.

This made perfect sense to George. But it wasn't he who was being naive. Rather it was Christine. The truth was that Raymond probably didn't want to go in the first place and was using him, if he had indeed articulated it, as an excuse.

'Why are you telling me this?' he asked.

'Because Christine thinks a holiday abroad would do your father a great deal of good and I'm inclined to agree with her,' said Stephen, butting in for the second time.

'Would you speak to him, George? Try and persuade him to come with me?'

Being put on the spot like this made George realise that he was in fact far from comfortable with the prospect of his father going abroad for a couple of weeks. What if something were to happen to him? He was getting on, after all. But what really concerned him was what would he do if something happened to him and Raymond wasn't around to talk to? This was a disconcerting thought, not just of itself, but because it was the first time he'd had cause to reflect on how much he relied on his father. It was something he'd been taking for granted all these years and now, faced with the truth of it, he wasn't at all sure how comfortable he was with the idea of such dependence. He wondered for a moment what Christine was expecting of him in this situation. He quickly figured out the perfect non-committal response.

'I'll talk to him,' he said.

This seemed to be exactly the kind of response she was hoping for, as she visibly relaxed.

'I was hoping you'd say that. Well, I must be going. If you could speak with him sooner rather than later, I'd be so grateful,' she ended by saying.

George didn't offer to walk her to her car. This was because he wanted to talk to Stephen about this new situation and solicit his advice. Stephen was glad, as he wanted the chance to speak to George. He felt his reaction to the idea of Raymond's going away with Christine was probably more complicated than he'd initially let on.

George would normally have spoken to his father, or at a stretch Ottey. Not by choice with the latter, but she had developed this annoying habit of being able to intuit when something was on his mind.

'It would be so great for Raymond,' Stephen began.

'But she's married. What about her husband?'

'I'm not sure what you're getting at with the first part of that remark. As for her husband, he's being well looked after. As you know he has advanced dementia which is hard for her to deal with. He's in a home just outside of Gloucester.'

'Have you met him?'

'I have.'

'Why?'

'I felt it would help Christine that when she spoke to me about him, which she does quite often, she knew I'd met him,' Stephen replied.

'What does she want? Why does she want Raymond to go with her?' Cross asked.

'She wants company. I imagine the last few years have been extremely difficult for her. She and Raymond enjoy each other's company. I mean, they were married once, let's not forget. They probably have a lot to talk about.'

Which was precisely what worried George. The one thing they had in common was him and it was natural they should talk about him, which he found unsettling.

'Will you talk to Raymond?' asked Stephen.

'It's none of my business.'

'She, by asking you, has made it precisely that.'

'He doesn't want to go. Why should I speak to him?'

'Because you said you would.'

This much was true.

'Why don't we talk about what's really happening here,' said

Stephen. 'You're obviously unhappy at the idea of him going away. Do you know why? Is it simply the idea of him going away? Or is it the idea of your parents spending time together that worries you?'

'It's very presumptuous of you to say that.'

'Are you trying to say it's not true? If so, what are you so worried about?'

'That is a question I don't have an answer for,' replied Cross.

'All right then, here's another. How would you feel if you knew that your father didn't do things he wanted to do, because of you?'

'He's a parent. Parents are expected to make sacrifices on behalf of their children,' said Cross a little self-righteously.

'When they're children, George. Not when they're fully grown adults; middle-aged men.'

George thought about this for a moment.

'Do you really want to be treated like a child by your father?' asked Stephen.

'Of course not.'

'Well then, you have your answer. Tell him to go, George. He'll enjoy it. But what he'll enjoy even more will be the fact that you encouraged him to do it. He'll love that.'

As he cycled home something occurred to Cross. The truth was he was actually quite concerned about being separated from his father. They had always been together in Bristol and even when he decided to leave home, he at least knew that his father was only a matter of minutes away. But he would have to 'get over himself', as Ottey was prone to say, and tell Raymond to go. He and Christine would have to travel by ferry and car, however. Letting his father fly was definitely a step further than he was willing to go.

22

Cross found a message from Clare the pathologist to call him. The post-it was written in her hand which meant she'd come over personally. It must be important. He'd asked her to look out for anything unusual or out of the ordinary. Something he often charged her with.

'DS Cross,' she said as she took the call.

'It is,' he confirmed. 'You left me a message to call. Have you heard that the neighbour has been charged?'

'I hadn't, no. Did you charge him?' she asked. A very perceptive question, Cross thought. Not untypical of her.

'I did not. It was DI Warner,' he replied.

'Are you happy he's been charged?' Clare asked.

'I'm never happy when someone has been charged with murder as it means someone else has been killed.'

'Fair point,' she replied, kicking herself. 'Were you part of the decision?'

'I was not.'

'Had you been, would you have agreed with it?' she asked.

'I would not.'

'Okay, in which case I think I may have discovered something which may be of interest to you,' she said, then paused for dramatic effect. Waiting for him to prompt her to elaborate. Which he didn't.

'I just received the toxicology report on Alistair Moreton. He had an unusually high amount of oxycodone in his system. It's a synthetic opioid,' she informed Cross.

'Enough to kill him?'

'No. Do you know if he was being prescribed it by his local GP?' she asked.

'I don't,' he said. 'Was that the reason for your call?'

'It was,' she replied.

He ended the call summarily. Not because what she'd said was of no interest to him. Quite the opposite, in fact. He wanted to follow up on this information urgently.

Cross got up and walked over to Mackenzie's desk.

'Alice, take me to Crockerne,' he announced at his door before turning back into his office. She hesitated. Wasn't the case closed? The pulsating headache knocking on the back of her eyeballs like an angry neighbour banging on the wall told her she'd gone to the pub the night before with the team and stayed too long. Until Warner's persistent advances towards her, despite the unmissable presence of Swift looming over him, had become too much and she left. She looked over at Swift, who had just fulfilled his daily caffeine run, for some assistance.

But instead of helping he volunteered, 'If Alice is busy, I can take you.'

'Wouldn't your forensic skills be best deployed somewhere other than at the wheel of a car?' replied Cross, who had turned at his office door.

'Of course, but as it happens, I'm here to inform you of some forensic findings I have which we could usefully discuss in the car,' said Swift.

'Michael, Barnaby Cotterell has been charged. If you've got any forensic evidence you should give it to Warner,' said Mackenzie mischievously.

'It's evidence that was requested by DS Cross and as something is obviously still bothering our great leader, I'd like to help him get to the bottom of it. Things are possibly not as clear as everyone in the pub last night thought.'

Cross thought about this for a minute, looked at the coffee on Mackenzie's desk then walked away from his office.

'Very well. I am convinced.'

Swift scampered after him, as well as anyone at six foot eight is capable of. A couple of seconds later Mackenzie also ran after them.

'What have you found, Dr Swift?' Cross asked as they drove out of Bristol.

'A couple of things which both revolve around our canine friends. The blood on Ricky's teeth and gums wasn't human.'

'Another dog?' asked Cross.

'Exactly, and it's obviously unlikely to be his own.'

'According to the vet, he also had a bite wound on his rear hip.'

'Which all but confirms the presence of another dog. Tricky thing is, I need a sample of Ricky's blood,' said Swift.

'Tom Holmes, manager of the Hobbler's Arms, will have it. I took the precaution of asking the vet to draw one when he was inspecting Ricky the other day,' Cross informed him.

'Wow, good thinking,' replied a relieved Swift, who couldn't have loved Cross more in that moment.

'Anything else?' asked Cross.

'Yep, the spare bed. I examined it as requested and found a number of dog hairs on it.'

'Are they a match for Ricky?'

'They are not, so the implication is that there was someone else there with a dog at some point. Unless he had a predilection for taking in strays,' joked Swift.

'Is there any evidence for that?' asked Cross.

'No, I was...' but Swift stopped himself. 'Not at the moment,' he said.

'We should check with Dr Hawkins to see if there are any dog hairs around the bites to Mr Moreton's legs.'

'We don't need to. I found some on Moreton's trousers at the bite sites,' he said a little too triumphantly.

*

Swift dropped Mackenzie and Cross at the GP surgery while he went to the pub to retrieve Ricky's blood sample from Tom Holmes. They had to wait until the end of an appointment before Dr Sebastian Gower was able to see them. Mackenzie reflected how different GPs' waiting rooms were after Covid. Before, they had been a real reflection of people in communities, both old and young. But now people seemed to come exactly on time for their appointment and not early. Surgeries had advised this as soon as they reopened but the pandemic meant that everyone now had an aversion to sitting in a roomful of other people's germs. That was if they could get an appointment with their doctor at all. Dr Gower was in his thirties and still had the earnest enthusiasm and concern of the young GP not yet worn down by the job. He had quite a pronounced bald patch and Mackenzie thought it wouldn't be long before the inch-long semicircle of hair around his head added a decade to his appearance. If she was his partner, she'd have given him a pair of hair clippers for his birthday. She tried to imagine what he'd look like with a shaved head and came to the conclusion he had a good pate for it. She made a mental note to check if there was a suggestion box in reception. If there was, she would leave a note offering some sage hair – or lack of hair – styling advice before they left. She then realised that Cross was talking. This brought her back to reality with a jolt.

'I'd like to talk to you about Alistair Moreton,' Cross was saying.

'I assumed that was the case but as you're aware I'm bound by doctor–patient confidentiality,' replied Gower.

'Is this the first time a patient under your care has been murdered, Doctor?' Cross asked.

'It is,' Gower replied hesitantly.

'Now, although confidentiality continues after death, this can be waived in the event it is in the public interest to do so. Would you think solving Mr Moreton's murder might be in the public interest?' Cross asked.

'Of course,' replied the doctor.

'Were you prescribing any pain relief for him?' Cross asked.

'I had been, yes.'

'What, exactly?'

'OxyContin.'

'Why?'

'To help him recover from his hip operation. He was in considerable pain.'

'When was the surgery, exactly?' Cross asked.

'About a year ago.'

Cross paused for a moment.

'When you say you "had" been prescribing it, does that mean you'd stopped?' Cross asked.

'Yes,' replied the doctor who then typed into his keyboard. 'I tapered his dose and took him off it six months ago.'

'Was he happy about you taking him off the drug?' asked Cross.

'Not initially, no. But that's not uncommon. People are often worried about the return of pain and not being able to manage without it.'

'And then there's the question of dependence,' Cross added.

'Yes, sometimes a physical dependence but mostly an emotional one.'

'Did you see Mr Moreton in the months after you took him off pain relief?' Cross asked.

'A few times, yes.'

'Why did he come to see you?'

'He didn't. It wasn't in the surgery. I saw him in the pub. I think it's important for a local GP to have a presence in the community. So I tend to pop into the Hobbler's once a week. It's also handy as it's where I tend to find my less cooperative patients who make a habit of missing follow-ups and hospital appointments there,' the doctor told them.

'Was Mr Moreton one of those?' asked Cross.

'No, far from it. He was very reliable.'

'Did you speak with him on the occasions you saw him in the pub?' Cross asked.

'A couple of times.'

'And how did he seem to you?'

'His usual self.'

'How was his pain?'

'He said he was managing it,' Gower replied.

'Did he say how?'

'No.'

'But he didn't complain?' Cross asked.

'Unlike other patients he was very good at being told no. Once I told him I would no longer prescribe him opiates, he never mentioned it again.'

Cross made a note of all this. Then looked up.

'Would it surprise you to know that a high level of oxycodone was found in his blood at the autopsy?' he asked.

'It would both surprise and concern me.'

'Why?'

'It's just not possible,' the doctor replied.

'Apparently it is,' said Cross.

The doctor thought about this for a moment then shook his head slowly.

'I didn't see anything,' he said quietly. 'I should've spotted it.'

'But it wasn't the oxy that killed him, Dr Gower. He was murdered,' said Mackenzie trying to console him.

'Even so. I should've spotted the signs he was using. It's my job, for heaven's sake.'

Cross agreed with his sentiment and was about to say so when he noticed Mackenzie shaking her head at him. As a result he said nothing. Not because he was doing as he was told, but because he was shocked at the possibility she might have known what he was about to say and had warned him off.

23

'What do you want?' was the curt response Cross and Mackenzie received from Tamsin Cotterell as she opened her front door.

'I'd like to speak with you,' replied Cross.

'And why would I want to do that when you've arrested and charged my husband for something he hasn't done?' she asked.

'I'd like to clear a few things up,' Cross said.

'Well good luck with that,' she replied as she started to close the massive door.

'Mrs Cotterell,' began Alice, stopping the door at the same time with her hand. 'I'm a police staff officer, not a detective. DS Cross is here, and he won't say this himself, because he doesn't believe the case against your husband is as clear-cut as his superiors. Who, incidentally, don't know he's here this morning.'

'Go on,' replied Tamsin, no longer pushing the door closed.

'You can't quote me on that, but if you want the best for your husband, I do recommend you talk to DS Cross,' Mackenzie insisted.

Tamsin Cotterell thought about this for a moment then said, 'Perhaps I should call my husband's lawyer.'

'By all means, but if you do that he'll just tell you not to talk to him and that'll be that.'

'Then why on earth should I?'

'Because the lawyer will just be doing his job. It's an automatic default response – don't talk to the police. He doesn't want you to have a conversation he has no control over,' Mackenzie went on.

'I'm sorry but I don't think this is a good idea,' replied Tamsin.

'Mrs Cotterell,' said Cross, 'I am not here to gather evidence against your husband.'

She hesitated again and looked at Cross, as people so often did in similar situations, trying to get a read off him. He did give off an unemotional, neutral kind of vibe. Yet it didn't seem to be in any way duplicitous or come across as some kind of ploy to gain their confidence.

She invited them in.

'In the couple of weeks leading up to Mr Moreton's death, did you notice any changes in his behaviour?' Cross began.

'Like what?'

'Mr Moreton was a man of predictable routine, he went to the pub at exactly the same time every evening. Walked to the shop to get his daily paper with his dog, every day at precisely the same time. Went to the pub for an evening pint at exactly the same time every night, except for Sundays, stayed for precisely the same amount of time, exactly an hour, before returning home. You must've been aware of these patterns, even if only subconsciously,' replied Cross.

'Maybe. It's not something I've given much thought to, to be honest. I can't see the front of his house, or the back door from mine. So, I wouldn't have noticed his comings or goings,' she replied.

'Did you notice anything else out of the ordinary?'

'Like what?'

'Any visitors, people calling round? People in the house?'

'There was a car parked in the drive for a few days,' she replied.

'Do you remember what colour? What make perhaps?'

She looked a little uncomfortable.

'I actually made a note of it. After the court case I started a log. I don't know why. I think it was because he had. Bit stupid really,' she said picking up her smartphone and swiping through it. 'It was a black Fiesta, an older model, but a sporty version. You know, with a spoiler and red go-faster stripes.'

'Do you have the registration?' asked Cross.

'I do, and a photo,' she replied, embarrassed. 'Bloody noisy it was. They used to rev it up outside the house for no bloody reason.'

'Could you send me that photo?'

As they reached the front door, something occurred to Cross. He turned to Tamsin.

'The night of the murder,' he began, 'as you left, did you see anything?'

'Like what?' she asked.

'Any other vehicles?'

'I don't think so, no. Barnaby was in such a state, I was concentrating on him and what he was telling me.'

'How about on the road?' Cross persisted.

'No. I can't remember anything,' she replied.

'When you turned into the road, did your husband ask you to check your side of the road to see if it was clear? So he could pull out?' Cross continued.

She thought for a moment, closing her eyes, trying to picture those moments.

'Yes,' she said slowly. 'There was a car. Parked to the side of the road. A Land Rover, I think.'

Cross made a note.

'Was there anyone in it?'

'I don't think so. But I can't be entirely sure.'

'A Land Rover parked on a small country road. Not exactly uncommon,' Mackenzie pointed out as they walked to the car. As they drove away Cross looked around.

'Not uncommon, certainly, but there are no other houses in the nearby vicinity,' he observed.

★

The next stop was the convenience store. Cross walked straight over to the drinks shelves as Mackenzie said hello to Patrick Withey, the owner. Cross looked at the energy drinks and alcohol. He then walked over to the counter.

'Do you sell extra strong lager and cider?' he asked.

'Only what you see,' replied Withey.

'Have you ever stocked this lager and cider?' Cross asked showing him a photograph on his phone of the crumpled White Storm cider bottle and a tin of Tennent's Super Strong lager.

'No. Not much call for it in a village like this.'

'Or this energy drink?'

Withey looked closely at the picture of Spike Hardcore and hesitated.

'What is it?' asked Mackenzie.

'We had a young kid in here a few weeks back. I'm pretty sure he was after that or something like it. Quite aggressive. Rude. Not from round here. But he came back a couple of times for a frozen pizza and milk.'

'Does your CCTV system record?' asked Cross looking at a monitor above the counter with a patchwork of different cameras in the store displayed on it.

'Yes, it's stored for two months then automatically deleted.'

'Can we download it?' asked Mackenzie.

24

They met Swift at the pub where he was waiting, drinking a coffee with Ricky at his feet. Cross handed him the USB from the shop which Swift plugged into his laptop.

'Tea?' asked Mary Holmes.

'Yes,' replied Cross.

'And for you, my dear?' she asked.

'Coffee? Cappuccino? Please,' said Mackenzie.

'No bother,' replied Mary.

'What are we looking for?' asked Swift.

'Go to Wednesday three weeks ago, thirtieth of August at 2.37 p.m.,' instructed Cross.

They looked at the screen. A couple of men in hoodies and sunglasses approached the counter. They looked completely out of place in Crockerne. For a start one of them was possibly of Caribbean descent and Crockerne had a small, predominantly aged and Caucasian population. They were also years under the average age of the village's residents.

'They're not from the village, surely,' observed Swift.

'Could've been passing through,' added Mackenzie.

'Except for the fact they returned a further four times. That would imply they were staying in the village somewhere,' said Cross.

'With Moreton?' asked Swift.

'Possibly,' replied Cross.

'Do you mind if I have a look?' asked Tom appearing from behind the bar.

'Sure,' replied Mackenzie.

He came over and had a look at the screen.

'I remember them. They came in a few times. Had a dog. A pit bull, staffie kind of thing. It kicked off with Ricky, but they calmed it down. Then, whenever they came in, they sat with Alistair,' Tom said.

'Which was odd, as no one ever sat with Al. I think it was the dogs they had in common,' said Mary as she returned with their tea and coffee.

'Did you ask him about them?' said Cross.

'I did,' replied Tom. 'He said he didn't know them, but he didn't seem particularly put out.'

'Would you recognise them if you saw them again?'

'I would, I think,' replied Tom.

'Alice, could you call the MCU and get someone to run this car's plates? See who the registered owner is,' Cross instructed her.

'It could be stolen,' Mackenzie suggested.

'Let's start with the facts,' Cross said dismissively.

'Were they the ones with the noisy little car?' asked Mary from the bar.

'What colour?' asked Mackenzie.

'Black. Sounded like it didn't have an exhaust.'

'Quite possibly,' replied Cross. 'Is there any particular reason you ask?'

'I saw them parked up outside Drew's copse, talking to him one day.'

'Talking to who?' asked Cross.

'Drew. He lives on Jonty Poll's land. They were childhood friends,' Tom explained.

'What does this Drew do?' asked Mackenzie.

The publican and his wife shared a look that was familiar to Cross. It was when people were unsure whether to share what they knew with the police.

'He's harmless,' Mary volunteered.

'He likes to think he's off grid, which he is to an extent. He's "rejected society and all of its oppressive strictures", according to him,' said Tom.

'He's a dreamer. Latest scheme is brewing his own beer. Even tried to persuade us to serve it, can you imagine?' Mary added.

'Claims he's now a microbrewer,' laughed Tom. 'Truth is, and he won't mind me saying this, he's our local pothead. Totally harmless stoner.'

'Where will I find him?' Cross asked.

'It's about a half mile further on from Alistair's. You'll find a cattle gate on the left. Open it and follow it down to the woods. You'll find his place there,' Tom explained.

'But there's no way he would've had anything to do with Alistair's death. They barely knew each other,' said Mary.

Cross's phone vibrated. It was Warner calling. Cross declined the call but the phone vibrated again immediately. He answered it.

'Cross.'

'Where are you, Cross?'

'I'm at Crockerne.'

'What? Why?'

'Just following up on a couple of things,' Cross replied.

'Like what?'

'Well—' Cross began.

'You know what, I don't give a shit. I need you back here. I want you to give me a hand preparing the case against Cotterell for court,' said Warner.

'Isn't DC Murray available?' asked Cross.

'He is. But I want you.'

'Why?'

'Okay, I hear you like things straight. So here it is. I want you in the office now. So I know you're not screwing around with my case. My *closed* case.'

'Then I have to decline. I think I'll be of more use elsewhere,' replied Cross cutting the call off before Warner was able to respond, ordering him back. Something he wouldn't be able to ignore.

'Dr Swift, is there a spare office at the forensics lab I might be able to make use of?' he asked.

'I'm not sure. I could check. But if there isn't you could always share mine,' Swift replied, enthused by the prospect.

'That won't do. Please check for other offices,' replied Cross.

Alice smirked at her boyfriend's look of love-struck hurt.

'Mrs Holmes, I would like to pay for the refreshments,' said Cross.

'Certainly not,' she replied.

'Is there a problem?' asked Cross.

'Not at all. They're on the house.'

'I cannot allow that. We have to pay.'

'Nonsense.'

'It's a rule that George is actually very strict about,' explained Mackenzie.

'Very well. That'll be a pound, please.'

'That can't be correct. Three doesn't go into a pound,' Cross pointed out.

'It includes the coffee he had before you arrived,' Mary replied.

'Well, it seems implausibly cheap. I'll need a receipt.'

Mary thought about this for a moment.

'When you go to people's houses and they offer you tea or coffee which you accept, presumably you don't pay for it?' she asked.

'Correct.'

'Well, you're in my house. I live here, so you can keep your money.'

'It's a pub,' protested Cross. 'A commercial premises in which people pay for refreshments, however cheap.'

'A pub which doesn't open till eleven o'clock. Until then it's my house,' countered Mary who then walked away convinced the argument was won. But she grabbed the charity jar off the bar and offered it to Cross.

'Why don't we compromise and you give the pound to charity?' she suggested.

Cross thought about this for a moment but Mackenzie, who had now had enough, leant over and put a pound in the jar.

25

Swift drove them out of the village. They passed Alistair Moreton's cottage and about half a mile later found the battered cattle gate. Mackenzie got out to open and close it. As she got back into the car her phone buzzed.

'The car belongs to a Terry Napier,' she said reading a text that had been sent in answer to her enquiry. They continued to drive down the lane towards a small, wooded area. A quick check had told them that Andrew Tite did have a criminal record. All of it drug-related. Nothing too serious in the wider criminal scheme of things, but there had been a short prison sentence for possession with intent to distribute. This was of particular interest to Cross and, together with his being spotted with Napier's car, warranted a visit.

Swift parked the SUV at the edge of the trees and they walked through to a clearing which was dominated by a run-down but still beautiful Airstream caravan.

'That is so cool,' observed Swift.

'It does have a certain aesthetic charm, despite its condition,' Cross had to agree.

The encampment was filled with what most people would consider to be junk. Cross knew, from his experience with his father, that Drew Tite would see it as an invaluable collection of recyclable essentials which, at some undetermined time, would be put to good use and the betterment of his daily life. Window frames with cracked glass, tyres, a couple of car seats, rusting engines were scattered around. A lot of metal pipes, corrugated iron, lead tiles leant against the silver metallic caravan. As if the Airstream was a powerful magnet that had been placed in the middle of a pile of metallic detritus, which had then flown through the air, sticking to its sides. There was a weather-beaten sofa outside the front door, opposite a couple of similarly battered armchairs. In the middle was a fire pit with blackened wood at its centre. The smell of woodsmoke lingered over the place.

'Andrew Tite?' shouted Mackenzie.

'Give me a minute,' came a voice from deep in the woods. They waited patiently and then with a rustle of leaves a man appeared brandishing a roll of lavatory paper and doing up a pair of baggy cargo shorts.

'Sorry, I was just in the bathroom,' he said, holding up the toilet roll as if it were proof. He was dressed in shorts and a T-shirt that was so faded it was impossible to tell what festival it had once celebrated. He wore strong ankle boots with thick wool socks rolled down on top of them and a filthy, floppy sun hat. He was tanned and quite muscular with pronounced veins, like large worms, on his arms and calves indicating perhaps that he did a lot of physical work.

'DS George Cross,' Cross announced, holding his warrant card aloft.

'This your band?' Tite asked, looking up at the six-foot-eight goth standing next to Cross. He spoke in a lazy drawl as if every word was an effort. Clearly intoxicated, Cross thought.

'Cool place you have here, man,' enthused Swift.

'Yeah? Thanks. And you haven't even seen the bath. Come and see the bath. You'll like this. At least I think you will,' he said disappearing round the back of the Airstream. They followed him to find a long cast-iron bath in the open air. There was a water tank above it and a wood burner at the base. It looked out over the fields to Avonmouth Docks in the distance. Swift began to clap, his grin pretty much reaching each side of his face. Tite turned to him.

'I know, right!' said Tite proudly.

'That's some view,' agreed Mackenzie.

'Isn't it? You'd pay good money for that in a hotel,' said Tite enthusiastically.

'Except for the fact that it isn't in a hotel, or indeed in any building of any kind,' said Cross.

'That's the point! I'm thinking of putting it on Airbnb,' he said.

Mackenzie looked back at the filthy and dented trailer.

'Obviously after I've cleared up a bit. Shall we go back to the sitting room?' he said, walking back to the front. Apparently, in a continuation of the alfresco theme, the sofa and chairs constituted his living room. This was obviously in keeping with the outdoor bath and lavatory.

'Have a seat,' he said, sweeping twigs, leaves and other dirt off the sofa. They ignored his offer.

'How do you know Terry Napier?' Cross came abruptly to the point.

'I don't. Who's that then?' he mumbled as convincingly as he could, taken aback by the directness of his inquisitor.

'You were seen talking to him,' said Mackenzie, joining in.

'Well, that'd be difficult as he's doing a twelve year stretch right now,' he laughed before realising his mistake.

'So, you do know him,' Cross pointed out. Tite's frustrated frown confirmed as much. 'If it wasn't him you were talking to, then who was it using Napier's quite distinctive car?'

'I don't remember talking to no one.'

'Double negative aside, perhaps you'd feel more comfortable talking to us down at the station,' said Cross magically producing his handcuffs.

'No, no, no, no, no need for that.'

'Who were you talking to, Mr Tite?' said Cross staring right at him in the way many people found disconcerting.

'It was Cal. Cal Napier. Terry's brother.'

'How do you know him?' asked Cross.

Tite sat down and stared at the ground for a few moments. 'I feel terrible about what's happened and if I've had anything to do with it, I'll feel even worse,' he said miserably.

'What's happened, Mr Tite? What are you talking about?' Cross asked.

'Al. Poor old Al. I mean, that's why you're here, isn't it?' Tite was almost whispering now.

'You'll have to speak up, Mr Tite,' said Cross.

'Drew. Everyone calls me Drew. It's what I'm used to.'

'Why don't we start at the beginning?'

'Am I going to be in trouble?' Tite asked pathetically.

'That, as yet, I do not know. Did you kill Alistair Moreton?' asked Cross.

'No. But it looks like I may as well have done.'

'Can you explain that?' asked Cross.

Tite thought for a minute as if trying to organise his thoughts into some kind of coherent order.

'When I lived in Bristol back in the day before Jonty let me use this place. We were school friends, see. I knew Terry.'

'Terry was a schoolfriend?' Cross clarified.

'No, Jonty. Terry was my dealer. Then I did some work for him. Got myself in a bit of bother that way and did some time. But I never grassed him up. He was always grateful. They've moved up in that world now. Bigger fish,' Tite said.

'Are they still your dealers?'

'No,' Tite protested. Just a little too much, Cross thought, but he didn't want to push it.

'So why were they here?' Cross asked.

'If I've got anything to do with this...' Tite mumbled, shaking his head and repeating himself. 'It was Cal.'

'Who?'

'Cal Napier. Terry's younger brother.'

'Why were they here in Crockerne?' Cross asked.

'They were looking for Alistair,' Tite replied eventually.

'Alistair Moreton? Why?' asked Cross. 'How did they know who he was?'

'A few months ago, I don't know, maybe six or so, Al came to me.'

'Were you friends?' Cross asked.

'In a way. That way outsiders immediately understand each other, if you know what I mean. He'd had his hip done, but was still in a lot of pain. Doc Gower in the village wouldn't give him any more pain relief. Oxy, it was. He's quite strict like that. Al asked me if I knew how to get hold of some. I felt sorry for him. I spoke to Cal. Got Al sorted. Even picked the gear up for him.'

'And added a little something for your trouble, no doubt,' said Mackenzie.

'Al was happy. Grateful even, though being Al he never said it,' Tite went on as if to justify himself.

'So, if you were getting the OxyContin from Napier and supplying it to Mr Moreton, why did he come to Crockerne?' asked Cross.

'Now hang on a minute,' said Tite prickling up at the mere mention of 'supply', 'I was just doing a friend a favour.'

'So, you told them where he lived?' asked Cross.

'Of course I did. These are dangerous people,' Tite protested.

'You do realise how wrong that sounds, Drew,' Swift opined.

'Did you see them again?' Cross asked.

'Not as such.'

'Explain.'

'I saw the car parked in his lane and driving about a bit. But I always hid.'

'Did you see Mr Moreton in the weeks that followed?'

'Nope.'

'Not even to provide his OxyContin?' asked Cross.

'Of course not.' Tite laughed.

'What's funny?' asked Cross. The smile quickly vanished from Tite's face.

'Because there was no need. They'd moved in, hadn't they? It's what they do. To avoid you lot. Poor old Al.'

'Why would they move in?' Cross asked.

'To do their business there without any danger of getting caught. It's like a safe place for them. They're under the radar. Al had no choice in the matter because he'd lost his head. The man was an addict. With them there he had oxy on tap. Did they kill him, do you reckon?' he asked nervously.

'I have no idea, Mr Tite.'

'They will have done. You mark my words. And now I'm a, what do you call it? A loose end,' he told them.

'I think you've been watching too much TV,' Mackenzie commented.

'I think I need police protection,' he said.

'Don't leave the area, Mr Tite,' said Cross, turning and leaving.

26

Mackenzie was delving as deep as she could into Alistair Moreton. It had been a tough search. As Cross had predicted the man had no digital presence at all. But she had just come across a Facebook page of alumni from the prep school Moreton had been headmaster of. The school, All Saints, was still open and most of the posts were from pupils in the last ten to fifteen years. News about reunions, old pupils' sports fixtures, weddings. But after a persistent trawl she came across a thread that immediately caught her attention. It was about Moreton's habits as a headmaster. There were links to other websites with names like 'boarding school survivors' and 'public school runaways'.

'Alice, where is the strange one?' Warner called out from his desk in Cross's office.

Mackenzie ignored him.

'Alice, I'm talking to you, so please do me the respect my rank demands and answer the bloody question.'

She continued to ignore him. He got up and came out of the office to her desk.

'Mackenzie, where's the bloody savant?' he asked.

'Oh, were you talking to me? I'm not sure who you're referring to,' she answered.

'DS Cross,' replied Warner, surrendering.

'Oh, is he not in his office?' she asked looking over at the empty room.

'Would I be asking if he was?'

'Then I have no idea. Sorry.'

Warner was going to let this go but he couldn't resist.

'What's he up to, Alice?'

'If I don't know where he is, how would I know what he's up to?' she asked.

'We're making a press announcement with Sandy Moreton about charging Cotterell at six,' he told her unnecessarily. It was as if reiterating this fact might get her to persuade Cross that the case really was over and done.

'Great. Congrats,' she replied.

Warner decided not to push the matter any further and retreated to his desk.

Cross was in fact in the basement of the building in a meeting with a DI Hammond from the county lines team. His colleague Edwin 'The Evidence' had found a spare storage room with a desk in it which Cross had now requisitioned as his temporary office until Warner decided to leave his. He recognised that this was a battle he wasn't going to win. He was perfectly happy in the windowless lime-green box he now inhabited, as it was so quiet. Silence was something he'd missed keenly over the past week or so.

27

DI Hammond was taken aback by Cross's 'office'.

'This is a temporary arrangement,' Cross explained.

'Blimey, maybe I should stock up on notepads while I'm here,' she joked.

'What size?' asked Cross perfectly seriously and turning to look at the shelves beside him.

'You called about Cal and Terry Napier,' she said, ignoring him.

'I did.'

'Why the interest?'

'It's linked to a current murder investigation.'

'But you're obviously aware Terry's in prison.'

'I am. Were you involved in the case?'

'I was. He's a nasty piece of work. Nowhere near the top of the food chain but a big cog in the wheel,' she replied.

'Do you always speak in clichés?' asked Cross.

She looked at him for a moment.

'Funny way to go about asking for help. Good luck,' she said, got up and left. Cross was puzzled by this and opened up his laptop. Hammond reappeared and just stared at him. Cross stared back. She came back into the room and sat down.

'I was warned about you,' she said. Cross said nothing. He'd heard this kind of statement before. 'And, as it happens, I need something from you so I'm going to ignore your rudeness.'

'I wasn't aware I had been rude,' said Cross.

'Which I was also warned about. Which murder investigation are we talking about?' she asked.

'Alistair Moreton, an old gentleman killed in the village of Crockerne.'

'Isn't that the case they just made a press statement about? It's closed.'

'Moreton's habits changed in the weeks leading up to his death. He stopped paying his nightly visit to the pub, didn't go to church.'

'Did anyone check up on him?'

'They did. Had the distinct impression someone was in the house as he wouldn't let them in.'

Mackenzie now knocked on the open door.

'This is police staff officer Alice Mackenzie, she's working on the case with me. This is DI Hammond from the county lines team.'

'Ma'am,' said Alice coming in and standing to one side as there was no room for a chair other than the ones Cross and Hammond occupied.

Cross turned his laptop around for Hammond to see. It was a still frame from the village store with the two men from the Ford Fiesta.

'That's Cal, Napier's brother, and Filip. They work for Terry,' she replied.

'So, I understand. Our victim had an oxy habit. They were supplying him through an intermediary, an individual called Drew Tite. Do you know him?'

'I don't,' she replied.

'They appeared in the village asking for Moreton's address a few weeks before his death,' Cross told her.

'Okay,' she replied thinking it through.

'We have evidence of someone living in the house with him,' Cross continued.

'It sounds like he's been cuckooed,' said Hammond. 'It's their MO.'

'Cuckooed?' asked Mackenzie, unfamiliar with the term.

'It's when a gang operating county lines moves into someone's property and starts using it as a base of operations. Normally the victims are vulnerable, living on their own and more often than not have an addiction. The gang use their dependency as their weapon.'

'That's what Tite said had happened with Alistair,' said Mackenzie.

'But to be honest with you, I've never heard of cuckooing ending in murder. Beatings yes, but...' Hammond added.

'A beating gone wrong?' asked Mackenzie.

'Sure, I mean absolutely that's possible. What was he like, the victim?'

'A loner, not particularly popular in the village,' replied Cross.

'Isolated, elderly and an addict. It makes perfect sense to me,' Hammond said.

'Do you know where these two are?' asked Cross.

'Not at the moment. To be honest our energies have been elsewhere, since we sent Napier down,' said Hammond. 'But we'll put them back on our radar and let you know what we come up with.'

'That would be helpful,' Cross acknowledged.

'Right,' said Hammond, realising this was all she was going to get from him. 'I'll be in touch.' She left. Mackenzie knew that Ottey would have thanked Hammond and then pointed out to Cross that he should do the same. She was also acutely aware how inappropriate it would be for her to do the same and so said nothing.

'Have you got five minutes?' she asked instead.

'I do.'

'I've come up with some stuff on Moreton's past as a teacher which I think might be relevant.' She waited in vain for some encouragement, which was not forthcoming, then continued. 'So according to a load of posts the man was a complete bastard as a headmaster. The scars run deep and have stayed in the memory. If these men are to be believed he was an absolute sadist. The things he did to them back then would end up with him in prison if he did them now. Words like "psychotic", "abusive", "violent", "insane temper" and "drunk" litter these posts. Some of them go as far as to say if they could get their hands on him they wouldn't care how old or frail he was they'd beat the shit out of him. I'm quoting there. These guys must be in their fifties by now and it still seems to have a real long-lasting effect on them.'

Cross thought about this for a moment. 'This is interesting.'

'He was a headmaster for ten years in Somerset when something obviously went wrong. There are all sorts of rumours on the boards, but no one seems to understand what exactly. But it was undoubtedly controversial. He was removed from his post in the middle of a school term by the board of governors. I could look and see if there was any media coverage of it. He then ran a crammer in London for a while then he seemed to fall off the educational radar,' she went on.

'Perhaps he retired,' Cross volunteered.

'It's unclear.'

Cross was well aware that past trauma was often a strong motivator in murder. Particularly when people suffered that trauma at the hands of another when they were powerless to resist, vulnerable. They often sought revenge or some kind of reckoning when older and able to do something about it.

'Has anything been posted since his murder?' Cross asked.

'I haven't finished looking yet. But Sandy Moreton also comes in for a lot of grief on certain threads. His father made him head boy. No qualms about nepotism there, obviously.'

Cross said nothing but just sat there processing what she'd just said.

'Also, Warner is getting twitchy about where you are and what you're up to. They're doing a presser at six. I got the feeling he expected you to be there,' she informed him.

'I have no intention of attending,' he said.

★

As Cross left for the night he saw Carson, Warner and Sandy Moreton MP talking in reception, having made their announcement. He walked directly over to them.

'Mr Moreton,' Cross began.

'Yes,' he replied.

'I'd like to speak to you about your father's time as headmaster at All Saints preparatory school.'

'Why?'

'As part of our murder investigation.'

Carson decided to intervene, prompted by Moreton's look of angry disbelief.

'George, are you on your way home?' he asked.

'No. I am on my way to my father's flat. It's Wednesday. I have dinner with him every Wednesday,' he informed Moreton.

'I'll bet that's the highlight of his week,' said Moreton. Cross considered this.

'I'm not sure I'd go that far. He has other interests that occupy him. But he has told me he enjoys it, so I certainly think it's something he looks forward to,' Cross explained.

'Please come and see me first thing in the morning, DS Cross,' said Carson, trying to bring the conversation to a quick resolution.

'Yes, sir,' replied Cross who then turned back to Moreton. 'Should I get in touch with your office, Mr Moreton?'

'What on earth for?'

'I believe I've already told you the purpose of such a visit.'

'Cross, stop making such an arse of yourself and bugger off. Accept defeat and move on,' hissed Warner.

Cross realised in the face of this hostility he wasn't going to get anywhere so turned on his heel and walked away but not before saying, 'Were you aware of your father's opioid addiction?'

'His what?'

'Specifically, OxyContin.'

'This is outrageous. My father was a great man who has been

savagely murdered and now you have the temerity to accuse him of being a drug addict?' Moreton spluttered.

'I'll be in touch, Mr Moreton,' Cross said finally before leaving.

'Is he being serious? What is it with that man?' asked Moreton.

'He's autistic,' replied Carson.

'Well, I suppose that's one word for it,' joked Moreton. 'But how the hell did he get through selection?'

'I think you'll find our ranks are filled with neurodiverse people,' replied Carson.

'Well, that would explain a lot about the current state of the police force,' Moreton responded. Warner laughed at this until he became aware of Carson's glare and he stopped.

'Sorry, not terribly woke of me,' said Moreton.

'No, not at all,' agreed Carson. 'Just terribly offensive.'

And with that he left, feeling just a little surprised at himself.

28

Raymond and George sat watching one of several editions of *Countdown* he had recorded for them. They did this every week, but he now had so many recorded that they were in fact almost a year behind the current transmissions. They enjoyed watching it together, Raymond armed with a pen and paper ready to form words out of the random letters the contestants were given. Or solve the mathematical problems. George had no need for such aids. He could do it all in his head. Something they both took equal pride in. But they were immensely competitive and had an ongoing scoreboard which Raymond kept in a notebook. This despite the fact that his son was so far ahead in the competition. Raymond had taken great pleasure in showing Christine how he could mention a *Countdown* transmission date and George would be able to say who won between them, for that particular episode.

Raymond could always tell whenever George was deeply immersed in a case, because on those occasions he didn't really concentrate on the quiz. It was at these times Raymond invariably won the competition. George never looked troubled when thinking about work, just distracted. Tonight though, George was troubled. Raymond sensed it immediately and knew why. But said nothing. He'd come to understand over the years that tricky conversations with his son were best had only when initiated by him. At a time of George's choosing and in a way that suited him. Tonight, George was obviously troubled by the prospect of Raymond going on holiday with Christine. Raymond had told her he couldn't go. Not because he didn't want to, but because he didn't want to leave George. She had probably thought this was an odd reason, as would most people. George was, after all, a grown man, an adult. He didn't need babysitting. Raymond had considered going, but only very briefly. This was because he'd been thinking, and worrying, with increasing frequency recently about his death. Raymond wasn't at all sure George would be able to cope in the aftermath of it and it troubled him greatly. Maybe going away for a couple of weeks would be a good thing. It might provide George an opportunity to be alone and find out how he got on. But in the end, he had decided to take the easiest way out and say no to Christine. She had taken it in her stride but did ask him if she could discuss it with Stephen. Raymond was pleased that there was a social support network building up around his son. The conversation between Christine and the priest had obviously taken place, and George was clearly aware of it, given the troubled expression on his face. An expression, it had to be said, no one else would have been able to discern. But they didn't know him as well as his father.

Raymond won their private *Countdown* competition that night and gleefully made a note of it with a good deal of satisfaction. George washed up the takeaway containers from their weekly Chinese meal and placed them in his father's recycling bin. Raymond's cupboard had a full quota of the agreed number of saved containers, so no more were added. This was just one of several small measures George was taking to prevent his father falling into his old hoarding habits.

'I have decided that you should go to Spain with Christine,' he said.

'I see,' replied Raymond.

'Good,' said George, glad the matter had been so quickly resolved.

'Do you want to discuss it at all?' Raymond enquired.

'There's no need. I've decided.'

'All right. As you wish.'

George went to leave but turned back into the room again.

'You will of course travel by ferry and car,' he stated.

'What? No!' replied Raymond.

'Yes. It's my only condition and my agreement to the trip is predicated upon it. Actually, that's not entirely true. There are several others. But after careful, considered deliberation I decided they were, on balance, probably unreasonable.'

'I no longer drive and Christine is too old to take on such a long journey by herself,' Raymond pointed out.

'It's not that far.'

'It's at least sixteen hours from Dieppe. That's two days' solid driving. Three, if you're sensible.'

'You could take the ferry from Portsmouth to Bilbao. From there the journey is under seven hours. Just like driving from Bristol to Scotland.'

'We don't want to go to Scotland,' said Raymond. 'And how long is that ferry crossing?'

'Thirty-three hours,' replied George as if it were nothing.

'So over forty hours in all?'

'Approximately, dependent, obviously, on how many breaks you take.'

'Rather than a two-hour flight and a one-hour drive from Alicante to Calpe.'

'Correct. Longer but much safer.'

'Even though she'll be driving a right-hand drive car rather than a left-hand one. On the right-hand side of the road, thereby considerably lessening her visibility when attempting to overtake?' Raymond asked.

George thought about this for a minute.

'Probably best not to overtake,' he replied unconvincingly.

'I'm sorry but that makes no logical sense to me. Do you happen to know the comparative numbers when it comes to the safety of flying to Spain for just over two hours and driving for seven hours on the wrong side of the road?'

This flummoxed George. He did not.

'You make a good point. I'll do some research.'

'George, we don't have time for this. This is her period of occupation. It's a timeshare, remember.'

'I'll get back to you tomorrow,' George said before he left.

Raymond realised that, for the first time in years, he felt frustrated by his son. He had a feeling, however, that the statistics, if George managed to find any, would prove him right. If George couldn't find any, he would doubtless look up statistics of air crashes and crashes on the roads in Spain, with the added factor of right-hand drive cars, and come up with his own number. Raymond felt logic was on his side of the argument and George would come to see that. George never argued with numbers, so maybe he would see that flying really was the only option. But he wondered why he felt a little irked. Then he realised why. It was the first time in decades that he wanted to do something independent of his son. Something else was now in his life, which he was glad of. A friendship with his ex-wife. But it wasn't going to be so easy for George to accept.

29

Cross was at his desk studying all of Mackenzie's material on Moreton's former pupils. He was becoming accustomed to his dark warren. He would occasionally stick his nose out into the outside world like a shy but inquisitive otter, before quickly retreating into the sanctuary of his holt. Although in normal circumstances he preferred to work without disturbance, he welcomed the occasional interruption when someone was in need of stationery. He was surprisingly happy to help them with whatever they wanted. It reminded him of playing 'shop' in his father's flat as a child. He would stock up from his father's collection of what everyone else considered to be junk – his collecting, or hoarding, hadn't been as pronounced when Ron, his father's partner, was alive – but it was enough to fill the shelves of George's retail enterprise. He then wiled away many an hour 'selling' goods to his father and Ron as well as keeping an immaculate sales register and stock book. It wasn't long into the occupation of his new workspace at the MCU before he spotted various flaws in the way the stationery cupboard had been organised. So, he'd spent some time after working hours one evening reorganising it in a way that he thought made more sense. Things were now more easily and immediately found. Things that were requested more often than others were now in places of easier access.

There was a knock at the door. Cross looked up and was about to ask what stationery might be required when he saw it was Carson. He looked at Cross and his desk shoehorned into the small space surrounded by shelves of pens, folders, papers and forms. He was obviously embarrassed. Something Cross didn't notice.

'I see you've made yourself at home,' was all Carson could lamely come up with.

'I have not. I don't sleep, bathe nor cook for myself here,' Cross pointed out.

'Of course.'

'I'm working here because you left me no choice after you reneged on our agreement. Do you require any stationery?' Cross asked.

'I do not. I just wanted to have a word with you.'

Cross stopped what he was doing and looked up, giving Carson his undivided attention.

'I know you think Barnaby Cotterell is innocent,' Carson began.

'I think no such thing. I merely have doubts about his guilt, which I have kept you fully abreast of.'

'Doubts which you continue to investigate.'

'It's my job.'

'But a man has been charged, George.'

'Prematurely, in my opinion. Even so, do you wish me to stop?' asked Cross, coming straight to the point. This was an awkward question for Carson. In his heart he didn't want Cross to stop as it was quite possible he was right. He couldn't, however, let him continue digging overtly as this would cause trouble with Warner. Which was the purpose of this visit. He needed Cross to continue without anyone else, specifically DI Warner, being aware of it.

'I would like you to be careful about drawing any attention to yourself when gathering evidence, whatever that might be,' he said, choosing his words carefully. 'If you can do that, I'm happy for you to continue.'

'Doing my job?' Cross asked. He was confused by the nuances of Carson's request and didn't have Ottey there to translate for him. He was about to go on when Carson interrupted him.

'Don't say anything, George. I'm simply suggesting that you should continue, but discreetly,' Carson said and retreated quickly. This left Cross quite confused. Why would Carson come to his office and just tell him to continue with his work? Maybe it had something to do with his conversation with Sandy Moreton in reception. Whatever it was he made a verbatim note of what Carson had said so he could run it by Ottey when he got the chance.

30

Ottey appeared at work the next day. She wasn't actually due back till the following week with the extension Carson had given her. But she'd had enough of dealing with her mother. Working a murder case would be light relief in comparison. The latest problem had been that Cherish did not like the red Ottey had chosen for the sitting room. She had described it variously as being like a Victorian funeral parlour or being back in her mother's womb. Ottey had pointed out that it was her sitting room and she'd paint it black if she liked. Cherish had muttered even that would be an improvement. Since then, she was incapable of entering the room without sighing and it was driving Ottey mad. She felt that if she didn't get out of the house and back to work, this new living arrangement with her mother had no chance of succeeding. Then it dawned on her that although she'd been kidding herself that her mother had come to live with them, she did actually half own the bloody house. She wasn't going anywhere, and in her heart, Ottey wanted her there. She thought once they got back into the routine of her being back at work, things would settle down and they would find a way of co-existing.

She felt an immediate comforting sense of familiarity as she walked into the open area until she saw Warner in Cross's office. She frowned and walked over. The door was open.

'DI Warner, I presume,' she began.

'And you are?'

'DS Ottey.'

'Ah, Oddball's partner.'

'Excuse me?' Ottey replied, not quite believing what she'd just heard.

'Just a little James Bond reference,' he explained.

'Don't you mean Oddjob?' she asked.

'Oh, that's right. Doesn't quite work, though, does it. Let's stick with Oddball.'

'Where's George?'

'I have no idea. Probably sulking somewhere.'

'I'm guessing you two didn't hit it off.'

'I'm guessing not many people do,' he replied.

'And you'd be wrong. Most people do. Those who bother to get to know him, that is. But then again none of them made the mistake of moving a desk into his office,' she replied.

'Oh, that's right. I just remembered you're the full-time secretary of his fan club.'

'Wow. Well good luck.'

'What are you talking about? I don't need any luck. The case is closed,' he said, looking up, so that she could get the full benefit of his veneered smile.

She turned away and saw Carson waving at her. He was indicating he wanted her to join him in his office.

'I thought you weren't back till Monday,' he said as she walked in.

'I needed a break.'

'I thought you were having a break.'

'I needed a break from my break,' she told him. He obviously didn't understand. 'Where's George?'

'In the basement. He's working out of a stationery cupboard in evidence.'

'That makes sense.'

'Does it?' he asked in a tone that implied he hoped she might explain it to him.

'I'm sorry, sir, but what did you expect to happen if you let Warner move a desk into his office?'

'They both put me in an awkward position.'

'Oh come on, George didn't do a thing. Well, at least the case is closed.' As she said this she saw that Carson was far from happy.

'George doesn't think it's closed, does he?' she said.

'No, and he's making waves.'

'So what else is new?'

'Do you know who the victim's son is?' Carson asked.

'Isn't he that arsehole MP that just got sacked?'

'Well, that would entirely depend on your view of the world,' he replied. He then noticed Ottey's enquiring expression and remembered his last unpleasant interaction with Sandy Moreton. 'Yes. That arsehole MP,' he said finally.

'So, what do you want me to do?'

'Well, you're his partner. Get him to be discreet.'

'Let me have a look at the case files.'

'Thanks.'

'A word of warning, sir. If George doesn't think this case is closed I'd maybe distance yourself from anything that's happening with it right now. Let Warner take his rightful credit.'

'Good thinking,' he replied after just a moment's consideration.

'Do you want to tell me what's going on?' asked Ottey as she walked into Cross's temporary sanctuary followed closely by Alice who had shown her the way down.

'I do,' he answered. Then said nothing further.

'Well go on then.'

Cross explained his findings. The change in Moreton's well-established habits, the black Fiesta, Moreton's oxy problem and the fact that Cotterell wasn't holding the chisel in his hand on the CCTV.

'Okay, and both Carson and Warner know all this?' Ottey asked.

'Yes, although Warner excluded me from the investigation, which of course he has every right to.'

He might have had every right, but it was a mistake on two counts, Ottey was thinking. One, he lost out on Cross's deductive skills; secondly, it just didn't work, removing Cross from a murder investigation, as Carson had found out on several red-faced occasions. Once Cross had seen the victim's body he'd made a subconscious, unspoken, irrevocable commitment to discover what had happened to them. He couldn't let go of it until he had.

'Okay, what can I do?' she asked.

'Have you been assigned to the case?' Cross asked.

'There is no case, George. It's been closed,' Ottey reminded him.

'Fair point.'

'I have been asked by our esteemed boss to find out what you're up to.'

'Esteemed in what sense?' Cross asked.

'What do we do next, George?' Ottey asked, ignoring him.

'Alice?' asked Cross. 'She's been looking into Moreton's background, particularly his time as a headmaster.'

'And it just got a lot more interesting. Quite a few red flags, in my opinion. The man was a complete bastard, by most accounts. A tyrannical sadist. I came across an online group of incredibly angry and scarred men who claimed he was a serial abuser,' Mackenzie began.

'Sexually?' asked Ottey.

'I don't think so. At least, not according to what I've come across so far. Mostly terrible beatings. He was a fervent believer in corporal punishment. Daily canings. Some of them talk about being locked in a place called "the hole".'

'What the hell was that?' asked Ottey.

'A small windowless room in the cellar.' The irony of her saying this in Cross's small windowless room wasn't lost on the two women. 'It's basically solitary confinement like you'd find in a maximum-security prison,' Mackenzie went on.

'Bloody hell.'

'You said it just got a little more interesting. What exactly did you mean by that?' asked Cross.

'Threats against Moreton and his son.'

'The MP?' asked Ottey.

'Yep.'

'Why?'

'He became head boy in an unashamed act of nepotism, apparently. He was the most unlikely candidate. Others were expected to get it. Natural leaders. Sports captains. Sandy Moreton was an unexceptional little weasel,' Mackenzie went on.

'We should talk to him and see if he has had any death threats,' offered Ottey.

'He likes to brag that he has them all the time. He attracts a lot of venom with his political beliefs,' said Cross.

'Great advocate for the restoration of capital and corporal punishment, he even talked about the replacement of ASBOs with the birch. He later claimed he was joking,' said Mackenzie.

'Couldn't these guys just be saddos who can't move on from a terrible time at school? I mean, it was bloody decades ago,' asked Ottey.

'It sounds more like a borstal. The only difference being it cost their parents a small fortune,' said Mackenzie.

'Where is all this stuff?'

'It started on an alumni page for the school. Then they set up a separate group called Victims of AFM – Alistair Franklin Moreton. There's also a page called Boarding School Survivors where some of them have shared their stories,' said Mackenzie.

'Has there been any online reaction to Moreton's death?' asked Cross.

'And how – comments about good riddance, people having no sympathy, couldn't have happened to a nicer bloke, et cetera. But there's one thread that begins with one of them joking that they hoped someone in the group was responsible for his death, which then descends into an "I'm Spartacus" moment with dozens of them writing "I did it!"'

'What make you think it was a joke?' asked Cross.

'I don't know. The sheer volume wanting to take credit. That and the "laughing so hard I'm crying" emoji that accompanied it.'

'We should talk to some of these people,' said Cross. 'I'm not saying one of them did it. But it might provide us with an insight into the man and who might have done it. Does the site have a moderator?'

'I thought you were pursuing the cuckooing theory?' asked Ottey.

'I'm not pursuing any theory,' he replied.

'You know what I meant.'

'I'm merely investigating all possible leads. I think this is a possible lead,' he continued in a way that made her think maybe she had come back to work too early and her mother's annoying interference at home was preferable to this.

31

Maurice Simpson, the moderator of the original Facebook group, lived in Cheltenham and was happy to meet that afternoon. Mackenzie was going to travel up with Ottey and Cross as she was across all of the posts. She gathered her things together and took her coffee cup to the office kitchen. As she went in she was aware of someone following her but washed the cup up, leaving it to drain. When she turned she was face to face with DI Warner. DC Murray was hanging back in the entrance like a faithful lackey.

'Mackenzie, I hear you have a little charabanc off to Cheltenham this afternoon,' Warner began. Mackenzie looked over his shoulder at Murray, the obvious source of this information, who just shrugged his shoulders.

'What about it?' she asked.

'What's the purpose of the visit?' Warner went on.

'We're visiting an ex-pupil of Alistair Moreton,' she explained.

'Why?'

'I don't know,' she lied. 'I just do as I'm told.'

He walked closer to her, not in any threatening way, but close enough that his breath blew against her cheeks. It had a sour, metallic smell of stale alcohol. No amount of polo mints nor coffee could camouflage the unmistakable odour of an excessive night on the lash.

'Okay. Well, why don't we meet up at the end of the day for a drink and you can fill me in on any developments,' he said.

'I'd rather do that in the office.'

'Understood. So why don't we go for a drink after we've met in the office. Make it strictly social.'

'No thanks.'

'Tomorrow night?'

'Also no,' she said, implying that any suggested night would get the same response.

He was about to say something, when Ottey appeared.

'Everything all right?' she asked with a quick look at Murray.

'Everything's fine,' Warner said, then turned and smiled widely.

'Okay,' she said, unconvinced. She instinctively didn't like his overbearing proximity to Mackenzie.

'I was just talking to Alice. Wasn't I?' Warner asked the young staff officer.

'Four,' Mackenzie replied. Even Ottey was thrown by this.

'What?' asked Warner.

'You have four really long hairs on your nose. They're so long and thick I was frightened you might have my eye out,' she replied.

'Let me see,' asked Ottey, walking up to have a closer look at his proboscis.

Warner looked at them both, maybe trying to come up with a witty put-down. But none was forthcoming. He smiled again and walked away with his wingman, Murray, in tow.

'Are you all right?' asked Ottey, unsettled by what she'd just witnessed.

'I'm fine.'

'What did he want?'

'What do all men like that want?'

32

Maurice Simpson was in his late fifties. He worked for a financial services company based in Cheltenham, advising people on pensions, investments and wealth management, according to the company website. He was working from home that day and invited them into his white-fronted Regency townhouse overlooking a garden square. He was dressed in rust-coloured corduroy trousers and untucked striped shirt. He wore brown suede loafers with tassels which made Mackenzie dislike him immediately. She'd known blokes like this at university. The well-heeled upper-middle classes who were on the verge of Hooray-Henrydom but had just managed to stay this side of the moat. Their lack of intelligence was compensated by a vastly expensive education which not only gave them a vital edge in life but also a sense of ill-founded superiority. He offered them refreshments, which they turned down.

'I read about an old man being killed near Bristol but didn't put two and two together until people started writing about it in the group. I had no idea where he even lived. Whether or not he was alive,' he laughed. 'Gosh, listen to myself. I sound like I'm trying to make up reasons why I didn't kill him.'

'Where were you on the night of the murder?' asked Cross.

'Which was when, again?' he asked.

'Sunday the seventeenth of September.'

'That's easy. We had the whole family here. I have three girls. It was the eldest's twenty-first birthday party on the Saturday. We spent Sunday night recovering with pizza and a movie. The girls still live here.'

'We've actually come to talk to you about your Facebook page,' said Ottey.

'But also about Alistair Moreton's time as a headmaster,' added Cross.

'Well, as I'm sure you know, the two are pretty much entwined.'

'Perhaps you could tell us what he was like as a headmaster,' said Mackenzie.

'The man was a complete nutjob. A monster whackjob, if you'll excuse the pun,' he began.

'Why is that a pun?' asked Cross.

'Because the bastard whacked us at every opportunity. You know what, that doesn't even sound right. Opportunity makes it sound like there was a justification in it. You'd like to think he wouldn't get away with it these days. That he'd be in prison.'

'Go on.'

'It's difficult to know where to start.' He laughed uncomfortably.

'It still upsets you,' Mackenzie observed, feeling instantly guilty about her initial judgement of him.

'A bit. Not as much as some of the others, mind you,' he said unconvincingly. 'There were so many obvious signs at the time but no one wanted to know.' He sounded as if he still couldn't believe this.

'What kind of signs?' asked Ottey.

'Well he had seven German shepherds, for a start. All named after Wagner operas. Who does that? And the drinking. He was always drunk after lunch. As a nine-year-old you don't notice but then the older boys tell you and you can't help but see it. Why didn't anyone else? But it was the beatings, mainly. Every day. For the smallest thing. Six of the best. He beat you as hard as he could. You hoped there'd be other boys, which there pretty much always were, because if he had more time he'd pause between each stroke just to let the pain seep in. And the noise. That swish. You never forget it. I can't play golf because of it. Can you believe that? The noise that club makes as it swishes through the air turns my stomach every time. You have to understand. We bled. He broke the skin on our backsides.'

'That's appalling, and you were only nine?' Ottey asked in disbelief.

'Seven, when I was sent away,' he replied.

'Seven? What parent sends their kid away at seven?' she asked.

'People thought it was the done thing. Some still do,' he said.

'I have two girls. I could never do that. Well, I couldn't afford to for a start. But they're kids for such a short time,' she pointed out.

'I know.'

'Did you send your girls away to school?' Cross asked.

'No. Nothing could've persuaded me to. Even when they were in their teens,' he laughed.

'Did you have to remove your trousers?' asked Cross.

'What? Oh, we wore shorts until we were eleven. Scratchy tweed things. No, we didn't. He didn't need you to. There was one boy always got in trouble. MacCallister was his name. One term he came back with a piece of foam cushion which he shoved down his shorts before he was beaten. He hired it out for 50p a time. Till Moreton found it on the chair next to his bed. He beat him just for that.'

'Sandy Moreton's name seems to crop up quite a bit,' said Mackenzie.

'Little shit, and look how well he's turned out. No surprises there. He was nothing, no one, except that he was the head's son. If anyone ever had a beef or a scrap with him they would invariably find themselves beaten for no reason by Moreton within a couple of days.'

'And then he was made head boy,' observed Cross.

'That was a joke. Except that it wasn't funny. He should never have been head boy. There were boys way more respected and suited to it than him.'

'That must've made him unpopular,' said Cross.

'He didn't care. He was untouchable. At least he thought he was.'

'What happened?' asked Cross.

'One night a group of the older boys grabbed him from his dormitory and duffed him up a bit. Nothing serious and it was so quick he didn't recognise any of them.'

'So the culprits weren't punished?'

'Everyone was punished.'

'What do you mean by everyone?' asked Ottey.

'The whole school. All one hundred and thirty, or thereabouts, boys were given six of the best. Even though the ringleader wanted to come forward, but we wouldn't let him. Moreton then beat the lot of us. But no one cared,' he said with undeniable pride. 'He lined us all up like an army on parade, outside his study in the stable block. It was a Sunday and after mass he beat us one by one. It took him over an hour and a half.'

'Bloody hell,' said Mackenzie.

'Who was the ringleader?' asked Cross.

'Boy called Brook. Everyone had assumed he would be head boy. He loathed Sandy Moreton. Beating us all kind of had a uniting effect. It made us all as one. We sat in the hall watching the others after we'd had our turn. As a boy came running in the one who'd been beaten before him would jump off this huge cast-iron radiator in the corridor to make way for him. And so it went on all morning.'

'Why?' asked Ottey.

'The heat of the radiator would have eased the pain a little,' said Cross.

'That's right.'

'Did you tell your parents?' asked Ottey.

'We all did. Most didn't believe their own kids. I think that screwed up a lot of people's relationships with their parents. Not being believed. I know it did with mine.'

'And now he's been murdered,' said Cross, almost thinking aloud.

'You know what? When you called, my first instinct was that you were just doing background into him. Unless of course you already knew about him. But I wasn't convinced that, despite everything he did to us, one of us would kill him. Then, the more I thought about it, I thought, why the hell not? Maybe one of us was more screwed up by it than the rest. Who knows?'

'Does anyone come to mind?' asked Cross.

Simpson thought about this for a moment.

'Not particularly, but here's the thing – even if they did, I'm not sure I'd tell you.'

'So, you have no problem with the fact that he's been murdered?' asked Ottey.

'I wouldn't go that far, no. But hey. Karma's a bitch.'

'I've heard about people having problems at boarding school before but, to be honest, I've always thought of it as a posh, privileged middle-class problem,' Mackenzie said in the car on the way back to the MCU. 'But hearing it from him. You could actually hear the terrified seven-year-old just under the surface.'

'You have to feel sorry for him. He was just a small child and it's not like he had any choice.'

'I feel bad. I didn't like him as soon as I saw him, thinking, it's turned out all right for you – what's the problem? But as soon as he started talking, I felt for him. How can it still be so raw after all these years? He's got his own family now. Very successful, by the look of it, but it's obviously so painful,' Mackenzie mulled.

'Because it was done to them all at such a young impressionable age. It must've been so frightening,' Ottey said.

'Did you enjoy school?' Mackenzie asked Cross who hadn't said a word since they got in the car.

'That's such a broad question, I have no idea how to answer it,' came the reply.

'Okay, how about – what did you like and what didn't you like about school?' Mackenzie specified.

'I enjoyed the lessons. I didn't enjoy the playground and the behaviour of some of the other pupils,' he said.

'Care to elaborate?' Mackenzie pressed.

'I do not.'

This response interested Ottey. Cross rarely gave anything away either in his professional or personal life. But something about the way he said this made her wonder if he did have painful memories of his schooldays. It wouldn't surprise her. Children can be so cruel, particularly when confronted by something they don't understand. She imagined George Cross the schoolboy would have been exactly that to his classroom contemporaries. Unfathomable.

Mackenzie had already made a note of other All Saints alumni on the online boards who seemed particularly angry and still deeply upset by their treatment at Moreton's hands all those years ago.

'Enquire about their alibis,' Cross instructed her, quickly changing the subject and hopefully ending Ottey's line of enquiry. 'No point in talking to them if they weren't around for the murder.'

33

As promised, George had done his statistical research into the comparative dangers of flying to Alicante versus driving on the right-hand side of the road with a right-hand side steering wheel. He explained that it wasn't entirely accurate as it was based on the data available to him and frankly the Spanish traffic fatality statistics were a little broad for his liking. But he had to concede that on balance with the data available to him, flying did seem to be the safest option. He wasn't at all happy about it, but in the end he gave them permission to fly to Alicante. Anyone else might have baulked at the notion of him granting them permission, but not Raymond. He and Christine then brought the date of travel forward to Sunday which put George into a complete spin. But as Raymond pointed out, George had accepted their desire to travel by plane and the date of travel was neither here nor there.

So, on Sunday night Stephen drove George, with his parents sitting in the back so he could take his preferred position in the front, to Bristol Airport. They were taking a direct flight to Alicante. George had tried to place obstacles in the way of this arrangement by pointing out that Sunday was Stephen's busiest day of the week and it was unreasonable of them to expect him to put himself out in this way. What was more they weren't even parishioners. Raymond then pointed out that it had in fact been Stephen's idea in the first place and that he was doing it in his capacity as a friend. As they drove George found himself becoming more and more unsettled and agitated. He gazed into the middle distance through the windscreen trying to calm himself, as Stephen asked Christine about Calpe, her flat and what their plans were for the holiday.

They finally arrived at the airport and Stephen stopped the car in the parking structure.

'Goodbye,' said George without turning round to look at Raymond and Christine.

'George, we're going into the terminal,' Stephen informed him.

'Why?'

'To say goodbye,' the priest replied.

'I just did.'

'It's what people do, George,' added Christine. They all got out, except for George who was busying himself on his phone. Stephen got the luggage out of the boot as Raymond went off in search of a trolley. George was texting Ottey and asking her if it was imperative for him to go into the airport terminal to bid Raymond and Christine goodbye. She was both surprised and rather touched to receive a text from him that was personal and not work-related. 'YES. DEFINITELY,' she replied.

Stephen pushed the trolley for his two older friends, like some divine porter, as Cross strolled reluctantly behind them like a sulky teenager desperate to be anywhere else. The air was filled with the sound of an aircraft taxiing and another taking off. The smell of aviation fuel, catnip to some world travellers, lingered in the atmosphere. This just exacerbated George's state of high anxiety. He had no problem with airports on the whole. He'd been to some in the course of work and as a child he'd often been taken to work at Filton by Raymond who was an aerospace engineer there. But somehow this was different. To his mind his father's life was at stake. And his mother's, of course.

Raymond was particularly impressed that Christine had her boarding pass on her smartphone. He'd had his printed at the check-in desk.

'I must get one of those,' he said, looking admiringly at her phone.

'You have one,' Cross retorted. 'It's in your right hand,' he added, looking at the boarding pass in his father's hand.

They walked to security. Raymond and Christine turned to Stephen and George.

'Right, well I suppose this is goodbye,' he said.

'I do hope not,' replied George, instantly alarmed. This made Stephen laugh.

'Only passengers are allowed beyond this point, George, so I'm afraid it is,' Christine told him.

'That's not what he meant,' replied Raymond. 'See you in a couple of weeks, son. It's no time at all. It'll soon fly by.'

This reference to flight made George wince.

'What I mean is, it'll all be over before you know it.'

Again, this just added to George's growing discomfort.

'You can go now, George,' Raymond said reassuringly.

'Right,' replied George who turned on his heel and left without another word.

'You'll keep an eye on him?' Raymond asked Stephen unnecessarily.

'I will, but I have a feeling he'll be just fine. So don't waste time on your holiday worrying about him.'

'Well, call us if there's a problem,' said Christine.

'Of course.'

When he got back to the car Stephen found George pacing up and down behind it.

'Come on, let's get you out of here,' he said.

'No,' replied George.

'Why not?'

'We should wait until the plane has taken off. Fourteen per cent of all fatal air accidents occur during takeoff and the initial climb.'

'All right but I've just paid for the parking so we need to leave the structure.'

Five minutes later they were parked up in a perimeter road with a clear view of the runway. The airport wasn't as busy as other hubs in the UK so it wasn't too difficult for George to work out which was his parents' flight. As it sped down the runway and took off Stephen noticed that George was standing ramrod stiff. Then he realised why. George was holding his breath.

In the car George began doing something the priest had never seen him do before. He started nodding up and down in his seat, like a worshipper at an altar or a holy monument. So violent was it at times that the seatbelt actually locked.

'I think maybe you should come back with me to the church, George.'

George made no reply.

They arrived back at the church.

'Why don't you come in and play the organ?'

George got out of the car and obediently followed Stephen into the church. But he went nowhere near the organ loft. Instead, he sat in a pew rocking backwards and forwards, his mind somewhere else completely. Every now and then he got up and paced the central aisle, constantly looking at his watch. Stephen stood in the shadows watching. Not at all comfortable about leaving him on his own, but also not wanting to be seen doing so by George. Finally, George stopped and looked at his phone. On it was a text from Christine. They had landed safely in Alicante and deplaned. Stephen received the same text. He walked over to George who seemed calmer but looked drained and exhausted.

'Are you all right, George?'

'I need you to drive me home,' George replied simply and left the church.

34

Terry Napier's brother Cal had gone to ground. The Fiesta was found at an address near Gloucester. The house belonged to his sister. She claimed it had been there since he'd gone inside. It was up for sale on *Auto Trader*. She pulled up the website on her phone to prove it. But the officer who had called on her noticed that the ad had been posted in the days after Alistair Moreton's death. She had no idea where Cal was. She hadn't seen him in weeks. But the county lines team were confident he and his partner would show up fairly soon on their normal stomping grounds, plying their trade. A couple of days later they were duly in custody in Gloucester and arrangements were made to transport them to the MCU. Animal control had also seized a pit bull terrier belonging to Cal when they arrested him at a tattoo saloon. He was very unhappy as it was midway through the inking session. As soon as Warner heard about this, he demanded a meeting in Carson's office. Ottey decided to tag along for good measure.

'Do you mind telling me exactly what's going on?' he began by asking Cross.

'You've called a meeting and we're here,' Cross replied. 'That is evidently what is going on.'

'Why do you have two men in custody?'

'I don't.'

'What?'

'They haven't arrived yet,' Ottey intervened.

'Why are they on their way here?' Warner persisted.

'I want to interview them,' Cross replied.

'How many times do I have to say this? We have our man and he's been charged,' said Warner.

'Who are these men, George?' Carson asked.

'Cal Napier and Filip Gallinis,' he replied.

'And why have you brought them in?'

'For questioning.'

'With reference to what?' Carson asked patiently.

'The Moreton murder case.'

Warner sighed and shook his head, exasperated. He looked at Carson.

'This is my case which, for the umpteenth time, is closed.'

'It's actually the unit's case,' Carson pointed out.

'A case in which I am the SIO.'

'Correct,' replied Carson.

'So why are you allowing this to happen?' Warner enquired as if it was such an obvious question, it almost didn't need asking. He was wrong.

'What, exactly?' Carson asked.

'Letting him interview further suspects. He's trying to undermine my case. Why, I have no idea.'

'I'm not sure that's entirely true, is it, DS Ottey?' he asked Josie, obviously in the hope that she had a better answer than he.

'He's gathering evidence, sir. These two men appear to have cuckooed the victim and lived in his house right up until his death,' she said.

'So what?' asked Warner.

'Seriously?' she said. 'Is that a serious question?'

'We have our killer.'

'And these men could be material witnesses.'

'To what?' Warner challenged her.

'Well, we won't know till we interview them. They could be witnesses to Cotterell's behaviour prior to the killing. You can't honestly tell me that if you have the right culprit, you're not interested in what two men, living with the victim, might have seen that could be pertinent to your prosecution? I mean, can you?' Ottey said.

Warner had no answer to this.

'I want in on the interview,' he said finally.

'Not a problem,' replied Carson. Cross looked up in surprise at this. 'Chain of command, George. Any questions?'

'Yes, I have two,' said Cross. He turned to Warner. 'Why are you so concerned about your case being undermined? It would indicate a lack of confidence on your part. If you're that convinced you have the right man, my investigations can only help your case, surely. Unless of course you're not. Also, wouldn't you rather your case be undermined if you have the wrong man?'

'I don't. I'm not wrong.'

'Perhaps you're more worried about your being undermined than the actual case. May I leave?'

'You may,' replied Carson.

Cross and Ottey left. Warner turned back to Carson.

'Do you know the first thing Cross does just before he closes a case? Drives everyone mad,' Carson said. 'Before he lets me go to the CPS and before the suspect is charged he does his damnedest to undermine his own case. He tries to find out if the suspect has an alibi even though he or she hasn't been able to provide one. And on more than one occasion he's discovered we've charged the wrong man.'

'So now you're saying I've charged the wrong man?'

'I'm not saying anything of the kind. You're just not listening, Bobby. He does this all the time. Even to himself. It's nothing to do with you. It wouldn't surprise me if the two men he has in custody add strength to your case. You never know, is all I'm saying.'

35

Cal Napier was a wiry, diminutive character. Quite fidgety, but with a lot of attitude and swagger. Cross wondered whether this was as a result of his lack of stature. Mackenzie had discovered a number of social media posts where he described himself as a 'gangsta'. He wore designer clothing that seemed way too big for him. His pit bull had a large gold collar and shoulder brace on him. It made the dog look dangerous but animal control hadn't reported any problems with it. Napier had cling film wrapped around his wrist, protecting a newly inked tattoo.

'Have you injured your wrist?' Cross asked.

'No, you dick,' came the terse reply.

'Are you sure? We could call a doctor for you if you wish.'

'It's a tattoo, mate,' he said, pulling the sleeve of his shirt up. 'Half done, thanks to you lot.'

'Oh,' said Cross surprised and leaning forward to have a closer look. 'What's it a tattoo of?'

'None of your business, mate.'

But Cross had noticed something else on the man's upper arm. There were a couple of faint yellow lines, like the last vestiges of bruising.

'Interesting. I've never seen a tattoo that's a work in progress. So they actually trace a pattern first. It reminds me of a Banda machine at school. Before photocopiers. Do you remember that, DI Warner?' Cross asked.

'I do not,' he replied.

'They looked just like that and in that kind of purple ink as well. My father used to have about twelve of them. But how interesting. So the trace gives you an idea of what it'll look like until the permanent inking is done. I do have a question. Would you mind if I asked it, Cal, or would you prefer Mr Napier?'

'I don't give a toss.'

'About the question or your name?'

'Look, can you just tell me why I'm here and then could we get on with it?'

'Do you ever consider what your tattoos will look like when you're older? Say, in your sixties or seventies?' Cross continued.

'People like me don't make old bones, bruv.'

'Is that right? Now you mention it, though, can you imagine what the old generation is going to look like if they go into care homes when they're older? There'll be saggy tattoos all over the place.'

No one said anything.

Cross checked his notes to make sure what he was about to say was accurate.

'You've been arrested on suspicion of murder and false imprisonment,' he said, looking up as if he expected Napier to confirm this.

'Are you asking me or telling me, mate? Is he for real?'

He turned to Warner.

'Does he know what he's doing, mate? Feels a bit like amateur time, if you ask me.'

Warner said nothing, sorely tempted as he was to agree.

'Do you know the village of Crockerne?' Cross asked.

'Never heard of it,' he replied. His solicitor leant over and whispered something in his ear.

'It's a small village on the River Avon. Almost under the Avonmouth M5 bridge,' Cross told him. There was no response. Cross looked at his script of questions, decided to move on and so turned a few pages over. He found what he was looking for and looked up.

'Did you go to Crockerne speculatively, in the hope that you might find someone elderly and vulnerable like Alistair Moreton, or did you just chance upon him?' he asked.

'No comment.'

'Maybe someone informed you of his whereabouts?' Cross suggested.

'No comment.'

'Do you know Andrew Tite?'

'No comment.'

'What was the date you moved yourself and Filip into Moreton's house?'

'No comment.'

'Are these your and Filip's choice of drink, Mr Napier?'

He showed him the photographs of the strong lager bottles and high energy drinks. He noticed a flicker of something on Napier's face. Either just recognition or sudden awareness that Cross was on his way to proving his being in the house.

'No comment.'

'Have you ever been to Crockerne?'

'No comment.'

'Look, we have two witnesses who say they saw you in the local pub with the victim,' Warner suddenly said, leaning forward in his seat. He was trying to bring the interview to an abrupt end as he thought it a pointless exercise. 'You're on CCTV in the local village shop. Your car has been seen by other witnesses parked at Moreton's house, sometimes overnight. Now cut the crap and tell us what you were doing there.'

'I'd like to speak with my client,' the solicitor said.

Warner got up and left. Cross was a little stunned and looked at his folder in front of him. His carefully planned and constructed interview narrative had just had a Warner-sized truck driven straight through it.

'Why did you do that?' Cross asked calmly in the corridor outside where Warner appeared to be waiting for him.

'To save time.'

'Whose time?' Cross asked.

'Mine.'

'Well, if you're concerned about saving time perhaps it would be better all round if you went back to your office and left me to waste my time on my own,' Cross replied, before walking off.

Ottey and Carson had been watching the interview on a monitor. She looked at him as if to ask what he was going to do about the situation. It was a clear case of one officer sabotaging another's interview strategy, and in this case when pursuing a line of enquiry he had no interest in. But Carson left the room without saying anything.

When Warner went back into the interview room with Napier and his solicitor, Cross wasn't there. Warner waited for a few minutes then indicated that the lawyer should start.

'My client acknowledges that he did know the victim. He was a friend and he'd been staying with him for a few weeks while he looked for new accommodation,' he said.

'Nothing nearer Gloucester?' Warner scoffed in disbelief.

'No comment.'

Warner actually had no plan of action. He did after all think this was a waste of everyone's time. He looked at his watch and realised that in all probability Cross wasn't going to make an appearance.

'Would you excuse me?' he said, getting up. 'DI Robert Warner leaving the room.'

He went into the open area and saw Mackenzie.

'Where's DS Cross?' he asked.

'No idea,' she lied.

'Bullshit. Where's Ottey?'

'No idea.'

They were in fact in the next-door interview room to Napier, with his associate Filip Gallinis. Cross had had a lightbulb moment regarding his frustration at Warner's interference in his interview earlier. He had realised he had two suspects in custody and Warner couldn't be in two places at once. So he didn't go back to interview Napier, he decided to interview Gallinis in another room. He and Ottey were in the process of going through the same initial questions he'd put to Napier. The door opened. It was Warner.

'DS Ottey, could I speak to you for a moment outside.'

She got up and left the room.

'What exactly is going on in there?' Warner asked.

'I would've thought that was fairly obvious. We're interviewing Filip Gallinis.'

'Don't piss me about. Cross and I were in the middle of interviewing Napier.'

'He must've thought this was a more efficient use of our resources, I guess,' she replied.

'That'll be all,' he said, dismissing her at the same time as grabbing the handle to the interview room in a pre-emptive strike, preventing her from going back into the room.

'DI Robert Warner has entered the room,' the detective announced as he came into the room and sat with a self-satisfied smile.

Cross said nothing for a moment, then got up saying, 'DS Cross leaving the room.' He went, leaving Warner dumbstruck. He then walked past Ottey in the corridor straight into the Napier interview room. Warner appeared.

'Where did he go?' he asked Ottey. She indicated the interview room. He disappeared into it. Moments later Cross appeared and went back into the other room. Warner appeared and followed him next door. Seconds later Cross reappeared and went back into the adjacent room. It was like something out of a Feydeau farce. Warner appeared looking quite angry now. He reached for the other door.

'I'd think very carefully about doing that if I were you, sir,' she said.

'Oh yeah? And why's that?'

'Because DS Cross is capable of doing this again and again for the rest of the day and well into the night,' she said.

'Well so am I,' he replied.

'The difference between you though, is that he genuinely won't be concerned about how ridiculous it makes him appear. The question is, will you?'

Warner thought about this for a moment then stormed off down the corridor.

36

'So, you admit to being in the village of Crockerne three weeks ago?' Cross asked the now bemused Napier, who was wondering what the hell the revolving doors routine had been all about.

'Yes.'

'In the convenience store where you bought pizza and the public house where you befriended Alistair Moreton?'

'I mean, who even says that? "Public house"?' Napier smirked.

'Just answer the question,' advised his lawyer.

'Yes.'

'Did you then visit his house?' Cross asked.

'No comment.'

'Your car was seen outside his house.'

'Not my car, mate.'

'So, you're admitting the car was there?' Cross asked.

The lawyer leant over and muttered in Napier's ear.

'No comment.'

'The victim's neighbour saw it and, thanks to an ongoing dispute with Mr Moreton, made a note of the registration.'

'No comment.'

'Having checked with the DVLA, it is your brother's car.'

The lawyer again communicated quietly with his client.

'We did stop off one afternoon. Yeah, I remember now.'

'One afternoon. Was that all?' Cross asked.

'No comment.'

'How do you know Andrew Tite?' Cross asked.

'No comment.'

'He says you were supplying him with OxyContin for Alistair Moreton.'

'No comment.'

'And that you arrived in Crockerne a few weeks ago asking where Mr Moreton lived.'

'No comment.'

'Before moving in for the weeks leading up to his death.'

'No comment.'

Cross ticked the question in his file and turned the page.

'Your dog Bert...' Cross began.

'I hope you read him his rights,' joked Napier, earning him a quick look of reproof from his lawyer.

'He's a dog. There's no need,' replied Cross. This threw Napier a little.

'You were seen in the pub with Bert. It seems he didn't take to Ricky, Alistair Moreton's dog.'

'No, he didn't. Can be a bit of a bully, Bert.'

'Nice name,' Ottey commented.

'Thanks. He's a softie, really. Unless he thinks he needs to protect me,' Napier said affectionately.

'Did he need to protect you from Alistair Moreton on the night of his death?' Cross asked.

'No comment.'

'The autopsy shows he was bitten twice on his calves. Was that your dog?'

'No. You should talk to the neighbours. Have you talked to them? They've got two vicious bastard dogs. Always having a go at Alistair. Barking at him, gnashing their bloody teeth. Talk to them. They probably killed him and all, if you ask me.'

'I didn't ask you.'

'No love lost there, mate. Right pair of wankers.'

'Bert means a lot to you, obviously,' Ottey said.

'Yeah. Go everywhere together.'

No one said anything.

'Is he all right, by the way? I mean, you're not going to put him down or nothing, are you? He's not a dangerous dog,' Napier asked, suddenly anxious.

'No, he's quite safe. In the pound,' Ottey assured him.

'Unless of course it's proved that he did attack Alistair Moreton, in which case euthanising the dog might well be ordered,' Cross observed.

'He didn't attack the old man,' Napier insisted, suddenly anxious. Cross noted his immediate worry about the dog. It was a weak point they could exploit.

'Are you one of those people that let their dog sleep on their bed?' Cross continued.

'Got no choice, mate,' Napier laughed. 'Bert'll howl the place down. Like a proper warewolf.'

'Werewolf,' Cross corrected him.

'Yeah, that's it,' he said, smiling.

'Where did you sleep at Moreton's house?' Cross asked.

'No comment.'

'Was it in the spare room? Where did Filip sleep? Must have been on the sofa in Moreton's study. Unless you shared the single bed in the spare room?'

'They don't strike me as… that close,' said Ottey mischievously.

Napier's hackles were obviously raised but he just managed to hold himself back.

'No comment.'

'Have you heard of DNA?' asked Cross.

'No comment.'

'I imagine you have, I mean it's all over the television these days, isn't it?' he asked Ottey, suddenly aware that as he didn't watch much television, he wasn't sure this was actually the case.

'It's awash with the stuff,' she replied. He looked at her. She definitely smiled. A joke.

'The advances in DNA technology are quite extraordinary. What you might not be aware of is the fact that it's now extended beyond humans to animals. There have been big advances in the US which unsurprisingly have found their way over here. We can tell from a single dog hair where a dog has been. Does Bert shed much?'

Napier said nothing.

'When he sleeps perhaps?' Cross suggested. Napier looked increasingly unsure of his situation.

'I'd like to speak with my brief,' he said finally.

37

Filip Gallinis was a little older than Napier. DI Becca Hammond had told them he was part of a Lithuanian crime family that had moved in on the south-west drug network a few years before. They were based in Luton but ran drugs in the Gloucestershire and Somerset area, at a safe distance from them. They had muscled in on the local gangs with a startling wave of violence, initially. Things had quietened down but had flared up again recently. Gallinis was known as an enforcer in the family. He never had any contact with the drugs, but kept the supply chain safe and made sure that the street operations were efficiently run. After he'd made a bloody example of two street dealers who were skimming off the top, the mere threat of violence from him was enough. They recruited kids to be drug mules, some as young as eleven, buying them presents and befriending them. Then when they had them firmly in their grasp, intimidation and blackmail replaced the gifts. Threats to tell their parents and their school.

With this information in mind Cross decided to take a different tack with him. Ottey's instinct was that he was more likely than Napier to have become violent with Moreton. So, Cross was going to let her have a go with Gallinis and see if her hypothesising might be effective.

'We know you were in the village of Crockerne during that last month. We know that you met up with the victim in the village pub and we know that you were enquiring about his address. Mr Napier has confirmed all of this. Did you reside in Mr Moreton's cottage?' Cross began.

'No comment.'

'Are you the muscle for your family's drug operation?' asked Ottey.

'No comment.'

'Have you ever killed a man, Mr Gallinis?'

'No comment.'

'I think you have. The county lines team certainly think you have. They think you were involved in a number of killings when your family moved your drugs business down here. Killings all related to one family, the Staffords, whose patch this was before you arrived. Three deaths, a number of beatings, stabbings. But they couldn't link you to any of them. Isn't that right? You covered your tracks well. But not so well, it would seem, when it came to an old man, a former teacher. Cantankerous but fairly harmless by all accounts,' she went on. Cross saw a flicker in the man's face as if he maybe wanted to contradict this description of Moreton.

'No comment.'

'You're no stranger to violence and no stranger to making yourself at home in the houses of the vulnerable people you decide to run your operations from. You've been in at least five residences in the south-west, according to DI Becca Hammond. You know her, don't you?'

'If that were true how come I'm not inside?' asked Gallinis.

'Because the residents you coerced wouldn't testify against you,' Ottey pointed out.

'Because I was living there with their permissions,' Gallinis insisted.

'That would be permission, singular,' Cross pointed out.

'Don't think so, mate. More than one resident. More than one permission.'

Cross was about to counter this when he realised a discussion about grammar was not only irrelevant, but with Gallinis, ultimately pointless.

'So, here's what I think happened,' said Ottey. 'You thought

Moreton was a perfect candidate for cuckooing. Lonely, vulnerable and, most important of all, an addict dependent on you for his daily supply of oxy. But you were wrong about him. You didn't know that Moreton was a tough old bugger and when he'd decided he'd had enough he fought back. Maybe it was the mix of oxy and alcohol. But whatever it was, it ended up with you stabbing him. I don't think you meant that to happen. But it did. Is that what happened?'

'No comment.'

'Mr Gallinis, remove your sweatshirt,' Cross instructed him.

Gallinis looked unsure what to do. His lawyer leant forward and advised him. He pulled the sweatshirt off to reveal a muscular torso. This man kept himself in shape.

'Turn round.'

He did so. Cross stood up to have a closer look at his back. There were faint yellow lines across the skin. Old bruise marks.

'Can I see your arms?'

On his upper left arm were more faint yellow marks.

'Bruises. A couple of weeks old, by the look of them. How did you get them?'

'No comment.'

'They would be familiar to Alistair Moreton's ex-pupils. Except they're in a different place, of course. With them, they'd be found exclusively on their buttocks. Are you right-handed?'

'No comment.'

'I think you are, which is why the bruises are on your left arm which you raised to protect yourself, leaving your right arm free to retaliate when he attacked you. With his weapon of choice. A cane. He still has his collection of canes in his sitting room. A reminder of better times. Well, for him, that is. Not his pupils. Mr Napier also has a couple on his upper arm. Did he attack him first and then you intervened? Stabbing him with a chisel?'

'I'd like to speak with my client.'

In the next-door room Warner was watching a monitor. He looked far from happy.

38

Swift hadn't been around the MCU for a few days. Mackenzie had had to get her own coffee. His absence made her realise that she actually liked his morning visits, despite the fact that she had protested profusely against them. She missed the puppy-dog eyes aimed endearingly at her from somewhere up in the vicinity of the ceiling. He was researching animal DNA testing in the US. Dog hair analysis had been used to convict various people in different cases over there. Less so in the UK. But he'd heard that Liverpool John Moores University had teamed up with North Wales Police to identify dogs that had been involved in attacks on livestock. Apparently British farmers were losing in the region of £1.5 million a year in such attacks. This programme was to identify individual culprits in an attempt to curb these incidents.

He called them, spoke to one of the team and asked if they could identify by breed the dog hairs found on the bed in the spare room of Moreton's cottage. They told him they could, and if it was a cross, the breeds it came from. He knew the blood on Ricky's mouth wasn't human but needed Ricky to be ruled out. A vet had taken blood from a very compliant Bert in the pound and also a hair sample. The lab said they could help. Everything was couriered to Liverpool.

While Napier and Gallinis were still in custody, Mackenzie was busy traipsing down various threads about men's experiences at All Saints in the seventies. This inevitably led to tangential, late-night strolls through people's lives that caught her eye. Fuelling a vicarious interest in the way their lives had panned out over the intervening years since they'd left school. She couldn't help herself as she digitally stalked men she had never met, and surely never would, for hours on end. Some had led what she thought of as ordinary, fairly unremarkable lives. Then she castigated herself for being so patronising. But there were also a few successful entrepreneurs, a couple of actors, one of whom she was vaguely familiar with through a TV series. A concert pianist, another MP who had lost his seat a few years before and had taken to making documentaries. One thing, though, did strike her. Which was that the more successful they were the less aggrieved they seemed about their treatment at the hands of Alistair Moreton. One thing also became clear. His abuse was widespread and non-discriminating. It was just a question of how some had processed it later in life and whether they had moved on or not.

She packed up her things late one night. It had been a long day and she needed her bed. She was walking to her car in the underground car park when she heard the door to the lift lobby slam shut. For some reason this made her instinctively quicken her step. Silly, really, she thought as she did it. This is a police station car park. She reached her car when a voice, unexpectedly close behind her, said, 'What's kept you at work so late?' It was Warner.

'Nothing,' she replied, feeling immediately uncomfortable. She opened the driver's door of the car.

'You and I both know that's not true. What's he got you looking into?'

'Who?'

'Cross.'

'Nothing. I'm working another case.'

'On your way home?' he then asked.

'I am.'

'So why don't we go for that drink you keep promising me,' he said, taking a slight step closer to her.

'I haven't promised you any such thing,' she replied, putting her backpack on the passenger seat.

'Look, I know we might have got off on the wrong foot but

why don't we put that right by stopping for a quick drink on the way out,' he said.

'I can't. My boyfriend is waiting at home for me. He'll have cooked.'

'I'm sure he can keep it warm. I'd love to have a chat. Get to know what your plans are, career-wise. See if I can help. Put a word in somewhere. At least offer you some advice.'

'No thanks,' she said as she went to get into the car.

He put his hand on her wrist. She pulled it away.

'Come on. Don't be so uptight.'

'Please don't touch me.'

He then grabbed her elbow as she leant down to get into the car, facing away from him. He pulled her forcibly round and towards him. Her hip banged painfully on the car door. As she instinctively put her hand to it he grabbed her other elbow, pinning them both to her sides and pushed her against the car. He leant forward to try and kiss her. She was so startled that she instinctively moved her head down to avoid it and accidentally dealt him a very impressive headbutt to his lips. He yelped like an injured dog and stepped back, dabbing at his lip. He looked at his finger covered in blood and back at her.

'You stupid cow. What the fuck did you do that for?' He then leapt forward again and tried to grab her. But he hadn't seen her reach into her handbag, which was still hanging off her shoulder, and bring out a small canister of pepper spray. She sprayed it straight into his eyes.

'Fuck you!' she yelled before getting into the car and starting it up as he stumbled around the car park lashing out blindly. She reversed quickly, having to swerve to avoid the staggering Warner. She then sped out of the car park. Her hand was shaking as she tried to put her electronic fob against the automatic barrier control panel. She dropped it on the ground outside the car and had to open the door to pick it up. But the seatbelt stopped her. She felt herself beginning to panic. Her mouth was dry. She finally managed to grab the fob, open the barrier and screech out of the car park. She drove for a few minutes before pulling over and bursting into frustrated, angry tears.

Swift was understandably incandescent.

'I know where he's staying,' he said, grabbing his coat.

'What?' asked Mackenzie. 'And what exactly do you intend doing?'

'What do you think?'

'Oh, don't be stupid. It'll only make things worse.'

'How could they get any worse? You've split his lip and temporarily blinded the bastard. What if he goes to Carson?'

'He's hardly likely to do that, is he?'

'Oh yeah, and how did you figure that out?'

She then told him about Warner's hitting on her in the office kitchen. How Ottey had come in at just the right time. It could be proved it was part of a pattern.

'Why are you only telling me about this now?' Swift asked her.

'Because I knew you'd react just like this.'

'All right, I get it.' He thought for a moment. 'But you need to call Ottey and tell her about tonight. You then need to email her and confirm what you said in the call.'

'Really?'

'Definitely.'

'Okay. I'll do it in the morning.'

'Do it now. If you leave it till the morning it could be said it didn't have that much effect on you. Wasn't as bad as you're making out. Trust me.'

39

By the time Ottey got into the MCU the next morning she was fulminating. Not so much at what Alice had told her the night before, but the fact that she hadn't been able to come up with a plan of action to deal with Warner. She'd decided to confront him, despite Alice's pleading with her not to. But she discovered that Warner had called in and informed them that he'd be working from home for the next couple of days. Presumably for his swollen lip to have shrunk sufficiently and his eyes to have lost their new bloodshot look, so that he wouldn't have to explain them away. One thing she had decided, though, was to tell Cross. Which she did in the stationery cupboard.

He then sat in silence for such a long time she began to wonder whether he'd been listening and heard what she'd just said.

'Were there any witnesses to last night's incident?' he finally asked Ottey.

'No. They were on their own.'

'So, it's her word against his.'

'He's taken two days out of the office,' she replied as if this was proof enough in itself.

'To work from home,' Cross pointed out.

'You and I both know that's not true,' she replied.

'Which is neither here nor there. What was said in the kitchen is also a case of his version against hers.'

'I'm a witness,' she protested.

'To what? You didn't actually hear what was said. He stopped as soon as you arrived. He could simply acknowledge the fact that he crossed a line in terms of normal acceptable social behaviour.'

'Again, both you and I know that's not true.'

'And again, that's neither here nor there.'

He then continued to think.

'Also, in the context of Warner having taken the Moreton case away from us—' he began.

'From you,' she corrected him.

'Indeed,' he conceded. 'However, there is a general perception that we work as a team.'

Ottey was impressed by this. It was the first time he had come anywhere near acknowledging that they worked in such a way. This was short-lived, though.

'Which, as inaccurate as it is, is still a widely held misconception,' he said. 'Any complaint from us about Warner's behaviour might simply come across as sour grapes that he solved the Moreton case without us.'

'But he didn't,' replied Ottey.

'The perception currently is that he has and this is all about perception at this moment in time.'

'So, what do you think we should do? We can't let him carry on like this on our patch.'

'I think his behaviour more than likely forms a pattern,' Cross said.

'No question.'

'You should find out who his subordinate female officers are in his Kent unit. See if you know any of them.'

'Unlikely, but I'll give it a go. Maybe it'll be like six degrees of separation from Kevin Bacon,' she said.

'Does he work for the Kent constabulary?' Cross asked.

'No!' she laughed. 'He's a Hollywood actor. Oh come on. Even you knew that.'

'I can assure you I didn't.'

'Six degrees of separation from Kevin Bacon.'

'So, you think someone in the Kent force knows Kevin Bacon

or someone who does. But why's that important when it comes to DI Warner?' he asked, completely confused now.

'No! It's like a game. Everyone in the world can link themselves to Kevin Bacon through six stages,' she explained.

'Well, I certainly couldn't.'

'Of course you could. Your father is Raymond, who worked on Concorde, a plane which Kevin Bacon flew on. There you are. Did you in three. What I'm saying is that using the same principle I can get to someone on the Kent force.'

'I still don't understand what it has to do with Kevin Bacon.'

'I give up. I'll talk to someone in the Kent force.'

'Good. We simply need to find out whether his behaviour with Mackenzie is part of a pattern. Then we can think about next steps.'

'Okay,' she said.

40

Napier and Gallinis were still in custody along with their continued pleas of innocence. Ottey's instinct was to push them each separately and see if they'd flip on each other. Her theory was that one of them had killed the old man and the other would want no part of it. Her money was on Gallinis as she'd informed Carson who was, it had to be said, keeping this line of enquiry at arm's length. Cross was content for her to go ahead. But he preferred to wait for the canine hair analysis to come back. This was always his way. To construct interviews with evidence in hand. The only evidence they currently had was that the two men had lived, presumably uninvited, in Moreton senior's cottage in the weeks leading up to his death.

'Okay. But let me ask you a question,' said Ottey, who couldn't help herself. 'Do you think they killed him?'

'I think it's a possibility. But it's not the only one. Dr Hawkins says the bites occurred at the same time as the stab wound. So, if the dog hairs found in the bites are a match for Bert, then we have a good case. Hence my inclination to wait,' he said.

'So, what do you suggest we do in the meantime?' Ottey asked with no rancour.

'In the meantime, we should talk about Sandy Moreton,' he said.

Cross and Mackenzie had been looking deeper into the MP. The problem was that there was so much material available. The man was a publicity seeker with an inordinate appetite for being in the public eye. At times it seemed like he homed in on ultra-sensitive issues and battered them with controversial opinions that generally caused a certain amount of outrage and therefore media coverage. Someone once accused him of being the Katie Hopkins of the Tory party. When Ottey had explained to Cross that she was a former *Apprentice* winner who had now gone on to pronounce hateful far-right views at any given opportunity, he was none the wiser.

Sandy Moreton was a bachelor and had been throughout his adult life. Never been married nor, it would seem, close to it. He'd been linked with various eligible women, the majority of whom seemed to have the 'Rt Honourable' or 'Lady' before their names. He was certainly aiming high in his social aspirations. He had been in the City for a while having left university – Oxford – where he worked as a hedge fund manager. He made a small fortune before going into politics. He was in a famously safe Tory seat in the politically blue belt of Dorset, the comfort of his sizeable majority giving him licence to be as outrageous or controversial as he liked on any volatile political issue. Whenever something newsworthy happened Moreton seemed to be on hand to give a succulent soundbite.

Recently there had been a flurry of claims of bullying on his part in the Commons. Firstly, as a chief whip and then as a junior minister. An inquiry was set up. The resulting report had led to him resigning the ministerial post in the summer. He protested that the untruthful and unfounded allegations being hurled against him were the direct result of a smear campaign led by the opposition. This, however, couldn't explain away the allegations of bullying that then surfaced from his time at the hedge fund. The bullying issue hadn't gone away by any means, even with his resignation, particularly with these new accusations from Canary Wharf. It had now led to the successful petition for his recall and a by-election in his constituency. Apparently he was going to stand as an independent. It seemed his self-confidence had no anchor in reality. Didn't he understand that the recall came from his constituency in the first place? Why would they vote him back in?

The story kept cropping up in the papers like a recurring yellowhead on an adolescent's chin. This wasn't helped by the government's initial failure to set up a proper investigation into the matter. There was one journalist in particular who had written several investigative pieces looking into Moreton. She was called Maggie Norman and obviously didn't like the man. She had proof of his links with various dodgy Middle Eastern princes, also his offers of getting businessmen sit-downs with the prime minister in return for a fee. This had come to a head when he was the victim of a newspaper sting. A tabloid journalist posed as a Russian oligarch who wanted to move a ton of money into the UK and wanted to invest in media outlets here. Moreton offered meetings not only with senior ministers in the Department of Trade and Industry but also with the main man himself. Cross set up a Zoom call with Maggie.

'Listen, he's one of those guys who got a bit of money, got bored with what he was doing, craved a bit of attention and notoriety and that's why he went into politics. Pure and simple,' she told them. It was difficult to tell on Zoom but she seemed to be a diminutive woman who could easily have been an academic with her unruly hair and oversized cardigan. She exuded a sense of unease. As if at any moment she could be the subject of an attack of some sort.

'Are you saying he had no political ambition?' Cross asked.

'Well, like everyone else when they go into that world, they have ambition when they first enter the House. Then they get worn down by the sordid and tawdry reality of Westminster and its internal politics. But he got into too many scrapes. The man just can't help himself. He often says the first thing that comes into his head with no thought for the political consequences. He's the definition of entitled and that doesn't work as well for people in politics as it used to. He's made too many mistakes. It's cost him his ministerial career. There could have been a lull or plateau before he returned to the front bench like so many of them. But that just won't happen now with the report and his recall. His political career is over but like so many narcissists he just can't see it. He jumps on any contentious issue he hears about on the political agenda like a massive wrecking ball. He's also been in trouble with the privileges committee, not declaring interests and gifts, like staying in people's Tuscan villas at their expense and not mentioning it.'

'I get the feeling you don't like him,' Ottey commented.

'The more you get to know him, the less there is to like. And to be frank, there wasn't a whole heck of a lot to like in the first place.'

'He's never married,' Cross observed.

'No, and that's another dodgy area. He's had to hush up a lot of sexual harassment cases both in the House and before, in the City. All female complainants. He likes to think of himself as something of a playboy.'

Warner immediately crossed Ottey's mind. Why did these men think they could get away with it? Because they so often did.

'Presumably you know about his father?' asked Cross.

'His murder? Yes. Whatever the old man did in the past he didn't deserve that,' Maggie said.

'What do you mean?' Cross asked.

'You must have come across all the claims of physical abuse at his hands in All Saints.'

'We have,' replied Ottey.

'The man was a tyrant. How no one saw it at the time is unbelievable. You know he had a load of German shepherds named after Wagner operas,' she said in disbelief.

'We did.'

'No wonder Moreton's so weird, growing up in the shadow of that,' Maggie added.

'We understand he's devoted to his father,' said Ottey.

'Absolutely. On the two occasions I've actually sat and interviewed Moreton he spoke about his father in almost reverential terms. Did I not know what a great man he was? It seemed to me he'd always sought his father's approval. He joked about how critical his father was about MPs. The old man was very opinionated and didn't care what people thought of him. According to his son he almost revelled in people's dislike of him. From the time he was a head teacher right to the end. Which he obviously thought was a good thing. They sounded pretty close.'

'That's interesting,' commented Ottey. 'We found several storage boxes filled with articles exclusively about Sandy Moreton both in the City and as an MP.'

'It's timely that you should be in touch now because I've been wanting to put together a piece about corporal punishment. But my editor said it belonged to another age and that the readership wouldn't be interested. But we are now a country ruled by people who thought it was the norm to be beaten with a cane by a teacher. Are they really fit to be in charge? With the report and the recall, the editor now thinks it might have legs.'

41

Things had been different between Alice and Michael since the Warner attack. He was overly protective and anxious. She was a little distant, partly through being immersed in the Moreton case, but also because she found herself now permanently on edge. As they sat down to eat one night in his flat, she looked up at him with an expression he knew well and was always wary of. It was the 'we need to talk' look.

'Michael, we need to talk,' she said. Alarm bells began in the emotionally ultrasensitive mind of Dr Michael Swift.

'Oh no. Are you breaking up with me?' he asked.

'What? How old are you? Twelve?'

'I won't bring coffee to your office any more. I promise,' he pleaded.

'Michael. Don't be stupid.'

'Okay,' he replied.

'I've decided,' she said with conclusive authority. Then said nothing more.

'Good,' he said with all the uncertainty that is inevitable when someone has no idea what the other person is talking about.

'I'm definitely going to apply for the DHEP,' she announced with pride.

'The what?'

'Michael, we've discussed this. The Degree Holder Entry Programme for the police. I'm going to become a detective.' She beamed.

'Are you sure?' he asked.

'Absolutely. It's what I want to do. That pig Warner made

me realise I'm not a victim. I won't be a victim. I want to help victims. I finally know what I want to do,' she said.

'That's fantastic. Really. I never imagined you as police, but I think it's wonderful,' he said.

'You're police.'

'I am not,' he replied firmly.

'Now you make it sound like a bad thing,' she said.

'I'm independent of the police. I work for the police. It's an important distinction.'

'If you say so,' she said, resisting the urge to call BULLSHIT!

'You have to promise me one thing though,' he said.

'What?'

'That I'm there when you tell your folks.'

'Oh, very funny,' she replied. But that was going to be one awkward conversation.

When they got into bed later, he turned to face her.

'I do actually have one question,' he began.

'Okay. Go for it.'

'Does this mean you'll have to be in uniform for a while?' he asked with a degree of licentiousness that rendered the overtly suggestive raising of his carefully curated eyebrows redundant.

'Oh, go to sleep,' she said, turning over with a smile that said this unspoken idea might hold its merits for her too.

42

Napier and Gallinis had been left alone with their thoughts, as another extension to their custody was granted to await the canine DNA results from Liverpool. When Swift went over to the MCU he delivered the habitual coffee to Alice and the results. They were having a break in the interview. Alice told him Cross was waiting for Swift's findings. This just made him anxious as he was fairly sure it wasn't what Cross was hoping for. He still didn't know Cross well enough to realise that Cross never hoped for or banked on anything when investigating a case. Even something which terminated a lead he was investigating was still progress for him.

He found Cross in his subterranean lair and looked around the room.

'No windows, nice,' he said approvingly. He found daylight and everything that went on in it outside his office an unnecessary distraction at work. Which was why he'd fitted blackout blinds over his windows. 'I have the results from Liverpool.'

'And what do they tell us?' Cross asked.

'The hair on the bed is a match to Bert, Napier's dog. So the likelihood is he was sleeping in the house.'

Cross nodded. It was an indication of this but far from proof of murder. The dog could have just slept up there during their visits.

'However, the canine blood on Ricky's teeth is not a match for Bert.'

'I see,' said Cross as he thought through the ramifications of this.

'Which does make sense, as the vet couldn't find any bite marks on Bert from any other dog.'

'Anything else?'

'Yes. The dog hairs on Moreton's trousers are not a match for either dog. They are, however, a match for this breed.' He handed Cross a piece of paper which contained all the results. Cross read it carefully.

'Please keep this to yourself for the next hour or so. You can then give it to Warner,' he said.

'Yes, boss.'

Cross had Napier brought up from the cells. He'd decided the best way to get anything from the young man was simply to tell him the truth.

'You were staying at Moreton's house as an uninvited guest. We know this because we found dog hair matching Bert's on the spare bed where you slept. However, we now have evidence that suggests someone else killed Alistair Moreton. Neither you nor Mr Gallinis murdered the victim.'

Napier looked at his lawyer as if needing confirmation of what Cross had just said.

'So, am I free to go?' he asked.

'You will be as soon as you tell me exactly what happened,' replied Cross.

'What are you talking about? You just said we didn't do it,' said Napier.

'I want to know how you and your associate came by those bruises on your arms,' Cross informed him.

Napier and Gallinis then gave them separate but almost identical accounts of their time with Moreton. There were enough small inconsistencies to lead Cross to believe they weren't at all rehearsed. Moreton, though never exactly glad of their company, got used to it and was reluctantly accepting of it, it seemed, despite pleading with them to leave and attempting to escape in the middle of one night. He'd even taught them a little Dickens, encouraging them to read *Great Expectations*. He introduced them to the music of Wagner. But as the two drug dealers relaxed, they let him drink more and more, until one night he completely lost it.

'We were asleep when he attacked us. Came at us with a cane. He was a madman. Completely insane. Smacking me on my arms. It hurt, man! He had some strength. Fil came up to find out what was going on and he had a right go at him. I thought Fil might smack him one. But it was weird. He just turned his back on the old man who kept hitting him and we left, quick,' Napier told them.

'I couldn't hit the old man. He was pissed,' Gallinis corroborated. 'I could've killed him if I hit him and we didn't need that kind of hassle. He had some power in those arms, man. I had to sleep on my stomach the next night.'

'Muscle memory and years of practice,' Ottey commented drily.

They also spoke about seeing a man in a car who was staking the cottage out. They thought it was the police at first. A man, it could've been the same bloke, had called at the door a few days earlier. Moreton did seem a little shaken by it, now they thought about it. That was when he really started to hit the bottle.

'There were others came round. The vicar, the man with his paper and another lady from the village,' said Napier.

'That would be the pub landlady in all probability,' said Cross.

'And then there was his son,' added Napier.

'Moreton's son?' asked Cross.

'Yeah, he came round one day.'

'Was this before or after the other man?' Cross asked.

'Next day, I think.'

'Did you meet him? The son?'

'No, Alistair wouldn't let him in. Said he'd met someone in the pub with Covid so it wasn't worth the risk. That got rid of him sharpish. Told us all about him though. An MP or something. Anyway, he didn't come back.' Cross made a note of this.

'Why did you leave the cottage when you did? Clear out all your stuff,' asked Ottey.

'Why d'you think?' Napier replied as if it should be obvious.

'DS Ottey has no idea. Hence the question,' said Cross.

'Because we found him.'

'What time?'

'I don't know. Maybe eleven or something. I didn't check the time. Look, he was dead,' Napier said.

'Why didn't you call for help?'

'Because you would've pinned it on us.'

'We didn't know he'd been murdered. It looked like he'd fallen down the stairs, pissed. Broken his neck.' Napier winced at the image in his head.

Cross made a note.

'You weren't there when he was killed?' Cross asked.

'Of course not. It wouldn't have happened if we'd been there. Swear to God,' said Napier.

'Are you religious?' asked Cross.

'No.'

'Then that's pretty meaningless,' he replied.

They both claimed to have left the night before Moreton was killed, the Saturday, and not returned till the night of the murder.

'Is that it?' Napier asked as the interview seemed to be coming to an end.

'As far as we're concerned, yes,' Cross replied.

'Sweet.'

'But we may have further questions for you,' Cross went on.

'No probs, bruv. Anything to help. Cheers, yeah?' he said, looked at his lawyer and then got up. Ottey opened the door for him. DI Hammond was standing on the other side with a pair of handcuffs in her hands.

'Cal Napier, I'm arresting you on suspicion that you have committed offences against the Modern Slavery Act 2015.'

43

Swift gave the other canine DNA result to Warner, who was talking to Carson. He read it and beamed broadly.

'What is it?' asked Carson.

'The blood on Moreton's dog's teeth came from a Rhodesian Ridgeback.'

'And...?'

'The Cotterells own two,' he said with barely concealed delight.

'Good work,' said Carson.

'Will you deal with Cross, or should I?' Warner asked.

'I'll deal with him,' Carson assured him. He'd heeded Ottey's advice initially, but this had to be conclusive, even for Cross.

44

Swift, Mackenzie and Ottey met with Cross in his temporary subterranean office. The three of them were deflated about the forensic results that had seemed to all but confirm Cotterell's guilt. But not Cross. For him this was simply a development. They had an explanation for Moreton's change in routine in the weeks leading to his death and although it wasn't linked to his death, they could now rule it out. He had two new questions, though. Who was the man Napier and Gallinis had seen watching the house and was this the same man who came to the door? From Napier's account Alistair Moreton seemed shaken up by the visit and began drinking heavily. Did this mean that Moreton knew him? Sandy Moreton had been round. Why hadn't the MP mentioned his visit to them? Cross was also curious to know whether the son's visit had anything to do with the other man's appearance at his father's door.

'We need to pay Sandy Moreton a visit,' Cross declared.

'Road trip!' Swift announced like an excitable teenager.

'Your services won't be required,' Cross responded summarily.

'What do you want me to do?' Mackenzie asked, trying to deflect their attention away from Swift's look of anguished disappointment.

'Keep digging into Moreton's past. See if anything else comes up. Where did he go after All Saints? We should look into any of the old boys that seem particularly angry,' said Ottey.

'Well, that doesn't exactly narrow it down,' Mackenzie replied.

'What about Malcolm Fisk, the stepfather of the not missing, missing girl?' asked Swift consulting his notes.

'He remains a person of interest,' replied Cross.

45

Cross and Ottey pulled up in front of Hinchwood Hall, a small Georgian country pile belonging to Sandy Moreton. Seven bedrooms, according to a quick internet search. There was a gravel drive up to the front door, which was flanked by two full-length windows on either side. The grounds were tidy, but certainly not indicative of someone passionate about horticulture. They were mostly laid to lawn with some box hedging here and there. It didn't give off the impression of an owner who had his hands up to his wrists in the Dorsetshire soil, trug on his arm. There was a turquoise 1970s Rolls Royce parked outside, together with a muddy Land Rover and a van belonging to a security company.

They pulled the bell pull. The door was then opened by a man who was unremarkable in every way except for a combover which might have embarrassed even Bobby Charlton. It was a thick strand of hair plastered from one side of his head to the other over a bald patch the size of a medium-sized dinner plate and just as pale. He was in his late forties, Cross estimated, wearing a pair of olive-green corduroy trousers, brown country brogues with thick leather soles, an army-type sweater with elbow patches, under which a tie was visible, all topped off with a brown tradesman's apron.

'Yes?' he enquired in, to Cross, a businesslike manner, and to Ottey a supercilious, perfunctory tone.

'We're here to see Mr Moreton,' Ottey explained.

'You don't have an appointment,' the man objected. It pleased Cross that he hadn't asked whether they had one, when he would obviously have been in full knowledge that they didn't. This was always a waste of everyone's time in his opinion so this demonstrated a welcome restraint.

'We're investigating the murder of Mr Moreton's father,' said Cross proffering his warrant card.

'But someone has been charged,' the man remonstrated.

'Who are you?' asked Cross now getting slightly irritated.

'I'm Reynolds.'

'And your function here is what?' Cross went on.

'I am the butler,' he proclaimed a little grandly.

'Then please buttle and tell your employer that we are here,' replied Cross.

Reynolds paused a moment as if to straighten out the creases of his trodden upon dignity, then ushered them into the hall.

'Please wait here,' he said before disappearing into the house.

'Is that even a word? Buttle?' Ottey asked.

'Of course it is. I would've thought you'd be aware by now that I'm not in the habit of using words that don't exist.'

The hall was floored with black and white tiles. The walls were dark green. The high skirting boards and dado rail were white. Various Stubbs-like paintings hung on the walls. A central staircase led up to an open landing. It had a sense of being confidently affluent, rather than ostentatious. But it didn't feel particularly lived in or homely. It had the air of a small country museum where perhaps a famous author had once lived and it had been preserved a hundred and fifty years ago for posterity.

Moreton appeared a few minutes later. He wasn't pleased to see them.

'Has something happened?' he opened with.

'Your father has been murdered,' Cross stated.

Moreton looked like he was about to respond to this statement of the obvious and then thought better of it. He must have remembered Cross from his previous meetings with him.

'I am well aware of that, DS Cross, as I am of the fact that my father's neighbour has been charged and is awaiting trial.'

'I did inform you that I would be in touch,' Cross continued.

'We're conducting further investigations for the prosecution,' Ottey interjected. 'DS Ottey. We haven't met.'

'We haven't. I would most certainly have remembered,' he said in an unctuous tone meant to flatter, which Ottey found mildly nauseating. 'Very well, come through. I am actually quite busy with these security clowns, who have come on the wrong day. But I'd have to wait another two weeks for them to return. So I had no choice. It's impossible to get anything done properly or on time in this country.'

'A result of Brexit, perhaps?' asked Ottey.

'Of course not,' he replied, scoffing at the very idea.

They walked into a room off the right-hand side of the hall. One of the large sash windows looking out onto the front of the property framed a grand mahogany desk and leather chair. There was a purple velvet sofa opposite the fireplace and a leather armchair. A large formal portrait in oil of Alistair Moreton in academic robes supervised proceedings from above the fireplace. The walls were lined with books. Cross realised very quickly why it was so familiar. It was almost a carbon copy of Alistair Moreton's living room in Crockerne. The two detectives sat on the sofa. Moreton chose not to sit on the armchair opposite them but behind the desk. Whether to give him a protective barrier between them or in an attempt to assert some posture of authority Cross wasn't sure. There was a desktop calendar for a local dog charity on the desk.

'I would offer you some refreshment but I'm short of time. This will have to be brief,' he said, looking up at Reynolds, who was hovering at the door and withdrew deferentially.

Cross turned to Ottey. They had agreed she would start the interview as she was less likely to accidentally cause offence and bring it to a premature end.

'Mr Moreton,' she began, pausing as people often made a point, at this early juncture, of insisting that they are addressed less formally. Moreton did not. 'You are presumably aware of your father's hip replacement last year.'

'Of course I am. How do you think he got to the hospital and back? Marvellous job they did. Classic example of the NHS working at its best,' he said, sounding like the politician he was.

'Did you know that he was on pain medication after the op?' she went on.

'Well, obviously. He was given them when he was discharged from the hospital. Do you know they have them walking forty-five minutes after they've come round from the op? It's incredible,' he said enthusiastically.

'To your knowledge, how long was he taking them for?' Ottey asked.

'Well, as long as they lasted, I suppose. What is all this about?'

'He was actually prescribed more by his GP,' Ottey went on.

'That's entirely normal, surely,' said Moreton.

'Yes, of course. Unfortunately, it would appear he became dependent on them.'

'How do you mean?' Moreton asked.

'He was addicted,' Cross said plainly.

'The GP tapered his dose to wean him off them. Your father pestered him for more drugs. He wouldn't take no for an answer,' Ottey said.

'Just like him,' said Moreton, laughing affectionately.

'But the GP refused to prescribe any more. So, your father went about procuring them through a local, illegal source,' Ottey said.

'Nonsense,' Moreton immediately refuted this.

'Your father was addicted to OxyContin. High levels of oxycodone were found in his blood at the autopsy. There's no question about this. His dealers preyed on his addiction and moved their operation into his house,' Cross continued.

'Have you heard of "cuckooing"?' Ottey asked.

'Of course I have.'

'Your father was a victim of it,' Ottey confirmed.

'I don't believe that, and what is more, I don't see what any of this has to do with my father's murder. It was the neighbour. You've now even identified the dog's blood and hair, apparently,' Moreton protested.

'You're remarkably well informed,' Cross observed.

'I am. Which makes me wonder exactly what you're doing here? Does DI Warner know you're here?'

'We're just making sure that every angle of the case is covered,' Ottey said.

'By accusing my father of being an opioid addict?' he asked.

'We're not accusing your father of anything. Those are the facts,' said Cross.

Ottey spoke again before Moreton had a chance to reply.

'Could we discuss your father's time as a headmaster?' she asked.

'What has this got to do with the neighbours?' Moreton asked.

'It shouldn't take long,' Ottey assured him.

'Very well,' he conceded.

'There's a lot of anger and resentment about your father as a headmaster,' she said.

'You're at it again. Demeaning a great, good man, who isn't here to answer for himself,' said Moreton.

'There's a Facebook group,' Cross pointed out.

'Oh, that lot. They really need to move on. I mean, how old are they? It's sad really.'

'Are you still in touch with any of them?' Ottey asked. Moreton laughed at this notion.

'I am not.'

'Did you not have any friends at school?' Cross asked.

'It was quite tough being the headmaster's son,' Moreton explained.

'Even tougher, I should imagine, when the headmaster was such a disciplinarian,' said Cross.

'There's nothing wrong with that, Sergeant.'

'A firm believer in corporal punishment, your father,' commented Ottey.

'A firm believer in discipline, yes – as I know to my cost.' Again he laughed. 'Of course, it's not fashionable now. But those were different times.'

'When you say to your cost, what do you mean? Did he cane you as well?' asked Ottey.

'Absolutely. No favouritism there.'

'Unlike when it came to making you head boy though,' Ottey went on.

'I hold my hands up to that one. Complete, unashamed nepotism,' Moreton joked.

Just like a politician, Cross thought. Choosing his battles and making concessions when there really wasn't much of a cost to be borne.

'You certainly seem to think there isn't enough discipline around in the modern world,' said Cross.

'I do and my views are widely known. Too many excuses for bad behaviour in modern Britain and not enough consequences,' he said, looking at his watch. 'But you're not here for a political discussion. Are we done?'

Cross noticed an umbrella stand by the door containing a fair number of umbrellas, walking sticks and, incongruously, a single cane. Some of the umbrellas and walking sticks had ornate handles. Two umbrellas had a parrot's head and one a dog.

'Very handsome umbrellas,' he noted.

'What? Oh, thank you.'

'James Smith and Sons, of New Oxford Street?' Cross asked.

'Some, yes, but there are also a couple of Briggs in there. My brolly of choice,' replied Moreton.

'Ah, a man who knows his umbrellas. The Brigg is the Rolls Royce of rain protection. A Brigg umbrella will cost you upwards of four hundred pounds,' Cross informed Ottey.

'What? I think I'd rather get wet.'

'They're handmade in Cambridge. Quite amazing

workmanship. Famous at one time for producing swordsticks and even once an umbrella containing a shotgun,' Cross went on.

'What, for a bank robber who didn't want to get wet?' asked Ottey, at which Moreton laughed.

'I don't think so. I think it was more for people who enjoyed outdoor pursuits. In fact, James Smith's glass Victorian advertising panels still advertise "life preservers, dagger canes and swordsticks".'

'Reassuringly out of date,' said Moreton.

'But not for as long as you might think,' said Cross warming to his theme. 'Swordsticks weren't actually made illegal till nineteen ninety-eight.'

'Really? I didn't know that,' replied Moreton, who noticed Cross still looking at the stand. He got up and walked over. 'These are actually mostly heirlooms. This one was my grandfather's. He was also a headmaster. Look, it has a pencil concealed in the handle.' He demonstrated by taking a small brass pencil out of the end of the handle and handing it to Cross.

'Intriguing,' Cross said, examining it. 'They concealed whisky flasks, all sorts of things.'

'That's right,' Moreton confirmed as he walked back to the desk. 'My father had one with a cane inside the handle.'

'Really?' asked Cross with an enthusiasm Ottey found both troubling and distasteful.

'Yes, it's over there somewhere. Never without a cane at his side, the old man. If he was out in wet weather with the boys and there was misbehaviour of any kind, the cane would appear out of nowhere from his umbrella, to dispense six of the best. Some of the boys were so amazed when they saw it for the first time they didn't seem to mind being beaten. I think there were occasions where the boys did nothing wrong and got beaten just so Dad could show off his umbrella cane. He called it Mozart.'

'The cane? Why?' asked Ottey, not at all sure she really wanted to know.

'He named all his canes.'

He noticed her look of horror.

'Like I said, different times. He called it Mozart because it had the composer's bust carved into the handle,' he explained.

'You've been burgled recently,' Cross observed.

'I have.'

'What went missing?'

'Nothing, oddly. At least, nothing obvious. Nothing I've missed.'

'Was there evidence of anything being disturbed?'

'Not in the house where you might expect it to be. But in here, yes. The desk was a mess, and the filing cabinet had been forced open. I can't say anything's missing. But I wouldn't expect it to be. It's just family stuff and estate admin.'

'What estate?' asked Cross.

'The one you're sitting in,' Moreton replied tersely.

'Oh, you call it an estate. That's overstating it a little, isn't it?' Cross asked.

'Do you keep any parliamentary files or papers here?' Ottey asked, trying to deflect.

'The local plod asked that, but no.'

Ottey was irked at the disrespect but said nothing.

'Presumably you used to have red boxes?' Cross asked.

'I did,' replied Moreton pleased at the reference.

'Before you were sacked as a junior minister,' Cross went on.

'I resigned,' Moreton pointed out.

'Anything in the filing cabinet to do with your father?' Ottey asked.

'Yes, of course. Various bits of administration. I look after all his bills, insurances that kind of thing. I mean, he pays them, but I make sure they're all in order. There's a copy of his will in there. I have copies of all the correspondence and paperwork to do with the Cotterell dispute.' He paused for a moment. 'Do you think it could be anything to do with that? The burglary, I mean,' he asked.

'It's certainly a thought,' said Ottey which threw Cross into a momentary spin as they didn't think anything of the sort.

'Tell me about your relationship with your father,' Cross asked. He noticed an immediate, slight change in Moreton's demeanour. He suddenly looked less receptive, more suspicious.

'What about it? What does that have to do with Cotterell?'

'Would you describe it as a good relationship?' Cross continued as if Moreton hadn't said anything.

Moreton thought about this for a moment. Whether it was because he was considering the question, or whether he was simply deciding to answer the question, Cross couldn't tell.

'My father was a tough taskmaster and yes, that included me. He had high standards which he expected everyone to uphold. But I loved him. He wasn't so good at showing it back, of course. But I know he loved me too. It's quite the comfort in these circumstances,' he answered finally with an emotional waver. Ottey wondered whether he was about to cry.

'Was he pleased with your success?' Cross asked. He noted enough of a hesitation to tell him that this wasn't the case. Moreton laughed.

'Unfortunately, neither of my choices of career in the City and then in politics met with his complete approbation. He disapproved of both worlds. I think he would much rather I pursued a career in academia, then he might've been happy.'

He seemed to be reflective for a moment. Then he got up, indicating the meeting was over.

'If that is all I really should be getting on,' he said.

Ottey stood but Cross remained seated. She sat down again with a barely perceptible sigh.

'How would you describe your reputation as an MP?' he asked.

'You'd have to ask others,' Moreton replied.

'I don't think so. I think someone who goes out of his way to get attention, to be so outspoken, opinionated and divisive on often controversial issues, has a fairly good idea of how he's thought of. I mean, it would appear to be one of your main preoccupations,' Cross opined.

'I'm popular with some people, less popular with others.'

'Merely less popular, or a figure of hate?'

'What has this got to do with Cotterell?' Moreton asked for the second time.

'Do you get threats made to yourself?'

'There is rarely a week that goes by without one,' he replied almost with an element of pride.

'Are those threats exclusive to you or do they occasionally include your family?'

'There is only my father.'

'Do they include your father?'

Moreton actually thought about this before answering.

'No, of course not. Why should they?'

'No reason. I'm just trying to evaluate the whole picture.'

As Cross and Ottey both stood she noticed the cane in amongst the umbrellas.

'Why do you have a cane?' she asked.

'Oh that, it's just a... I don't know, a souvenir perhaps. A relic from my schooldays,' he replied.

'Is it one of your father's?' she asked.

'Good lord no. It was mine.'

'Yours? I don't understand.'

'As head boy I was allowed to cane junior boys,' he replied matter-of-factly.

Ottey was momentarily speechless.

'You caned other boys when you were thirteen?' she asked appalled.

'No, no, I was twelve.'

'And you've kept it as a souvenir?' she asked in disbelief.

'I know. I shouldn't have. But I never seemed to get rid of it.'

He ushered them to the study door. Cross turned back into the room.

'Oh, before we go could I have a look at Mozart?' he asked.

'Yes, of course,' replied Moreton who seemed pleased by Cross's interest. He turned to the umbrella stand and rummaged through it.

'That's odd,' he said.

'What?' asked Cross.

'It's not here.'

'Really? Do you remember when you saw it last?'

'Can't say I do, but it wasn't that long ago. I was showing it to someone else.'

'Are you thinking about the burglary?' Ottey asked Cross as they drove back to the MCU.

'No.'

'Chances are his brolly cane has just gone missing somewhere in the house. The bedroom probably,' she said, laughing quietly.

'Why would it be in his bedroom?' Cross asked.

This made her laugh again. Which just made Cross all the more confused.

46

Mackenzie looked up at them with such speed as Ottey walked into the open area that she knew immediately something was up. But before she had a chance to ask her young colleague, DI Warner appeared from his office and said, 'Ottey. Carson's office now. Where's the savant?'

'I have no idea what you're talking about,' she said, walking straight past him in the direction of the DCI's office.

'Then text him and tell him to come up,' Warner instructed her.

'You have his number,' she replied.

She realised his tone was neutral. Not at all pissed off. She and Cross had discussed the fact that Moreton would undoubtedly have made some calls after their visit. But his attitude meant that Warner felt he was in an advantageous position. He had obviously had time to confer with Carson and the resultant plan of action suited the DI.

The first thing Ottey noticed when she walked into Carson's office was a strong smell of Tuberose. She wondered where or who it was coming from and then saw it on the bookshelf. A lit scented candle. The world was often divided into distinct groups of people, to Ottey's mind. Take lanyards, for example. There was one group where people wore them, as designed, round their necks, and another who stuffed them casually into their pockets. Even this group had a subgroup – those who put them away so that they couldn't be seen and those who let it be seen hanging from their pocket scruffily as if to ensure their small gesture of rebellion was visible to everyone. Cross and Ottey were both lanyard wearers. Warner was a visible lanyard pocket stuffer. But was it a subversive act against an enforced homogeny or a considered, sartorial choice?

Another division in life, pertinent to that morning's meeting, was about people's attitudes to their office at work. There were two groups, essentially. The first group treated the office at work as just that – an office at work. Functional, serving a purpose, existing solely to accommodate the occupier while at their job, with rudimentary accessories to facilitate work: a desk, a chair, maybe two for meetings, filing cabinets, wastepaper basket, coat hook on door and, depending on their seniority perhaps, a whiteboard attached to the wall. The other group in this equation were nesters. People who added personal touches to their office, from simple things like photographs of their partner, or children, maybe even primitive paintings with indecipherable dedications on them. The next level up in the group though was the person who tried to make their office like an extension of their home. These people inhabited their offices rather than simply occupying them. Some brought their own chairs, sofas even, potted plants, framed prints. They might even paint the walls. Carson was one of these. He even had a collage of photographs of himself. From Hendon recruit to uniformed constable, photobooth quads with friends pulling the requisite looks of surprise or fake hilarity. The scented candle was just one step further. Was it another iteration of the post-natal euphoria Carson seemed to be currently enveloped in? She noticed it was a well-known quite expensive brand. Probably a gift, she thought. Such was the strength of the candle's scent in such a small, confined space she was tempted to ask whether he'd lit it because someone had farted. But she refrained.

Carson began the meeting in silence. He did this habitually when things were serious and he wanted the people in front of him to realise exactly how seriously he was taking the matter in hand. If it was really top of the serious scale, this silence would be accompanied by his fingers being formed into a spire which reached up to his lips. This morning was one such moment. There was also a knowingness imparted in this gesture. An unsaid acknowledgement that the silence was a product of them all knowing why they were there, and that this was a chance for them, the ones on the other side of his desk, to ponder things for a moment.

He finally looked up.

'Do you know who I've had on the phone this morning, George?' he asked.

'I do not. Do you want me to find out for you?' Cross replied.

'The chief superintendent, who had had a call from the assistant chief constable, who had himself received a call from the chief himself, who was calling because he'd had a very irate call from Sandy Moreton MP.'

'Is he still an MP?' Cross asked. 'I'm not sure what the form is when someone has been recalled.'

Carson went on, ignoring this.

'All of them wanting to know why I, yes that's me in the firing line, thank you very much, am letting you continue an investigation into a case which has been closed by DI Warner here. Closed with a man in custody, awaiting trial with a fairly formidable amount of evidence against him.'

No one said anything.

'Do you two really have nothing to say in response?' asked Warner.

'I do not, as a response by its very definition requires a question to initiate it,' replied Cross.

'All right, George, it's a little early in the morning for your semantics. But I know how you like clarity, so let me ask you this directly. Do you have any firm leads or avenues of enquiry backed up with recently discovered new evidence that might indicate or give some weight, indeed any weight, to the idea that DI Warner has charged the wrong man?' Carson asked.

'No, sir. I do not,' Cross answered honestly.

'Fine, then I'm giving you a direct order, both of you, to cease making any further enquiries into the case. Is that clear?'

'It is,' replied Cross after a moment's thought.

'DS Ottey?'

'Crystal.'

'Presumably this countermands the instruction you gave me to continue investigating the case discreetly so as not to alert DI Warner's attention?' Cross enquired.

'That will be all, George,' said Carson, glancing nervously at Warner. 'We have a body in a housing estate in Longwell Green. You'd better get down there sharpish. Both of you.'

47

The following Thursday George was at Stephen's church settling into the organ loft for his weekly practice. The murder of a young man in Longwell Green had been settled quickly. Another sad case of young knife crime that was growing in alarmingly senseless numbers. In this case the teenager charged wasn't even aware his victim had died. He'd stabbed him in the thigh but severed the femoral artery. He was pronounced dead at the scene, not even making it to the hospital.

The priest wasn't at the church. What George didn't know was that Stephen was at Bristol Airport waiting for the arrival of Raymond and Christine back from Alicante. The reason George was unaware of this was that after Stephen had told them about the state George was in during their outward flight, they had decided to bring their return forward by twenty-four hours. They didn't want to put George through that again and reasoned that if he didn't know they were flying, he wouldn't become so agitated. He wasn't expecting them back till the next day.

George finished practice and seeing Stephen's car wasn't in front of the presbytery, gathered up his bike and belongings to head home. As he got to the end of the church path he saw Stephen's car driving down the road towards him. He was about to cycle off when he saw Raymond and Christine also in the car. This was puzzling. So he pushed his bike up to the priest's house.

'Hello, George!' his father greeted him enthusiastically as he got out of the car.

'Hello, George,' said his mother, joining in.

'Why are you here?' was the welcome they received. 'You're

not due back for…' he consulted his watch, 'another twenty-two hours.'

'We just decided to come back a day early, that's all,' Raymond replied innocently. But there was something alien to George in his father's delivery. The pattern of speech he was so familiar with sounded off. He realised what it was almost immediately. Artificiality. He looked over at Stephen who just shrugged his shoulders in a non-committal kind of way.

'But why?' George persisted.

Raymond and Christine hadn't exactly thought this through. They had neglected to take into account the inevitable interrogation they would suffer at the hands of George, with this late change of plan. A sudden alteration like this was something Raymond knew full well his son hated and had difficulty coping with. They should have discussed a plausible excuse on the plane.

'It's my husband, George,' Christine explained. 'He's not been so well in the last week. I felt we had to come back.'

'What's wrong with him?' George asked.

'A chest infection.'

This was in fact true. But it wasn't something they'd had to come home early for.

'I see,' replied George.

'Could you help me with the luggage?' Stephen asked him, thereby preventing him from pressing the matter any further.

They sat in the familiar setting of Stephen's kitchen. Normally this offered Cross some sense of comfort. He felt more at ease in places he knew well, particularly this one when Stephen was offering up his famous salted caramel cake with a pot of tea. Raymond and Christine chatted away, ensuring there wasn't a moment of silence. But Cross was still preoccupied with his parents' premature return. There was always a reason for change in situations like this. His mother had ostensibly supplied him with one; her husband's ill health. But the logistics, the timing of it, didn't quite stack up for him. For example, why was she here and not on her way to Gloucester, if the situation was urgent enough for them to have had to come home a day early? The main question he had, though, was why hadn't he been told?

'When did you decide to come home early?' he asked.

'Just a couple of days ago,' Raymond replied.

'Why didn't you inform me?'

'We knew from Stephen that you were working a brand-new case and so didn't want to disturb you,' his father explained.

'You were in contact with Stephen while you were away?'

'Yes.'

'But not with me,' he pointed out.

'At your own insistence, if you remember, George.'

This was undeniably true. George had reasoned that 'out of sight, out of mind' was definitely the best coping strategy for his father's absence. He knew himself well enough to realise that daily communication would have only caused him stress. Worrying about his father. Even setting up times to make the calls would have caused him anxiety. Better all round to have a policy of no communication.

'We had a lovely time,' said Christine trying to divert the conversation in a different direction.

'You should come with us next year, George,' said Raymond.

'You're going back?' George exclaimed.

'I think probably, yes,' said Raymond.

'Wasn't once enough?'

'No, there's plenty more to see.'

'I don't think so.'

'Well, you don't have to decide now, George,' said Christine.

'The other good thing is it's at the same time every year. You know, being a timeshare.'

Cross said nothing. He was thinking about the possibility.

'I'd have to travel by train,' he said after some consideration.

'We could all go by train,' exclaimed Raymond, obviously excited by the prospect. 'It would be quite the adventure.'

Christine didn't look at all sure.

As they drank the tea and ate cake, the couple described how they'd spent their time in Spain. The daily routine they quickly adopted, the markets they shopped at, the restaurants they frequented. But George couldn't help notice a discomfort in the way they were speaking. In the same way a group of suspects talked with heightened animation when they were trying to cover something up. One clue was the absence of small periods of silence that normally cropped up in the conversation of people so familiar and comfortable with each other. Every hint of a pause was leapt on by one of the others to keep the conversation flowing. All conducted with a slightly enforced hilarity.

Christine finally ordered an Uber.

'That's quite an extravagance,' George observed. 'A taxi to Gloucester.'

'Oh, I'm not going to Gloucester. I'm staying with Raymond tonight,' she replied breezily.

George couldn't initially work out why this disconcerted him. It wasn't the fact that she was staying the night with his father. After all they'd been staying together in Spain. Added to the fact that he now knew his father was gay. No, it was the fact that having come home twenty-four hours early on account of her husband's health she wasn't going straight to the care home.

'What is it, George?' Stephen asked after they'd departed. He sensed his guest wasn't about to leave before he got something off his chest. George was still thinking about the circumstances of his parents' early return from Spain. What was running through his mind was the fact that at work the answer to a fundamental question in a case often lay within the question itself. In this instance that question was why they hadn't told him, and there was the simple answer. Why wouldn't you tell someone something? Because you didn't want them to know.

'They lied,' he said finally. 'About coming home early.'

'They did.'

'As did you.'

'Actually, I think you'll find that I didn't say a word, so you can't accuse me of lying. Anyway, I'm a priest.'

'Then you lied by association.'

'I did, and gladly so.'

George thought about this and why they would do it. Then it struck him.

'You didn't want me to know they were in the air.'

'Correct.'

George thought about the implications of this.

'It was Christine's idea,' Stephen told him.

George was pleased by this. Not because he was touched by her thoughtfulness. Of course not. Such sentiments never occurred to him. The reason he was pleased was that the idea of the deception, as small as it was, had not been his father's. And this was where he understood what was perplexing him about the whole situation. His father never deceived him about anything. He was always honest and direct. Had flying home early been Raymond's idea, he wasn't sure he would ever have been able to trust him in the same way ever again. He also realised in that moment how trust was unequivocally at the centre of his relationship with his father. How up until this point it was something he had taken for granted. That it was something he valued intrinsically.

On the way home this thought created a sense of deep unease in George. A sense that without his father in his life there would be no one for him to trust and he found himself wondering how he would cope without him.

48

The following months reverted to relative normality at the MCU as much as that was possible for a unit that dealt with murder. This was partly because Warner had returned to his own division in Kent and wasn't due to darken their doors until early in the next year when *R* v *Cotterell* came to trial. Cross had been initially horrified when he moved back to his office to find Ottey occupying the trespassing desk.

'What?' she'd asked innocently as he enquired what she thought she was doing. But she couldn't keep the charade up for long. It was too cruel. Particularly as the target had no sense of humour. She then laughed and went back to her own desk. Cross realised her laughter meant that it was supposed to be a joke, one he didn't find funny. Mackenzie organised for the offending desk to be removed later in the day. Another case after the Longwell Green murder landed on their desks and occupied a few weeks of their time. Even though they had a confession at the outset, at the crime scene itself, which had been repeated under caution at the MCU, it still required days of work to assemble and collate all the evidence into an orderly shape.

One thing had been agreed between Cross and Ottey early on in their working relationship, which was that they would always be open with each other in work-related matters. This mostly worked on Ottey's part. She kept to it pretty much all the time and was able to forgive any transgressions on Cross's part, as she knew he had no secret agenda. So she told him that Mackenzie and she were reaching out carefully to people in Warner's Kent division. She simply couldn't let the car park incident go. Cross appreciated that it was probably best done initially by the two women, but made it clear that if they needed his help they had only to ask.

For his part he was concentrating on their current case. He still wasn't entirely happy or reconciled with the conclusion of the Moreton investigation. But he'd put it at the bottom of his mental in-tray. His focus had to be elsewhere currently. Every case deserved and got his full attention. There was also the not inconsiderable consideration that he and Ottey had been ordered off the Moreton case and forbidden from making contact with any of the parties involved. But then he received a call from the Reverend Alison Smith in Crockerne.

Cross had decided that it would only cause more trouble internally if he, Ottey or Mackenzie attended Alistair Moreton's funeral and so they had stayed away. He had, however, asked the vicar to call afterwards so they could discuss it. She had initially been curious as to why, but after the funeral it made complete sense to her. Alistair had left instructions that his funeral service be held at the church in Crockerne. Alison was amazed and touched by the turnout for the service. The entire village, it seemed, had filled the church. All except for Malcolm Fisk, that was. The heavily pregnant Tamsin Cotterell was even there, which had surprised Alison, but not Cross. It was a clear statement of her belief in her husband's innocence and a compassionate expression of her sorrow about what had befallen their combative neighbour. Tite had also skulked uncomfortably at the back of the church throughout.

Alison had stood at the door of the church and bade farewell to all the mourners as they left. Moreton had requested that he be buried in the churchyard and Alison had bullied a reluctant parish committee to accede. Whatever they thought of him, she told them, he had been an important part of their community for over a decade. One they had talked about endlessly and so he deserved his place there, as well as it being the Christian thing to do. She knew all of the mourners, of course, which included

Sandy Moreton with a very glamorous woman and a couple of people from his constituency office. But there was one individual she hadn't seen before. He wouldn't give his name, but told her that he'd been a pupil of Alistair Moreton's at All Saints. When she commented how nice it was that Moreton had had such an effect on his life that he'd come to pay his respects all these years later, she was taken aback by his reply. He said that Moreton had indeed had an effect on his life, which was why he was there to make sure the old bastard was definitely dead.

Moreton senior had uncharacteristically left money in his will, to be put behind the bar at the Hobbler's Arms for the attendees of the funeral. According to Tom Holmes it wasn't a huge sum, not because the old man was mean, but because he obviously didn't expect many people to attend. The ex-pupil was there and had a few pints. He then proceeded to have a voluble argument with Sandy Moreton.

'What was the argument about?' Cross asked.

'His father's treatment of this man when he was a pupil of his. How he'd been physically abused. How his father had got away with it for years and justice had finally been meted out. The MP fella threatened to call the police. I told him there was no need and persuaded the bloke to leave. But then Alison found him standing next to Moreton's grave later that afternoon,' Tom said in a follow-up call.

'That's interesting,' observed Cross.

'All the more so when you consider it was pissing with rain. But the other thing was the guy was crying. Standing by the grave crying, like he'd lost someone he loved.'

This was strange indeed.

'How's Ricky?' Cross asked before ending the call.

'He's all right. Fine. But you probably won't believe this. He went missing one day. We looked all over for him and guess where we found him?'

'I have no idea,' said Cross who found these types of questions irritating. It would be far simpler, quicker and easier for all if the inquisitor just shared their information instead of this ridiculous dance.

'In the churchyard, lying next to Al's grave. He goes up there every day around the time Al used to come to the pub.'

'That is remarkable,' replied Cross before moving on. 'This man, the ex-pupil, did he buy a drink, or did he not have to with the money behind the bar?'

'Oh, he did. Refused to take one from Moreton's pot. Insisted on paying himself. You'd have to ask yourself why he bothered to come,' said Tom.

'Did he pay with cash or card?'

'Cash. I remember it, because so few people do these days.'

Cross called Maurice Simpson, the administrator of the All Saints alumni page.

'Has anyone posted on the board saying they attended Moreton's funeral?' he asked.

'No, and to be honest with you I can't think of anyone in the group who would have wanted to go.'

'An ex-pupil did go. It's possible he's not in your group. But he's obviously still very angry.'

'I'll keep my eyes open. But one thing you should understand, Sergeant, is that we often go for months, sometimes a year or so, without any activity on the board. There have actually been a few times recently where I've thought of shutting it down. But that didn't go down very well. People like it being there. When it started it really was an alumni thing, people getting in touch, posting old school photos, before it morphed into a Moreton abuse support group.' He laughed at such a notion.

'But presumably there's been a lot more activity since the murder?'

'That's true.'

'Anything stand out?'

'Not really, no.'

Cross wasn't sure he believed him but didn't press any further. He asked whether, as the moderator of the board, he'd had to delete posts. He had but wouldn't divulge what and from whom. Data protection and all that. He would willingly, with a warrant, but wasn't sure it was worth Cross's time and effort. Cross couldn't get a warrant in the current circumstances as it would have got straight back to Carson.

As convincing as the evidence against Cotterell seemed to be, Cross was still far from sure the man was guilty. There were too many imponderables, too many unanswered questions. But frustrating though it was, there was only one thing he could do. Wait until it came to trial and hope that the legal system did its job properly. Unfortunately, as Cross knew well, that wasn't always guaranteed.

49

There were dozens of advantages for Ottey having her mother live in such proximity – literally downstairs – to her and her girls. Childcare was no longer something she had to fret about. Although her mother was at pains, constantly, to remind her daughter that she did have a life of her own. When Ottey pointed out that the only times her mother left the house were to do food shops and go to choir rehearsals and the Sunday service, Cherish held this up as proof of her already hectic life. One thing they had agreed on, though, was that weekends were sacrosanct family time, unless there was something really urgent at work. Ottey had argued that as she dealt with murder her work was, by definition, urgent. But she agreed to the sentiment about weekends, in principle.

Mackenzie and Ottey had been bashing the phones and emailing women in droves over the last few weeks, talking to people in the Kent force. Not exclusively women either. But it was Warner's sexual harassment that had hit a chord with the female members of the Kent constabulary. Finally, a DI who described herself as the 'mother' of the Major Crime Department called them. She'd been made aware of their enquiries into Warner. She agreed to meet off the books and out of hours, which meant it had to be a weekend. This was fine for Mackenzie but a little more delicate for Ottey who had only recently had another conversation with Cherish about the ring-fencing of weekends. She never discussed her work with her mother, investigations were obviously confidential. But she felt she was able to tell her about the Warner problem and her need to go to Kent that weekend. This wasn't strictly speaking work, though work-related. This was part of a bigger problem in the police force. Cherish was appalled that a policeman could behave in such a way. They were supposed to be figures of trust. Mind you, the killings of black people by the police in the US and the rise of the Black Lives Matter movement told a different story. But was Josie absolutely sure about it? Yes. She had witnessed it herself. They thought briefly about making it a family day out to Canterbury. Cherish had never seen the cathedral. But the prospect of the girls being in the car for eight hours in total didn't seem that much of an attractive prospect, added to the fact that they doubtless had a full social diary, yet to be unleashed on their mother and grandmother amidst a chorus of high-pitched pleas for lifts.

So, Michael Swift found himself a long-distance chauffeur. Ottey was particularly impressed, as he'd said at the outset that he was well aware that a male presence in their actual meeting probably wasn't a great idea. That was okay, he would occupy himself. She thought it a mark of good character. Either that, or he was definitely still in the smitten-with phase of his relationship with Mackenzie. A relationship she, like everyone else in the MCU, pretended to be ignorant of.

They met DI Jacky Collins – 'I know, I know, it's been the bane of my life, especially with wise-arses in the interview room' – at her home on the outskirts of Canterbury. She was from Dublin originally, divorced, had two grown-up kids and now lived with her partner Sandra, a former probation officer.

'So, what's happened? Jesus, Warner was only with you for a few weeks,' she began as Sandra produced a cafetière of coffee and some biscuits.

They explained.

'Pepper spray!' She laughed out loud as she pictured the scene in the MCU car park. 'I'd've paid to see that. I'm sorry, I shouldn't be laughing. It must've been frightening. Having said that, you can obviously look after yourself.'

'That's okay,' replied Mackenzie.

'We just felt, like I said on the phone, that this was probably part of a pattern and if it was, we should do something to put a stop to it,' added Ottey.

Collins nodded slowly. 'I think the timing's right. Women are more willing to come forward right now. The force as a whole seems to finally want to do something about it.'

'So, tell us about him,' said Mackenzie.

'He started off in uniform in the north-west, in Manchester. He moved down to us about six years ago when he became a DI. Didn't have room for him in Manchester although it has occurred to me that they might have promoted him to get rid of a problem. Rumblings started almost as soon as he got here. Maybe his promotion made him worse or just more blatant. It's difficult to say. Harassing junior female officers, members of staff like yourself. He claimed it was all harmless banter. But it progressed quickly. He had a couple of relationships, if you can call them that, at work. They quickly fizzled out. Both women said he was controlling and violent when drunk. But none of it went up the chain.'

'Why not?' asked Ottey.

'Well, did you tell anyone, Alice? Would you have told Josie had she not walked into the kitchen?'

'No.'

'There's your answer. At the beginning maybe women thought they were one-offs. But remember he always targeted young women at the start of their careers. Women who'd only just joined the unit, who weren't sure how complaints would go down. Whether his behaviour was just the norm that they were expected to put up with. They worried it could prejudice their career if they complained. How would other people in the force react to them if they reported him? Then he overstepped the mark. He became close to the sister of a victim in a murder. It was completely unacceptable. Which isn't to say when it happened at work it was. But this crossed a line. I worked that case. The woman was emotionally vulnerable, which he simply exploited. I reported him after he'd slept with her. But the man was closing cases left, right and centre. He's even been heard to say he prefers putting villains away to sex,' Collins said.

'So, he was untouchable?' asked Ottey.

'Yes and no. Upstairs knew there was a problem. HR had been involved. He'd been sent on safety at work courses. He tried to cop off with the instructor. Can you believe that? I mean, it's a problem. That is to say, he has a problem. He's even followed women into the ladies' washroom here. He seems to think such a brazen attitude makes him more attractive. He's done it so many times it's not even funny.'

'That's unbelievable,' commented Ottey.

'Yes, but I've been keeping a log. When women come into the unit they are specifically warned by me or another female colleague about him. So they're forewarned and can be guarded. It hasn't stopped him though. But they at least know it's not a problem unique to them. The trouble is that in the last eighteen months things have taken a turn for the worse. It was almost as if as it got more difficult for him, the stakes were raised. The more of a challenge it became. The more alluring it was. I'm really sorry, I should've reached out to you. But then again, I didn't know who to reach out to in Bristol.'

'How do you mean, things have gotten worse? What are we talking about here?' Ottey asked.

Collins paused before she said it. As if hearing herself saying it out loud made it all the more real and terrible.

'He's raped three women, possibly four,' she said finally.

'What?' Mackenzie said, shocked. She wasn't sure whether it was just the fact of it, or how close she may have come to it herself.

'Why didn't you do anything?' asked Ottey.

'It's an ongoing process. But you know why. Two of them had rape kits done though,' she said.

'Do you know them?' Mackenzie asked.

'One of them. I have contacts for the other two. One is police, the others civvies.'

'What about the one you know? Is she persuadable? To come forward I mean?'

'She feels that as an isolated case it has less weight.'

'But she has DNA proof,' Mackenzie exclaimed.

'It was at her flat. He could claim it was consensual. She'll come forward if the others do. You know how it is. She doesn't want to get on the stand and face a cross examination where they basically tell her it was her fault.'

'Is she still with your unit?'

'No, she got a transfer.'

A few days later Collins sent screenshots of a WhatsApp group of police officers in Kent of whom Warner was one. It was another piece of ammunition for the time they thought they could bring Warner down. The chats pretty much covered all the bases of inappropriate and actionable behaviour of the group. Racism, sexism, jokes and comments about female officers and what they'd like to do to them. Bragging about sleeping with witnesses and junior officers.

'This is appalling,' said Ottey, genuinely shocked.

'Makes you wonder what goes on here, doesn't it?' asked Mackenzie.

'No, surely not.'

'I don't know. You don't know. Isn't that the terrifying truth of the situation?'

50

Barnaby Cotterell's trial for the murder of Alistair Moreton came up on everyone fairly quickly. Tamsin Cotterell had given birth to a healthy baby girl. Daisy-May. Cotterell wasn't there for the birth which had hit him hard.

Carson thought the speed may have something to do with Sandy Moreton's claims that he had friends in the justice department. It was strange, because there was still a lengthy backlog of cases piled up at the court. But someone, somewhere, obviously thought this one needed fast-tracking. There was the usual press interest for a murder trial, but scaled up. Not only because the victim's son was a public figure. But he was a controversial public figure who was also in a spot of trouble having suffered a resoundingly humiliating defeat in the recent by-election. The press interest was national not just local. Ottey and Cross kept their eyes on the trial and had the occasional discussion about it. They couldn't help it, even though they weren't involved. It was a bit like a jilted lover who can't keep their eyes off their ex's Instagram feed with its endless photographs of them and their glamorous new partner.

Ottey kept in touch with the in-court machinations through DC Murray. She didn't particularly like him, mainly because he was firmly in the anti-George camp in the department. This small, exclusively male club had grown in numbers since Warner's secondment. Murray's personal reading of the first few sessions in court was, unsurprisingly, that it was a slam-dunk for the prosecution. The jury was clearly taken by the narrative the prosecuting KC was putting in front of them. Painting a damning picture of a well-to-do young London couple who were classic second-homeowners. No interest in the local community. Entitled, snobbish and self-righteously affronted by an elderly local resident defending his property from their metropolitan encroachment. The case was definitely heading for a conviction. From her own reading of the media coverage, she thought Murray might be right. It did seem to be coming over like a case of a neighbour dispute getting completely out of hand and resulting in a tragic death.

As the prosecution built their case Cross received a phone call from Maurice Simpson, the administrator of the All Saints alumni page. He had some important information for Cross. So important that he insisted on travelling down from Cheltenham to meet Cross at the MCU in person. This wasn't a problem for Cross, as both Carson and Warner, who had reappeared for the trial, were in court. Warner, because it was his investigation, Carson because he wanted to be available for any media opportunities that presented themselves. For him, even being filmed walking into court and not making any comment was an important piece of self-promotion. He'd been known to time his entrances into court for the moment a national TV reporter went live on air. Carson would then be seen walking with grim determination through the back of shot.

Cross had observed over time that people wanted to travel, often some distance, to meet the police at their HQ, when they thought they had information that they felt might well be crucial to an investigation. It wasn't so much a question of maintaining secrecy, or there being a practical need to meet face to face to, say, hand over a piece of physical evidence. It was because they wanted to witness first-hand the amazed reaction of the police officers when presented with their undoubted case-cracking gold.

Cross and Ottey met Simpson in the VA suite.

'Since we spoke last I've been keeping my eye on the alumni board and any posts that have cropped up,' he said, pausing to give Cross an opportunity to express his thanks. Cross didn't take it, so Simpson was forced to continue. 'I've had to delete a lot of messages which were frankly just disrespectful. Whatever you may think of him, the man has now died. In the end it got so bad that I threatened to close the board down permanently. I have to tell you it's had quite an impact on my mental health. The vitriol. People seem to think they can say the most vile, vicious things online. As if it doesn't really count. It's as if social decency and a moral compass fly out of the window as soon as they are in front of a computer. As for the grammar and spelling, well, don't get me started.'

'Was there anything specific you wanted to tell us that meant you felt the need to travel here?' Cross asked.

'I can show you this because it wasn't actually posted on the closed group. It was posted on the individual's personal page. But he tagged the group. His page is set to public, whether he knows that or not I have no idea. But anyway, he posted this at the weekend and frankly it's beyond the pale.'

He showed Cross his phone. On it was a photograph of a certain Peter Montgomery standing over a freshly filled grave. The caption read 'Ashes to ashes, dust to dust, Alistair Moreton is no more! May the bastard rot in hell.'

'Is that definitely Moreton's grave?' Ottey asked.

'Good question,' replied Simpson. 'Hadn't thought of that, to be honest. If it's someone else's, that's almost worse.'

'I can't say for certain,' said Cross. 'There's nothing identifiable in the background. We can confirm with the vicar though.'

But what Cross was more interested in was what Montgomery had protruding from his right hand. It was an umbrella. Cross zoomed in on the handle. It was a small carved bust. From images he'd seen of the composer on the internet, Cross was fairly sure he was looking at Wolfgang Amadeus Mozart. He now definitely needed to meet with Montgomery, but thought it could and should wait until after the conclusion of the trial. Simpson was duly thanked by Ottey and asked not to tell anyone of the Montgomery post. Pleased to be part of a, in his eyes, crucial, confidence with the police, he readily agreed.

51

DI Warner's mood changed noticeably during the time the defence's case was being presented in court. It wasn't so much that the momentum had altered. It always did when the defence started to try and disassemble his investigation. But the reason he was so discombobulated a few days after the prosecution had closed was that the defence had called DS George Cross to the stand as a witness. This was practically unheard of. It was an unusual move to say the least. No one had been more surprised than Cross himself. He'd had nothing to do with the case, having been effectively sidelined by Warner and then ordered away by Carson.

Warner was of course immediately suspicious. As he was the investigating officer on the case he couldn't speak to Cross, as that could be seen as interfering with a witness. He'd discussed it with Carson the day before. Carson was as alarmed as Warner.

'Can you think of any reason they'd call George?' he began by asking Warner.

'None. You?'

'None at all.'

'Can you ask him?'

'You know very well I can't,' answered Carson, amazed that Warner had even suggested it.

'What the hell's he up to?'

'I've no idea. But knowing George I suspect he's got nothing to do with this.'

'Then why are they calling him?' Warner persisted.

'He was the first officer on the scene,' Carson suggested by way of a possible explanation.

'With you,' Warner pointed out.

'No,' began Carson. 'Oh yes...'

'Have you been called?'

'Obviously not.'

'Have Cross and Ottey carried on working the case?' Warner wondered.

'I don't think so.'

Carson leaned out of Warner's appropriated office.

'Josie, can you come in for a moment please?'

Ottey got up from her desk and walked over reluctantly. Not only because she knew what it was about, but also because she wanted to keep as far away from Warner as possible. Not out of a fear for her safety; she just found him repellent. She hoped this time round it was she who looked like she had the upper hand.

'What's going on?' Warner began by asking.

'I don't know. You tell me,' she replied.

'You know George has been called as a witness.'

'I do.'

'Why?'

'Because he told me.'

'You know what I mean,' replied Carson.

'I have no idea.'

'Why has he been called, Josie?'

'I just said. I have no idea.'

'Have you spoken to him about it?' asked Warner.

'Of course not. Why would I?'

'Are you not in the least bit interested?' asked Warner.

'Of course I am. It's just that you know as well as I do that he's a stickler for the rules and wouldn't tell me even if I did,' she said before returning to her desk. 'If I were you, I'd be more concerned with the defence's intention to call Dr Swift.'

★

Cross had been called to the defending barrister's chambers to discuss being a witness. He understood that it had come at the behest of Cotterell's wife after his visit to her.

'Is it true you weren't entirely happy with the charging of my client?' asked Cotterell's defence barrister.

'It is, yes,' replied Cross.

'Can you tell me why?'

'Of course, but I don't think you'll be able to use it in court.'

'Perhaps you'll let me decide that.'

Cross then explained his view of the CCTV of Cotterell outside Moreton's cottage. The barrister listened intently.

'That's a convincing interpretation,' said the barrister.

'It's not *an* interpretation. That implies there could be others. It is the only interpretation based on the evidence,' Cross retorted.

'Did you have an expert analyse the footage?' asked the barrister.

'I did.'

52

Cross sat patiently in the witness suite in the Bristol Crown Court building. It was somewhere he was quite familiar with. He was eventually called by an usher and taken into the modern courtroom. He entered the witness box and affirmed that he would tell the truth. He opted to stand. The jury were opposite him. He saw Carson and Warner in the public gallery. He had specifically asked Ottey and Mackenzie not to come. But Alice had insisted, as she was coming to see her boyfriend perform, not Cross. It had taken ages to choose Michael's outfit for court. His devotion to all things gothic meant he'd wanted to come in a feather coat and wear make-up but was persuaded that not only would this mean the jury might take him less seriously but also if Cross saw him like that he would probably never work with him again. That clinched it. He wore a black suit with a black shirt and black tie. He still looked like a large raven in a suit, she thought. But quite a sweet one.

'DS Cross, you're a member of the Avon and Somerset Police. Is that correct?'

'It is.'

'Specifically, the Major Crime Unit or MCU. Yes?'

'Correct.'

'Were you the first officer on the scene on the 18th of September last year?'

'Together with my CO, DCI Ben Carson, yes.'

The barrister paused for a moment then asked, 'Tell me, is it usual for a detective who is first on the scene to be removed from an investigation?'

Cross thought about it for a moment.

'That would depend on a number of circumstances,' he replied.

'Such as?'

'If the deceased was a family member or in some way connected to the decedent.'

'Of course, but in a normal course of events you wouldn't expect this to happen.'

'I wouldn't have thought so, no.'

'DS Cross, were you removed from this investigation?'

'I was not.'

'But you became less involved in the investigation after DI Warner took over. Is that correct?'

'Yes.'

'Do you know why this was? Perhaps I should explain to the jury, Your Honour, and indeed yourself, that DS George Cross is an incredibly successful police detective. In fact, he has the highest conviction rate in the Avon and Somerset Police.'

'By far,' said a voice from the witness box. The barrister turned to Cross who then repeated, 'By far. The highest conviction rate, by far.'

'Indeed. So why were you sidelined in this way by DI Warner?' asked the barrister.

'I don't know.'

'Any suspicions?'

'It might have been my objection to his smoking in one of the pool cars. It's against department policy, you see,' he said directly to the jury, as if to make sure they had the whole picture. 'Because of the passive smoking effects on other occupants. It does also leave an awful stale odour in the car for days.'

There was laughter in the court which puzzled Cross. This was a murder trial after all.

'Isn't it true you were moved off the case because you didn't like the direction the investigation was taking?' continued the barrister.

'Why the hell isn't the prosecution objecting?' Warner whispered to Carson.

'I suspect it's because they've come across George before and know there's no need,' he answered quietly.

'No, that's not true,' replied Cross.

'Then why?'

Cross thought about this for a moment.

'I think it's probably because Warner doesn't like me,' said Cross. Again, some titters in the court. 'He moved a desk into my office and I made a complaint. I'm allowed an office of my own as I find working in open areas difficult.'

'We understand you expressed reservations about the charging of our client to his wife. Is that correct?' the barrister asked him.

'Objection. Hearsay.'

'Overruled.'

'Why was that?'

'It mainly concerned my conclusions from viewing the CCTV footage from Mr Moreton's camera the night of the murder,' replied Cross.

'Which were?' asked the barrister, chancing his arm.

The prosecution barrister decided to bring this to an end.

'Objection. The opinion of the witness of the footage is irrelevant to this court, Your Honour. He isn't an expert witness as far as I know.'

'Sustained.'

'Your Honour, I simply want to ask the witness about a factual observation which doesn't require any expertise. As my learned friend is well aware I have an expert witness coming to the stand shortly.

'DS Cross, could you tell the jury your concern when you first saw the footage?' the barrister asked.

'It wasn't just the first time. It was each and every time I saw it,' Cross specified.

'Indeed. Please tell the court.'

'My concern is that the defendant doesn't seem to have anything in his hand. Specifically, the chisel.'

'We've been told he lost it.'

'Which presupposes he went into Mr Moreton's house for some reason, saw the chisel in plain view, picked it up and killed him,' said Cross.

'That is the prosecution's suggestion, yes.'

'If we accept that assumption or narrative, how does the chisel end up in the front garden?' Cross asked. 'He entered by the quickest route, the back door. Why would he then leave by the front, on the furthest side of the house from the car?'

'Perhaps he threw it?' suggested the defence half-heartedly.

'Only if he's able to throw it round the corner of a building,' replied Cross.

It was obvious to Carson what the defence were trying to do. They were trying to build a picture of the investigation team being at odds, with some of them not at all convinced by his guilt. Cross's observation about the chisel was simply a way of introducing an element of doubt into what had up until this point been pretty damning evidence. The barrister was opening their minds up to be receptive to Swift's analysis of the CCTV.

Michael Swift was then called to the stand.

53

Mackenzie had instructed Swift to look relaxed in his suit which he attempted to do with moderate success. He moved across the court to the witness stand with as much reverence as an undertaker approaching a coffin at the end of a service. Albeit an undertaker from a very fashionable funeral directors. On account of his size the barrister had asked him to sit throughout his testimony, as he thought his height might be a distraction for the jury.

'Dr Swift, what is your role in Avon and Somerset Police?' the barrister began.

'I'm a forensic investigator,' he replied.

'Any particular field of expertise?'

'Several,' came the deadpan response. This caused Mackenzie to giggle involuntarily, earning her a withering look from Warner, which in turn made her even happier.

'Does that include analysis of CCTV footage?'

'It does. But in this case as there has been no claim of digital manipulation or interference of the footage my remit was purely geometrical analysis.'

'Can you explain to the jury what that means?'

'It means I analysed the footage together with the geography of the immediate location to ascertain as accurately as possible what happened.'

'Perhaps you could lead us through it in some detail?'

'Of course.'

The footage was replayed on several monitors in the

courtroom. Swift controlled it with a remote control given to him by an usher.

'As you can see, the defendant comes out of his barn with a bag which he places on the rear seat of the car. He then stops and looks up at the cottage.'

'When you say "up", where do you mean?'

'He's looking at the upper part of the cottage.'

He then brought up various stills with lines of sight drawn on them.

'As you can see from the calculations the defendant is looking at the top of the cottage.'

'So, you would say, in your expert opinion, that he is not looking at the end of the path as the prosecution claims.'

'Definitely not. The angle is completely wrong for that. His face would be angled further right in the picture, to his left.'

'So, you would dispute the prosecution's claim that the victim came to the end of the cottage path to shout at the defendant?' the barrister asked.

'That is out of my remit. What I can tell you categorically is that the defendant never looked at the end of the path at any moment for the duration of the footage.'

'Perhaps the victim appeared at an upstairs window.'

'There are no upstairs windows on that side of the cottage.'

'But something happened that made him look up?'

'That's one interpretation, yes.'

The barrister turned to the jury.

'I would suggest that Dr Swift's observations and technical analysis contradict the prosecution's claim that the defendant was reacting to something shouted at him by the victim at the end of the cottage path. That what actually happened was entirely in line with the defendant's claim. That he heard a commotion upstairs in the cottage, thereby attracting his attention. Dr Swift, from the timings stamped on the footage, how long would you say the defendant was in the victim's cottage?' the barrister asked.

'He was inside the cottage for roughly thirty-one seconds.'

'Thirty-one seconds,' the barrister said, turning to the jury. 'That's just half a minute in which, according to the prosecution, to go inside, presumably look for the victim downstairs if he was at the end of the path, realise he has to be upstairs, find him, have an altercation with him, see the chisel, pick it up and stab the victim in the chest. Watch as he falls down the stairs, then run out of the front door, not the back door which was nearer, drop the chisel in the garden and get back to the car.'

'But the fact is he came out of the back door. Had he used the front door coming from the front garden, he would be entering the camera's field of vision from the right. As it is he reappears almost directly below the camera which is mounted directly above the back door,' Swift concluded.

'Indeed. Thank you for that further detail. But going back to the period of thirty-one seconds. Is it really long enough to go in as I described, look for the victim, find him upstairs, stab him, watch him fall down the stairs, then climb over him and leave the cottage? Or is it more likely to be just enough time for the defendant to go into the cottage, discover the victim's body at the bottom of the stairs, feel his pulse, ascertain he was dead and leave?'

He posed this question to the jury, some of whom made notes.

'Dr Swift,' the defence barrister continued, 'in your role as forensic investigator, did you attend the scene?'

'I did.'

'And did you examine the body?'

'I did.'

'Just for clarity: although you observed the wounds they are not within your remit. Is that correct?'

'Yes, that is the job of the forensic pathologist whom I work alongside. My work with the body was to examine it for any trace elements, any evidence such as cloth fragments, blood, DNA.'

'And what did you find?'

'On the body?'

'Yes.'

'There were two bite wounds to the victim's legs.'

'These were later identified as dog bites, is that correct?'

'Yes.'

'Did you examine the bites?'

'I did not. That was done by the forensic pathologist, Dr Clare Hawkins, who found some hair as well as DNA from saliva.'

'And what did that evidence tell you?'

'The hairs and saliva were both canine. From the DNA we were able to specify the breed. The dog, and the evidence suggests there was just the one, that bit the victim was a Rhodesian Ridgeback.'

This caused a slight murmur in the courtroom.

'I see, and of course we are all aware,' the barrister said for the benefit of the murmurers, 'that the defendant is the owner of two such dogs.'

'That is correct.'

'Could I take you back to the CCTV footage?'

'Of course.'

'Could you go back to the moment the defendant walks from the car into the cottage?'

Swift did so, the image appearing on the various monitors.

'Are you able to zoom in on the back of the vehicle? Specifically, the luggage compartment.'

'I can.'

Swift zoomed in on the footage till he reached a silhouette of two dogs' heads looking over the back seat of the car from the luggage compartment.

'And what can we see there, Dr Swift?'

'The defendant's dogs in the car.'

'Are you sure?'

'Yes, you can tell from their large floppy ears which is characteristic of the breed,' Swift replied.

'Where they remain for the entire time the car was parked on its return. Just to clarify, they were also in the car upon its return.'

'Yes.'

'So, we can safely conclude from that, that the defendant's dogs didn't bite the victim that night?'

'We can.'

'Let me save my learned friend the bother of remembering to ask the next question. Could the dogs have bitten the victim at another time, say earlier the same day?'

'It would be possible, had the forensic pathologist not determined that the bites were inflicted on the victim at the same time as the stab wound and the skull fracture.'

'You also examined the victim's dog.'

'Ricky, yes.'

'Why was that?'

'He had some blood on his teeth. Not his blood nor his owner's blood. It was canine blood.'

'Dare I ask whether you know which breed?'

'It was a Rhodesian Ridgeback and the DNA was a match for the canine saliva found on the victim.'

'So, we're back with the Rhodesian Ridgebacks?'

'We are. But not the defendant's.'

'Go on.'

'A vet drew blood samples from both of the defendant's dogs. Neither of them are a match.'

The barrister paused, as if surprised by this information although he was obviously familiar with it, to ensure it had truly sunk in with the jury.

'What does this mean?'

'It means another dog attacked the victim at the time of his murder.'

'Another dog, belonging to someone else?' the barrister asked for the sake of clarity.

'Unless the defendant owns a third dog of the same breed we don't know about.'

'He does not. So, the dog belongs to someone else. Someone else other than the defendant who was in the cottage that night. The actual murderer.'

Warner looked a little shell-shocked.

'Did you check any of this with Swift?' Carson hissed at Warner.

'Which?'

'Well, the footage for a start.'

'No,' he said almost inaudibly. But the barrister wasn't finished yet.

'One further question if I may, Dr Swift?'

'Of course,' replied Swift all the more genially having noticed Carson's snatched exchange with Warner.

'The murder weapon,' the barrister stated.

'The chisel?' asked Swift.

'Yes. I believe you found traces of the defendant's DNA on the chisel.'

'That's correct.'

'Which is hardly surprising as it's been established that it was his chisel that he'd misplaced.'

'Yes.'

'Was there any other evidence on the chisel?'

'Yes, a partial fingerprint.'

'The victim, or the defendant's wife perhaps?' enquired the brief.

'No. Neither were a match. It's an, as yet, unidentified third party.'

'Perhaps the owner of the unidentified dog,' the barrister suggested to the jury.

The existence of this print had of course been disclosed to the prosecution who obviously didn't want it brought up. The defence had bided their time and, judging by the look on the faces of some of the jurors, had done so to good effect.

The defence rested its case and the court adjourned for closing statements in the morning. Carson turned once again to Warner.

'Were you aware of the partial print?' he asked.

But Warner didn't answer. He just got up and left the courtroom.

54

Cross and Ottey watched the news coverage of the case that night. Moreton was filmed trying to make his way through the massive, heaving throng of media that had assembled. They knew from the past weeks that Moreton was never one to offer 'no comment'. That would presumably just be a wasted opportunity in his book. Swift's and Cross's evidence had been a hammer blow for the prosecution. The media used it as an excuse to ask him again about his by-election result.

'How do you feel the trial is going after today's bombshell from the defence?' he was asked.

'I'm not sure it's appropriate or even legal for me to comment on the proceedings at this juncture,' he replied.

The seat-warmer out of the way, the reporter came to the point immediately.

'Will you be seeking another seat to stand for election, if one comes up?'

'Of course. Why on earth shouldn't I?' he scoffed.

'Self-respect?' suggested another reporter over the heads of others. This made Moreton stop as if accepting a challenge.

'And what source of drivel are you from?' he asked.

'The BBC,' came the reply.

'Well, there's a surprise. Now if you'll excuse me.'

'Were you surprised by the margin of defeat in your constituency?' asked another reporter.

'Disappointed. None of this would have happened without the so-called bullying report. It was a complete put-up job.'

'Are you saying there's no truth at all in the report?'

'Other people's truths, not mine.'

'What makes you say it's a put-up job?'

Again, Moreton stopped as if signalling he had something worthwhile and important to point out.

'Look, the civil servant at the centre of this witch hunt and I have a long history.'

'You were at school together – is that correct?'

'Yes, and he was as much of a troublemaker then as he is now.'

'In what way?'

'He's been a constant source of conflict. My father would tell you as much. But as you know he can't as he's been recently murdered by his neighbour,' he said with outrageous grandstanding. A collarless-shirted individual with wig hair whispered urgently in his ear.

'Allegedly,' he repeated with obvious reluctance.

'Your father was a headmaster.'

'Have you been attending the trial or read any newspapers recently?' he asked combatively.

'I have.'

'Then that's a somewhat pointless question, isn't it?'

'It was actually a statement not a question.'

'Well, pointless, whichever way you frame it. It's all on record. My father was indeed headmaster. What might not be on record is that Richard Brook never got over my being appointed head boy and taking a sound beating at my hands in front of the whole school. If that sounds small-minded it's because that's exactly what he is.'

'Brook! That was the boy Maurice Simpson told us about. He's the civil servant mandarin,' said Cross out loud, angry at himself.

'How did you miss that, George?' asked Ottey, tongue in cheek as she had no idea who this Brook was. She immediately regretted it as she saw his crestfallen face.

'Are you watching this?' asked Mackenzie as she came into Cross's office. 'The civil servant behind the report is the boy,

Brook, Maurice Simpson told us about,' she stated in amazement. She took one look at Cross's face and said, 'Ah...'

'My question is this. Is this report just another indication of how far Richard Brook would go to get back at me and my late father? As childish as that sounds I believe it to be the truth,' Moreton finished by saying.

Cross wasn't entirely sure what to think at this point. He had read the reactions, of which there were plenty online, in print and on TV about the conclusion of the Moreton bullying report. But not the report itself. He'd had no reason to. Moreton's reaction was the fairly predictable denial of everything, discrediting the inquiry itself, that modern politicians obviously learned on an updated media course somewhere. Moreton blamed a conspiracy in the civil service which now opened the door for anyone to have a go at ministers in office. It had become open season. But all the separate allegations, from different people, at different times, in different locations had many striking similarities. Too many. Some of the instances were just verbal, shouting and swearing, humiliation of people and their work in front of others. But some were also physical. Mobile phones being thrown, a computer screen smashed, even a wastepaper basket, into which he had thrown some 'inferior' work, being set on fire. Some instances of humiliation had occurred in public and had been caught on people's camera phones. Moreton claimed the footage had been digitally altered. The fallback for any ultimately desperate denial. But Richard Brook being the author of the report was definitely of interest.

55

The closing statements in *R v Cotterell* were finally made by the prosecution and the defence. The representatives from the MCU – Carson, Warner and Murray – were all in attendance. To Carson's mind, sitting next to Warner again, it felt like the pendulum in the case had swung firmly in the defence's favour after Cross's and Swift's appearances in the witness box. He was quietly furious that Warner had been so cavalier with the loose ends such as the DNA, and had clearly not examined the CCTV footage in detail. He knew that none of these were mistakes that George Cross would have made. Warner had utilised the evidence which suited his case and ignored what didn't. His overriding concern should this go the way of a 'not guilty' verdict was damage limitation and blame avoidance for himself. Thankfully, bringing Warner over from Kent had been the chief superintendent's idea not his. So at least he was in the clear there. But he knew that his supervision of the investigation didn't show him in a good light. As they sat waiting for the judge to appear, he filled the anticipatory vacuum by trying to put himself in the position of one of the jurors, having listened to the closing statements and the evidence they'd heard. What he concluded was that the defence hadn't just demonstrated that there was sufficient doubt over Cotterell's guilt. He felt Swift's analysis of the CCTV and the presence of a third party's DNA being on the murder weapon were fairly emphatic. Added to this, the fact that the defendant's dogs remained in his car throughout the duration of the time he was supposedly killing Moreton was the final nail in the coffin of Warner's case. There was no doubt in

Carson's mind now that they had got the wrong man.

The judge finally appeared and made his closing remarks. He then left followed by the jury who each seemed to stand up slowly as if the weight of their impending decision bore down on them.

It was Carson's turn to stand up and leave without a word to his neighbour.

Back at the MCU, Carson summoned Cross and Ottey.

'Right, there's no easy way to say this but I think DI Warner's case is not as watertight as we might have thought when we charged him.'

'Just to clarify. When you say "we" do you in fact mean "you"?' asked Cross.

This of course immediately caused Ottey to smile, which she attempted to hide with an involuntary cough. Carson noted it but turned to Cross and answered reluctantly, 'Yes. In retrospect Bobby's rush to arrest, and charge, does seem a little precipitate and short-sighted as I'm aware you pointed out at the time.'

'Do you think the jury will come back with a not guilty?' asked Ottey.

'I certainly hope so,' Carson replied.

'But I thought—' she began.

'Whatever happens, I'm reopening this investigation,' Carson interrupted.

'Even if they find him guilty?'

'Particularly if they find him guilty, because then I believe we'll have sent the wrong man to prison.'

'Okay, so thinking this through... If they do find him guilty, how are you going to square reopening the investigation with the brass?' Ottey asked.

'Let me deal with that. But you should both consider the case reopened. George, what are your thoughts?'

'That you shouldn't have charged him in the first place.'

'Yes, yes, I think we've covered that. How do you want to proceed?'

'I have no idea. I need to go back to my office and formulate a plan of action,' he said, getting up in order to do just that.

'All right. Get to it. Oh, and, George, for what it's worth, I'm sorry.'

Cross thought about this for a moment then just nodded, said 'yes' and left.

Ottey smiled at Carson. 'Good for you, boss,' she said.

When Ottey got back to Cross's office she asked Mackenzie to join them.

'Well, I'm not surprised,' was her immediate reaction when informed of Carson's new instruction. 'Michael is convinced Cotterell is innocent. The CCTV evidence just doesn't stack up with the prosecution's narrative.'

'I think Dr Swift's testimony was crucial to the defence case,' replied Cross.

'So, George, where do you want to begin?' asked Ottey.

'I think we need to bring Peter Montgomery in for questioning and search his property,' he replied.

'The bloke who posed over Moreton's grave?' asked Ottey.

'Yes,' Mackenzie replied.

'Shouldn't we wait until the verdict is in?' asked Ottey.

'Why?' responded Cross. 'Carson told us to investigate whatever the verdict.'

56

Peter Montgomery was in his late fifties and lived in Winchester. Ottey informed the Hampshire Police that they wanted to make an arrest and conduct a search. She asked for their help. When Cross had applied for the warrant, the magistrate expressed some surprise that it related to a case already in the crown court. One in which the jury was out considering a verdict, moreover. The magistrate, however, knew Cross quite well and Ottey sensed an amused admiration in him, that Avon and Somerset's most intriguing detective was yet again swimming against the tide, together with a curiosity to see how this one panned out. He granted them the warrant.

Montgomery lived on a suburban, weary-looking, life-worn estate just outside the city in the top half of a sixties house that had been converted into two flats. They rang the doorbell early in the morning, deeming that a forced entry wasn't necessary. He opened the door in a pair of pyjama shorts and a string vest. He was visibly and understandably alarmed at their presence, but no more alarmed than Cross, Ottey and the other officers. The man was wearing a white sweatband of the John McEnroe era round his forehead. The sweatband was bloodstained, as was the majority of his scalp which was covered in red, bloody scabs. He looked like he'd been dipped upside down in a chip fat fryer.

'What on earth has happened to you, Mr Montgomery?' asked Ottey.

'I've just come back from Turkey,' he replied.

She wanted to ask him if he'd forgotten to pack his sunscreen but held back just in time. 'Right,' she replied.

'I've had a hair transplant.'

'When?'

'Just this last weekend,' he replied. 'My wife left me, you see,' he said as if this was an understandable reason.

'Because you went bald?' asked Cross.

'Not just because of that, no. But I don't think it helped, in all honesty. I'm back on the market now so I thought I'd do some renovations,' he said, as if discussing property and directing it at Ottey on the off chance she might be interested.

'We have a search warrant,' Cross informed him, holding it up.

'What for?'

'To search your flat,' Cross replied.

'No, I meant what are you looking for?' he asked as he walked up the stairs to his flat and they followed him.

'Well, if we told you, that would spoil all the fun. The clue's in the word "search",' Ottey said.

This comment perplexed Cross and it wasn't for the first time. Why did Ottey always talk about fun when they were investigating a murder? It just didn't make sense to him. Of course, Ottey had replied in this way because she herself didn't even know what they were looking for and couldn't have told Montgomery anyway.

The first noticeable thing about the flat was that it was lined from floor to ceiling with wooden and cardboard cases of wine. All the way up the side of the stairs and in every single room including the bathroom.

'I don't have a drink problem if that's what you're thinking,' Montgomery said.

'I'm not. I know you run an online wine business and with the recent change in your circumstances, both domestic and financial, it looks like you've lost your storage facilities,' Cross replied.

'Yes, that's all true. Except for the wines in bond.'

The flat had an acrid, vinegary, smell of spilt wine. It was almost overbearing.

'Sorry about the smell. A few bottles got smashed in the move. It happens.'

Several surfaces in the kitchen and the living room were covered with open bottles of wine, all about two thirds full, with corks stuffed in the top.

'I have a wine blog and do live tastings and recommendations,' he explained as he saw them looking at the bottles. 'Can I get dressed?'

'Yes. A constable will have to go with you though,' said Ottey.

'You haven't asked us why we're here,' observed Cross.

'What? Oh no. I suppose it was the shock. Why are you here?'

'We're investigating the murder of Alistair Moreton,' replied Cross. This seemed to throw Montgomery.

'I see. But isn't that at trial? The jury are deliberating their verdict, aren't they?'

'Correct.'

'Okay, so I'm confused. I had nothing to do with that. I mean, you have your man, so why are you here?' he asked.

'The verdict isn't in,' replied Ottey.

'True. What's more, that CCTV footage did seem pretty good for the defence,' said Montgomery.

'You've been following the trial?' asked Cross.

Montgomery hesitated.

'Only like everyone else. You know. On the news and such. In the paper, that kind of thing,' he said. 'Just like everyone else,' he repeated as if to justify and underline the obvious innocence of his interest. 'I'll go and get changed.' Cross looked at the man for a moment and tried to ignore the fact that he looked like he'd been recently scalped. He seemed familiar. Then it came to him. He'd been in the public gallery when Cross gave evidence.

Cross and Ottey looked round the flat. It didn't take long as not only was it small, but all of his things seemed to be in packing boxes. It looked like he'd either not lived there long or he'd just packed and was moving out. There were no pictures on the walls. But there was a packing case filled with framed photographs. Cross found a box that immediately interested him. It was marked 'SCHOOL' in indelible black ink. In it were framed formal school photographs with their years and names embossed on them. What stood out in various team photographs was the fact that Montgomery was something of a peripheral figure in all of them. On closer inspection, in a football team photograph he was wearing a referee's uniform. Various cricket elevens in which he stood to one side at the back with a large book under his arm. He was the scorer. It was as if he wasn't a true participant but, having kept them, he obviously didn't feel this way.

At the bottom of the box were photographs from All Saints. Three photographs of the entire school with Alistair Moreton sitting plumb centre flanked by the second master and the head boy. In one of the photographs the head boy was Sandy Moreton. Cross ultimately found what he was looking for, leaning against the wall near the front door, and placed it in an evidence bag. Mozart. They must've walked straight past it on their way in.

The boxes marked 'SCHOOL' were all seized, as were a few others marked 'correspondence', together with a laptop, a desktop computer and journals. They were all logged and put in the boot of Ottey's car. Montgomery finally appeared from the bathroom. He then slept the entire way to Bristol in the back of the car. The two officers had seen this happen many times. Experience told them that there was nothing to be read into it. Some people slept because they were sleeping something off. Some because they didn't want to speak. Some, because they were so confident they hadn't done anything wrong that they were completely relaxed. Some, because they very much had done something wrong and had decided there was nothing they could do about it, so were resigned to their fate.

He had expressed no surprise when they finally informed him that he was being arrested on suspicion of the murder of Alistair Moreton. He didn't object. Didn't react in any way. But

Cross got the distinct impression from the way his eyes were just fixed in the middle distance, not reactive, not following anything going on around him, that the man was considering his options.

57

'Mr Montgomery, are you clear why you've been arrested?' Cross began in the interview room back at the MCU.

'You think I murdered Alistair Moreton.'

'We think it's a possibility, yes. Just to be entirely clear. I don't *think* you murdered Mr Moreton. But I do think it's a possibility which your being here gives us an opportunity to explore.'

'It's not like you gave me a choice,' Montgomery retorted.

'That is true. You've been arrested on suspicion. The reason for this is that you can be interviewed under caution in case it turns out that you did indeed kill the victim,' Cross informed him.

'Mr Montgomery, where were you on the evening of seventeenth of September last year?' Ottey asked.

'I was at home.'

'Anyone else with you?'

'You seem particularly clear in that recollection,' interrupted Cross.

'That's because I've had plenty of time to think about it this morning.'

'Mr Montgomery, did you kill Alistair Moreton?' asked Ottey.

'I did, several times,' Montgomery stated and then seemed to smile with satisfaction that he'd momentarily silenced the room. 'In my head. There's hardly been a day in my life when I haven't imagined causing that man harm.'

'Did you kill him on the seventeenth of September?' Ottey persisted.

'Unfortunately not, no.'

'Why unfortunately?' asked Cross.

'Because I would've liked nothing more than to put an end to the bastard.'

'Why's that?'

'Payback.'

'For what?'

'The way he treated me, us. All of us in that hellhole. It was criminal. He'd be locked up if he did that these days.'

'Mr Montgomery, have you ever been to Crockerne?' asked Cross.

'I have not.'

'Are you sure about that?'

'I am. Don't even know where it is,' Montgomery went on.

'It's on the River Avon, next door to Shirehampton,' Cross explained.

'Means nothing to me.'

'How long were you at All Saints school?' asked Cross.

'Four long miserable years.'

'At what age?'

'Nine to thirteen.'

'And how old are you now?'

'Fifty-three.'

'So, you left school forty years ago this year.'

'I did.'

'An anniversary of sorts,' Cross observed.

'If you wish.'

'Is that why you chose to kill him now?'

'I didn't kill him.'

'Why, after so long, are you still preoccupied with the headmaster of your prep school? I mean, it was so long ago,' Ottey asked.

'I suppose you could say that the experience scarred me.'

'Did he beat you?' asked Cross.

Montgomery scoffed at this question. 'You'd be hard pressed to find anyone, not a single pupil, who wasn't beaten. No one got through that school without feeling that bastard's cane across his arse.'

'Some people would argue that's just how it was then. Different times,' said Ottey.

'Whatever,' Montgomery dismissed this with a weary tone, which suggested it was something he'd heard many times before.

'Why has it remained with you so keenly?' asked Cross, who was genuinely interested in the answer.

Montgomery took his time to answer this one.

'Because he was so cruel. So relentlessly, appallingly, maliciously cruel. He clearly enjoyed it. He must've. He put so much time and energy into it.'

'It sounds terrible,' Ottey offered.

'It was. But it wasn't just the beatings. The man was insane and it was even worse when he was drunk. Like the infamous fire alarm night,' he said.

'What was that?' asked Cross.

'As a boarding school you had to have a fire alarm drill once a term. The alarm would go off and we all had to troop to the gym across the courtyard and do roll call. One night we all went to bed as usual at eight. It was the Easter term, February, I think. It had been snowing. The alarm went off at nine and we trooped across the courtyard in our dressing gowns and slippers in the snow. I mean that, for a start – why choose that night? He could've waited till the snow had thawed. But no. We had the roll call, which he took. A hundred and fifty names, it took a while. Then back to bed, everyone freezing and shivering under their sheets. Goes without saying the central heating was switched off in the dorms at night. Then at ten fifteen the alarm goes off again. Same routine. All troop through the snow in our now damp slippers. Roll call. Back to bed. Bit odd, twice in a night like that, we thought. But he'd only just got started. Eleven thirty the alarm went off again. All troop out. He's there again, glass of whisky in hand this time. It happened again at one fifteen, quarter to three, four forty-five and finally just before six. He was there every time. Well, I assume he was because at six I never made it to the gym. I went half asleep to the bathroom and started cleaning my teeth, thinking it was time to get up. Matron came and told me it was another fire alarm, but I think she must've seen how exhausted I was and took me back to bed. She probably got into trouble for that,' he told them.

Ottey looked horrified. 'That's unbelievable. Are you sure—' she began.

'And there you are!' he interrupted. 'That's what still upsets me to this day. It can't be true. It's so unimaginable, it has to be just that. The imagination of a small boy. It can't have really happened. Surely not. No one in their right mind would do that. My parents happened to come down the next day to take me out to lunch at my grandmother's. I fell asleep in the back of the car. I was so sleepy at lunch. Could hardly keep my eyes open. My mother asked me why I was so tired. I told her. They didn't believe me. My mother said I had to be exaggerating. My father told me not to lie. They didn't believe me. They never did. I've spent my whole life worrying whether people think I'm telling the truth. I have a problem trusting people with things because, what if they don't believe me? Shouldn't my parents have believed me? My father didn't believe me till the day he died. It was like he couldn't. Because in some way it was a criticism of him. But it meant he was sceptical about anything I said even as an adult. Alistair Moreton instilled that in him.'

'You're claiming it's affected you psychologically?' asked Cross.

'You see? Look how you frame the question. With doubt. Too fucking right it did. It's left me always thinking I've done the wrong thing. That I might be in trouble somehow. Because with him you never knew when you were in trouble. But the consequences were always painful and humiliating. Nowadays if I send an email or a text and don't get a speedy answer, I'm convinced I must've said something wrong. I'm anxious all the bloody time and yes, I do blame him. He tortured us at such an impressionable age. You have no idea what it's like not to be listened to.'

Cross thought about this for a moment. 'I do actually, it used to happen to me all the time. But not any more,' he said.

'Really? Why's that?'

'Because I tend to be always right,' said Cross.

Ottey smiled.

'Why are you still so bitter?' asked Cross.

'Why? Because that man cost me everything.'

'Such as?' Cross asked.

'My wife and kids for a start. She divorced me. Told me she'd had enough. That I should move on with my life. What she meant was she couldn't stand the man he'd made me into.'

This was a little too much for Ottey, who wanted to grab him by the shoulders and give him a good shake. She wanted to point out that he'd had plenty of opportunities to shape the man he'd become after leaving that school at the age of thirteen. Even though he was irritating the hell out of her, she decided against it.

'It makes you wonder about the people running this country and their outlook on life,' she said later. 'How it and they were formed at such a young age. So many of them grew up in a system like Montgomery where being beaten was the norm. Where you weren't believed. Then you become an adult with all those issues. It's deeply worrying that a privileged education can screw you up so much. But you still end up in positions of authority.'

'You and my folks would really get along,' was the only response she got from Mackenzie. Ottey hoped Maggie Norman would get her piece written. Not that it would make any difference probably.

58

'The All Saints alumni page on Facebook. Are you a member?' Cross asked Montgomery.

'I am.'

'Would that include membership of the closed group Victims of AFM?' Cross continued.

'Yes.'

'Who is AFM?'

'Alistair Moreton, obviously,' Montgomery answered.

'Did you interact with this group on a regular basis?'

'You wouldn't be asking if you didn't already know.'

'Please answer the question,' said Ottey.

'I do.'

'Quite a few of your posts were deleted or not approved by the group's moderator – is that true?' asked Cross.

'Maurice Simpson? He's a wanker, that man. He knows nothing. I was only saying what others were thinking. He doesn't understand, because he's persuaded himself it was all okay. That most of it never happened. He's in denial.'

'Were others thinking of killing him? Inflicting violence on him?' Cross paused. Montgomery held his look. The solicitor looked slightly alarmed. 'You made several unambiguously violent, abusive threats against Mr Moreton. Which I would imagine were against Facebook's policies as much as Mr Simpson's. Also, bizarre fantasies about retribution, which for the benefit of doubt I'm going to imagine were made under the influence of alcohol or some other substance. Do you take drugs, Mr Montgomery?' Cross asked.

'I do not.'

Cross drew a line through something in his notes.

'Did you really want to get a bamboo cane and "shove it so far up his arse it would give his tongue a splinter"?' Cross asked.

'Probably,' said Montgomery laughing. 'You have to admit that is quite a good one.'

'This one I don't quite understand. Albeit it's on a similar theme. "I'd like to get hold of Mozart and shove it up Moreton's fundament so far his head comes out of his mouth." What does that mean?' Cross asked.

Montgomery thought for a moment before answering, 'No comment.'

'What has a composer of some genius got to do with all this?' Cross asked.

'No comment.'

'Is it a typo?'

'No comment.'

'But a typo of what? I've tried to work it out. I'm quite a fan of puzzles. Jigsaw puzzles, sudoku, cryptic crosswords. Are you a fan of puzzles, Mr Montgomery?' Cross went on. 'But I've studied a computer keyboard and tried to see if maybe the keys adjacent to M-O-Z-A-R-T might form another more plausible instrument that you might want to use in this way. But to no avail. Then I thought it probably wasn't a typo at all as you specifically say you want to see Mozart's head protrude from your chosen victim's mouth.'

'No comment.'

'My father used to have a collection of busts of composers. Mind you, he had a collection of lots of things,' Cross reflected.

'Tell us about Sandy Moreton,' Ottey chimed in.

'A loathsome little man. What about him?'

'Were you a direct contemporary of his?' she went on.

'I wasn't. He was three years above me, unfortunately.'

'Why was that unfortunate?' asked Cross.

'As a senior he always picked on the junior boys. He became even worse when he became head boy.'

'When he beat other boys himself?' asked Ottey.

Montgomery laughed.

'Why's that funny?' asked Cross.

'Because, to his credit I suppose, he never did. I mean, I think he did once or twice but that was it. Always threatening to. Walking round the place swinging his cane about.'

'Why do you think that was?' asked Cross.

'You'd have to ask him. Maybe he realised the perversity of the idea, even at that age.'

'Unlike his father who was rather partial to a beating,' suggested Ottey.

'I've never heard it put like that before. But I think you're right. I think there was, I mean there had to be, an element of gratification in it for him. It was like the man was obsessed with the idea of beating us.'

'Have you seen Sandy Moreton recently?' Cross asked.

'Yes.'

'When?'

'At the funeral.'

Cross paused very deliberately and then flicked through his notes very carefully.

'That's odd. Because you just told us you'd never been to Crockerne,' Cross said.

'I didn't put two and two together,' Montgomery replied weakly.

'That the funeral was in Alistair Moreton's village?' asked Cross. Montgomery said nothing.

'Did the two of you speak?' Cross continued.

'No. I kept my distance.'

'Why was that?'

'Well, I was hardly going to offer him my condolences, was I?'

'Isn't that the point of going to a funeral?' asked Cross.

'No, and I wasn't paying my respects either.'

'So, what were you doing there?' asked Ottey.

'It was, what's the American word for it? "Closure". It felt like I was finally closing that chapter of my life.'

'You're in your fifties. That's a bloody long chapter, Peter. It's practically a whole book,' Ottey commented.

'You sound like my wife,' Montgomery replied.

'Isn't that the point though? You couldn't put it past you. It's obsessed you all your life. The physical abuse. No one believing you when you told them. The effect it's had on you long term. A never-healing sore of injustice,' commented Ottey.

'I suppose so,' came the quiet reply.

'You didn't speak to Sandy Moreton at all?' Cross asked again.

'Like I said. No.'

'Did you go to the pub after for refreshments?' Cross asked. Montgomery paused slightly before answering.

'Yep.'

'Yes, you did. Where, according to several witnesses, you had an altercation with Sandy Moreton. Who you claim you didn't speak with,' Cross pointed out.

'No comment.'

'Have you ever been to Sandy Moreton's house?' asked Cross.

'Oh, on several occasions. I'm hardly ever out of there,' Montgomery replied sarcastically.

'Really?' replied Cross who hadn't expected this.

'Oh yeah. Parties, dinners, tennis weekends. You name it. I was first name on the guest list.'

'So, you were a friend then, despite your experience at school?' Cross asked.

'Mr Montgomery is being sarcastic, DS Cross,' Ottey explained.

'I see.' He crossed out the sentence he'd just written in his file. 'Have you ever been to Sandy Moreton's house?' Cross repeated as if he hadn't already asked the question.

'No comment.'

'Did you break into his house in Dorset a few weeks ago?'

'No comment.'

Cross looked at the suspect for a long moment. Then went back to his file. He looked through it like someone who's lost their place in a book they're reading.

'Let's go back to Mozart. Is it not true that Alistair Moreton named his canes? The canes he used for beating boys?' Cross asked.

'Yes. Sick bastard.'

'And one of those was called Mozart. Is that correct?'

'I don't remember.'

'Really? That seems odd. Mozart the cane was infamous. Almost a novelty. Rather a special cane, was it not?'

Montgomery said nothing.

'Because it was concealed inside an umbrella. Moreton would take it on walks. The joke among the boys was that Moreton was never further than a hundred yards away from a cane. It's claimed by some old pupils that boys would misbehave deliberately on these walks to provoke Moreton into unsheathing Mozart. Is that true?' Cross asked.

'No comment.'

'You have no recollection of Mozart the umbrella cane?' Cross persisted.

'No comment.'

'Could you explain this photograph?' Cross asked, suddenly changing the subject. He showed him the picture of Montgomery standing over Moreton's grave. 'Could you tell me where you are in this photograph?'

'At Alistair Moreton's grave,' Montgomery replied.

'It looks more like you're *over* his grave. Why pose like that? Standing with your legs each side of his freshly dug grave?'

'I don't know. I suppose it is a bit childish in retrospect.'

'Looks like the pose of someone who's glad whoever is in the grave is dead. Victorious even. The pose of the occupant's killer,' Ottey suggested.

'No. I mean I can see what you're saying. It could look like that. Except I didn't kill him,' Montgomery protested.

'What's in your hand?' asked Cross.

The lawyer furrowed his brow and leant forward for a closer look.

'An umbrella,' replied Montgomery.

'And can you describe to me how the handle is fashioned?'

'No comment.'

'It's a bust of Wolfgang Amadeus Mozart, is it not?'

'No comment.'

'It is in fact this umbrella, isn't it?' said Cross as he produced it from a large evidence envelope. 'Or, more accurately, this umbrella cane. Alistair Moreton's Mozart?'

'No comment.'

'The very same, notorious Mozart from your schooldays. Schooldays which have scarred you so badly. Have affected the course of your life. The same Mozart you wanted to anally rape Alistair Moreton with? You really don't recognise it? That seems strange as we retrieved this from your flat when you were arrested. Sandy Moreton kept it at his house as some kind of morbid souvenir, until you broke in and stole it.'

'I'd like to speak with my client.'

Later that afternoon Cal Napier returned to the MCU. Napier and Gallinis had walked free from the county lines investigation. They had been unable to prove that they had occupied Moreton's cottage against his will. It was obviously an area of the law that needed reframing. Cross was surprised that he wanted to help and came voluntarily back to the station. Somewhere he would normally avoid like the plague.

Napier had offered to help the investigation into the murder of Alistair Moreton in any way he could. Despite having taken a beating at the old teacher's hands, both he and Gallinis seemed to have developed a fondness for the old man. If they could help bring the killer to justice, they were 'up for it' they'd told Cross.

He was taken into a room with a monitor which showed Montgomery in the interview room next door with Ottey.

'Weird being on this side of it,' he joked.

'Is the man sitting with DS Ottey the individual who came to the door of Mr Moreton's cottage while you were there?' Cross asked.

'Nope,' Napier answered confidently.

'Are you certain?'

'Definitely, because that's the geezer who was sitting in his car in the road outside. The one we thought was police. But he didn't come to the door. No way.'

59

'My client admits he did break into Sandy Moreton's house, where he obtained the umbrella cane.'

'"Obtained"? That's certainly a novel way to describe a theft,' Cross commented.

'What was the real reason for breaking in? I mean, you can't have known he had Mozart. It would have made more sense if Moreton senior had been in possession of it, wouldn't it?' asked Ottey.

'The truth?' asked Montgomery.

This response always puzzled Cross. Obviously, they wanted the truth. Why would they want anything else?

'Yes,' replied Ottey.

'Curiosity.'

'About what?' asked Cross.

'I don't know. To see how he lived. How things had worked out for him.'

'So, what happened?'

'Well, nothing. I did just that. But then I saw Mozart sticking out of his umbrella stand and I couldn't resist.'

'Why did you go through Mr Moreton's private correspondence?' asked Cross.

'Like I already said. Curiosity.'

'What was the real reason for the break-in?' asked Ottey. The two detectives had upped the tempo of the interview and started to dovetail with each other.

'I just answered that,' Montgomery spat.

'Isn't the actual truth, rather than the version you're attempting to fob off on us, the fact that you were looking for an address? Alistair Moreton's address?' Ottey pushed.

'Mr Montgomery, had you ever been to the village of Crockerne before the funeral?' asked Cross.

'I had not.'

'Had you ever been in the vicinity of Crockerne?'

'No.'

'Can you explain this Airbnb booking for the first of September of last year then? Two weeks before the murder? A room in the village of Shirehampton?'

'I was taking a break.'

Cross addressed the lawyer. 'You remember Shirehampton. I mentioned it earlier the first time your client lied about never having visited Crockerne. It's the neighbouring village to Crockerne.' He turned back to Montgomery.

'Quite the coincidence. A visit to the next-door village, just weeks before the murder. Don't you think?'

'No comment.'

'You were staking out the property, weren't you?'

No answer.

'To observe Moreton's movements. What you didn't know was that Moreton had two unwelcome guests staying in his cottage at the time. As a result, he never left the property for the two days you were there.'

'No comment.'

'Is this your car?' asked Ottey. She showed him a photograph Napier took on his phone from Moreton's cottage. It showed a car parked in the road outside with someone sitting in the driver's seat.

'No comment.'

'I suggest it's time for you to hold good to your offer of telling the truth, Mr Montgomery.'

'No comment.'

'Mr Montgomery, would it help you in your recollection of your recent movements if you knew that we have an eyewitness who saw you sitting in your car outside Mr Moreton's house?'

Montgomery's lawyer leant forward and whispered in his ear.

'It is my car. Yes,' Montgomery finally said.

'Why were you there?' asked Ottey.

'I wanted to confront him.'

'Why now, after all these years?' Ottey pushed.

'Why do you think? My wife had left me, my business was in trouble. He'd screwed up my life. I wanted him to know.'

'And did you? Confront him?' asked Cross.

'No.'

'But you went to the door,' suggested Cross even though Napier had said it wasn't him.

'No.'

'Well, someone went to the door and spoke to him. According to our witnesses he was quite shaken up,' said Cross.

'Then maybe you should find whoever that was and talk to him. Because it wasn't me. That's your bloody killer right there,' he said looking at his solicitor as if he'd stated a blindingly obvious solution to the crime. 'I didn't go up to the house. He had two real dodgy-looking men there. So, I kept away.'

'Until you went back a couple of weeks later and killed him,' suggested Ottey.

'I did not kill Alistair Moreton. I almost bloody wish I had. But I didn't. Am I glad he's dead? Yes! But I didn't kill him!'

'Do you own a dog, Mr Montgomery?' Cross asked.

'And that's another thing!' Montgomery answered with a bitter laugh. 'You know about his dogs, right? All seven of them. He used to walk around with them at night like a prison guard checking the perimeter wall. So, I hate dogs. I'm terrified of them. Even a small thing like a Chihuahua will have me cross to the other side of the road to avoid it.'

'They can be quite vicious, Chihuahuas. Don't be fooled by their size,' said Ottey, who wasn't a particular fan of dogs.

'You're cynophobic,' Cross commented.

'What?' asked Montgomery.

'You have cynophobia. A morbid fear of dogs. Not to be confused with cinephobia, a hatred or fear of watching movies,' Cross informed him.

He studied him for a good few moments. No one said anything. Then Cross got up and left.

60

Cross and Ottey sat with Carson in his office. She knew better than to ask if Cross thought Montgomery was guilty but did think things were stacking up against him.

'So, this is what we have, sir,' she began, after Carson had asked them for a progress report. 'A man who is deeply affected by what happened to him at the hands of the victim when he was a young boy. He blames him for his lack of trust in people, for always thinking he might be at fault, for losing his wife and for his business being in trouble. He's posted a photograph of himself posing at the victim's grave holding some weird umbrella cane which he stole from Sandy Moreton's house when he broke in there. He also went through his correspondence. He said he was just curious. But I call bullshit. He was looking for something and I'd put money on it being Alistair Moreton's address. We have an eyewitness placing him in a car outside the victim's cottage. It feels like it's all beginning to point at him.'

Carson listened but didn't say anything, which was unusual for him. He normally leapt on any possibility of charging a suspect. Maybe his doubts about Cotterell were making him more cautious.

'What's bothering you, sir?' Ottey asked.

'I don't know. On the one hand I can see that he might've snapped and decided to get justice for himself, as it were. The wife, the divorce, could have been the trigger. That went through recently, yes?'

'A month before the murder,' answered Cross.

'Or, he could've gone to confront the man, yell at him about the impact he'd had on his life, and it got out of hand,' Carson continued.

'In that scenario, how did they end up upstairs?'

'That's a good point. I don't know. I may be going out on a limb here and I'm sorry. It's not evidential, George. But each to their own. The reason I'm not entirely convinced is I'm wondering if this might be a case of Stockholm syndrome. He's obsessed with his abuser. You can view it that during his time at that school he was virtually imprisoned and subjected to Moreton's abuse. This obsession maintains a relationship with Moreton. It's one of the longest associations he's had with anyone throughout his life. It seems like there's not a day goes past that he's not thinking about the man. But if he killed him for retribution, revenge or whatever, that relationship has now gone. It would no longer exist. Does that sound idiotic?'

'No,' said Ottey.

'On the contrary, sir. I think it's one of the most intelligent things you've said,' replied Cross.

Ottey couldn't help but smile as she was thinking the same thing but would never have said it out loud.

61

The Cotterell jury was back with a verdict.

Carson was in court again, sitting next to Warner and Murray. None of them spoke. The atmosphere was febrile as is often the case when a murder verdict is expected. So many different opinions as to the outcome bounced invisibly around the courtrooms between people, like silent, charged atoms. The judge appeared and was handed a piece of paper which he read. He nodded and handed it back. He then looked up at the jury and asked the foreperson to stand. They had reached a unanimous verdict, he told the judge.

'Not guilty,' she announced.

There was a pause. A moment of silence engulfed the courtroom. It was almost a physical sensation. Then, as if a pressure valve had been released, a spontaneous smattering of chatter. The judge pounded his gavel.

'Mr Cotterell, you are free to go,' he said.

Cotterell stood up and embraced his lawyer and the team. His wife rushed forward to hug him. Carson stood, was about to say something to Warner along the lines of 'you can't win them all, good work, you did a good job, but we don't always get the verdicts we want...' but realised he had no inclination to say anything, so just left.

'What a load of bollocks, sir,' Murray said to Warner. But Warner wasn't listening. He was watching Alice Mackenzie who had been sent by Cross to observe the verdict. Tamsin Cotterell was signalling to her. She walked over to be swept into a grateful embrace by the now-free man's wife. Warner watched as Tamsin introduced Mackenzie to her husband who listened intently amidst the noise of the court clearing. Then an expression of grateful recognition swept across his face, and he shook her hand enthusiastically. He began talking to her in earnest. Warner couldn't help feeling there was something of a smug victory dance in all of this, with Mackenzie at the centre. This wasn't entirely surprising as her wretched boyfriend had swayed the jury towards the wrong verdict with his theoretical analysis of the CCTV.

'Drink, boss?' Murray asked Warner.

'Sure. I need one after this bloody fiasco.'

62

Ottey looked at the text from Mackenzie announcing the result and smiled. She walked over to Cross's office, who was also reading something on his phone.

'Is that the text from Alice about the case?' she asked him.

'No,' he replied. He looked momentarily fixated on his phone.

'You heard though? Not guilty,' Ottey said brightly.

'Yes,' he said, leaving the office.

'Where are you going?' she asked, following him.

'To talk to Montgomery.'

'Okay. I guess this means it's not looking so great for him just now.'

As they walked down the corridor, she noticed Cross was still looking a little perplexed.

'What is it, George? What were you reading on your phone?'

'A text from my father.'

Ottey knew this meant it was important. Raymond never texted his son at work because he knew it distracted him. He also never wanted to worry him with anything that could wait until the end of a working day.

'What did he want?' she asked.

'Nothing. He didn't want anything.'

'Then what did he say, George?' she asked.

'It's my mother. Her husband died this morning.'

'Oh no. Well, you need to call her.'

'I don't. I didn't know him.'

'But she's your mother.'

'Who I also don't really know.'

'George, she's your mother and you need to call her to offer your condolences,' Ottey insisted.

'I don't think so. It's none of my business.'

'So why did your father text? Ask yourself that.'

'To inform me. Which he's done.'

'No, it was to let you know so that you could call her.'

'If he'd wanted me to call her, he would have said so specifically.'

They arrived at the interview room and, in classic fashion, he immediately surprised her.

'Mr Montgomery, I'm releasing you on police bail. I no longer consider you to be a person of interest in the murder of Alistair Moreton. However, the Hampshire and Isle of Wight constabulary want to discuss the burglary of Sandy Moreton's house.'

'So that's it for the murder? I'm no longer a suspect?' asked Montgomery with obvious relief.

'For the time being,' said Ottey, looking quizzically at Cross while rapidly playing catch-up. 'New evidence may come up and if it does you may well be rearrested.'

'Well, that's not going to happen,' Montgomery retorted.

'I'm glad you're so confident,' she replied.

'I am, because I didn't do it.'

Cross turned to leave the room. Neither he nor Ottey had sat down. She turned to follow as she wanted to find out exactly what was going on and wasn't going to do so in front of Montgomery.

'DS Cross,' Montgomery said. Cross turned at the door. 'Have you had a look at Richard Brook for this?'

'Why?' Cross asked.

'Well, for one thing, those two have had a beef since I knew them at school.'

'I'm aware of that.'

'They've been at each other's throats ever since and now it

looks like Brook might have done Moreton's political career over with his inquiry.'

'It would certainly seem so. But what is your point?' Cross asked.

'You know about his brother, yes?'

'I didn't know he had a brother.'

'Well, you wouldn't. He doesn't seem to talk about it much. Richard's a real high-flier. You can see that from what he's achieved. But it was always going to be so with him. You could see it at thirteen, unlike Sandy Moreton or Richard's brother. Adam he was called. Bright and able, but nothing like his older brother. I knew him at prep school and then we went our separate ways. I didn't hear anything about him again till I was eighteen. I'd just got into university with pretty decent A levels but it seems Adam Brook didn't. Didn't have the grades for Oxford.'

'How do you know this if you'd gone your separate ways?' Cross asked.

'My best friend from prep school was at senior school with him. It was the sister school to All Saints, which is why I didn't want to go there,' Montgomery continued.

'So, your parents did listen to you at some point,' said Ottey.

'Yes, I suppose they did,' he said, as if this had never occurred to him before now and smiled. 'Anyway, Adam was sent to a crammer in London to get the grades for Oxford. He lasted just four months there,' he said quietly.

'What happened then?' asked Cross who had over the years recognised a pause for a feed question from someone telling a story they thought crucial to an enquiry. Asking it, he'd learnt, simply sped the process up.

'He killed himself.'

'I see,' replied Cross. 'And what does that have to do with this case?'

'The headmaster of the crammer was Alistair Moreton. It was the only job he could get after he'd been removed by the All Saints governors.'

Cross said nothing.

'Richard Brook never got over the loss of his brother and laid the blame fairly and squarely at Alistair Moreton's door.'

63

Carson assembled a meeting of the entire MCU team in the MCU. Cross, as usual, sat at the back next to the door in case the meeting and accompanying noise became too much for him and he needed to make a hasty retreat.

'As you all know, the Moreton murder is an open case once again. It's no higher a priority than it was before. But it is clearly at the front and centre of current media and public interest. The facts are still the same. A man has been murdered. However, because in essence we charged and took the wrong man to court there is added pressure from upstairs to get it right this time. We need to rectify the situation as quickly as possible in the public eye. We need to prove that we can do our job properly, bring people to justice and prove that the public have good reason to trust us,' he said.

'Is DI Warner still leading the investigation?' asked Ottey.

'No.'

'Is he aware of that, sir?' she continued.

'No. I can't get hold of him at the moment. But just as soon as I can he will be told and be returning to the Kent force,' Carson replied. 'DS Ottey will be leading the investigation with DS Cross. They will report directly to me, in effect now the SIO on the case. So, if there are any questions or queries and you find they're out of the office, my door will be open.'

'What about Montgomery? What the hell's going on there? I liked him for this,' asked a detective, known to be suspicious of Cross and his way of working.

'George, perhaps you could answer that as I'm assuming you had a good reason to let our prime suspect walk,' said Carson.

'He didn't own a dog,' Cross said, causing a couple of people to laugh. Ottey had noticed since her return that Warner's presence in the MCU had had quite an effect on people feeling freer to question or disrespect Cross.

'Right...' said Carson.

'Whoever killed him had a dog,' Cross went on.

'So, we're looking for a man who owns a Rhodesian Ridgeback?' asked Carson.

'Possibly,' Cross replied enigmatically before disappearing through the adjacent door.

64

Bobby Warner had seen the text summoning him to Carson's office several hours ago, but had seen fit to ignore it. He'd go into the MCU after a couple of pints of reflection with DC Murray. On balance he was still fairly sure that he'd made a good case against Cotterell and that the CCTV footage was speculative at best. He didn't buy the defence's version of events or even the timeline. In retrospect he should probably have anticipated the defence's objections to his narrative. But that was the prosecuting team's job, not his. He'd resume the case first thing in the morning. He was angry, as this meant he'd have to spend more time in Bristol, with all eyes on him. People would be openly questioning his ability. But the fact was that sometimes verdicts didn't go the way they should. Even so, Cotterell was out of the frame now. He had to accept that it was possible he'd been wrong. Not an easy thing for a man of his character. He listened to Murray's consolatory protestations in the pub for as long as his ego needed stroking, then decided it would be politic to go and see Carson before the end of play. He wanted to lay down some ground rules for the investigation going forward. The first of which was that he wanted neither Cross nor Ottey anywhere near it. It was a simple case of him or them.

Carson recognised the look of a detective who'd spent the best part of his day in the pub, the moment Warner knocked on his office door. The loosened collar, the slightly sweaty skin, the small red veins on his cheeks and nose a little more pronounced. The rheumy eyes, constantly trying to focus.

'Bobby. Come in. Been consoling yourself in the pub?' Carson asked.

'Not exactly. Just chewing the cud with Murray,' he replied.

'Did you put the world to rights?' Carson was trying to break the ice. Warner didn't reply. 'Well, thanks for stopping by.'

'No problem. I was going to come in anyway. Before I saw your text. I think we should have a grown-up conversation about how we go forward in light of the verdict,' Warner mumbled slightly.

'Oh good. I completely agree,' said Carson allowing himself to believe for a moment that this was going to be a lot easier than he'd thought.

'I still think Cotterell was good for it,' said Warner causing Carson to pause.

'Except for the fact that he was found not guilty in a unanimous decision,' he pointed out.

'Sure, and I accept that. So, we must look elsewhere and I'm more than happy to do that. But in order for me to agree to that I have certain conditions,' he went on.

'Bobby—' said Carson, in an attempt to interrupt him.

'No, hear me out, sir. Like I say, I'm happy to reopen the investigation. It's unfinished business for me, if you like. But I cannot do it with DS Cross. We're just not a good fit and that goes for Ottey as well.'

'Who, it should be pointed out, you haven't actually worked with.'

'That's as may be. But they're partners and I'm sure you'd be loath to split them up. It would be easier for everyone if they had nothing to do with it. So just assign me other detectives from your roster and I'll be a happy chappy.'

Carson looked at him for a moment. In truth he was thinking that people who wanted to conceal the fact that they had been drinking would do well to construct their sentences with less sibilance.

'So, here's the thing, Bobby. You don't have to worry about working with Cross or Ottey.'

'Oh, great.'

'Because you won't be working the Moreton case from here on in.'

'What?'

'You're going back to Kent.'

'Then who's going to be leading the investigation?' Warner asked.

Carson said nothing.

'You are fucking kidding me.'

'Call it a need for fresh eyes, if you like.'

'The idiot savant?'

'That is offensive, Bobby, however much you've had to drink.'

'You're replacing me with that freak? What does he have on you? He must have something.'

'I think you should go before you say something you'll come to regret,' Carson warned him.

'I've never seen another officer so indulged in the way you indulge that man. He's like a teacher's pet. No one here likes him but they're afraid to say it. It's just weird.'

'I do indulge him, yes. Absolutely. He does get special treatment yes. On account of his condition. He has his own office. Yes. Because of his sensory issues. Something you clearly have no interest in, nor consideration of. He has all of this because as challenging and infuriating as he often can be, he is the best detective I've ever had the privilege of working with,' Carson replied. 'For what it's worth he's actually a lot more popular in the unit than you'd like to believe.'

'Oh, is that right?' spat Warner.

'Do you want to have a look at his numbers? Or maybe we should just look at the case you have just failed in. Watch him as he solves it and, what is more, gets a conviction instead of just an arrest. I don't like you, Warner, and so let me put this in language you might understand. He is Sherlock Holmes to your Inspector Clouseau.'

Warner sat there for a moment taking in what had just been said. The alcohol in his bloodstream was encouraging him to turn the desk over in Carson's lap. But as pissed as he was, his innate survival instinct kicked in. So instead, he got up with as much dignity as he could muster and, with a slight sway, sashayed out of the room, leaving Carson reflecting pleasantly on his surprisingly choice analogy.

As Warner left the building with his overnight bag and jangling his car keys, he saw Alice Mackenzie get into her car and drive out of the car park.

65

'Right, I'm off,' announced Ottey as she poked her head round Cross's office door. 'Did you see Warner? He just left, tail stuck firmly up his arse.'

'I did not,' replied Cross who was studying his phone.

'What are you doing?' she asked.

'Checking train times.'

'Where are you off to?' she said looking at her watch.

'Gloucester.'

'Now?'

'Yes.'

'Why?'

'I called Raymond. He's up there with Christine. I thought about what you said and told him I'd go up.'

'He must've been pleased.'

'On the contrary. Christine insisted that I didn't.'

'So why are you still going?' she asked.

He flicked through his personal notebook until he found what he was looking for.

'You told me on the seventh of August 2021 that,' he began to read from the book, '"in emotionally charged situations people will often lie about what they want and what they don't want." Christine was lying in response to my question,' he said, rather pleased that on this occasion he could demonstrate that he did pay attention to Ottey and was constantly trying to learn. She thought for a moment.

'Come on, I'll take you. It'll be a lot quicker.'

'Yes, it will,' he agreed.

'Let me just call my mum.' She then stopped and turned to him.

'You should probably make a note of this as well, George. When someone makes an offer which will obviously inconvenience them, or cost them in some way, not necessarily financially, the polite and usual response is to insist there is no need, even if you don't believe it,' she said as he busily scribbled it down. 'George, now would be that time.'

He thought for a moment, looked up and nodded before quickly writing down what she'd said in his notebook. Exactly. Word for word.

She sighed and went to call her mother and endure the polite unspoken reprimand that would inevitably come her way. At the same time consoling herself that the need for her not going home for dinner had come from the fact that George did actually listen to her.

'Richard Brook. Should we be paying him a visit?' she asked, as she drove them to Gloucester.

'I think so. I'm not sure we have any other leads currently.'

'Do you believe Montgomery?'

'I'm not sure what there is to believe or not believe. Brook did have a brother who did indeed take his own life at eighteen. Montgomery has no need to lie to us.'

'It seems out of character for a lifelong civil servant, though, don't you think?' Ottey asked.

'Dennis Nilsen was a civil servant,' Cross pointed out.

'That's different. You know what I mean,' Ottey insisted.

'I can assure you I don't,' he replied.

66

They arrived at the care home on the south side of Gloucester. As they parked Cross noticed the private ambulance stationed by the front entrance. Such a plain, ordinary-looking vehicle whose deliberately nondescript appearance, designed to make it invisibly discreet, screamed, DEAD BODY INSIDE! They found Christine and Raymond waiting in the corridor outside a room.

'George, I told you not to come. There was no need,' Christine began by saying.

'I didn't think there was a need either but then I realised that people have a tendency to lie in situations like this and there was every possibility you were doing so,' George replied. Josie gave Christine a comforting hug.

'It was quite quick in the end,' Christine told her.

'Well, that's a blessing,' Josie replied.

'Yes. It's all a bit of a blessing really. He would never have wanted to just exist in this way,' Christine told her.

'I'm so sorry for your loss,' said Josie, more as a prompt for George than anything else.

George picked up on it immediately. 'I'm so sorry for your loss,' he repeated automatically. He knew that social protocol called for him to embrace his mother at a moment like this. But he didn't like that kind of social proximity with anyone. Nonetheless, he held out his arms stiffly, as if he was going to hold her away at arm's length. She smiled.

'It's all right. We don't have to do that, George,' she said.

'Oh good,' he replied.

Raymond couldn't remember the last time he'd felt this proud of his son. He and Josie shared a private, knowing smile with each other.

Christine turned to Josie. 'Thank you for bringing him up. It means a great deal to me, George, that you're here, despite what I said on the phone. I mean, you didn't know him. Had never even seen him.'

George was aware from experience that agreeing with her might sound wrong in this context. So, he simply said nothing. At that point the door opposite them opened and two undertakers, dressed in simple black suits, white shirts and ties, manoeuvred a steel trolley with a black plastic body bag out of the room. Christine let out a small mournful sob, a sigh almost. Raymond took hold of one of her hands, Josie the other. When they turned to follow the undertakers out of the home, they saw that the corridor and the reception leading to the front entrance was lined on both sides by the staff of the home, in a guard of honour. Nurses, carers, cooks, cleaners all stood in line and bowed their heads in respect as the trolley went past. This was an unexpected gesture that took Josie completely by surprise. What was even more surprising, perhaps, was that this experienced police sergeant, who had witnessed countless bodies being removed in bags from crime scenes, started crying.

As they watched the plain, black van drive Duncan's body away, Christine, Josie and Raymond all wiped the tears from their eyes.

'Gosh, I wasn't expecting that. The guard of honour. That completely floored me,' said Josie.

'Yes, very touching,' agreed Raymond.

'Will you come to the funeral, George?' Christine asked.

'No, I don't think so.'

'He will. I'll come too,' said Josie.

'I'd like you to, George,' said Christine.

'Oh, I see. Yes, well in that case I shall certainly make every effort. Work allowing,' he replied.

'It's just that I don't think there'll be many people there. So many have died, and Alzheimer's seems to alienate your friends. They all visit for a while, but as things get worse, I can understand them thinking what's the point? He no longer recognised anyone. Not even me, really. Occasionally, but mostly not. So, you can't really blame them for staying away. It's so distressing and everyone has their own lives to lead and problems to deal with,' Christine went on.

'But he knew you at the end. Right at the end,' said Raymond.

'Do you think so?' she asked.

'I know so.'

The carers at the home were obviously well versed in death and the signs that it was imminent. Duncan's pneumonia never really cleared and a couple of days earlier they had warned Christine that his death would be soon. That's when she'd called Raymond. Then, just before he died, the nurse saw that Duncan's fingertips had become discoloured, almost black. This was a sign that death was just minutes away. His breathing became shallower and shallower. His chest rattled slightly. Then with a sudden spasm, his body tensed, and he opened his eyes for the first time in five days. He looked directly into his wife's eyes as if he'd known instinctively where they were even before he opened his.

'It's all right, Duncan, my darling,' Christine had said, taking her dying husband's hand in hers. 'It's fine. You can go now, sweetheart. It's time.'

Raymond thought he saw gratitude in Duncan's pale blue eyes as he then closed them and died. Just like that. With a sigh. Almost of relief. That she'd given him her blessing. That it was all over.

He stayed up in Gloucester with Christine that night. He didn't want her to be alone and also wanted to help with all the death administration that she would have to do the next day.

George and Josie drove back to Bristol in silence. He was thinking how enormous an event death actually was. Even when it came to someone you didn't know, like Duncan. It was so significant. The emotional tectonic plates of life shifted. Josie had cried at the gesture of the home staff, but he thought it was more than that. He knew it was a spontaneous outpouring of all the emotions she was always suppressing about the things she saw and heard at work. He had felt something himself. He wasn't sure what. But it was significant, if not emotionally then for some other reason. He wondered whether this feeling explained his determination when investigating someone's murder. Was that what urged him on? What it also brought home to him was how death was a profound event to those close to the deceased. There was a sense of time moving on. The end of an era. It brought out different reactions and often uncharacteristic emotions in people. Look at Josie's tears. He couldn't remember having seen her cry before. He himself had imagined what his life would be like without his father recently, prompted by his being out of the country and also Duncan's death. But how would he react to the actuality, the fact, the event of his father's death? He simply had no idea. It made him wonder what effect Richard Brook's mother's death had had on him.

Ottey's phone rang. It was Swift.

67

Alice Mackenzie had hoped that she and Michael Swift could go out for dinner that night and celebrate the verdict in the Cotterell trial. She thought, as she drove home from the MCU, that this was an example of her job achieving something good. Something that would demonstrate to her socialist parents, who still thought the police were just an oppressive tool used by whichever authoritarian government happened to be in power at the time, the worth of her chosen career path. Something that might smooth the path to inform her parents of her intention to become a detective. She was proud of her contribution and thought that her conversation with Tamsin Cotterell and Cross had been the instigator to having him called as a witness. He obviously couldn't testify to the CCTV footage but what he'd told them prior to the trial had encouraged them to call Michael to the stand. His evidence had been the deciding factor in the acquittal. It made her all the more determined to go ahead with her application for the DHEP programme. To become a fully-fledged police officer and not just a police staffer. She wanted to be a little more hands-on. Closer to the action. With the power to make change for good.

She parked in the gravelled area outside Michael's flat in Pembroke Road, gathered her bag and the bottle of wine she'd bought on the way home and got out of the car. She walked up the steps to the front door and searched for her key, balancing her bag awkwardly on her knee. She found it, opened the door and went in. She looked at the mail that had been stacked on the radiator cover in the hallway and walked to Swift's flat door at the back on the right. She opened that door with another key. She became conscious that the front door hadn't clicked shut. As she pushed the flat door open she suddenly became aware of the smell of cigarette-infused clothing, stale alcohol and minted breath enveloping her from behind. She turned to look at the front door but as she did so was shoved violently into the flat. Her wrist was immediately wrenched as her hand was still pressing the key in the door. A huge shadow pushed her against the wall of the small hall in the flat. DI Robert Warner then hissed in her ear.

'You and your boyfriend think you're so fucking clever, don't you?'

'Get off me!' she screamed.

'So bloody superior,' he continued.

She yelled in pain as he grabbed her wrist with his hand and twisted it back. He pushed her into the sitting room and onto the sofa, face down. He put his knee into her back painfully and with his free hand grabbed her handbag. She could hear him rummaging through it before emptying its contents onto the floor.

'What do you want?' she managed to say despite the air in her lungs being compressed by his sheer weight. She felt oddly calm despite the fact that her heart rate had gone through the roof and was beating like a bass drum in her ears. She knew he was going to rape her and she began to think rationally what to do. She'd recently had a manicure done. Her nails were long and in good shape. Whatever happened she'd try and scratch the bastard's face.

As he hauled her back up off the sofa, she became genuinely terrified. It was the thought of this man, this shit of a pig, taking her by brute force. She felt helpless and repelled by the idea at the same time. She might not be able to fight him off but she could still talk.

'You're pathetic, you know that?'

He said nothing but frogmarched her through the sitting

room into the bedroom. Her arms really hurt where he had hold of her.

'How long do you think you'll actually get away with this?' she asked him. 'I know there have been others. Ottey knows there are others. We went to Kent. Did you know that? Spoke to Jacky Collins. You do this and you're going to prison, you sad, bloated old fuck.'

He then did something which she wasn't expecting. He turned her round and threw her onto the bed. In that second she saw what he had in his hand. The pepper spray from her handbag.

'Your turn, sweetheart,' he said, spraying it directly into her eyes. 'How does that feel?'

She screamed. He covered her mouth. Her hand reached up to her eyes which were streaming. The pain was excruciating but more frightening was the fact that she now couldn't see a thing. He moved his hand from her mouth onto her sternum and applied all his weight. She heard him fiddle with his belt using his other hand.

'We all know what happens to rapists in prison,' she said in short bursts, trying to catch her breath as adrenalin coursed through her body. 'But a rapist who's a policeman!' She laughed. 'You'll have no chance.'

She could hear him pulling at his zip and the change or keys in his trouser pockets rattling as they fell to the ground.

'Bet you didn't bring a condom. That's your first mistake. Soon as you're done, which I imagine shouldn't take long, I'll be straight down to casualty for a rape kit.'

'I'm not that stupid, bitch.'

He pulled her jeans' zip open and yanked them off like he was undressing a reluctant child refusing to go to bed. Then tore her knickers off so roughly, the elastic caught on the back of her leg like a tourniquet. He pulled it violently using both hands. She screamed again. She felt so exposed, so vulnerable. She reached up blindly for his face. When she found it, she dug her nails into his cheek and scratched him painfully with three gouges that immediately started to bleed. He yelled and slapped her hard with the back of his hand. Drops of his sweat fell on her face. She spat at him. He hit her again. She sensed him leaning back. There was a pause. He was fiddling with something. But he needed both hands. It had to be the condom. She sat up as fast as she could and her face smashed into his nose with a distinct crack. As he stood up straight, she leant forward and reached blindly for his cock. She grabbed it and sank her nails into it as hard as she possibly could. He screamed but she wouldn't let go. Then he suddenly seemed to pull away from her, her nails making their mark on his engorged penis. There was a loud thud and yelling as two bodies crashed into the wall beside the bed.

'Michael?' she shouted hopefully and immediately burst into tears, pulling her legs up around her, still unable to see.

'You sonofabitch!' Michael screamed. He was on top of Warner now, on the floor, pounding his fists into the side of the man's head as he knelt on him. Warner, with a huge yell of effort, managed to turn himself round. Michael still held him down.

'Alice, call the police!' he shouted.

'I can't see,' she yelled back.

'What?'

'He pepper sprayed me!'

As Michael turned to look at her, Warner managed to pull him off and trip his way out with his trousers still round his ankles. Michael gave chase.

'Michael! Leave him. I don't want you getting hurt. Call the police!' Alice shouted after him.

68

When Cross and Ottey arrived at Swift's flat there was already an ambulance outside and a couple of patrol cars. There was no room left for them to park. She saw Carson's car parked at the side of the road as she parked. Inside they found Alice giving a statement to a detective. She was wearing a white paper forensics suit and her right hand was sealed in a clear plastic bag taped at her wrist. Carson had insisted on her statement being given as soon as he got there. He wanted it to be as contemporaneous as possible.

'She was extraordinary,' Swift told Cross and Ottey. 'As soon as I'd called the police and you, she made me photograph the room and her, as if I were working a case. Her legs, her eyes and face, her hands, her pubic area, her torn knickers on the floor.' He faltered as if saying this out loud made it worse. 'She made me bag her hand. Melissa,' he said, pointing to a forensics officer, 'took her clothes and put her in the suit. She was brilliant, very businesslike.'

'Did she scratch him?' asked Cross, looking at the bag on her hand.

'Yep. I think she's in shock,' Swift replied.

'Of course she is,' said Ottey. 'She'll need to go to hospital for—'

'He didn't rape her, thank God,' he interrupted.

'She'll still need to go.'

'Yeah, I know. She...' He laughed despite himself. 'She managed to grab him. She couldn't see a thing, but she grabbed his... stuck her nails in. He was bleeding. I saw it.'

'She's a brave woman,' commented Ottey. 'How could she think straight? It's amazing.'

Cross had wandered over to the bedroom. He knelt by the bed.

'Evidence bag. Tweezers,' he announced to no one in particular.

Swift grabbed his work bag and provided them. Cross picked up the discarded condom from the floor and carefully placed it in the bag. There was blood on it.

As the detective was finishing Alice's statement, Carson asked Cross and Ottey to go outside.

'I can't believe this is happening. Has happened. But they both positively ID'd Warner,' he said. Then listened as Ottey told him about the kitchen incident and the night Alice pepper sprayed him in the car park.

'So that's why he pepper sprayed her.'

'Yep. Payback,' replied Ottey.

'Josie, this is terrible. I feel responsible. But I can't do anything if I'm not told. You have to report this kind of behaviour. You're a senior female officer in the department. You have to come to me. Why didn't you?'

'These kind of complaints from young women against senior officers don't have a great track record in being seen through. Alice didn't want to,' she replied.

'I see. Well, that's awful. I get it, of course. But it's not okay. We'll talk about this later. I mean, if that's all right?' he asked plaintively.

'Of course.'

'So, what about Warner? Something tells me this behaviour hasn't come out of the blue.'

Ottey then explained their trip to Kent, the existence of the WhatsApp group, Warner's behaviour in Manchester and the other victims who were unwilling to come forward.

'Will Alice press charges?' Carson asked.

'By the look of things, I'm almost certain of it,' replied Ottey. 'Perhaps that'll encourage the others.'

'Hopefully.'

'Well, this isn't the Met,' Carson announced a little grandly. But Ottey was willing to forgive him. 'We're going to put a stop to it.'

'Will you go upstairs with it, sir?' Ottey asked.

'I'm not sure. George, you haven't said much.'

'I haven't said anything,' Cross pointed out.

'Should I go upstairs with this?' Carson asked. Ottey was impressed with his openness and appeal for advice.

'Not immediately, no. As soon as you do, it becomes a different problem. Their priority will be about how to manage this outwards. I think we should just concentrate on arresting as we would any other sex offender. The fact that he's a police officer should have no bearing on it.'

'Are you suggesting they'd cover it up?' Carson asked.

'I'm not suggesting anything. It just becomes a bigger, different question, upstairs. For us it's a simple one. Get him in a custody suite and assemble the evidence before we go to the CPS,' Cross replied.

'Do we hand it over to the rape team?' Carson went on.

'I think we should make the arrest and, as I say, get the evidence together. It makes sense to then have specialist officers interview him though. So yes, we should hand it over to them. It also makes it cleaner if we're not involved in the interview itself. It won't give the prosecution any distracting ammunition.'

'Agreed. I'll put out an APB.'

'No, don't,' said Cross.

'Why not?'

'Aside from saving valuable and scarce resources, let's lull him into a sense of false security. Make him think he's got away with it. He has done so before, let him think he's done it again. That way he'll resume where he left off. As normal. Going back to work as if nothing has happened, which is where we'll pick him up.'

'That'll involve informing his superiors.'

'No. Don't.'

'They'll be mighty pissed off, George,' he said, laughing at his naivety.

'So what? When this comes out and the fact emerges that they've let this happen on their watch, they'll have a lot more to worry about than our arresting him on their turf.'

Alice was taken to hospital in the ambulance which she thought was completely unnecessary. But they pointed out that as they were there, they might as well. Swift and Ottey went with her. Carson drove Cross to his flat as it was on his way home. Melissa, Swift's forensic colleague who had been in the flat, came to the hospital and took cells from under Alice's fingernails. She also swabbed her dried tears for traces of pepper spray, and her face for any residue of Warner's sweat.

69

Cross and Ottey went over to Swift's flat the next morning. Swift and Mackenzie had taken the day off work. It struck Cross that Swift was more upset by the attack than Mackenzie, which led him to conclude that she was holding everything in, keeping things in check. He knew this couldn't last. Ottey wanted to talk to Mackenzie alone.

'Perhaps Michael could show you his collection of crime scene books?' Ottey suggested. Swift had a sizeable collection of these books together with his cellophane-wrapped rare comics that were catalogued in various storage boxes.

'Sure, no problem,' replied Swift, aware of what Ottey was up to. For Cross, however, it just seemed a wholly inappropriate thing to suggest at such a time. Nevertheless, the two men sat engrossed in crime scene photographs from the past while the two women spoke.

'You know I worked in the sex crimes unit for a few years,' Ottey began by saying.

'I didn't know that, no.'

'So, if you want to ask anything about the process or just talk, you only have to ask,' Ottey went on.

'Oh sure,' said Mackenzie, as if the idea of not taking her up on this would be just daft. 'But I'm good. Honestly. I'll be back in after the weekend.'

'You're still in shock, Alice, and it'll wear off without any warning. When you're least expecting it. Like suddenly coming off painkillers too early when you've hurt yourself. You don't have to be brave and put on a strong front. It's just not a requirement.'

'I felt so calm, I mean not so calm but calm. Is that weird?'

'Not at all. Unusual, but not weird.'

'Maybe it's because I knew who it was.'

'Possibly.'

'I can't imagine what it must be like if it's a complete stranger. So much more terrifying. I just thought, what can I do to prove it was him? Then he peppered me.'

Ottey said nothing. She knew all too well that commenting on events like this often had an unintended effect on the victim.

'Alice, are you going to press charges?' she asked.

'Of course I bloody am. They got DNA from my fingernails. I wasn't just fighting back doing that. I wanted his DNA.'

'Good.'

'It was intentional,' said Mackenzie, trying to make sure there was no doubt.

'I know. Michael told me. Quick thinking. We need to talk to Jacky Collins in Kent and get her up to speed. See if the others will come forward in the light of this. I think it's only fair to give her a heads up that we're going to arrest him.'

'Sure. Is there a warrant out for him?' Mackenzie asked.

'No.'

'Why not?'

'George. He thinks Warner's pattern of behaviour means he'll just go back to work after a few days, thinking he's got away with it again. When Collins tells us he's back, we'll go and pick him up. Unusually for George, he wants me and him to go and do the honours.'

'Wish I could be there. Does he really think the bastard's that arrogant? That he'll just go to work?'

'He does. Just be patient. You'll get your chance to stare him in the face again in court. The man's time is up.'

70

The next day was understandably a little subdued in the unit. Word had got round the office about Warner's attack. People were horrified. None more so than DC Murray, who appeared in Cross's office as soon as he got into work.

'I don't know what to say,' he began.

'Were you with him all afternoon?' Ottey asked.

'I was.'

'How much did he have to drink?'

'Too much. That man can put it away.'

'Were you drinking as well?' asked Cross.

'Yes, but I was driving. So, I just had the one pint then pretended I switched to G&T but drank soda water. He didn't know because he never put his hand in his pocket, tight git. He started drinking whisky chasers, but he just seemed a bit pissed off about the case. I had no idea he'd—'

'He has history,' said Ottey.

'Really? That makes sense, I suppose. I mean, these things are never one-offs, are they? Look, if there's anything I can do,' he offered.

'There is,' said Cross. 'You can go and sit down, make a note of the time and the date and write down everything you remember about yesterday after the trial. What was said. What was drunk. Timings. Everything.'

'Sure.'

'You might have to testify to his state of mind and inebriation in court,' said Cross.

'You want me to take the stand?' he said, suddenly uncertain about that prospect.

'You have a problem with that?' asked Ottey a little more aggressively than she perhaps intended.

'No, no of course I don't.'

'Did he mention Alice yesterday?'

'Not that I recall.'

'All right, go and make your notes.'

'What about the Cotterell case?' Murray asked. 'Sorry, I meant the Moreton case.'

'You'll be reassigned,' Cross told him.

'Really? Why?'

'I think the initial phrasing of your question should answer that,' said Cross.

Murray stood there for a moment wanting to protest, but thought better of it and withdrew.

Ottey made no move to leave the office. She just sat opposite Cross, deep in thought.

'You're upset,' he observed.

'Hardly surprising. What is surprising is that you noticed,' she replied.

'You're frowning and picking your lips. Two sure-fire signs.'

'I'm just thinking how upsetting and disturbing last night's events really are.'

Cross thought about this for a moment.

'But I'm all good,' she added.

'I'd like to do some further background on Richard Brook before we request an interview,' Cross said.

'Okay.'

'You should spend your time talking to your contact in the Kent force and forming some kind of plan for Warner.'

'Exactly what I was thinking.'

'Do you trust her not to alert everyone in her unit?'

'Oh yeah. I think she'll just be happy something's finally going to happen. I'll tell her that Alice is pressing charges and ask her to reach out to the other victims she knows. See if that encourages them to come forward.'

'You should also put together all the information they have and everything we have on Warner. So we can collate everything for the interviewing team.'

'Oh right, sure. I hadn't thought of that,' she said sarcastically.

'Just as well I asked then,' he responded.

She was more relieved than annoyed at being patronised by him. It suited her emotional state to put everything together for the Warner arrest. Little did she know that Cross was thinking exactly the same thing. That in her current state she would be better focusing fully on Warner. It would be restorative. It also freed him up to work on his own, which was something he felt he needed to do to make progress on the Moreton murder. It annoyed her a little that he thought that they shouldn't conduct the interview with Warner. An overcautious move, in her opinion. But then again, she didn't want anything to jeopardise their chances of putting Warner away.

As she walked back to her desk, she had to admit that the one person who had come out of all of this surprisingly well was her boss Carson. Someone who generally infuriated her before she'd even got into work and before he'd even opened his mouth to speak. He'd made a quick decision about Michael Swift's expert witness evidence without waiting for the verdict. He'd also made an uncharacteristically perceptive judgement call which was not to alert his superiors and keep the arrest in-house. His first thought, normally, was how to manage upwards and what effect any decision might have on his image and career. So, kudos to him, she thought, as she sat down and called Jacky Collins.

Sir Richard Brook was a very accomplished individual. A happy family man with a beautiful wife and three children. He was at the top of his game in the civil service. He was a great sportsman at school and university. No slouch academically either. He left with a double first in Philosophy, Politics and Economics (PPE) from Oxford. He had played hockey, cricket and rugby for the first teams at school. He gained a blue in both hockey and boxing. Then came top of his year in the notoriously tricky civil service exams on leaving Oxford. Many of his contemporaries thought he might end up as a diplomat, or an ambassador somewhere. Some even suggested he would have made a great spy and should have joined the security services. The general view was that he would have excelled at any career he chose.

He had worked at various departments during his ascent to revered, senior mandarin status, with the requisite knighthood. But had settled at the Department of Trade and Industry which was then renamed the Department of Business, Enterprise and Regulatory Reform (BERR), subsequently the Department for Business, Innovation & Skills before recently being rebranded Department for Business, Energy and Industrial Strategy (BEIS). Cross thought these meaningless changes, presumably wrought out of the desire to look as though progress was being made in some way, must have cost millions in stationery alone. Brook was well respected and had had the ears of several prime ministers over the years. It seemed to Cross that he had hardly put a foot wrong in a long career. Evidenced by the fact that he had disappeared almost completely from the general public eye in the corridors of Whitehall for decades, before reappearing at the top of the civil service pyramid. He had been in the news recently because of the Moreton inquiry of which he appeared to be the main architect. Although it had been carried out by an eminent KC it was Brook who had commissioned it. He felt that Moreton's behaviour as a junior minister was simply inexcusable. Cross noted that the civil servant had talked about an institution-wide systemic culture of intimidation and bullying which was no longer acceptable or fit for purpose. He stated his desire to eradicate this culture once and for all.

Cross thought this was interesting from a man who had kept his head firmly below the parapet, and taking on the ministerial club was a risky move. But in the end, it had paid off. Cross had been aware of the inquiry before the Moreton murder and had read that if the inquiry came up empty-handed, it would be the end of Brook's career. Resignation would have been inevitable. An illustrious career would come to a quick end through a self-inflicted wound, many political commentators adjudged.

Cross then began a painstaking process of going through Brook's career and life since he left Oxford. There were huge gaps as he pulled the strings of government under his mandarin's cloak of invisibility. What Cross was interested in was if and when his and Sandy Moreton's paths crossed. This took hours of cross-referencing with little success to show for it. This never worried Cross because in his mind the less he found, the more significant what he did find would prove to be.

After All Saints, the two men went on to attend the same senior school, Downside. All Saints was a feeder for it. But Cross then noticed that Moreton was in the year below Brook at Oxford. It was possible that Moreton had taken a year off to travel, a gap year. But he hadn't spoken about it anywhere. He did say how his GCSEs had been disastrous but that everything had turned round in the sixth form where he blossomed to such an extent that he got into Oxford. Cross highlighted this in his file.

Another thing that interested him was that Brook hadn't taken up boxing until his second year at Oxford. He'd already got a hockey blue, but seemed to have dropped that for boxing. Sandy Moreton had been a boxer at school and joined the Oxford University boxing club in his first year. Cross searched for photographs of the boxing teams at the time but found nothing online. He got in touch with Gillman and Soame, an Oxford-based photographers who seemed to do all the college and sports teams photographs. He gave them the years he was looking at and half an hour later three photographs of the university boxing teams of the time came through.

They all looked so young and fit, smartly dressed in their blazers and ties. One of them had a black eye. But Brook and Moreton were together in two of them. In the first, Brook's second year, they were both in the team, standing at either end of the back row as if they'd had to have distance put between them. In the second photograph Brook was now captain, sitting in the centre of the front row. To his right on the end was Moreton. In the final photograph Brook had now left university and Moreton had taken his place as captain of the boxing team.

Cross made a note of the coach of the team. He looked like he would have been in his forties at the time of the photographs so there was every chance he might still be alive. A former professional boxer himself and part of the Olympic squad in the Munich Olympics of nineteen seventy-two, his name was Bob Richmond.

'Of course, I remember them two,' the old coach laughed hoarsely on the other end of the phone. 'I remember all of my captains. Keep in touch with most of them.'

'Are you in touch with Brook and Moreton?'

'Not so much. I mean, they're busy people. Richard more so than Sandy. Lovely man. Always keeps tabs on what's happening with the club. Helps in any way he can, does Sir Richard,' said Richmond, dropping Brook's title with a chuckle of pride. 'We have reunions now and then which they sometimes come to. Not too often, you understand. We think the less frequent the better the attendance, if you know what I mean.'

'Do they get along socially?' Cross asked, causing another cackle of laughter.

'No. I don't know what it was with them two. Always at each other's throats.'

'Did they ever box each other?' Cross asked.

'Did they ever! Sparred, if you can call it that. It got so full-on at times we had to step in and stop them. They were the same weight, so often were put together sparring. But more often than not technique would go flying out of the window and they went at it hammer and tongs. It became pointless after a while, so we had to stop them sparring with each other altogether.'

'No love lost between them then,' commented Cross.

'It went back to their schooldays, someone told me. But I don't know if that's true.'

'I noticed Brook didn't box in his first year.'

'No, he was a hockey blue. He was one of those people who could just turn their hand to any sport and excel at it, I reckon,' said the old coach.

'But Moreton boxed at school. Is that correct?'

'Yes. Brook once told me, after he'd left, and he'd had a glass or two it had to be said, the only reason he took up boxing at Oxford was so that he could have a pop at Moreton on a regular basis. Legitimately. Maybe he was joking. And, of course, there was all that nonsense with the girl. That didn't help,' added Hazell.

'What girl would that be?' asked Cross.

'Richard Brook's wife. She was Moreton's girlfriend at Oxford. Completely besotted, he was. She was an absolute beauty. Everyone knew who she was. If you'd had to put money on any two students getting married it would've been those two.'

'What happened?'

'Richard Brook happened. I mean, you couldn't blame him. People used to say she was out of Sandy's league. But he was heartbroken. I'm not sure he ever got over it. Boxed in a completely different way in his third year after she'd left him. Ruthless, he was. And of course she was in his year so he kept seeing her around – when she wasn't in London, that is.'

'You seem to know an awful lot about it. Did Moreton talk to you about her?'

'A little. It was the other lads who filled me in.'

'And they're still married?' Cross observed.

'Yep. And Moreton never married himself. That tells you quite a lot. Maybe he never got over it. But that's probably just the romantic in me.'

Sandy Moreton left Oxford and became a manager in a well-known hedge fund, Kendall, Bowes and Crisp (KBC), where, apparently, he continued to box in City charity boxing nights. He left just under a decade later by 'mutual agreement' to pursue other opportunities. As Cross knew full well, separations by 'mutual agreement' were almost always anything but. Someone was pushed or someone jumped. He made a note of the date and started a major trawl through the business pages of the time. He finally came across a parliamentary report on hedge funds misreporting returns to cover up losses. It was a widespread practice, the report concluded, but one firm in particular came into the report's sights: Kendall, Bowes and Crisp. Their reporting was found to be systematically at fault. Large swathes of data were unearthed to show that they regularly misreported. The company held up its hands and said systems had been put in place to ensure this never happened again. Changes were also being made in their corporate offices. This meant that a number of people were sacked. Sandy Moreton himself left four weeks after the publication of the report. Obviously no coincidence. But what was of more importance to Cross was buried in one of the appendices. It was a list of the contributors to the report alongside the main authors. There, in the middle of a long list, was Richard Brook, a middling civil servant at the time.

It seemed to Cross that the next time these two men's paths crossed again was at the BEIS where Brook was the leading civil servant and Moreton became a junior minister. This meant that he was, in effect, working for Moreton and reported to him. Cross could imagine how little this would have appealed to Brook. It was this final connection with his old rival that seemed to have led to Moreton's current problematic situation. It really did seem that his political career had come to an end thanks to Brook's inquiry. On the balance of his research thus far Cross did wonder whether Moreton's claim that the inquiry had been a witch hunt with a personal agenda might have more than an element of truth about it.

72

Sir Richard Brook had an effortless, urbane and immaculate appearance which had doubtless been honed over the years and occurred now on a daily basis with little or no thought. He was wearing a three-piece blue pinstripe when he met Cross in his grand Whitehall office. The stripe was a chalky one and Cross noticed it was an English drape cut. He wore a white shirt with the cuffs protruding just the right amount from below the jacket to display his cufflinks. He wore a woven silk tie, blue with the smallest of white dots.

'Anderson and Sheppard?' asked Cross.

'A man who knows his suits. Yes, it is,' said Brook standing up at his imposingly large mahogany desk and offering his hand, which Cross ignored. This didn't put the man out at all as he magically morphed the gesture into an indication that they should sit at the large leather sofas on the distant side of the acreage of his office. It was as if he hadn't been offering a handshake at all.

'From afar. A man who certainly can't afford bespoke tailoring. Are they your main tailor?' Cross had a genuine interest in the traditional arts, whether it was the construction of church organs or that of a fully bespoke suit.

'Mostly. But I also use Ritchie Charlton if I want something with a more contemporary look. I could introduce you if you like.'

This was a classic example of someone trying to put someone else at their ease. This was Brook telling Cross they were equals. That he should not be put out by the vast grandeur of his office.

That said, if the square footage of the office and the view from the window were indicators of seniority or success, then Brook was at the top of his particular tree.

'As I said, beyond my budget and possibly inappropriate. A detective in bespoke tailoring.'

'I've ordered tea and biscuits. You are this afternoon's excuse for me to indulge.'

'I'm surprised a man in your position needs an excuse,' observed Cross.

'Well of course I don't. That was a joke, Sergeant.'

Cross now became aware of a strong waft of cologne coming from the man opposite him. He recognised it immediately as he himself wore Penhaligon's Blenheim Bouquet from time to time. He decided against commenting on it, thinking it might make him sound like a Sherlock Holmes wannabe showing off his deductive skills.

'The purpose of your visit, Sergeant?'

'Sandy Moreton. You and he have a long association,' Cross began.

'We do. I can't seem to get rid of him.'

'Well, it seems as though you might have succeeded finally. Was that the purpose of the inquiry? To get rid of him?'

'No, that was careless phrasing. Let's put it this way: Sandy Moreton is my Widmerpool,' Brook replied by way of explanation.

'Anthony Powell's *A Dance to the Music of Time*,' said Cross.

'You've read it?'

'I have not. But I'm aware of the character of Widmerpool and what he has come to symbolise. That's quite the indictment of Moreton.'

'This conversation is confidential, yes?' Brook enquired.

'If you wish it to be, yes.'

'It has to be. I'm a civil servant. Mr Moreton was a Member of Parliament.'

'Was, thanks to your report. Your mutual antipathy goes right back to your schooldays.'

'It does, as everyone now knows. Thanks to him. He can't stop going on about it.'

'There was a fight at the school, between the two of you. Is that correct?' Cross asked.

'Yes.'

'And he came off the worst.'

'He did. Even though he boxed for the school. I gave him a good whooping,' Brook corrected him.

'What was the fight about?' asked Cross.

'I can't remember. It must've been about something. But I think it more likely just came out of a general resentment among the schoolboy population of his sense of entitlement. He was the headmaster's son and wanted everyone to know it.'

'The entire school was beaten for that fight. Is that correct?'

'Yes.' Brook laughed at this. 'It was a bit of an "I'm Spartacus" moment. I wasn't given a chance to admit to it. It was a rather wonderful moment of rebellion. Everyone was beaten except for Sandy. The alleged victim.'

'It seems like an extreme measure.'

'Not for Moreton senior.'

'Did his methods have a lasting effect on you?' Cross asked.

'Good lord no. It was so long ago.'

'Not everyone feels that way.'

'Ah, you've spoken to Maurice and his safe space board,' Brook replied.

'I didn't know he called it that.'

'He doesn't officially. But he says it so often it's become a kind of nickname for it. However, I do think, and I've said this to him, that they really need to move on. It's a bit pathetic. Yes, it was terrible. But it was so long ago. Just deal with it.'

'One question I've been meaning to ask. Didn't the teachers object to his methods?' Cross asked.

'Sometimes, yes. Matrons, the women who looked after us

at school, left constantly. It was like a revolving door. I heard from one recently who got in touch. She told us she was fired by Moreton for taking him on about the beatings. She'd just cleaned up the bleeding buttocks of another child, had had enough and told him so. Others just resigned, apparently. You know he had names for them. His canes, Mussolini, Genghis, Roosevelt were the ones I remember. Just weird,' he went on.

'Mozart,' Cross volunteered.

'Yes, that's right,' said Brook who, Cross thought, seemed to be becoming a little reflective. His speech had become slightly hesitant and he rubbed his hands together, as if to comfort himself.

'What about other teachers?' asked Cross. Brook thought about this for a while before answering. If he was thinking about whether to answer at all, or just about what he was going to say, Cross couldn't tell.

'Moreton had a stripe system. If you misbehaved or needed punishing a teacher could give you a stripe. You'd be given a chit and it would be written in a book in the staffroom. You then had to go give Moreton the chit and ask politely for a beating. Which you then duly got. He didn't even want to know what it was for, most of the time. But the thing was, you couldn't take the stripe to him till the end of the day, after five. So, if you were given it in the morning you had it hanging over you all day, with this sick feeling at the pit of your stomach. It was a nightmare.'

'Why was it called a stripe?' asked Cross. 'I always thought stripes were something you earned.'

'Which is exactly right. You earned your beating. But they were named after the stripes that were left on your backside. Great big red weals that would go dark blue then yellow.'

'And the teachers went along with this?'

'Some, not all. In fact, when they realised how dreadful the beatings were they stopped giving out stripes and gave detention instead. As fewer and fewer boys went to Moreton and he saw more and more of us in detention, he banned it. Abolished detention. It was a stripe or nothing.'

'He sounds deranged.'

'Deranged and drunk.' He looked down as he thought about it all.

'Are you upset?' asked Cross as he couldn't tell.

'I was nine, Sergeant. You were prevented from seeing your parents for the first half of term, which could be as long as seven or eight weeks. We were entirely at the man's mercy.'

'Did the teachers leave?' asked Cross.

'A lot of them, yes. He replaced them with retired army officers, most of whom saw nothing wrong with the occasional beating. But even some of them had a problem with it, I think.'

'Sandy Moreton was made head boy rather than you,' said Cross steering the conversation back to Moreton junior.

'Well, firstly there was no guarantee it was mine for the taking. That might have been the pervading popular opinion at the time. But it was more of an assumption. Others' assumption, I should point out,' he said and looked at his watch. 'Sergeant, you do realise this meeting is scheduled for just the one hour?'

'I do. Were you angry about not being head boy?'

'Not at all. It was such an act of blatant nepotism it didn't really matter.'

'How did you feel about him being able to beat other boys?'

'Well, it was an appalling thing for Moreton to impose on his son. Can you imagine anything worse for your popular standing? To be fair to Sandy, he never beat anyone.'

'He seems to claim that he did.'

'Because he's trying to be controversial. It's simply not true. Typical of him not to see the upside of refusing to do it. But that's Sandy. Say one thing he'll immediately say another. Everything has to be a battle, a confrontation,' said Brook.

'You were at senior school together. You did become head boy there.'

'I did.'

'Did you come across him much?'

'Sure, but we were in different boarding houses. I took some classes with him. But other than boxing he was pretty hopeless at sport, so that was about it, really, in terms of paths crossing.'

'Then you were both at Oxford.'

'Correct.'

'One thing interested me. He was a year below you at university, yet you were in the same year at school. Why was that?' Cross asked.

'Simple. He became a bit of an academic mess in the senior school. We were both scholars going in from All Saints. But it seemed without his father's presence and encouragement, albeit in the form of a regular beating, he went to pieces academically. Flunked his GCSEs quite impressively. Then did moderately all right in his A levels. But not good enough for Oxbridge which his father was obsessed with. A bit like my mother, to be honest.'

'So how did he get into Oxford?'

'A number of factors, really. He attended a crammer in London to improve his grades,' replied Brook.

'The crammer his father ran?' asked Cross who already knew the answer. He noticed a slight hesitation and a catch in Brook's voice when he answered.

'Correct. His father got the grades out of him at the crammer. He also knew people at Oxford. You couldn't call them friends. Moreton wasn't very popular, even in academic circles.'

'How do you know that? You're not in academic circles yourself, so how did you find out?' Cross pressed.

'I can't remember now,' Brook replied with the first evasive answer of the day. 'But his father pulled a few strings, identified a subject that was easier to get in with and a college that was short of applications in it.'

'Which was?' asked Cross.

'Divinity.'

'I thought he read Philosophy, Politics and Economics.'

'Changed after the first year. He always neglects to say that he didn't get in on PPE, which is one of the most difficult subjects to get into Oxford to read,' Brook said a little scathingly.

'That must've rankled,' Cross suggested.

'It's the way of the world, Sergeant. I've had to put up with a lot more egregious abuses of position in my career than a father helping his son get into Oxbridge.'

'Why did you give up hockey at university?'

Brook eyed Cross up before he decided how to answer.

'I had my blue,' he answered.

'So why not cricket or football? Two other sports you excelled at.'

'Not good enough.'

'But why boxing?'

'I just felt like it was something I would be good at.'

'Nothing to do with the fact that Sandy Moreton was on the team.'

'Absolutely not,' Brook said unconvincingly.

'Did being teammates make things a little more amicable between the two of you?'

'No.'

'Bob Richmond said,' Cross consulted his notebook, 'that you'd told him you took up boxing so you could "beat the shit out of Moreton legitimately and on a regular basis".'

Brook laughed. 'Did I? I must've been drunk. I don't recall that.'

'He was president of the union.'

'Only because the woman who was supposed to be president that year came down with glandular fever. Look, I don't know where this is all going. But no, I didn't like the man. I didn't join the boxing club because he was in it, I'm not that petty. In truth, I liked the sound of being a boxing blue. But did I enjoy being given the chance to hit him when sparring? Absolutely. He was more loathsome at Oxford than school. Always showing off. Wanting to be the centre of attention. Much like now. Not a lot has changed,' Brook said, a little more animated now.

'You entered the civil service and he went into the City. It was another decade before your paths crossed again,' Cross quoted from his notes.

'Well, I wouldn't go that far,' Brook pushed back.

'The hedge fund report.'

Brook studied the detective for a moment and realised that the man had done his homework.

'I was neither the instigator nor the author of that report,' he replied slowly.

'Even so, it cost Moreton his job and you were one of the accredited contributors,' Cross pointed out.

'I have to say I really don't understand what you're after here, Sergeant,' Brook said.

Cross made no response. It made no difference to him what Brook felt and as he hadn't been asked a question, he simply sat there and said nothing.

'All right, full disclosure. I hadn't been aware of Moreton since I left Oxford. He was out of my orbit, my social circle, my work. I didn't know Moreton worked at KBC until I started working on the report. Something I was assigned to do, by the way. Not something I volunteered for. But it was natural I would be asked, as the department I worked in at the time had hedge funds within its purview. As it happens my work on the report didn't cover Moreton's work whatsoever. I cannot take any credit for his resignation, or more likely sacking. That course of action wasn't a recommendation of the report. It was taken independently of it by the company.'

'Did Moreton make contact with you after the publication? After he was sacked?'

'Not directly, but he started making statements complaining personal agendas were behind the report. All of which was untrue.'

'Then you meet again when he becomes a minister in your department. How did you feel about that?' asked Cross.

'To be honest with you, it simply confirmed to me how the

most appallingly mediocre and unqualified people can succeed in politics.'

'That seems a surprising verdict on a world in which you work and have spent the majority of your life in,' Cross commented.

'I work in government, Sergeant. I am a civil servant. I do not indulge in politics,' Brook answered a little grandly.

'So, you now found yourself in a position of having to work for him.'

'In effect.'

'How was that?'

'No different to working for a lot of the third-rate individuals over the years. On a personal level, however, it was difficult to accept initially. But my job is to put my personal feelings to one side.'

Cross made a note, then turned a page in his notebook. After he carefully read what was written on it, he looked up.

'The bullying inquiry,' he said.

'Yes,' sighed Brook.

'From all that you've said about Sandy Moreton and with the history between the two of you, it would be easy to view the report and its conclusions as some form of retribution,' said Cross.

'DS Cross, you told my secretary that you were coming here to discuss the murder of my former headmaster. Why? I have no idea. But I have made time in my incredibly busy day to talk to you. What, may I ask, does any of this have to do with the murder of AFM?'

'You have granted me an hour which I will not exceed. How I decide to utilise that hour for the purposes of my investigation is entirely up to me, Mr Brook.'

'Even so—'

'Would you prefer to continue this conversation back at my unit in Bristol? A six hour round trip?' Cross asked.

'No, of course not,' replied Brook, sensibly deciding to stop complaining.

'How did the inquiry and the subsequent report into Moreton's behaviour come into being?' Cross asked.

'I take full responsibility for it all. I like to think I run an open and fair-minded department. That if any misconduct occurs people feel they can come right to the top and report without any splash back on them or their career. Rumours had started swirling around Moreton's conduct within days of his arrival which was, to say the least, unusual. It wasn't long before two of them landed on my desk. By then I had seen several examples of his unacceptable behaviour with my own eyes. Yelling at junior civil servants. Tearing up papers that people had been up all night to get ready for him, theatrically, in front of the whole office. I wondered whether my relationship with him was the reason for it. That he was demonstrating his power for my benefit. But a few calls to other places he'd worked in all confirmed a similar pattern of behaviour.'

'Did you talk to him about it in private?' asked Cross.

'I did on several occasions. But I think he felt he was able to do exactly as he liked and he sort of revelled in it.'

'Were you ever subject to it?'

'Oh yes, to all the usual ministerial tirades about people not doing their jobs properly, not being briefed properly when he had, but just hadn't paid attention. About the civil service obstructing the proper running of the country. Constant references to the Circumlocution Office from *Little Dorrit*, not that I believe the man has ever read a page of Dickens. The final straw was when a civil servant showed Moreton a report on his iPad in my office. Moreton was well known for wanting everything printed. Moreton took the iPad, screamed at the young woman and hurled it at the wall.'

'What happened then?' asked Cross thinking secretly that he had some sympathy for Moreton's preference, if not his behaviour.

'I adjourned the meeting and spoke with him again. I told him there was no room for that kind of behaviour in my department and that I would not only report it, but would be suggesting an official inquiry into his behaviour.'

'What was his response?' asked Cross.

'He had that same smug, entitled look he had as a twelve-year-old boy. A look that said he was untouchable. He told me to do whatever I wished. He was a minister of the crown and could behave as he liked. But this time he didn't have his father's protection as headmaster. I think he felt he had the PM's. But he was wrong.'

'How did you feel about his eventual resignation and recall?'

'I was glad he'd been found out. Relieved it was all over. Happy that we'd demonstrated that such behaviour was unacceptable in government, whoever you might be. But also, that it showed complaints would be listened to and acted upon. I hoped it would discourage such behaviour and encourage others to come forward, if they had a concern without worrying about a black mark appearing against them. I also think Parliament is better off without him marring its benches.'

Cross found himself thinking about Warner as he listened to this sentiment and feeling unsure that the same could be said about the police.

'What was Moreton's reaction?'

'Well, it's been well documented in the press. I'm sure you've read the coverage.'

'I meant to you personally. Have you heard from him?'

'Oh yes. He confronted me in the street in Whitehall. Completely orchestrated. He had a trail of cameras and press behind him like some kind of media Pied Piper. It's on YouTube. He was furious. Held me personally to blame. Announced to the press that I was the weasel, I think he said, or the quisling, I can't remember which, behind the witch hunt. As with most bullies in life, he was looking for excuses and deflection.'

'But the man's political career is over,' Cross pointed out.

'Oh, it is, and his character has been fully exposed. I don't think his next step will be an easy one.'

Cross nodded thoughtfully.

'One thing has surprised me with regard to his father's murder. Why hasn't he used it for more political capital, more media exposure? Gained the public sympathy. I would've expected that of him,' observed Brook.

'I think he did at the beginning,' Cross remarked.

'True, but since the "not guilty" verdict at the trial he's been unusually quiet.'

Cross thought about this. It was indeed true.

'I would've expected him to launch a full-on assault on the ineptitude of the police. About the need for justice in this country. He's always so quick to point the finger at people. But not this time.'

'Where were you on the ninth of September this year?'

'September the ninth. Was that the night of the murder?' Brook asked.

'No, a couple of weeks before.'

'Let me check,' he said, walking over to the computer on the corner of his desk. 'Oh yes. I took a long weekend that weekend.'

'Did you go away?'

'I did not.'

'Were you in London?'

'I was.'

'Did you leave London for any reason?'

'I did not.' Brook looked at his watch. Cross had no need to. He knew he had just over five minutes left.

'The crammer Sandy Moreton attended to get his grades for Oxford, run by his father,' Cross began.

'Yes,' Brook answered enquiringly.

'Is that the same crammer your brother attended?' Cross consulted his notes and looked up. 'Adam?'

For the first time Brook looked discomfited. He leant forward with his elbows on the desk as if unsure what to do with himself, but confident that this posture normally exuded authority. But this time it was wrapped in a cloak of uncertainty as if he was unsure what to do with himself. Whether he should get up and go over, stand to assert himself and bring the meeting to a close or just stay where he was. He decided on the latter.

'It was.'

'And was it before or after he sat his exams that he took his own life?'

'Before. Three weeks before.'

'Was it expected?' Cross asked.

Brook sighed then laughed in a puzzled, resigned way and shook his head all at the same time.

'Um, no. I mean, had it been in any way expected I'd like to think one of us would've stepped in and tried to help.'

'Were you aware he was unhappy?'

'Yes, of course.'

'Why was he there? His grades were good enough for university.'

'Because they weren't good enough for Oxbridge.'

'And your father sent him there despite everything you'd told him about All Saints.'

'It was my mother, actually. I come from a very matriarchal family. My father married money, my mother always said, a little unkindly. She believed she'd married below her station in life, for love. Made her the romantic heroine in her eyes. I adored her, but boy, was she a tough old thing. She was obsessed with both of us going to Oxbridge. There was simply no point in going anywhere else in the UK if we wanted a proper university education. It was either Oxbridge or the States, for her.'

'He was four years younger than you?'

'Correct.'

'Why was he sent to All Saints after your experience there?'

'My mother didn't listen to either of us. Or she did listen, just didn't believe us. Because let's face it, it was pretty extreme. She thought on the whole Moreton's methods, whatever they were, had stood me in good stead for life, so there was no debate in her mind. Adam had to go to the crammer where that bastard tortured poor Adey. There's no other word for it. Beat the shit out of him all over again. At seventeen, can you believe the humiliation? You're beginning to feel like you're growing up and suddenly you're a nine-year-old on the end of a beating again. If boys were troublesome at the crammer, I mean not all of them were as easy to bully as boys between the ages of seven and thirteen, AFM just told the parents to withdraw them, or he expelled them. It was all about keeping the overall grades up.'

'And did they?'

'Some did. Remember, just being there was an act of despair on the part of the parents. But Moreton's results spoke for themselves. He succeeded in improving grades, he bullied the boys into academic excellence, or rather excellence at sitting exams.'

'Your brother hanged himself,' Cross stated baldly.

'He did.' Brook grimaced. The pain of the memory obviously still keen. 'Can I ask, how is this relevant to Moreton's murder?'

'Do you blame Alistair Moreton for Adam's death?'

'Oh, I see. Of course I fucking do,' Brook answered with force. The use of the expletive seemed so out of keeping with this man, his suit, his perfectly cut and combed hair, his carefully put together demeanour, the surroundings they were in. Cross looked at his watch.

'My time is up,' he announced leaving his chair and walking towards the door. He stopped and turned before he opened it. He'd spotted a photograph among a number of framed pictures on the window behind the desk of Brook with, presumably, his wife and a dog.

'Do you own a dog, Sir Richard?'

'I do,' the mandarin replied, looking at the photograph fondly.

Cross didn't need to ask what breed the dog was. He already knew.

It was a Rhodesian Ridgeback.

73

Over the next couple of days Ottey was in regular contact with Jacky Collins in Kent. The three other victims were willing to come forward now, in light of Alice's attack and her determination to press charges. As were dozens of other women, some of whom claimed to have been sexually assaulted by Warner. Others were the subject of inappropriate touching or the recipients of unwelcome indecent texts from him. Collins was more than happy not to tell her DCI or detective superintendent of the imminent arrest of one of their lead detectives. She felt they had been complicit in allowing Warner to get away with his behaviour for all this time, simply because he 'got results'.

Warner duly returned to work the following Thursday morning as if nothing had happened. As Cross had predicted. He had scratch marks on his face which he laughingly, in Collins's opinion, blamed on an elderly neighbour's cat he had rescued from an old coal flue. Collins thought he might have come up with something more original than a cat. She also couldn't believe how he was welcomed back into the fold like a returning hero, despite the fact that the verdict in the Cotterell case had gone against him. She was also aware that he'd been dismissed by Carson and so to hear him claim that he'd decided for himself that fresh eyes were needed was galling. But she comforted herself with the knowledge that his self-satisfied smile would be wiped from his face soon enough when he was arrested the following morning. She wondered whether his confident smile emanated from thinking he'd gotten away with it once again. That to his mind, he really was untouchable.

Cross and Ottey sat in her car at eight thirty the next morning outside the building which housed Kent's serious crime office. It had been an early start from Bristol. They watched as Warner pulled up an hour later, parked, got out of his car and stubbed a cigarette out on the ground. He tightened his loose tie and went into the building looking like he didn't have a care in the world. He didn't realise that world was about to be turned on its head. Cross had been happy to arrest him in the car park. But Ottey and Collins wanted it to be done in front of all his colleagues and, more importantly, their superiors.

Ottey received a text from Collins. Warner was at his desk.

She met them at reception and walked them through security. They went upstairs and then through an area that was not too dissimilar to the MCU. Desks, computers, cork- and whiteboards. If you'd taken a photograph and shown it to someone, then asked them what business or organisation worked from that office, they would probably be hard pressed to answer. Warner was at a desk at the far end of the room, which afforded him the opportunity to see the two Avon and Somerset detectives enter and walk the length of the room towards him. Interestingly, he made no disparaging gags at their expense, just waited till they reached him.

Cross spoke first.

'Robert Warner, I am arresting you on suspicion of sexual assault and attempted rape.'

The reaction round the room was immediate. Everyone stopped what they were doing, looking up from their computers, cutting off phone calls abruptly. Some of the men stood up, as if this was in some way a supportive action. Then Collins and six other women walked forward and formed a semicircle behind the detectives from Bristol. Presumably they had all been subjected to advances from him, maybe more, and this was a tacit demonstration for him of how serious things were. That they were not going to back down. Ottey produced her handcuffs.

'You've got to be kidding,' Warner said in disbelief.

'I am not,' she replied firmly. 'Put your hands behind your back.'

'Boss!' yelled Warner like a small child in need of help from a parent, as Cross read him his rights.

A man appeared from a side office.

'What the hell is going on?' he asked as he saw Warner being cuffed, and strode across the room.

'We're arresting Mr Warner,' Ottey replied, deliberately not using his rank.

'For what?'

'Sexual assault and attempted rape,' said Cross.

'And I have a feeling that's just for starters,' added Ottey.

'For Christ's sake,' spat Warner.

'You've been cautioned, Bobby, don't say any more. As for you two, you can't just come in here and arrest one of my detectives.'

'DI Warner being in handcuffs would suggest otherwise,' replied Cross handing him their warrant.

'And why didn't you, or for that matter your CO, have the courtesy to forewarn me?' DCI Hart, as the badge on his lanyard proclaimed him to be, asked.

'The general thinking was not to forewarn you in case you forewarned him,' Cross replied candidly.

'Names. Your names.'

Cross handed him their cards which he had ready in his pocket for exactly this.

'Were you in on this?' Hart asked Collins.

'Very much so,' she said, with no apparent regard for any possible consequences.

Hart looked up from the warrant. 'Who is your CO?' he asked.

'I've written it on the back of my card together with his mobile number which he was very insistent you had,' Cross told him.

'Let's go,' Ottey said to Warner with a suggestive nudge.

'Boss, are you just going to let this happen? They can't bloody do this!' Warner protested over his shoulder as he was led away. Hart didn't answer, instead he turned to Collins.

'My office in five,' he barked, before leaving the open area.

Ottey and Cross walked Warner through the open area. Cross was conscious of how slowly Ottey was walking, as if to make the very most of this walk of shame. Warner said nothing further, probably mindful of having been cautioned and that any ill-advised comments might not look great for him later. The other detectives stood, looking on in silence. Whether they saw it as a salutary warning or simply something that should have happened long ago, it was impossible to tell.

When they got to the car Warner turned to Ottey.

'Josie—' he began in a conciliatory tone.

'You've been cautioned, DI Warner. I suggest you say nothing till you've spoken with a lawyer.'

She opened the door and gently pushed his head down as he got into the back seat, as she would with any other suspect. Then she re-cuffed him with his hands in front of him for the journey.

74

Carson had been fully aware of their journey to Kent and so wasn't in the least surprised when the call came in from DCI Hart's superior in Kent, a Detective Superintendent Miller.

'Were you aware that two of your detectives marched into my HQ this morning and arrested one of mine?'

'I was, sir, yes,' Carson replied.

'So would you mind explaining why you didn't pay me the courtesy of informing me?' Miller asked.

'Let me answer that with a question. Do your detectives make a point of calling a suspect's employer to let them know an arrest is going to be made in their place of work?' Carson asked.

'That's completely different and you know it. We're the bloody police. We're on the same team.'

'I think that answers your question, sir.'

'What are you trying to suggest?' Miller asked indignantly.

'I'm not trying to suggest anything.'

'Then let me ask you a question you might want to reflect on. How do you think your chief constable is going to react to the call he's going to receive from mine?'

'When availed of the facts, I'm sure he'll be completely supportive.'

'I'm not sure mine will be so accommodating.'

'With respect, sir, these allegations are very serious. What is more, I'm reliably informed three victims claiming to have been raped by Warner are now willing to come forward. Two of whom worked in your force. So, you might want to consider very carefully what you say to your chief, if you're at all worried what side of history you land on.'

The call was ended abruptly by Miller.

'Annie, can you get me the chief constable's office on the phone?' Carson called out to his secretary. He'd made the decision during the call to go straight to the top rather than through his immediate superiors, as he wanted the chief to hear it directly from him.

As Warner got out of the car at the MCU building he looked up and saw dozens of faces looking down from the windows that overlooked the car park. Word had spread quickly. One of those faces was Alice Mackenzie, now back at work. This was the closest she would get to Warner before the trial. Ottey had asked her to keep well away. But she needed to see her attacker in cuffs.

There was an unusually quiet and sombre atmosphere in the custody suite as Warner was asked if he understood why he'd been arrested. He was photographed but excused the additional humiliation of being fingerprinted as his prints were already in the system. (As a police officer, his prints had been put in the database for reasons of elimination at crime scenes.) Melissa the forensic investigator then arrived with a male colleague to photograph the scratches on his face. She also swabbed his hands for any traces of pepper spray although it was a long shot considering the amount of time since the attack. This was the last Cross and Ottey would see of him. Two detectives, who had been briefed, read the crime report, read Alice's statement and also interviewed her, arrived. They would be conducting Warner's interview.

75

The day had been a long one and that night Cross went to practise the organ. As always in situations like this, where cases became more difficult and the solution didn't seem anywhere in sight, he found playing cleared his mind. At these times he would always play pieces that were familiar to him, so he didn't have to think. He just played instinctively, freeing up his mind to juggle the facts of the case in hand. The sounds of the organ, particularly the low pedal notes reverberating off the walls, in an almost physical way, put him in a familiar safe and comforting solitary place. He began thinking about the Moreton case. For him there were currently only two possible leads to follow. Who came to Moreton's door in the days leading up to the murder? A visit which threw Moreton, according to Napier. The other was the dog. Moreton was bitten by a dog during his fatal attack. Swift had concluded categorically that it was a Rhodesian Ridgeback. Did it belong to Brook? He was surprised to learn that there were now over eleven thousand of that breed in the UK.

As it was the first Thursday of the month, he had been expecting his mother that night. But neither she nor Stephen were there after he finished practice. So, he cycled home. Back at the flat he made himself a cup of tea and a ham sandwich. He only ever had a sandwich after organ practice because Stephen normally gave him a slice of cake and his appetite was thus diminished. The sandwich had become part of his routine, a habit, and habits were something Cross had a problem changing.

He sat down and began looking at several links about Richard

Brook he'd saved on his laptop. There was as little information about his private life as you would expect from a man who had spent his entire career in the civil service. People like that had a tendency to be in the shadows and deliberately not seek the limelight. It made their job easier and less complicated that way. But it was on his Wikipedia page, not always an entirely reliable source of information, Cross felt, that he saw a tiny detail which had hitherto evaded him. In his biography were the names of his parents, Martin and Hilary. His father was still alive but Cross noticed that his mother had died that year – just a month before Moreton's death. The mother who had been so insistent on sending Adam Brook to Moreton's crammer. It was exactly the kind of small detail that Cross knew often proved to be significant.

He picked up his phone and dialled Cal Napier's number.

'Mr Cross!' exclaimed the voice on the other end of the line.

'DS Cross,' he corrected him.

'That's the one! What's up? What can I do for you, sir?'

'I'm going to send you five photographs of different men. I want you to tell me if you recognise any of them as the man who came to the cottage and discombobulated Alistair Moreton,' Cross said.

'Disco—what?'

'The man who came and seemed to upset him. But I want to make it clear that it may well not be any of them,' Cross stipulated.

'Okay, bro. Fire away!'

Cross then sent over five pictures of various men taken from recent online articles which he numbered one to five. Three minutes later his phone rang.

'That's him, definitely,' Napier said.

'Which one?'

'Number four.'

'Are you certain?'

'Definitely. I had eyes on him the whole time.'

'Were you able to hear what they were talking about?'

'No, but it started out all right then the man, number four, he got quite upset. Started shouting and jabbing his finger at the old man. Filip thought he might have to step in at one point.'

'Did Gallinis see him as well?' Cross asked.

'Yep.'

'Give me his number,' Cross demanded.

'What? I can't do that. Data protection an' all that,' Cal protested.

'Mr Napier, this could be vitally important.'

'Okay, because it's you, right? And remember this is a favour. You owe me, man,' Cal laughed.

Ten minutes later Gallinis confirmed the same thing. Cross double-checked that he hadn't spoken with Napier about it, and he swore he hadn't. He confirmed that the man in the picture who had a confrontation with Alistair Moreton at the cottage was Sir Richard Brook.

76

Brook's secretary refused to put Cross through the next morning which, though he found it annoying, he thought was completely understandable. He told her who he was and that it was urgent. Ten minutes later Brook was on the phone.

'Sergeant, how can I help?' he asked with the perfected equanimity of a civil servant who, although irritated at being pulled out of an important meeting, gave no indication of it whatsoever.

'I need to speak to you again,' Cross informed him.

'Which is why I'm on the phone.'

'In person.'

'When?'

'Today.'

'Well let me look at my diary for the day. How long will it take you to get to London?' he asked.

'In Bristol,' Cross answered.

'What? No. That's impossible. You'll have to come to me, I'm afraid.'

'You need to come to Bristol, Sir Richard,' Cross said with a neutral calmness that implied there was no room for negotiation here.

'Why?'

'I will tell you why when you get here. By my estimation if you left fairly promptly, you could be here by twelve. That's on the assumption you're driven here. I'd need to recalculate if you were to come by taxi and train.'

'You don't seem to understand. I deal in government business at the very highest level, Sergeant Cross. My day today has been planned months in advance. I can't just drop everything with no notice.'

'I think the lack of understanding seems to be on your part, sir. You have a choice. You can either be driven down here with the minimum of fuss, or you can be arrested in your office and driven down by my colleagues in the Met.'

'What?' the civil servant replied in disbelief. Cross said nothing as he was happy he'd made himself perfectly clear. 'DS Cross, I had nothing to do with Alistair Moreton's death.'

'Murder,' Cross corrected him. 'Which is it to be?'

'I'll be with you by twelve. Text me the address,' he said tersely before ending the call.

DI Bobby Warner had answered every question put to him during his interview with a 'no comment'. He obviously intended doing all his arguing, or have it done for him, in court. Statements had now been obtained by the three alleged rape victims and others were in the process of giving their statements about various assaults and harassment at his hands. He was formally charged and, when he appeared in court later, bail was denied. He was remanded in custody till his trial, which wouldn't be for several months.

Carson had been summoned to the chief constable's office. He was questioned about the whole Mackenzie incident and his handling of it. As to whether the chief and his surrounding council of senior officers thought he had acted as he should have done, they kept very close to their chests.

Carson had then called a meeting of the whole department to brief them in full about the Warner situation. He also made his unease clear. His unease that harassment and inappropriate behaviour might exist in the Avon and Somerset Police. He himself wouldn't tolerate it and wanted both women and men to feel comfortable in going to their immediate superiors with any concerns or complaints. They would be taken very seriously and confidentially.

77

'Shit,' was Ottey's immediate reaction when Cross told her about Brook being on his way to Bristol. 'Shit,' was her reaction when then told of the timing of his mother's death and her matriarchal role in the Brook family. By the time he told her Brook owned a Rhodesian Ridgeback she seemed to have no exclamations left. He arrived in a chauffeur-driven Jaguar. He was as immaculate as the day Cross had seen him in his office. Different suit and tie but the same elegance. He was taken into an interview room with a lawyer he'd brought down from London with him. Cross and Ottey came into the room. Cross organised his folder. The lawyer spoke immediately.

'Is my client going to be placed under arrest?'

'He is not. But this will be an interview conducted under caution,' replied Cross.

Ottey then cautioned Brook. Cross noticed that, although in a completely different environment from his palatial Whitehall office, Brook was nevertheless undiminished. He sat upright and confident. Was this his natural bearing, or was it because he had nothing to worry about?

'How would you like to be addressed? Sir Richard? Richard? Mr Brook?' Cross began.

'Thank you for asking. Richard will be absolutely fine,' he replied cordially.

'Richard, when was the last time you saw Alistair Moreton?' Cross asked.

'I've already answered that question.'

'Sir Richard, as you are now being interviewed under caution, you may well have to answer some questions you've already been asked,' his lawyer advised him, with the noticeable use of his title as if to remind everyone in the room of his client's status.

'At my brother's funeral, probably. I'm not entirely sure,' Brook replied, as before.

'You blame Alistair Moreton for your brother's death, do you not?' Cross asked.

The lawyer leant forward and whispered in Brook's ear.

'No, I'd like to answer that,' Brook replied, disagreeing with whatever he'd just been advised. 'Yes, I do. Alistair Moreton was a monster as a headmaster. His behaviour was completely unacceptable at All Saints, yet he got away with it till he was sacked. He bullied and tortured Adam at the crammer in London.'

'Why was he there? Your brother?' Cross asked.

'Because my mother was obsessed with Oxbridge and my father, as always, just fell in line.'

'But you had both presumably told your parents of Moreton's methods, his incessant beatings?'

'Yes.'

'And yet they went ahead. Why was that?' asked Cross.

'I think in part because Mother thought we exaggerated, but also because she thought his methods were successful.'

'Did Adam protest at the decision?'

'Absolutely. We both did. But my mother could be very persuasive. She told Adam it was only for a few months and then it would all be over.'

'But your brother left early and killed himself,' Cross stated matter-of-factly.

'Correct.'

'Did your mother blame herself?'

'She never said as much. But I think so, yes. I mean, who wouldn't? But it never occurred to us, any of us, that Adey would do such a thing.'

'Did you discuss it with your parents after it had happened?'

'No. Not after the funeral. They weren't great like that. Showing their feelings, let alone discussing them. They just felt it had happened and we should get on with life. My mother, though, never got over it.'

'So, to be perfectly clear. You never discussed Moreton, your brother's suicide and the possibility that his treatment of him had something to do with it, with either of them?'

'Possibility? That man was almost solely to blame.'

'Did your brother have other mental issues?' asked Ottey.

'I didn't think so at the time but now, obviously, we have to accept that he must've done. The fact that I didn't know, or even worse, didn't notice, just makes it all the more painful.'

'Are you over your brother's suicide? Emotionally?' asked Ottey.

'Of course not. You never are.'

'Did you ever consider confronting Moreton?' asked Cross.

Brook paused momentarily.

'No. What would be the point? And like I said, that would have been tantamount to blaming my mother,' he replied.

'Is that why you waited till after she died?' Cross asked.

There was a significant pause. The lawyer remained completely poker-faced.

'Did you wait until after your mother's death to confront Moreton?' Cross repeated.

'Of course not,' replied Brook, his mask of composure slipping for the first time in the interview.

'I mean, a man with the many resources you have at your fingertips in government would surely have little or no trouble tracking him down. But then, you had no need. You saw Peter Montgomery had posted Moreton's address.'

Brook made no response.

'Unfortunately for you, but quite usefully for us, you didn't initially make a note of it before Maurice Simpson deleted it. So, you private messaged him and asked him for it,' Cross explained.

Again, Brook said nothing.

'To be fair to Montgomery,' said Ottey chipping in, 'even when we arrested him, he said nothing about you. The old boy network at work. But we had his computer and found the messages between you.'

'Did you go to Alistair Moreton's cottage prior to his murder?' Cross asked.

Brook's lawyer leant over and whispered in his ear at length. Brook then turned back to Cross and stared at him. Cross simply looked straight back and read Brook as being conflicted. But the civil servant said nothing.

'What are you thinking about, Richard?' Ottey asked.

'He's calculating whether we only have his asking Montgomery for the address or we have more evidence,' observed Cross. It had become a familiar poker moment in an interview for him.

'I did not.'

Cross noted a slight blink of surprise in the lawyer's eye.

'Do you want to reconsider that answer?' he asked.

A lengthy pause followed.

'I do not.'

'We have two eyewitnesses that put you at Moreton's door the week before his murder,' Cross informed him.

'Who are these witnesses? Moreton lived alone. He was notoriously antisocial,' commented the lawyer, who was obviously very well briefed.

'That is immaterial,' Cross responded, while at the same time curious as to how the lawyer may have come across this information.

'They have both, independently, picked you out of a photo lineup, Richard,' Ottey told him.

'Why did you just lie?' asked Cross.

'My apologies,' came the suave, assured answer.

'Why then?' asked Cross. 'Why, after all this time, did you choose to go to Moreton and confront him?'

'As you correctly pointed out, my mother had just died. I was no longer held back by that.'

'What happened when you went there?'

'I told him who I was. But there was no need. He knew. He proceeded to tell me how proud he was of me. He'd been watching my career from afar. I was his star pupil. It was so offensive to hear that coming out of his mouth. Didn't even mention the Sandy situation. But that didn't surprise me. I always felt that he didn't think much of his son. That maybe he was always a disappointment. Anyway, I just came right out with it. I told him he'd killed my brother and that I'd never be able to forgive him. I just wanted him to know that's what we all felt. I lambasted him for the way he'd treated us children. Told him I thought he was a barbarian who should've ended up in prison for what he'd done. It got quite heated quite quickly. The old temper rose to the surface in him, and I saw the tyrant I recognised. He pushed back hard, tried to defend himself, which only made things worse. He was quite agitated which, I don't know, maybe that was enough for me. So, I left.'

'How did you feel after that encounter?' Ottey asked.

'In all honesty, I felt a little ashamed. But also liberated.'

'Why ashamed?' she asked.

'He was an old man, a little frail. I'm not sure what I expected. But actually, I'd do it again. Just because he got old shouldn't be a reason to think he should be able to get away with it. That there'd be no consequences for what he'd done to us and for Adam's death.'

'Which is why you went back on the seventeenth of September and killed him,' said Cross. 'The ultimate consequence.'

'I did not kill Alistair Moreton, nor did I go back to his house,' he replied calmly.

'You have lied to us on a number of occasions. Why should we believe you now? You see how difficult you've made it for yourself?' Cross pointed out.

'Because it's the truth.'

Cross simply looked back at the man blankly.

'Where were you the night of September the seventeenth?' asked Ottey.

'Now I've actually checked this. It was a Sunday, and I was at home.'

'Were you alone?' she asked.

'No. My wife was away for a weekend jaunt with her girlfriends. I was at home alone with my father,' he replied.

'Will he testify to that?' asked Cross.

'No. He has Alzheimer's.'

'I'm sorry to hear that,' said Ottey.

'Does he live at home with you normally?' asked Cross.

'He does.'

'Presumably you have help?' Cross asked.

'Yes. Carers come in. They get him up in the morning. Spend time with him in the afternoon and then put him to bed in the evening.'

'Does he go to bed at a regular time?' Cross asked.

'Yes, like clockwork. He may have lost his mind but he likes his routine and gets very upset if it isn't adhered to. He tends to go up around seven.'

'Do you use an agency? For the carers?'

'We do.'

'Could we have their details?'

'Of course.' He wrote a name and number on a piece of paper. Ottey disappeared for a few moments to ask Alice to check the agency's roster that night. Find out who was caring for Martin Brook and speak to them. Cross continued, meanwhile.

'Richard Brook. Did you kill Alistair Moreton?' asked Cross.

'I did not.'

'But as you've told us, you had a major issue with him. Not only because of the physical abuse you received at his hands as a young boy, but you're convinced he drove your brother to his death,' Ottey pointed out. 'It would be completely understandable if you had. Like you said, his actions should have consequences.'

'I didn't mean it in the way you are putting it. My brother's been dead a long time. Moreton was an old man. What would be achieved by doing that?'

'Is it true to say you hated the man?' she asked.

'It is. Yes. But if that were grounds for suspicion for his murder, you'd have hundreds of suspects around my age.'

'You have history with Moreton's son, Sandy,' said Cross changing tack.

Brook sighed. They'd already talked about this, but he knew he'd have to go over it again. He had no choice.

'Our lives seem to have collided at various points, yes,' he conceded.

'Are you pleased that it would appear you have ended his political career? That in the end, perhaps, you came out on top?' Cross asked.

'Pleased would imply a level of personal satisfaction,' Brook replied.

'It would, yes, which is why I phrased it that way.'

'No, I'm way beyond that. I was simply happy his behaviour had been brought to an end and that was that.'

'Are you happily married?'

'I am.'

'Does it surprise you that your wife was Sandy Moreton's girlfriend at Oxford?'

'Of course not. I knew at the time.'

'I didn't phrase the question correctly. That's not what I meant. Does her choice surprise you? That she found him an attractive enough personality to spend time with him in a relationship,' Cross clarified.

'Oh, I see. Yes, I suppose so. To an extent. I joke it was her one lapse in taste. But he made a great effort to be sociable and that was alluring. She met him early on and he introduced her to a lot of people. Took her to parties. It made sense.'

Mackenzie now brought in a note and gave it to Ottey. She knew from experience that Cross didn't like to be interrupted in any way in the interview room. Ottey read it and when she judged it a good time passed it on to her colleague. He read it, then turned over the pages in his file to get to a different point in his notes. He then seemed lost in thought for such a length of time that it occasioned Brook to look over at his solicitor enquiringly. The lawyer simply shrugged. Cross finally looked back up at Brook.

'Do you know anything about Sandy Moreton's relationship with his father?' he asked.

'I don't think it can have been very easy.'

'Because he was his headmaster?' asked Cross.

'In part. But the way his father treated him at times made it quite difficult for him at school. Now that I'm a lot older I think, well, I almost feel sorry for him back then. His aggressive, superior attitude to the rest of us was simply self-protection. But one's character is formed in those impressionable years. I think it damaged him for the rest of his life.'

'Do you think he liked his father?' Cross asked.

'You'd have to ask him that,' Brook replied, perfectly reasonably, Cross felt. He then thought for a few seconds, assembled his papers and left the room. Brook looked at Ottey.

'You're free to go, Richard,' she said.

'I see. Is that it?'

'Yes. Thank you for your time,' she said, standing up. He also did so.

'For what it's worth and despite my feelings about Alistair Moreton, I do hope you find who's responsible. He didn't deserve this, whatever he did in the past.'

78

'Well, that's disappointing,' said Carson who had been viewing the Brook interview on a monitor.

Cross never thought of moments like this as a failure. To him it was progress. It meant their focus had been further narrowed. Ruling Brook out was a positive development. The note from Mackenzie had informed them that Brook's father's carer had left their house in Chelsea at around eight in the evening and that Richard Brook was there. She had seen him as she had told him that his father was asleep. Brook had been working on some papers in his study, she said. There was no time for him to have travelled to Crockerne and killed Moreton.

'Back to the drawing board, George?' Carson asked.

'No,' Cross replied. 'We're somewhat past that.'

'Well to be honest with you I could really do with some good news to take upstairs right now. Not to put too fine a point on it but with Warner's futile prosecution of Cotterell and his subsequent arrest things aren't looking so rosy for me upstairs,' he said with such candour that Ottey was beginning to wonder, not for the first time in recent weeks, what was going on with her boss.

Over a number of days Cross had systematically and slowly gone through all the case files and his notes. Progress in his investigation had been hijacked and stalled by Warner's conviction that Barnaby Cotterell had killed Alistair Moreton. As a result of this and their subsequent, fruitless, line of enquiry with the All Saints alumni, it meant that one person in particular had fallen by the wayside. Malcolm Fisk. Cross had him picked up. But he wasn't sure. It was speculative at best which was why he didn't have him arrested. Arrest was a power that Cross used with caution. To him it was a draconian measure which was often unpleasant, particularly if the suspect was innocent. There was also one detail which was a stumbling block for Cross. Fisk didn't own a dog. But he was a loose end in the investigation, as Drew Tite had once described himself, that needed tidying up. One way or another.

'You took your sweet time,' Fisk proclaimed, as Cross and Ottey came into the interview room.

'What makes you say that?' replied Ottey. 'Did you kill Alistair Moreton?'

'Take the wrong bloke to court. Run out of ideas and realise you have to pin it on someone else, have you?' Fisk asked, ignoring her but staring at Cross.

'Mr Fisk, you have been asked to come and answer some questions under caution. You have not been arrested,' Cross pointed out.

'Yet,' replied Fisk.

'Indeed, as you point out, yet. But you can see our problem here. You had a history of antagonistic encounters with our victim. You have been barred from the local pub after several altercations with him. You accused him, falsely as it transpired, of abducting your former stepdaughter. Accusations you maintained till his death, despite her coming forward and proving it not to be the case,' Cross said.

'Why wouldn't you just want to put an end to it?' asked Ottey.

'Because I'm not that clever,' came the retort.

'I'm sure that may be the case,' said Cross. 'But could you put it in context?'

Fisk gave his lawyer a perplexed look, then turned back to Cross.

'I'm not clever enough to murder someone I disliked as much

as that bastard and get away with it. Particularly in a small village where everyone knows everyone and were well aware what I thought of the old man and would point at me as an obvious suspect,' Fisk said.

'But you can't account for your whereabouts on the night of the murder,' said Ottey.

'I can and I have. I was at home, blackout drunk.'

'Quite convenient,' she observed.

'Did anyone see you? Did you have a delivery that night? Did anyone come to the door?' asked Cross.

'Nope.'

'Did you go out? Maybe to the shop, to get food or more alcohol?'

'Not that I remember. Look, I got pissed. Passed out on the sofa and woke up at five. When the sun was up,' he said.

'You didn't go to work the next day,' Ottey pointed out.

'Called in sick,' he confirmed.

'Maybe you were in shock after what had happened the night before?' she suggested.

'I called in sick because I knew I'd be over the limit to drive. I'm not going to risk my job, or anyone else on the road, because I got bladdered on my day off.'

'How very considerate and responsible of you,' Ottey added.

Cross's confidence in Fisk being a valid suspect was further undermined when Mackenzie texted him with the result of the fingerprint comparison. The print on the chisel was not Fisk's. They had pretty much known this as it hadn't come up in the initial search of the database, but they needed to be sure. He looked back up at Fisk.

'You don't have anything, do you?' Fisk asked him. 'You know how I know that? Because I've never been in Moreton's cottage. Not once. So you're not going to find even the tiniest trace of my DNA in there. What's more, I know you know that. You know how? Because you haven't asked to swab my mouth for a DNA sample. You did when we first met, but not today. Because you know there's no point. You've identified all the DNA you've found.'

Cross was surprised by this astute appraisal of the situation.

'I may not be clever but I'm not stupid. I followed Cotterell's trial in the paper. I may not be able to prove where I was that night or remember anything about it. But I do know one thing. I don't own a dog. No dog, no killer, eh, Sergeant?' Fisk finished by saying. He was released later that afternoon. Cross found himself thinking that in another life Fisk might have made a good detective.

79

Cross was in his office early the next morning studying his notebook. Again. He'd been doing this a lot recently. Today he concentrated on the notes he'd made on their visit to Sandy Moreton's house. The burglary had naturally been of interest to them at the time. Particularly with the missing umbrella cane, Mozart. It then turning up with Montgomery had led them down a dead end. Again, nothing stood out to him. He began a trawl of all the social media accounts that Moreton's constituency office ran for him. Photographs of him at his country house, working in his study. Frame grabs of him speaking in the Commons. Hospital visits, hugging sick children clearly confused as to who he was. Opening fetes, at local sports events, drinking a pint of local beer in a pub. Then one caught his attention. Moreton cuddling two homeless dogs at a local dogs' home. He looked up the sanctuary's website. It was called PAWS and was a dog trust and charity. In the news section there were a couple of mentions of Moreton. Closer examination revealed the board of trustees and its honorary patron – Alexander Moreton. It appeared he was actively involved. But it was one paragraph in particular that caught Cross's eye. Moreton frequently fostered dogs while they were waiting to find their permanent homes. Sandy Moreton, it would appear, had frequent access to dogs despite the fact that he didn't own one.

Cross and Ottey arrived at PAWS just after lunch. They were greeted at a very modern reception. The whole place had an air of being well-run, clean and well-funded. On the journey down Cross had found a lot of photographs on the internet of their fundraising endeavours and Moreton was omnipresent. At one point a post described his fundraising efforts as 'Herculean'. They asked to see the manager and were shown into the small office of Meghan Bairstow. It was a well organised room. On one wall were dozens of photographs of dogs that had been successfully rehomed, some with their new owners. Cross reflected it was rather like the office of a fertility or paediatric consultant, several of which he'd been in over the years as part of his work, who had photographs of impossibly small babies next to others with them as fully grown teenagers.

Bairstow was immediately sympathetic and eager to help when they said they were investigating the murder of the father of their leading fundraiser and patron.

'We met with Mr Moreton recently,' Ottey told her.

'Oh, Sandy...' she exclaimed with a smile and a sigh of commiseration. 'I don't know where we'd be without that man.'

'Is he very involved with the charity?'

'Oh yes. He devotes a good deal of time to us. He says it's purely selfish as he loves dogs so much.'

'I'm thinking of getting a dog,' Ottey announced out of nowhere. Cross knew this wasn't the case and was immediately confused.

'Really?' Bairstow asked.

'Really?' Cross repeated.

'Yes, I've just moved. I have a bigger house now and a garden.'

'But as a police officer your hours must be quite irregular and time-consuming,' Bairstow observed, as if the suitability interview of Ottey as a potential dog owner had already started.

'Yes, but I have two daughters and my mother lives with us in the downstairs flat,' Ottey said at the same time, wondering why she was justifying herself to this woman, when she had absolutely no intention of getting a dog.

'Well, you should bring them along,' said Bairstow as if Ottey had passed the first hurdle.

'Mr Moreton is patron and trustee. What does that involve?' Cross asked slightly irked by what he saw as Ottey's unprofessional dog adoption enquiries.

'He sits in on board meetings when he can and advises us on all kinds of things. His position also means he can open all sorts of doors for us and he's a ferocious negotiator with our suppliers,' she replied.

'As well as fundraising,' Cross commented.

'That's what I mean when I say I don't know what we'd do without him. He's raised thousands of pounds. Just recently we've been able to fund a new operating theatre, largely down to his efforts. It means we can treat the dogs here without them having to undergo all the stress of a transfer somewhere else. He has an annual garden party at his home for us. We are very, very lucky to have him.'

'You sound very enamoured of him,' Cross said, choosing his words deliberately. It immediately made her uncomfortable and possibly defensive.

'I'm not sure what you mean,' she said blushing. 'I'm just immensely grateful.'

Cross calculated there was more to it than this, but it wasn't relevant to their visit.

'Does he often foster dogs from here?' he continued.

'Yes, he does foster quite a lot. I mean, when he can. He loves them. Particularly ones with behavioural problems or difficult temperaments. He has a way with them and they often come back to us completely different animals, well behaved, calm.'

'Do you keep a record of the dogs who are fostered and the people who look after them?' Cross asked.

'Gosh, yes. We wouldn't know where we were otherwise. We're quite overrun and need to keep a proper record,' she replied.

'Would that include Sandy Moreton?' Cross went on.

'Of course,' she replied, sounding a little offended. 'We keep a strict record of everything.'

'Could I see it?' he asked.

She thought about this for a second and then said, 'Yes, I don't see why not.'

She handed him a book.

'We keep a record on our computers, but I like to write it all down. It seems to make it stick somehow,' she explained.

'Kwekwe,' Cross said out loud as he looked through the book.

'Ah, Kwekwe, yes, a troubled soul. But as soon as Sandy saw him he said he'd take him. I did warn him but he insisted.'

'This was on Wednesday the thirteenth of September,' Cross read out. 'But he was back with you within a few days.'

'That's right. Sandy said he just couldn't cope with him. He was way beyond the most aggressive dog he'd had from us. Thought he was a lost cause.'

'What breed was he?' asked Ottey.

'A Rhodesian Ridgeback,' she replied. 'Hence the name. Kwekwe is the name of a city in Zimbabwe.'

80

Ottey and Cross set off for Dorset immediately with two uniformed officers in a separate car, just in case. The door was opened by Reynolds, who invited them in. Moreton appeared at the top of the staircase and welcomed them with a superior condescension.

'Good morning, or is it afternoon?' he began and looked at his watch. He arrived at the bottom of the stairs. 'I don't remember your names, I'm afraid,' he said to Cross.

'Alexander Moreton, I am arresting you on suspicion of murder,' began Cross.

'What?' laughed Moreton in disbelief. Cross then read him his rights. 'Is this some sort of joke?' He turned to see Reynolds was already on the phone. 'The murder of who?'

'Whom,' Cross corrected him. 'Your father, Alistair Moreton.'

'What? This is crazy. Is this some kind of act of desperation because you've already charged the wrong bloody man?'

Reynolds was now talking to someone on the phone. He turned to them.

'Where are you taking him?' he asked calmly.

'The MCU in Bristol,' replied Ottey, giving him a card.

He went back to the call.

'I'll have your badges for this, it's outrageous,' said Moreton.

'In that case you'll be needing my name. DS George Cross,' said Cross as Ottey took the MP by the elbow and led him out. She had decided cuffs weren't necessary.

'Reynolds, call the chief constable and tell him what's happened,' Moreton barked over his shoulder.

Reynolds waited a moment, then put the phone back in his pocket. He was about to close the front door when one of the uniformed policemen asked if they could have a quick word with him before they left. He took them into the kitchen, made them a pot of tea and gave them some biscuits. He seemed most hospitable and calm for someone whose employer had just been arrested for murder.

Moreton's outrage had in no way abated when they sat in the interview room a few hours later, after his solicitor had arrived. He had the attitude of a man who has been slighted and affronted in the most egregious way.

'Mr Moreton, where were you on the evening of the seventeenth of September?' Cross began by asking.

'I have no bloody idea,' came the angry response.

'That seems very peculiar. That you cannot remember what you were doing or where you were on the night of your father's murder,' Cross observed.

Moreton thought for a moment. 'Of course I remember. It was the date that slipped my mind.'

'Were you in court for the Cotterell trial?' asked Cross.

'You know very well that I was.'

'I don't, actually.'

'I was on the news every night. Do you not watch the television?'

'I don't. I prefer the radio. Generally, Radio Three or Four, depending on my mood when I return from work. Do you watch the news, DS Ottey?'

'I do.'

'What's your point?' asked Moreton.

'The date. September the seventeenth must've been mentioned dozens, if not hundreds, of times, during that trial and yet it didn't stick in your mind,' Cross said. Moreton just sat there. 'Where were you on the night of September the seventeenth?'

'I was at home.'

'In London or Dorset?'

'At the country house.'

'Were you alone that evening or did you have company?'

'I was alone. Except for the staff of course.'

'By "staff" do you mean Mr Reynolds?'

'That's correct.'

'And he can corroborate that?'

'Yes. Absolutely,' he said confidently, and with an arrogant dismissal that it should have been obvious to this dullard of a police detective.

Cross paused for a long time as he read a piece of paper carefully. He knew what it said already but was making absolutely sure. He looked back at Moreton.

'Mr Moreton, where were you on the night of September the seventeenth?' he asked again.

'Is he stupid or just being deliberately obtuse?'

'Neither. He's just giving you the opportunity to answer the question truthfully,' replied Ottey.

'I'd like to see your senior officer. The one I met before. Immediately.'

'Mr Moreton, this isn't a department store or a restaurant where you can ask for the manager if you are dissatisfied with the service,' said Cross.

'I am a former member of His Majesty's government,' he replied as if this should still count for something.

'That may be so. But in here you are a suspect in a case of murder, and you would do well in the next few hours to remember that. Where were you on the night of September the seventeenth?'

'At home in the country.'

'Did you go out that night?'

'I did not.'

'Mr Moreton, who is Mr Reynolds?'

'He is my butler.'

'How would you describe him?'

'An absolute stalwart. A diamond. I couldn't manage my life without him.'

'Is he trustworthy and honest?' asked Cross.

'Of course. I wouldn't employ him otherwise.'

'This is a statement taken from Mr Reynolds this morning after we left. He was asked about the night of the seventeenth, which of course he remembers well. He told our officers that you left the house shortly after seven and didn't return till just before eleven. Where were you?'

Moreton was obviously flummoxed by this development and was momentarily silenced.

'Mr Reynolds also said that you seemed very agitated on your return. Quite upset. You went directly to your room. He fixed you a drink and took it to your room, where he found you in tears. Why was that?'

'I don't recall,' Moreton mumbled.

'Kwekwe,' Cross stated out of the blue.

'I beg your pardon?'

'Do you recollect Kwekwe?'

'Of course. A rescue dog. Lots of problems with that one.'

'He was with you on the night of the seventeenth.'

'That's right. That's what I was doing. Walking the bloody thing. Trying to grind him down. Bully the bugger into submission,' he laughed unconvincingly.

'But you went in the car. Your Land Rover,' Cross observed.

'Yes. So?'

'How much land is your house situated in? How much land do you own?'

'About thirty acres.'

'So why on a Sunday night drive anywhere to walk the dog? Surely that's enough land for any dog?' Cross asked.

'A change of scenery.'

'What breed was Kwekwe?'

'I have no idea.'

'Really? Not at all curious?'

'No.'

'He's a Rhodesian Ridgeback.'

'Was.'

'What do you mean "was"?' asked Cross.

'He was uncontrollable. I couldn't do anything with him. So, he was put down,' said Moreton with obvious satisfaction.

Cross didn't react. He simply made a note and passed it to Ottey, who read it and left the room.

This seemed to please Moreton, who suddenly looked a little more assured.

'Why did you choose to foster Kwekwe?'

'I can't remember.'

'Really? Meghan Bairstow says that when you discovered they had a Rhodesian Ridgeback at the kennels you were immediately interested and wanted to see him. She warned you that he had behavioural problems. But despite that, you insisted on fostering him. She thought it was quite odd at the time. That was a couple of days before your father's murder. But it made complete sense to me. You'd met your father's neighbours, the Cotterells, and one of their dogs went for you. You were remarkably good about it, they said, and very keen to know the breed.'

Moreton said nothing.

'You knew that the Cotterells, engaged in a now public dispute with your father, owned two Rhodesian Ridgebacks. I thought they're not too common in this country but do you know there are over eleven thousand? There were only seven hundred when they were registered as a breed with the Kennel Club in 1954. But when you saw the dog at the kennels a plan formed in your mind. You went there that night intending to kill your father.'

'I did not.'

'Which? Kill him? Or intend to kill him?' Cross pushed.

Moreton looked at him for a moment and then launched into a diatribe about his father.

'You have no idea what it was like to be brought up by that man. Right from the beginning. All the way through school. Nothing was ever good enough for him,' he began.

'It must've been hard for you to be at the same school where he was headmaster,' Cross commented.

'Are you kidding me? It was awful. Everyone hated me because of it. I couldn't make any friends. No one wanted to be my friend. He beat them so badly. I got away with it a bit. But he beat me as well. Then he tried to get me to beat them, when he made me head boy. When I wouldn't he was furious and beat me instead. I begged him not to make me head boy. Pleaded with him. Even my mother, bless her soul, told him it was a dreadful idea. But oh no, he knew best. I wanted to go to Exeter university, but he insisted I went to Oxford and tortured me when I resat my A levels.'

'This was at the crammer?' asked Cross.

'Yes. He'd been thrown out of All Saints by then. But he never accepted it. If anything, it made him worse.'

'But he got results,' Cross pointed out.

'But at what cost? It was a miserable place. It worked on misery. Studying was a way of taking your mind off the abject misery that surrounded you. He still treated us like eleven-year-olds, but we were seventeen, eighteen.'

'And then there was Adam Brook,' Cross added.

Moreton said nothing, then shook his head slowly.

'Adam Brook. Poor old Adey. What am I talking about? Old? He was so young. That's the truth about me and Richard. He could never forgive my father for Adey's suicide and maybe took it out on me. Who could blame him?'

He sat there lost in thought.

'All of this anger, all of this lifelong resentment resulted in you killing your father,' said Cross.

'No comment.'

Ottey came back into the room. Cross looked at her and gave her a cue that was invisible to everyone else in the room.

She reached down into her briefcase and brought out a plastic evidence bag in which was Cotterell's chisel.

'Do you recognise this?' she asked him.

'I do not.'

'It's Barnaby Cotterell's chisel. The one that was used to stab your father in the chest, fatally wounding him.'

Moreton didn't look at it but just stared at her.

'Did you use this chisel to stab your father?' she asked.

'No comment.'

'We found two sources of DNA on the chisel. Barnaby Cotterell's and your father's. But there was also an unidentified fingerprint on the handle. Unidentified until you arrived here. It's yours. How can you explain that? Your fingerprint on the handle?' she asked.

'He could have picked that chisel up on any visit to his father's house. Maybe helping him with some DIY. You have nothing. No eyewitnesses. You cannot place him at the scene of the crime,' insisted Moreton's lawyer.

'Maybe we can't, but Kwekwe can. Not only the breed of dog can be determined from its hair but the DNA within that hair can identify an individual dog.'

'Like I said, poor old Kwekwe is no longer with us, so you'll have nothing to compare it with,' replied Moreton.

'So that's two deaths you're responsible for,' observed Ottey.

'We have a forensic investigator at your house right now who is even more patiently persistent than me. He can find the most amazingly small, microscopic pieces of evidence invisible to us mere mortals. I think Kwekwe may well have the last word in all of this.'

81

Swift spent almost six hours in Moreton's study where he found several dog hairs, but none of them were a match. It was when combing the back seat of Moreton's Land Rover that he finally found one, late at night.

Cross came back into the interview room with Ottey. He laid his folder carefully on the table, opened it and studied a document carefully. It was the lab report from Swift.

'Mr Moreton, a dog hair we found in the boot of your car is a match for the dog hairs found around the bites on your father's legs. These bites were inflicted at the same time as the fatal stabbing,' Cross began.

Moreton said nothing.

'The fingerprint on the chisel which was used to stab your father matches the prints we took from you when you were booked in. Why did you kill your father, Mr Moreton?'

Moreton seemed to be processing all of this. Trying to work out how the ground now lay. Finally, he sighed. A long sigh of despair, surrender. Acknowledgement, perhaps, that it was all over. But he needed to explain. Needed to put such a horrific act like patricide in an emotional context.

'I loved him. I idolised that man. It was hard. But I did. I even commissioned an oil painting for his seventieth birthday to commemorate his time as a teacher. He was against the idea right from the start. Practically refused to sit for it. Then when he finally did, he was so objectionable the artist almost walked away. When it was finished, he refused to take it. Said it was dreadful. That's why it's hanging in my study in the country. You've seen it. It's not dreadful at all, is it?' he asked rather pathetically.

'I would say it's a good likeness,' replied Cross.

'He despised the City, the financial institution, that is. When I went into it he told me I didn't have a proper job. Called my salary and commission "theft". Can you believe that? He was scathing when I bought the country house. Called it pretentious and nouveau money. There's a lovely cottage in the grounds, part of the reason I bought the bloody place, which would have been ideal for him. But he wouldn't hear of it. I told him he could free up the little capital he had and live with me rent free. He told me I was just after his money. When I became an MP things became even worse. He despised politicians and reminded me at every available opportunity.'

'So, you decided to kill him.'

Moreton thought about this for a moment.

'No, it wasn't like that. I hadn't gone there to kill my father.'

'Explain Kwekwe to me then. Why did you take Kwekwe there that night?'

'The dog wasn't as bad as Meghan made out. Not aggressive. Just confused.' Moreton sounded almost sympathetic, as if the dog had been misunderstood. 'When I heard he was a Rhodesian Ridgeback I leapt at the chance of having him. I wanted to take him over to the Cotterells.'

'Did you think they might adopt him?'

'No, not at all. They already had two. I just thought the dog might be common ground. That I could appeal to their vanity, present him as a problem dog and ask for their advice. I wanted to appease the situation with my father. It wasn't doing him any good. He wasn't going to back down, even though he'd won. I just thought Kwekwe might be a kind of an ice breaker. But I was delayed by the press that day. The news of the successful recall petition had hit the news that morning. I had all that shit to deal with.'

'So, what happened that night? The Cotterells had already left?'

'Yes, there was no one else there. I was pretty tired after the day I'd had. I almost didn't go. God, how I wish I hadn't, now. But I needed to see him. I thought, I don't know. I thought... well, the truth is I didn't have anywhere else to go. Animals are extraordinary, aren't they?' he said, almost changing the subject. 'Kwekwe could sense something was up. He was very calm. Affectionate even. My father's reaction to the recall was of course predictably awful. No sympathy. He told me what a pitiful specimen of a man I'd become. Whose fault was that? I asked. But he was drunk and incoherent. I told him he should ease up on the whisky which he was chucking back. I didn't even know about the painkillers. He suddenly started talking nonsense. I actually wondered if he was having a stroke. Slurring his words and making absolutely no sense. And so violent.'

'In what way?' asked Cross.

'With what he was saying and the way he was saying it. It wasn't like him at all. Even at his worst. This was something else. On an altogether different level to what I'd seen before. The more agitated he got the more confused he became. He became almost incomprehensible. Ranting and raving. He completely lost it.'

'A mix of whisky and opiates,' suggested Ottey.

'He started asking me and my friend to go. I assumed he meant Kwekwe. But it felt like he was actually talking about someone else. Another person. He'd had enough of us being in the house. We were abusing him. He wanted his house back. We couldn't live there anymore.'

Ottey looked at Cross.

'I refused to leave, so he went upstairs. I followed him. Thought maybe he was going to bed. But he came raging out of the bedroom with a cane, slashing it about like a sabre. He kept hitting me, again and again. Around my head, my back, my legs. It was so painful. I tried stopping him, but he was beside himself. Kwekwe then attacked him, biting his legs. Ricky went after Kwekwe. The noise was terrible. Dad came at me one final time, swinging at me. He hit me round the head so hard I swear I saw stars. Then I saw the chisel on the top of the banister. I wanted to get him to just back off. But he lunged at me and instinctively I just stabbed him. He fell backwards against the wall. He made the most sickening noise. Blood was bubbling in the corners of his mouth. It was so terrible.' At this point Moreton broke down completely. Cross realised the beating would account for Mackenzie's mistaken observation that he had a love bite on his neck on his first visit to the MCU. It was obviously a fading bruise from his father's assault.

'What happened then?' asked Cross, pushing on.

Moreton pulled himself together a little.

'I heard someone approaching the back door. I got hold of Kwekwe and took him into the sitting room. We waited while someone came in, presumably looked at Dad, then legged it.'

'That would be Cotterell,' said Ottey.

'So it would seem,' Moreton muttered. 'I didn't mean to kill him. Despite everything, I never wanted to kill him. It just happened in a second.'

'Why didn't you tell us, Mr Moreton?' asked Cross.

'I was going to. I thought about it for a few days. Then when you arrested Cotterell. Well, I suppose I saw a chance of at least delaying the inevitable, if not the chance of getting away with it.'

Cross looked at Moreton for a while then back at his folder. He ticked off a couple of things, and left the room.

Sandy Moreton was charged and remanded in custody. The media interest was immense. It was all over the papers and on all television news channels. Ottey thought it was a desperately sad outcome. Despite her innate dislike of Moreton his father had had a devastating effect on his life, made him the man he was. By killing him Moreton had just completed the project.

'If I was Watson to Cross's Sherlock, I would write this story, make Moreton an alcoholic and call it *The Hair of the Dog*,' said Michael Swift to Alice that night as they reflected on the events of the last few days.

He was rewarded with a long low groan of complaint from Alice. Something he was getting quite used to of late. It wasn't just a reaction to the poor quality of his joke. She'd been to a counsellor that day and was talked out.

82

Christine had asked Stephen if he would conduct the funeral service for Duncan. It was held at a crematorium near Gloucester. It was a simple service, and the turnout far exceeded her expectations. There were people from the care home he'd been in, both carers and residents. Friends from work and their former social circle all expressing guilt that they'd lost touch since his illness. All met with a genuinely compassionate understanding from her. George had come as requested with Raymond. Also Josie and Cherish, the latter apparently could never resist a good funeral, even if she didn't know the deceased, as in this case. She had startled George as she sang the two hymns at the same volume as if she'd been singing in the choir at her Baptist church while everyone else mumbled self-consciously. Swaying and belting out 'The Lord's My Shepherd' with complete, worshipful gusto. She even muttered 'Amen!' and 'Hallelujah' constantly through the service in response to Stephen, whenever the spirit took her. All to the accustomed embarrassment of Josie who had grown up with this all her life.

They adjourned to a local hotel for tea afterwards, which George was pleased about. He was dreading the idea of a noisy pub, and this suited him perfectly. Raymond came over to George who was sitting on a chair near the door having a perfectly enjoyable time on his own. He'd exhausted the little amount of small talk he had, with Josie and her mother, and so had retreated from the room. He stood up as his father approached.

'Are you ready to go?' George asked his father.

'Actually, I'm going to keep Christine company tonight. I don't think she should be alone on a day like today,' Raymond replied.

'Very well.'

'George, there's something I wanted to tell you. Christine has decided to sell up in Gloucester and move to Bristol.'

'I see,' replied George. 'And why is that?'

'So she can be closer to her family,' said Raymond.

'Oh, I had no idea she had family in Bristol.'

'That would be us, George. You and me.'

'Everything all right, George?' asked his mother as she appeared at their side.

'Perfectly acceptable, thank you. I thought Stephen performed a nice service. Anyone would've thought he'd known your husband,' he said, fairly confident that Josie had told him to say something along those lines.

'It was very nice of him to do it,' Christine said.

'Well, it is his job,' George pointed out, not unreasonably he thought. 'I understand you're moving to Bristol.'

'Yes, that's right,' she replied. 'But don't worry, I won't impose on you any more than I already do.'

'Oh, good,' he said.

'I want to be closer to Raymond,' she went on, smiling at George's father. Raymond smiled back a little awkwardly.

'Why?' George asked. She looked at Raymond uncertainly.

'Have you not said anything?' she asked him.

'No,' Raymond replied.

'You really need to hear it from him, George,' Christine said, walking away to leave them alone. George was suddenly panicked. He looked at his father.

'Shall we sit down, George?' Raymond asked him.

George thought about this for a second and was suddenly overwhelmed with a mix of anxiety, irritation and confusion. It was almost physical. Was there something wrong with his father? He'd frequently been thinking about life without him of late. Now this.

'No,' he suddenly said, then turned away and looked for Stephen. He walked straight up to him, interrupting his conversation, and said, 'I need to leave.'

'George, oh, I wasn't aware I was giving you a lift. Don't you think we should stay a little longer?' asked Stephen who looked over at Raymond.

'No. It's Thursday. I have organ practice at seven. If we leave now, we should be in good time,' replied George, who then promptly left the room. He was watched anxiously by Raymond who then nodded at Stephen, as if to say all was okay.

But for George Cross, the conversation that required his sitting down with his father was one which would have to wait for another day. He felt decidedly odd, but it wasn't until the fresh night air hit him that he realised what it was.

He was frightened.

Acknowledgements

Thanks as always to the team at Head of Zeus for their continued help in bringing George Cross to a wider readership. Bethan Jones for her encouragement, perceptive notes and always being on hand to talk. Peyton Stableford, Andrew Knowles, Polly Grice, Ben Prior, Matt Bray, Emily Champion, Nikky Ward and Daniel Groenewald for all being an important part of Team George. Lucy Ridout for her great notes and invaluable suggestions. My social media team Sarah Oldman and Lilly Hill for their wonderfully inventive posts. Emma Finnigan, my PR, for doing her best not to take 'no' for an answer from people.

I feel it incumbent upon me to make it clear that the experiences I have drawn on in this novel are based on my time at my first prep school and not at Clifton College or prep where things were quite different and I was happy. I still find it unbelievable and inexcusable what happened to me and my contemporaries in a quiet corner of Somerset many years ago. The writing of this novel has been surprisingly cathartic.

To my wife Rachel, thank you for putting up with the writer in the attic, and my daughters Bella and Sophia, for supporting their crazy old man in his literary endeavours.

Finally, to all my readers. Thank you for getting in touch. Hearing from you and reading your affection for George makes the whole endeavour worthwhile on a daily basis.

About the Author

TIM SULLIVAN is a crime writer, screenwriter and director who has worked on major feature films such as the fourth *Shrek*, *Flushed Away*, *Letters to Juliet*, *A Handful of Dust*, *Jack and Sarah*, and the TV series *Cold Feet* and *The Casebook of Sherlock Holmes*. His crime series featuring the socially awkward but brilliantly persistent DS George Cross has topped the book charts and been widely acclaimed. Tim lives in North London with his wife Rachel, the Emmy Award-winning producer of *The Barefoot Contessa* and *Pioneer Woman*.

To find out more about the author, please visit TimSullivan.co.uk.